By Gwen Davis

FICTION
NAKED IN BABYLON
SOMEONE'S IN THE KITCHEN WITH DINAH
THE WAR BABIES
SWEET WILLIAM
THE PRETENDERS
TOUCHING
KINGDOM COME

POETRY
CHANGES

THE MOT

BY
GWEN DAVIS

HERLAND

Simon and Schuster
NEW YORK

SBN 671-21738-0
Library of Congress Catalog Card Number: 73-20547
Designed by Irving Perkins
Manufactured in the United States of America

1   2   3   4   5   6   7   8   9   10

TO THE HOFFMANNS
OF VIRGINIA

He who has issued from thee teacheth thee reason.
  —BABYLONIAN TALMUD: JEBAMOTH

So doth she.

PROLOGUE

BASIC BLACK was perfect for setting off Evelyn's neatness of figure, contrasting the white brilliance of her smile, emphasizing her thick red-black hair, picking up the small darts of darkness in the glowing hazel of her eyes. The times and the fashion industry had been kind enough to raise skirt lengths back up to show her remarkable legs, which could not go unnoticed even at a funeral.

Even a funeral such as this: Arlington National Cemetery, Virginia. Strewn with the markers of Civil War dead, cordoned off by Secret Service men who set up protection around the gravesite itself, keeping the curious and unidentified away, limiting the number of photographers and television cameramen, because of the presence of the President.

Tourists were there in amazing number, to visit the Death-place of American heroism. A few of the bolder sightseers tried to get close to the funeral procession, most of them not knowing what exactly it was. Some who had read the papers broke across the cemetery from adjoining roads and tried to get closer to the eerie orderly movement of mourners moving down the hill. But the honor guard and the color guard and the Secret Service and the proud posture of Senators and Congressmen kept them in awe, at a distance.

Colleagues and family of the deceased had gathered at the Memorial Chapel, North Post, Fort Myer. The services for the dead Senator had been brief, affecting, the minister and the rabbi both limiting their oratory to one subject—the greatness that could now never come to full fruition, at least not in the halls of American government. Perhaps (they held out the funeral dream) it would bloom in more hallowed halls.

The stature of the man to be mourned had catapulted in the few days since his death. There was no doubt, according to informed sources, that he would have risen to very high office, maybe the highest in the land, in spite of his being a Jew. Even those who were critical while the Senator was alive—those who had called him ruthless, ambitious, conscienceless, and an outright crook—were subdued by the reality of his disappearance from the ranks into whispering how much he had added, being among them.

After the service the pallbearers put the closed coffin draped with the American flag onto the old caisson positioned outside the chapel door. And, to the beat of a muffled drum, the horses drew the caisson. The procession moved off into the cemetery, winding slowly down the hill, led by the President, walking bareheaded behind the casket.

They kept on moving until they came to a place under a tree where an empty rectangle of raw earth was covered with a green cloth. Chairs and a canopy had been set up for the mourners, but as there were too many to seat and Evelyn looked her best standing, she positioned herself to the right of her husband, on her feet, her left hand on his shaking shoulder, partly to give herself better balance, and partly a closer connection with the bereaved, some fingertips of consolation. He was weeping openly, silently, colorless tears coursing steadily from his gray-blue eyes, the kind of eyes with splintered dreams in them. Seated, his shoulders rounded with sorrow, he was still a tall man, handsome except for the distorting bloat of too much emotion.

The salute was fired. Taps was played. The color guard removed the flag from the coffin, folded it in a neat triangular gathering. The captain of the honor guard took the folded flag and handed it to Evelyn. She nodded in aristocratic acceptance, stately in being part of a ceremony of state, the surviving female of the family, in basic black, holding the red, white, and blue.

"Hey!" A short, stocky man in a blue pinstripe suit and a white-on-white shirt and a white-on-white tie flashed a card at the Secret Service man, and made his way over to Evelyn. "What's this shit, they didn't leave me a permit to park, I had a hell of a time getting in here." He was trailed by a woman in too high heels, with harlequin sunglasses that seemed to set the occasion askew.

Evelyn's husband looked up, his big square jaw resetting itself from despair to anger. "Get out of here, Rosey," he said very quietly.

"Why?" Rosey said. "This is one funeral I'm really going to enjoy."

The big man sprang to his feet, arms that had a moment before been limp with mourning and grief now strong and upraised and reaching toward Rosey. "Get out of here," he wheezed. "Get out of here, you son of a bitch."

"How are you, Evelyn dear?" said Daisy di Bonaven, trying not to sink into the sod with her spiky heels, trying to set her glasses straight. "Isn't it nice that Rosey let me come?"

"Who the fuck do you think you are?" said Rosey di Bonaven as Evelyn's husband grasped his lapels and started moving him away from under the canopy. "Get your lousy hands off of me."

"Get out of here."

"Big man," said Rosey. "You and your brother. Really big men. I come to enjoy how big a man your brother is."

The tall man covered his eyes with clenched hands, lifted his half-obscured face to the skies, let out one cry of rage, and crashed his fist against Rosey's jaw. "Get out of here!"

Rosey held the side of his face, fought to get his breath. "I like this funeral. I'll go to any funeral I like. It's a free country."

"If you knew some of the things going on even inside the Oval Room," whispered Daisy to Evelyn.

But Evelyn wasn't listening. She was moving between the two men, who were squaring off and bashing angrily at each other like two aging little boys, oblivious to the stares, the frozen honor guard, the snapping of shutters on cameras permitted to photograph, the pointing fingers of tourists who had hoped only for a glimpse of the ancient honored dead, the newly honored dead, nothing so exciting as a living battle.

"Oh honey, don't." Evelyn reached for her husband's upraised fist, and put it near her heart, and made it a hand. "Don't do this to your brother's funeral. Don't do this to yourself. You could have a heart attack," Evelyn said. "And with my luck, you'd live."

BOOK ONE

ONE

When Evelyn started speculating it was in the midst of the Great Depression, as it was known, just as the war that had ended had been called the Great War, since no one could imagine there being another one worse or Greater. Overnight poverty hit Pittsburgh as badly as it hit anyplace, but that didn't make much difference to Evelyn's family.

Trusts and high finances and the failure of various stocks and bonds were as alien to the fruit and vegetable stand at the corner of Craig and Centre as the idea of a college education had been to Pappy and Grandma, cleaning out behind the stalls. Pappy, having made his original fortune of twenty-four dollars investment capital by loading stones in the bottom of the barrels in his wagon, covering them with new potatoes, weighing in for the Irisher who bought by the bushelful, was singularly unalarmed by the hullaballoo in New York. As long as people had to eat, he was in business. And as long as he had what to eat, and Grandma cooked it like only Hungarians could, he was happy.

He had been a little upset at first when Evelyn went to college. But it turned out to be all right because the city put her through free, for nothing, and all it cost him was two dimes a day lunch money. She saved it, never telling him, until she completed her education, when she gave him back all the dimes she had collected, because she loved him more than eating in the cafeteria. It totaled up to three hundred dollars, enough to pay for his false teeth, which he needed that year.

"Robbers!" he cried through bright pink gums. "Only a couple was rotten altogether. You should send Sammy and Murray to be dentists, they could steal all the money in Pittsburgh, Pennsylvania, and we move from Centre Avenue to Easy Street!"

But Sammy and Murray weren't smart enough to get their education free like Evelyn. So they helped Pappy out at the market: open stalls with a striped canopy hanging over the most colorful of the fruit, produce hosed off, polished for the occasional sunlight. A number-one quality store, polkadotting the grayness of the street with red and yellow and green.

There were two other sisters, one named Sadie who was still in high school, and one who came late, by accident. ("Even without teeth. What do they know how good a man is? Robbers!") Grandma ran back and forth between the stand where she swept and cleaned and brought her boys lunch, and the second-floor apartment where her baby was. And Evelyn went downtown on the number twenty-three streetcar to work in the department store. She gave the family most of her salary, except what she spent on dresses so she could look nice at lunch hour, which she passed eating egg salad sandwiches with Corinne White, who came from one of the finest families in Squirrel Hill, where the best people lived. ("You see," Grandma said to Pappy, "even from a top-shot family the girls have to work in Kaufman's. Life isn't easy." "Where is it written it's supposed to be easy?" Pappy said.)

One night Corrine asked Evelyn to dinner in Squirrel Hill. It was there that Evelyn met Corinne's older brother Walter.

"What's he like?" Sadie asked the next night at dinner.

"All right," said Evelyn.

"What's he do?" asked Sammy.

"He just got out of dental school."

"Marry him!" Pappy exclaimed, and dipped his bread in his soup.

"So how's the family?" Grandma never sat down during dinner. There was room for her at the long, brown, varnished wooden table, when the leaf on the far end was put up, the tablecloth pulled over so no one could see the crack. But she was too busy getting everybody food and running back to check on the baby. Afterwards, she could eat in the kitchen, standing up, while whichever boy wasn't watching the store washed the dishes, and Evelyn dried, and Sadie ran the carpet sweeper under the table in the dining room. "They nice people?"

"What, you don't know?" Pappy said. "They're Kings and Queens."

"Stop it, Moisch," Grandma said. "You shouldn't make fun."

"Who's making fun? It's a fact! Everybody in Squirrel Hill is Kings and Queens. Especially the Roumanians."

"They're a very prominent family," Evelyn said.

"They knew this on Ellis Island." Pappy scratched the stubble on his chin. "The police knew this. That's why they gave them a new name."

"The immigration officials couldn't read the old name. They couldn't make it out," Evelyn said. "It started with W. So they wrote down 'White' when Walter's father came to this country."

"That's his story. The old man was probably wanted by the law." He ran a hand over his shiny bald dome.

"Stop it, Moisch."

"All Roumanians are crooks. It's right his son should be a dentist."

"So what are you?" Evelyn said. "Putting rocks in the bottom of potato barrels."

"Who told you?" Pappy slammed the table with his fist, jarring the soup in his bowl so it lapped like waves in a chicken ocean, making the candle flames stir in his angry wind. Grandma lit the

candles every Friday. She couldn't remember the prayer anymore, and there wasn't really time, but they looked nice and she
always Thanked God. "Who told you such a terrible lie about
your father!"

Pappy had told her so himself, many times. It was one of the
things he was proudest of, cheating an Irishman.

"So what are they like?" Grandma came back from the
kitchen with more matzoh balls for the soup. "Are they a nice
family?"

"Very nice." Actually, the Whites had fought all during dinner. The old man had scared her, he was so well-mannered and
good-looking, with black eyes under heavy brown brows and a
big, neatly trimmed moustache, and such fine diction even as he
yelled. By the end of the meal the three oldest sons and daughters
had slammed out of the house, because they had "no respect," all
except Corinne, his only "obedient child," and Walter, who was
"on his good behavior. Because we have such a pretty visitor,
obviously," the old man had said.

"So how come you don't get married?" asked Pappy.

"Moisch, they only met each other the first time."

"So?" Pappy leaned back and belched. "How long did I take
with you?"

"We were on a boat."

"That must have been very romantic," Sadie sighed.

Sammy laughed.

"What's so funny?" Pappy said.

"She thinks it was an adventure," said Sammy. "Pretty good,
an adventure. Two thousand people like cattle on a ship, and
Sadie sees moonlight."

"We were on a boat," said Grandma. "And then it took seven
years."

"That part I forgot," said Pappy.

"Remember," said Grandma. She brought a bottle of schnapps
to the table. "So you like this fellow from Squirrel Hill?"
Grandma asked Evelyn.

"He's all right." He was better than all right. Walter was dark like his father, tall, with deep brown eyes. And he wrote *poetry*. Evelyn didn't know too much about poetry, but he had shown her some of it, and the words were multisyllabic and cleverly rhymed.

"So why are you fooling around?" Pappy said. "Get married already. You're twenty years old. It's time. But don't give him an inch. Believe me, you shouldn't trust a Roumanian."

"Walter's American," Evelyn said.

"Says who?"

"His birth certificate," Evelyn answered. "We're all Americans. When you're born in America, you're an American. If you weren't so ignorant, you'd understand that."

Pappy put down his shot glass, reached over, and slapped her across the ear. She did not flinch.

"That's for you, Miss American."

"She didn't mean it, Moisch." Grandma stood behind her daughter and touched the girl's shoulder.

"Where I come from, *without* a birth certificate, we respect our father," Pappy said. "You'll apologize."

"Apologize," said Grandma.

Evelyn said nothing.

"Have a drink, Moisch." Grandma went to him and poured another schnapps. "You shouldn't ruin your digestion."

Pappy raised the glass to his lips and made a terrible grunting, swallowing sound. "For this I needed the United States of America. So my children should grow up and their family isn't good enough. All right. So I don't mind. Move to Squirrel Hill. Run to those crooked Rumaneets. Marry that robber dentist." Pappy shrugged. "You're too good for this family, go! Run." He scratched his chin. "What can I lose?" He smiled, very wide, removed his upper plate, and his lip caved in on his smile. "He can't get my teef."

It was a Sunday when Walter finally came to their house to dinner. Sunday was a very good day, brightened with the funny papers, not to be looked on lightly, as they were one of the few bonuses Murray got for working all night Saturday in Silverman's drugstore. Funny papers, and the radio, gave an occasional aura of amusement, waste of time to their lives. (Thank God KDKA started in Pittsburgh, and Pappy could hunch over the yellow dial in his long underwear, or there would have been violence. "Is this what a man's life is?") By the time Walter had started courting Evelyn ("Courting?" Pappy said. "Very fancy words they have for things, these robber Roumanians"), Evelyn was praying they wouldn't discuss that week's events in the comic strips at table. ("Pretend you read books," she said to Pappy. "Walter's a poet.")

Pappy stared at Walter's impeccable table manners, watching him touch his soup spoon to the back of the bowl and bring it gracefully, undrippingly to his lips. Evelyn watched how Pappy's surveillance was affecting her newfound friend. She contented herself with Walter's smile over her mother's lentil soup, and his generous acceptance of their crassness.

"So how you like it here in Oakland with the peasants?" Pappy finally said.

"Father!" said Evelyn.

"Who is she talking to?" Pappy said to Sammy. "It isn't enough she's been hanging around Squirrel Hill. She's also becoming a Catholic?"

"Mother, make him be quiet."

"You talking to me?" Grandma asked, bringing in a steaming plate of pot roast and vegetables from the kitchen.

"Certainly she's talking to you," Pappy said. "Otherwise she'd start with Hail Mary."

"Don't fill up on soup, Mr. White," Grandma said. "The pot roast is very nice."

"So you still haven't told us, Walter M. White," Pappy smiled, "how you like it in this neck of the woods. It's all right, if I say 'woods,' isn't it, mein darling daughter? Woods could be anywhere. Russia. Poland. Squirrel Hill."

"They have plenty of woods in Schventiensky," Sadie said.

"Will you stop talking about Schventiensky," Evelyn said, and clattered her spoon on the table. "I am my own source."

"Like the Amazon River," Pappy said, and grinned, surprising himself as well as Evelyn. "Lowell Thomas," he said, with a modest lowering of his eyes.

"I'm afraid I don't know what Schventiensky is," said Walter.

"It's a place where people come from when they have hearts," Pappy said. "You have any Schventienskians in Squirrel Hill, Walter M. White?"

"Excuse me." Evelyn left the table and went into the kitchen.

"She went to *collitch*," Pappy said. "They taught her a lot of strange languages. She has many ways now of telling me to go to hell."

"*Sha*, Moisch," Grandma said, and filled his plate with vegetables. "Eat, you'll feel better."

"I feel fine!" Pappy slammed the table. "Listen, Mr. Walter M. White. Are you serious about this daughter of mine, who suddenly starts calling me 'Father'?"

"Well . . ."

"They've only started seeing each other, Moisch."

"We've only started seeing each other," Walter said.

"Because if you're serious, there's something you ought to know. She isn't really a member of this family. Don't let that interfere with your honorable intentions. Who she really is is the long-lost Princess of Schventiensky, where only the royalty are excused from feeling. Kidnapped at birth. Sold to the gypsies. Brought here under a spell by a wicked magician who deposited her on our doorstep. And because my wife, who she suddenly calls 'Mother,' is such a soft heart, we kept her. But one day she'll reclaim her true kingdom, and then she won't have to have anything to do with us anymore."

"Make him shut up!" Evelyn shrieked from the kitchen. "Grandma, please make him shut up!"

"Here, Moisch," Grandma said, and handed Pappy a small glass filled to the brim with dark brown liquid. "A slivowitz. Like it's an occasion."

Pappy drank the brandy and coughed. "You better give me another one, I forgot to make a toast."

Grandma refilled the glass, and Pappy lifted it into the air. "To the long-lost Kingdom of Schventiensky and its princess. May they find each other soon."

From the kitchen came the noise of angry sobs and fists hitting wood. Grandma turned to Walter, took away his soup plate, put it on the sideboard, and hesitated. The steam from the pot roast with its rich drippings and tomato gravy, carrots and celery and potatoes, rose into the silence.

"Maybe, Mr. White . . ."

"Walter, Grandma."

"Maybe, Walter, it might be a good idea, if you took Evelyn out to a restaurant."

"Why?" Walter asked. "The pot roast looks wonderful."

The romance of Evelyn and Walter M. White proceeded very charmingly indeed. As he was a poet, he wrote her three sonnets in the style of Elizabeth Barrett Browning, whose poems he also read to her aloud. She fancied she had touched his heart. So she let him touch the inside of her thigh. No higher.

She felt something for him she was quite convinced was passion, especially when he read her the poems, and when she ate dinner at his parents' house, where there were three bathrooms. But she controlled herself, and him, until they were officially engaged.

He did not give her a ring, as things were still a little slow getting a dental practice started. But when they told Walter's family at dinner that they were going to be married, Old Man White, with sonorous voice and a moustache that decorated his words like a dark brown velvet ribbon, proclaimed that he was welcoming a beautiful daughter. Reaching over to his wife's neck, he drew from it a gold chain with tiny amethysts, no bigger than beads, and put it around Evelyn's throat.

"That was my mother's," he said. "Now it will be yours."

"That was supposed to be mine," Walter's older sister said.

"When I got engaged to Helen, you gave us nothing, *nothing*," said the brother, throwing down his fork.

"Maybe because you asked," said Walter's father, who had not been a success in the credit business for nothing.

"And maybe it was because you didn't want to put your hands down Helen's blouse," the brother said.

"Leave the table," Old Man White shouted, but his son had already left.

"That was supposed to be mine," Rachel, the older sister, said again. "Mother was going to leave it to me."

"I'm not dead yet," said Mrs. White, but nobody heard.

By that time, Rachel had slammed out of the house.

"I hope you'll both be very happy," said Corinne.

"My only obedient child," said Old Man White. "Except for once my son Walter has done something to please me." He reached over and touched his fingers to the chain dangling from Evelyn's neck. "Pretty. Very pretty."

"Why don't you just stick your hand down her toots?" said the brother from the doorway.

"Out of my house!" screamed the father, but the son was already gone.

Afterwards, when Walter tried to kiss her in the parlor, Evelyn was still shaking. He imagined it was from passion, and agreed that they should be married as soon as possible. She thought of all the rooms in the White mansion (which was how it was referred to where Evelyn lived—in Oakland almost every house in Squirrel Hill was a mansion): a sitting room, and a parlor besides, and a full dining room with no rollaway bed for Sadie to sleep in in the corner, a rollaway bed intruding its striped mattress into the only lovely part of her day—Grandma's cooking. Also a kitchen with two iceboxes, two, and loaded with ice all the time (one of Old Man White's debtors was an iceman), and a *schvartze* who came in once a week to do the laundry in the basement, the basement, not bent over the kitchen sink on Mondays like Grandma. Evelyn thought of all these things and she thought of the three bathrooms, and suddenly the food she had eaten for dinner did not seem so bland, or the shouting she had heard quite as loud, or as frightening.

"We are going to be happy," she whispered.

The ceremony took place on the 11th of May, 1934. Evelyn was too stunned from the actuality of the proceedings, the hearing of words which, when uttered, would free her from the greatest American curse: OLD MAID, OLD MAID. "I now pronounce you man and wife"—they had said that about her—she was too drunk with relief and wine to pay much attention to what anybody said. The only important thing had been said, and made her someone's wife.

The Whites had wanted a small orchestra in the tiny hall. But Pappy and Grandma were paying for the wedding, and they would have been too proud to give the bill to someone who could afford it, so they settled for a phonograph.

The in-laws had had the pale green walls decorated with flowers. ("The Roumanian's got some poor florist by his credit," Pappy said.) Pappy and Grandma did some of the food and got the rest from friends, some bought, some received as gifts, and some traded for the fruits of summer soon to come in. Herring in sour cream next to a big tub of chopped chicken livers (the delicatessen would have traded for cucumbers, but Grandma's was better), rolls and cakes, gefilte fish brightened with horse-radish on a borrowed silver-plated tray, little stuffed cabbages in sweet and sour sauce, meatballs ("Everything a person could ask for with plenty left over," Pappy said)—all this was on the three card tables set up to the side of the room.

The tables were pushed together and looked to be just one, covered with a gift Grandma's mother had given her when she left Hungary, two fine white linen tablecloths, miraculously saved, traveled, beautiful. It looked like a great banquet in Pappy's eyes, and Evelyn's eyes, which were misty from salvation. In the eyes of the Whites it looked like a modest spread, but Walter had eaten Grandma's food and knew better.

"Where are we going after this is over?" Evelyn said, as Walter whispered words of love in her ear that she couldn't quite make out. He had kissed her on the lips in public. And let everybody know. He had made it official with God and her parents.

After the food and the wine and most of the people were gone, Walter drove her downtown in his new white DeSoto and they registered as man and wife in the William Penn Hotel. He had told her to bring only her overnight things. She assumed it was because he intended keeping her in the room for the entire honeymoon, and the thought was so depraved she loved it. She did not know it was because they were going home the next day.

"Are you very disappointed?" Walter said in the morning. "I would smother you with honeymoons, but it's so expensive and I'm just getting started . . ."

"It's all right. I'm sort of looking forward to getting settled." There were enough rooms so she could stay out of old Mrs. White's way.

"You don't have to do a thing. Grandma's already done everything for you."

"You mean, moved my things over to your house?"

"Rearranged her place so there'd be room for me."

"In Pappy and Grandma's?"

He touched her chin and turned her face toward him. And he was actually smiling. "I wanted it to be my surprise."

"Well, it's that," Evelyn said. "It certainly is that."

She could not kill him just then. To be a widow was no disgrace, not the cold disgrace of an old maid. A widow could even be merry, but not if she was in jail.

Her rage was so great, she was trembling. But she couldn't speak it. Women didn't say such things.

Sammy doubled up with Murray, Grandma and Pappy took the bedroom by the kitchen and moved the little one in there, so that Sadie on her rollaway bed in the dining room wouldn't hear Walter and Evelyn making love.

They did not make very much love, even though it was their honeymoon there in Grandma and Pappy's apartment. Walter imagined it was shyness and virginity. Evelyn was still so awed that he had actually married her, she could not express her fury that they were not in Squirrel Hill. After a few days of tolerating her lassitude, Walter stopped kissing her breasts so much, and just got his own business out of the way.

"Why?" Evelyn asked finally, six o'clock one yellow-shaded morning, when she could stare at the crack in the ceiling no longer, afraid to close her eyes lest she slip back into another of those dreams: caged in a box with her own excrement, everything foul.

All through college she had eaten lunch in one of the toilets in school, locking the cubicle door, wolfing without chewing, almost choking to conceal the sounds of swallowing, for fear that one of the other girls would come in and know what she was doing in there. Find her greasy brown paper bag, when all it cost for lunch in the cafeteria was twenty cents. Twenty cents, and all along Evelyn had saved that, so she could give it to her father, and be free. Free to leave the single toilet bowl that with all Grandma's scrubbing and bleaching would never be clean, not with the germs of God knew how many penned-in refugees, climbing up rickety flights of steps, their only airing in the Pittsburgh soot on pathetic back porches, cement, with iron swings and fire escapes.

"Why?" she screamed, and hit Walter with a pillow, in his sleep.

"Huh?"

"Why are we here?" she wept. "What are we doing here?"

"Well, God created us to do the best we can. As Emerson said . . ."

"Oh, damn Emerson," she shouted. "Damn all your goddamn poets. Damn God."

"Evelyn," he said. "Your mother might hear."

"Grandma's almost deaf, and you know it." The whole family ran to otosclerosis, which was what they didn't know they had yet, the word being too fancy and the operations later to come being, for the moment, out of their grasp. They all just contented themselves with thinking they were "hard of hearing," something that Evelyn was sure was what gave them their gentle quality, all except herself who could hear perfectly, denied even the small blessing of missing some of the pain, and Enid, the baby, who already showed signs of being a bitch, and Pappy, who had thrown an alarm clock at Evelyn twice, getting her both times on the ear, which still hadn't made her deaf, dammit. Damn him, whom she loved best of all.

"What are we doing here?" she said again to Walter. "And don't give me any of your poetry. I mean what are we doing in this bed?" She jumped up and down twice on her buttocks to illustrate with creaking mattress. "What are we doing in this apartment? What are we doing in this goddamn slum? Cracks in the ceiling and window blinds! Why have windows when they have to be blind, because what's outside is so ugly? And what's inside is uglier. Why do we have those hideous pictures on the wall? Because the wall is uglier than the pictures."

The pictures to which she referred were two lithographs, heads, of women with hoods. One woman with a black hood, the other with a deep red one. Their outstanding characteristic was the one feature they had in common: no eyes. Just the outline and the whites of two terrifying almond-shaped holes with nothing in them. Evelyn despised the pictures, although she had picked them out herself from a store where the dealer owed Walter's father money.

"What are we doing here?"

Walter was silent for a moment, studying his wife's shoulders as they heaved. It was the greatest display of passion he had seen in her since their marriage.

"Don't you dare touch me, you son of a bitch," she screamed at his suddenly lively hand. "Don't comfort me, when you can't even answer a simple question."

"What was it again?" he said.

"What are we doing here?"

"Why, dear, you're in the arms of your family, who love you."

"I always had them. Why am I here with *you?*"

"You didn't want to live here?" he asked.

"That's funny. Why would anyone not want to live here, just

29

because it's a slum with five children and a mother and father and one bathroom and any normal rich son-in-law would choose it as the ideal place to start his marriage?"

"So then you don't like living here?"

She had always attributed his slowness to a philosophic, poetic stance. She laughed, very suddenly; it caught in her stomach and she had to run to the bathroom, all the way down the hall, and started retching emptily into the bowl.

She felt his hand on the back of her head. "Are you all right?" he said.

"Oh my God," she gagged. "Oh my God."

"Maybe you're pregnant," he said. "Wouldn't that be wonderful?"

"Oh my God," she said.

After she stopped throwing up, when she could calm her laughing and halt her weeping, she went back to their room and lay face down on her pillow, open-eyed. He was still near her, she could tell that, and she didn't dare turn her head for fear that she might start vomiting again.

"So you don't like living here?" he said.

"But you do," she managed. "You really do."

"They're a wonderful family," he said. "Grandma's a great lady. I enjoy Pappy, even if he does try to needle me. And your brothers . . ."

"I didn't ask you for an endorsement of my family. Look at where we're living. Look at how we're living."

"I thought it was very nice here," Walter said.

"I'm beginning to understand that," Evelyn said.

"But you're not happy?"

"That's thirty-two dollars. Would you like to try for sixty-four?"

"Well, then, I guess we'll just have to move."

When they finally moved, their daughter was three years old. They moved to a small apartment in Squirrel Hill, around the corner from the Whites, where Walter did not like going to dinner as much as he liked going to Grandma's. Also, things were still not so terrific in the dental trade, he was eventually to admit to Evelyn, and he was finding it hard (laughter) to make plates meet. After four months, they moved back to Grandma and Pappy's.

By now Sadie had gotten married to Hymie ("Another bum," Pappy said), and they were using Evelyn and Walter's old bedroom. So Walter and Evelyn now slept behind the sliding doors in the parlor, and, in the small niche that Grandma called the living room, their daughter stayed on the sofa, except on warm days when it was pleasant and she could sleep on the back porch swing.

There were some very temperate, pleasant evenings; it would stay light for a while in the back yard, and Evelyn and Walter could stretch a badminton net from the two poles where neighborhood women strung washlines on Mondays. It was during such a game that Evelyn looked down and caught the movement of her own legs, the slimness of thigh, the soft curve of the shapely calves, and the full tide of her disappointment flooded over her. The birdie fluttered to earth between her small feet.

"That was an easy shot," Walter said. "How could you have missed such an easy shot?"

"That's a very interesting question," she screamed, and ducking under the net, brought the badminton racquet crashing to the side of his head. It was not a very hard blow, as the racquets were secondhand, and she was not as strong as she wanted to be. But it did hit his ear. When he suffered the first case of otosclerosis in his family fifteen years later, he was to attribute it to this moment.

At the exact time, however, he did not react with philosophic horror, or pain, or the deafness that might one day come. Instead, he brought her instantly to earth and started grinding her face into the little patch of grass in between the mud and the soot, while she kicked up backwards toward his genitals.

Their daughter Chris was conducting a costumed charade with the neighborhood children on the back porch. At one point, Gene Kelly had come back to his hometown of Pittsburgh and given tap dancing lessons in a studio downtown. Chris couldn't get her foot up to the bar for the ballet part, couldn't move her feet fast enough for the tapping; her legs were too chunky. Evelyn and Gene Kelly both agreed it was a fairly hopeless task, so Chris was retired as a tap dancer at the age of two and three-quarters. Pittsburgh was asparkle with three- and four-year-old Shirley Temples, and Chris had been abruptly cancelled from the midst of their clicketing ranks. Still, she conducted charades and pageants, one of which she was holding now, as her parents beat each other up, and she saw it and screamed.

The terrified yelling brought Pappy and Sammy and Murray and several people who were not related down the fire escape. By the time they managed to separate them, Evelyn had the beginnings of a black eye and a welt on her chin, and Walter had several good bruises on his inner thighs.

That night they made love to make sure his equipment could still function. It was the best it had ever been. After that, Evelyn and Walter would have a physical battle at least once every other week, instead of foreplay.

Neck and neck with violence, the thing that excited Evelyn most was the stock market. Because of her poverty, she had very early learned thrift; if one could save what amounted to a handsome sum in those days from two dimes a day lunch money, managing a household account could yield a small fortune. Very small, and not an actual fortune. But Evelyn dwelt meaningfully on the word. Fortune. Chance. There had to be chance or there was nothing. The land of opportunity, whether or not her parents were willing to seize it.

The papers were filled, like Pappy's meandering cursings, with news of robber barons, men who had built empires from beginnings almost as simple as rocks in the bottom of potato barrels. Even her father-in-law, that son of a bitch who had given them nothing, *nothing,* it was right his children didn't speak to him, could have been more than just a big man in Pittsburgh. So it followed that someone with brains and imagination could build from a tiny pearl a necklace, and eventually mount it on a crown.

The pearl, like all good pearls, stemmed from a minor irritation: stealing. Evelyn did not consider it so, except sometimes late at night when she realized she wasn't dealing a hundred percent fairly with Grandma. She didn't mind pulling the wool over the eyes of her husband. Walter M. White had already pulled the wool over her eyes, robbing them forever of their open innocence, putting darts of suspicious black into their hazel, seeking the same lazy comforts she had wanted so desperately to escape. Also, he was being unfaithful, she was sure of that, leaving his office early in the afternoons, driving around town in his white DeSoto sedan, screwing widows and orphans and probably his own sister, or her own sister, she didn't really care, not having time to follow him anymore. She was too busy with the stock market.

In the five years of their marriage, she had accrued twenty-eight hundred dollars, which, considering how stingy he was, gave renewed substance to her early conviction that she was remarkable. Two dollars a week from grocery money, three dollars a week from clothes allowance, four from rent, a dollar from cleaning. (Grandma still insisted on doing all the laundry herself, so there was no way to short that account.) The bulk of the money she got from charging shoes to Old Man White at the shoe store chain that owed him, bringing them back to a different store, sometimes miles away, where she wasn't known and could return them for cash.

Walter complained in the beginning when the bills came through from his father, to whom he wasn't speaking. But eventually Evelyn worked it out so she wouldn't buy more than five pairs of shoes at a time, and when Walter asked where were they, these shoes that were enough to sole and heel a harem, she would throw something at him and ask him who he was screwing that afternoon. At such times, Pappy and Murray and Sammy and now Sadie's husband Hymie would pull them apart after minor bloodshed; they would be very busy cleaning up the battleground and seeing what was broken and afterwards making love, so Walter forgot to ask her to show the shoes again, until the next bill came due.

She did have minor pangs from time to time about not letting Grandma have all that was due her. But Grandma was filled with a happy acceptance of her life, a joy that a baby was there again, she didn't know any better.

So Evelyn took her capital in small paper bags down to the offices of companies listed on the stock exchange, and played the market as she had once played the violin—without virtuosity, but with a great deal of intelligent devotion, especially to her teachers.

These last were any of the big men involved in finance who were kind enough to speak to her, which many of them were. She was dark and young and pretty, and her look and smile were still filled with the naïve, eager aspirations that had long ago been stifled in their souls. She would ask their advice, and they would advise her, and she would buy a few issues at a time, selling them the next day, or two days later, when they were up a few dollars. When her counselors told her to wait a while longer, that this issue was really good for a long-term gain, she would sometimes listen to them. If the issue plummeted, the black-flecked hazel eyes would fill with quiet tears, and the perfectly even dazzlingly white-toothed smile would disappear. At such moments, men who had watched relatives jumping out of windows a few years before in 1929 were moved to remember that those had only been brothers and cousins, but this was a young pretty woman who had believed in them like a child, whom they had disappointed. So they would offer to stake her to another small block of stock.

"Oh, I couldn't do that," she said, but usually did. She wouldn't let any of them lay a finger on her, nor would she meet them for even a cup of coffee outside the actual place of business. She didn't believe in adultery, and she didn't believe in whoring; besides, she had enough excitement in her life making money.

At the end of six months of speculative investing, she had over ten thousand dollars in cash scattered in various boxes in various banks around Pittsburgh, and one in Turtle Creek, where she never visited her sister-in-law who had married a *shagitz*. She was too smart to open any regular accounts, because banks failed, and banks sent statements, and then Walter might find out. Nor was she foolish enough to buy any presents for the family, although she fully intended to take care of them when the time was right.

Evelyn did buy a very expensive doll for her little girl after the croup kettle tipped over in her tent and then the tent tipped over, and Chris wasn't found for three hours, and when they untangled her from the hot sweaty mess she had pneumonia.

"I'm sorry," Grandma said in the waiting room of the hospital. "It got busy at the store, and I had to help out, and I didn't realize . . ."

"Don't blame yourself," Walter said. "She isn't your child. Where was her mother?"

"Don't start that crap," Evelyn screamed. "Where were you, you son of a bitch, and don't give me that crap about being at the office, because I was there, I was there looking for you, and it was closed—where were you, out screwing your receptionist?"

"Oh, please," Grandma said. "Evelyn, please. It's a hospital." She looked around the waiting room, at the huddling groups waiting for death, because nobody came to a hospital except to have a baby, or die.

"If she dies," Walter said, "I'll kill you. I'll kill myself."

"Do that first," Evelyn said. "We'll all be better off."

"Bitch!" Walter screamed, while Pappy held his right arm and Sammy and Murray held his left. Sadie and Hymie were home babysitting with Evelyn's youngest sister Enid, who had signs of a cold which Grandma was now terrified would turn into pneumonia. Also Sadie thought she was pregnant, and God forbid she should be in a hospital when somebody died. God forbid.

"Let me loose," Walter yelled, crying. "I'll kill her. Leaving that child alone."

"And where were you?" Evelyn shouted. "And don't give me that crap—"

"Evelyn, please," said Grandma, putting her arms around her daughter, trying to cushion the bleatings of that mouth with her great warm breast. But she was too short. Tiny as Evelyn was, her mouth came to Grandma's eyes, not her bosom. And Grandma wasn't strong enough to pull Evelyn down.

"Where was he?" Evelyn wept. "Where was he while my little girl . . ."

"Don't pretend to be a mother at this point," Walter cried. "You never went a foot out of your way for that child."

"And where were you?" Evelyn shouted. "Where was he?"

Grandma couldn't tell Evelyn. It was an *entente* between them, even though she didn't know that was what it was called. Where Walter White was every afternoon was in the little room behind Pappy's fruit and vegetable stalls, eating Indian nuts. Business was very slow in the dental trade, he wasn't lying about that. And he loved Indian nuts. So every day he would hide out in that little room. Hundreds of husks accrued around his feet while he spoke of philosophy with Pappy in between sales, and Grandma came in and swept up after him. All those shells.

Little mountains of shells. And both of them sworn never to tell Evelyn where he was. Walter had too much sadness to let his wife know he didn't have enough customers to fill an afternoon, too much pride to hide at his own father's, too much shame to spend the afternoons at home. Besides, he said he found Pappy stimulating, which nobody had ever done before, even without Indian nuts.

"Murderer," Evelyn screamed. Grandma sat Evelyn down and drove her bosom closer to the profligate mouth.

"Jezebel!" shouted Walter.

"Judas!" said Evelyn.

They had run out of anything but civilized appelations, and Grandma strained with her bad ears not to hear any more terrible words, and with her heart to the Lord not to provide them, since God alone knew where they picked up such language. The doctor came then, his stethoscope hanging like the armor of a medieval knight, shielding him against twentieth-century tragedy.

"I think she's going to be all right," the doctor said.

Evelyn went to the window, the yellow-painted dingy-framed

3 6

panes that opened on a bitter black sky. "Thank God," she whispered.

"No thanks to you . . ." Walter began.

"Enough," said Pappy, and started to cry.

None of the family had ever seen him break before except in rage, and the spectacle of him, his graying one-piece underwear visible to them all underneath his shirt, Pappy crying, like a mere defenseless mortal, sobered even Evelyn. She stared out the window, at the pieces of red steel-eating flame gobbling the night sky above the mills, and bowed her head, and tried to cry with as much selfless relief as her father.

It was not that she was not a good mother. It was not that she was not a good woman. It was not what she was *not* at all: It was what she *was* that was so elusive.

She had been raised to measure her success based on the success of the man she married. She had loved not wisely but not too well, either. Still, she had the ability to throw off the narrow conditioning of her background. What bothered her was she had no idea of where to go. She wanted only to be the lovely, powerful, contented woman she knew she could be. But she wasn't sure at the time who that was.

As for her own daughter—she had nothing against that little girl. Chrissie was pretty, Chrissie was bright, what more did a girl need to be? Especially as she had seemed to sense even from infancy that she ought to stay out of Evelyn's way, since Evelyn didn't know quite where that way ran.

Chris watched her mother with too bright eyes while Evelyn went through an occasional display of those maternal chores that only Grandma could effect without effort, because Grandma was born to do them. Born to boil water for diapers, to keep diapers clean. Chris' diapers. Chris who looked at Evelyn with dark adoration that Evelyn could rarely return. What was she doing with a daughter, even one who showed signs of being exceptional? Christine, for Christ's sake.

It suited the child, oddly enough, perhaps quite simply because it was not the usual name, especially for the spawn of a Moskowitz and a converted White from Pittsburgh. The little girl was unusual, that was apparent from the start. She was quick to talk, and even quicker to listen, the greatest blessing, once she had been potty-trained.

The last had been accomplished by the time Chrissie was nine months old. Evelyn took it as confirmation of Walter's conviction that the baby was brilliant, not bothering to point out to him that it had taken something like genius on Evelyn's part to get her that way. From the moment Chris was advanced enough to sit, Evelyn had fed her on a high chair that was also a potty seat, on which she would place her, first thing in the morning, feed her breakfast, and on which she would leave her till after the last meal of the day. So she would only have to empty the dirty bowl once.

Playthings were placed on the small wooden overhang from which plates had been removed, baby rhymes were read to Chris until she dozed off for the afternoon nap, still sitting. Grandma feared for Chris' spine, not knowing, except by instinct, any more sophisticated kinds of damage. Evelyn told Grandma, now that she was finally, legitimately a grandma, that she was the older generation, and if it was her martyred pleasure to wallow in diapers, that was her business. This was Evelyn's baby.

By the time Chris was five months old, she could say "Ma-Ma" and "Da-Da," "Mam-maw" and "Doo-dy." When the elder Whites insisted the nine-month-old baby be brought over for a family gathering where everyone fought, and there was no way Evelyn could carry with them anything but a portable potty seat, she noted to her pleasure that after lunch the infant's face went quite red from the strain of holding something in. Evelyn put the portable seat on the toilet in one of the three bathrooms, and said, "Doo-dy. Good girl. For Mummy." And as simply, and complexly as that, the connection was made in the tiny head, reinforced with a cover of kisses. And never again were Evelyn's hands to be touched with the soil of a child.

Once in a while, Evelyn would have a terrible dream in which Chris' diapers were dirty again, especially after a period of constipation. So she would give Chris an enema to ensure its all going into the toilet. "Hold it in until I count to fifty." As the child grew older, the count grew longer. By the time she was three Chris could count to a hundred by herself, very fast.

"My beautiful little girl, my clever little girl," Evelyn would say. "You're right about her, Walter dear," she told him at dinner. "She is brilliant, even if she can't tap dance. She can count to a hundred all by herself. Go ahead, sweetheart," Evelyn said. "Count to a hundred for your daddy."

It seemed a minor accomplishment at three, being able to count to a hundred, since Chris had been reciting the Gettysburg Address from the time she was two and a half. Walter had read it to Chris once, he claimed, and Chris had told it back to him, although Evelyn later insisted she too had read Chris the Gettysburg Address whenever it seemed feasible. Whatever the truth of the learning process was, there was no question the little girl was eager to hear and remember.

She would sit for hours on her father's lap, her outsize black eyes fixed on his lips, while he read her the great poems, as categorized by himself. She actually looked as if she could hear the hoofbeats, as over the cobbles they clattered, up to the old Inne door—seemed as if she could feel the sadness for the lost Lenore, and believe that a Raven could speak, even the same word over and over. And in spite of the child's rapt reverence for poetry, she still appeared to accept that Walter should never see a poem lovely as a tree. Astonishing, really, especially as in that neighborhood, ugly dwarfed trees stood silent witness along the gray cement sidewalks, giving the lie to the sentiment of Joyce Kilmer, as did the chosen poems themselves give verbal testimony to the truth of it.

Evelyn didn't really care, she was just grateful. At least with his daughter on his lap, Walter would stay off Evelyn's back. So she was free to go into the small bedroom and study the newspaper columns of stocks and bonds as lesser dreamers did the stars. Watching their daily movement up and down, and sometimes sideways, Evelyn could feel her heart jump as a stock she had fantasized buying the day before for, say, two thousand dollars' worth made her a four-hundred-dollar profit overnight.

When she started putting her reveries into actual motion, and the paper bags grew fatter with accrued cash, her dreams began to burgeon as the dollars did.

They were not dreams such as anyone around her understood dreams. A place of her own, like Sadie and Hymie wanted, was too little for Evelyn now. He had deprived her of that, the poet-dentist, bypassing that might-have-been serenity with his lack of understanding for her feelings. No, she dreamed of something that none of them would dare begin to think about: freedom. Freedom from the past, freedom from him, freedom from them, freedom from anything the responsibilities of her heritage insisted she deliver. Maybe even from love. Love was the biggest legend of them all, fed to you with the matzoh balls, to lay heavy on your spirit, so movement would be impossible.

Movement up, movement down, movement sideways. Movement. It was not intended that she be like the rest, like everybody, or she would not have been gifted with so much imagination and drive. What she might be driven to, she could not yet fully imagine, which was why she spent so much time running downtown. Movement implied motion, and immobilized thought, so she could not perceive she was getting nowhere. Whatever her fate was, wherever it was, she knew only that it was *away,* from what they tried to make her believe she was destined to be.

She would not be like the others, restless only in her soul, regretting the whole of her life over cups of coffee in girlfriends' kitchens with everyone wearing print dresses. She had too much inside her for that. The only thing missing was the plan and the courage.

The courage began to come to her the night Chris didn't die from pneumonia. There had to be significance in a child's not dying, just as there had to be no significance in death, no matter what the rabbis tried to put over on their diminishing congregations. Death was death—over. Life, when there was supposed to be death, was a reprieve from things being finished. A reprieve was another chance. Chance was everything. Chance gave you courage to continue.

Also the weapon. Before that night, with Pappy sobbing in hitherto unrevealed weakness, Chris had seemed to be only a little girl. Now all at once she was a sword which Evelyn could brandish at whatever fates had condemned her to Pittsburgh, a knife with which she could cut out a piece of unsmoked sky, and the heart of Walter M. White.

Not that she was bent on revenge: it was the furthest thing from her thoughts, she was sure. But a good girl from a nice family didn't simply set sail like a breast-plated Viking, barbarically severing ancient ties, sacred bonds, and traditions, no matter how sloppily the last were observed. Candles were lit on Fridays whether or not you remembered the accompanying prayers. Marriages were kept intact whether or not you could remember why you got married in the first place. Ancient, mysterious rituals held people together, because most people didn't have the courage to ask why they had to be tied. Or the weapon to slash the rope.

"Not too many at a time," the doctor cautioned, the next evening. The orderlies had taken away Chris' oxygen tent, and survival was assured. "She must rest."

"You go on without me," Evelyn told the rest of the family. "I'll wait. I want to see her alone."

"She'll ask for her mother," Walter said. "She always wants you. God knows why. She'll want to see you."

"I'll wait," Evelyn said. She was holding the doll in an unobtrusive box, wrapped in plain paper, as if it had only come from a drugstore, its expensive price tag carefully removed.

Evelyn looked at the hands that held the box with the doll inside. They were not as good as her legs, but then there was little that could be. At least her fingers were not red or coarse—Grandma still washed while she dried. And Sadie ran the carpet sweeper under the dining room table, after dinner.

The family. They were really very sweet, in their meaningless way. For a moment a wave of loss passed over her, as when Walter had made her stop smoking, because it would stain her teeth, and who could afford caps?

But it passed. The moment she connected to and pictured

vanished was, after all, only a meal. Her hungers were deeper than those of the stomach. Besides, her youngest sister Enid was getting old enough to dry the dishes.

"She wants you," Walter said, as they shuffled silently, red-eyed, back into the waiting room.

"Thank you," Evelyn said politely, and kissed Pappy's un-shaven chin, squeezed his suddenly thin shoulders. She had never realized before how small he actually was. Then she hugged her mother, felt the velvet of that cheek, smelled the incredible combination of warmth and light cologne and food.

"I love you," she said, without meaning to, and realized she actually did. "You're a wonderful mother."

It was true. Besides, it sharpened the knife she was preparing. What could they say when a woman did things for the good of her child? It wasn't as if she were Medea, for God's sake.

Chris was sitting on a bedpan in the middle of white hospital sheets, a blanket pulled up over her legs, the smell pervading the room. "They gave me an enema," she said.

"That's so you'll get well," counseled Evelyn, and touched the small, dark face, moved her fingers through the black curly hair. Near-loss and future excuses gave it sudden poignant texture.

"Daddy was crying," Chris said. "Why was Daddy crying?"

"Well, he loves a good drama."

"What's a drama?"

"It's something you can hold your heart from, even if it doesn't rhyme."

"What's that box?"

"It's a present."

"It isn't my birthday."

"It's an occasion."

"What's an occasion?"

"It's like it was both our birthdays," Evelyn said. "Yours and mine. Our life begins today."

They unwrapped the present together. Evelyn lifted the lid. She let her daughter stare at the doll for a minute before she took it out of the box.

"She's beautiful," Chris said.

"She's almost as big as you are."

"What's her name?"

"Whatever you want it to be."

"Evelyn," said Chris. "Her name is Evelyn. She's too beautiful to be anybody else."

For a moment Evelyn felt something so real, so unfamiliar, it weakened her. She turned her back to her daughter. She moved to the cold, white drapes that shut out the evening, pulling them open, hoping for stars—anything she could fix her eyes on that would not be her own heart. She *did* have one. How could he have said she didn't have one? Too many tear-jerk movies made from too many Fannie Hurst stories, swallowed whole on top of Edgar Allan Poe's worst nightmares, in rhyme, had turned him into a highwayman of the boring. Who would come to her by moonlight? I'll come to thee by moonlight. Look for me by moonlight. Not on his ass.

The darkness of unmoonlit sky was brightened by holiday windows, wreaths and trees lighting up apartment buildings, and homes, high on hills, bulbs delineating the roofs and walls of houses, transforming them into a two-dimensional fairyland. The city of Pittsburgh, so oppressive by ordinary day—built on hills and industrial hopes, shored up with darkening bricks, only streetcars on wire cables electrically sparking the dullness of the air, those grim hovels built for two and three families with ashened dreams, reality made more ugly by the occasional white-fronted, newly painted, colonial facades of Rich People's Houses—this dinginess was curiously dazzling by Christmas season night. Evelyn's eye could not move for more than a fraction of an inch without a gay multicolored patchy intrusion, or an outline of a blue gingerbread cottage invading it.

"There," Evelyn said to Chris. "Now you can see all the pretty lights."

"What are they for?"

"Christmas," Evelyn said. In their own neighborhood there were no lights, outside the houses or in. "Some people put up Christmas decorations and lights on Christmas trees."

"Do we have a Christmas tree at home?"

"No."

"When am I coming home?"

"In a little while."

"I have to stay here?"

"Just so you'll get well, darling. Just till you get well."

"And then will we have a Christmas tree?"

"No."

"Why not?"

"Because we just don't, that's all."

"Why?"

"Because we don't believe in Christmas."

"Why not?"

"We're Jewish," Evelyn said.

"What's Jewish?"

Evelyn wasn't sure. She understood it was a religion. But religion was something you practiced, and Evelyn never did. At the moment some screamer in Germany was calling it a race. Race was not Jewish, it was Caucasian, a very fancy word when every other race was yellow and brown and red.

"Jewish is what some people are," Evelyn finally said. "And it means you can't have Christmas trees."

"Are you Jewish?"

"Yes."

"Don't you like Christmas trees?"

"They're very pretty. Colorful. Gay. I like things to be gay."

"So why can't we have one?"

"We just can't, that's all. It's the law."

"What's the law?"

"Rules. What you can do and what you can't. People have to live by the law. They have to obey it." Who Said, Who Said, and if He really did, where the hell was He, putting her here like this, with all these questions?

"Or else they'll be punished?" Chris asked.

"Well, not always, darling. But it's a good idea to keep the law, because otherwise . . ." She was not sure what to tell her daughter would happen otherwise. She could not tell herself what would happen otherwise. She doubted God was in the sky, and she knew He was not in the White House, no matter what Grandma thought.

"Do you like your doll?"

"I love her. Yellow hair. Why don't I have yellow hair?"

"Because Daddy and I have dark hair."

She saw Chris moving uncomfortably on the bedpan, and rang for the nurse.

"Am I being punished?" Chris asked her mother when the nurse was gone.

"Of course not, darling. You're a good little girl."

"Then why do I have to stay in the hospital?"

"Because you're sick."

"When can I come home?"

"As soon as you're better."

"And then can we have a Christmas tree?"

"Maybe one day," said Evelyn. "When you want something badly enough, maybe one day you can have it."

"When I grow up I'm going to get you everything you want. I'm going to buy you a diamond necklace."

"Do you mind putting that in writing?" Evelyn foraged in her purse, took out a pencil and a small pad which she carried for her stock market calculations. "I'm not entering into any more contracts I can't sue on." She handed the paper and pencil to Chris.

"I can't write."

"How old are you anyway?"

"Four."

"Well, it's time you learned to do something," said Evelyn. "You've been hanging around long enough."

Naturally, Evelyn was only kidding. It was enough that the child was there, as Mount Everest was later to be, so that when Evelyn provoked Walter into calling her terrible things, she could scream back, "I won't have my child exposed to this kind of filth," at which point she could break a milk bottle over his head. It got to the point where Pappy ordered an extra bottle a week, so they wouldn't start using anything hard to replace, like lamps. But with all Pappy's planning, his constant haranguings that people should not be behaving like animals, the day did come when the nearest thing handy was a cut-glass vase that Grandma's mother had sent all the way from Hungary, via a friend.

"*Fiend!*" Evelyn shouted, hurling it the length of the room, missing Walter by inches but shattering the framed photograph of President Roosevelt in front of the American flag, cut from the Parade Section of the Pittsburgh *Sun Telegraph.*

"She's blinded me!" shouted Walter, covering his face, which was several feet away from the actual spray. "The bitch cut out my eyes."

"It was nowhere near you, you bastard. You're just such a fairy you're afraid of a little noise."

"Shut up! Shut up!" Pappy ordered, while Grandma went to get the broom.

"Powdering your parts," snorted Evelyn. "Your own dear fairy Godmother, little Cinderella."

"Shut up! Shut up! The two of you are crazy!"

"*Whore!*"

"*Pansy!*"

"*Bitch!*"

"*Bastard!*"

"*Genug!*" Grandma said, tears in her eyes, sweeping the debris into the dustpan. "What's the matter with the both of you, you've got a child listening here."

Chris was concentrating very hard, trying to figure out the reference to Cinderella, which she didn't understand at all. Evelyn saw her watching, wide-eyed. She seized the opportunity almost as quickly as she had grabbed the vase.

"That's right, you bastard. I'm not going to have my child exposed to such language."

She went to grab Chris, but Walter had moved faster. His arms were under Chris' legs, sweeping the little girl from the chair.

"Your child?" he screamed, as he headed out the kitchen door, toward the back porch. "When was she ever your child?"

4 6

It was a summer evening, so the sun shone behind them as he carried Chris, running down the fire escape. Chris could not help noticing that the shadow she cast on the wall, as her father whipped her down the metal, winding stairway, had a curly-headed outline that could have belonged to Shirley Temple, as in silhouette it was impossible to tell that she didn't have yellow hair. It would not be enough to teach herself to read, as she was already doing, or to write, which she hoped to accomplish soon. Even though she could not dance, perhaps she could learn to sing, and then her mother would really be pleased.

"Maniac!" Evelyn shouted, mutedly, outside the window of the car. It was another DeSoto, cream-colored this year. Walter had locked his daughter inside it. Maybe he couldn't get to her, but neither could Evelyn.

"Call the police!" Evelyn shouted, and several neighbors did, while Pappy phoned the cops and told them to pay no attention.

"Why is Chrissie locked in the car?" one of the little boys in the neighborhood wanted to know. "Has she been a bad girl?"

"She's a very good girl," said Evelyn, embracing the locked window. "She just has a very bad Daddy."

Walter sat down on the curb of the sidewalk and started to cry.

"You big, ball-less wonder," Evelyn hissed, "using a child. It's all right, my darling," she purred through the glass. "Mummy will save you."

The actual salvation did not occur until several weeks later, by which time Evelyn had carefully collected all her cash from the various boxes in different banks, and some timetables from the Pennsylvania Railroad. The exact moment of departure, in spite of the assiduous attention that Evelyn devoted to the train schedules, imagining the comings and goings with the same studious air she had given to the stock market's motion, was difficult to determine.

In the first place, she and Walter had made up, colossally, after the locked-car episode, abetted in their passion by the appearance of several police officers who had not received Pappy's deterring calls. It was the first time they had had the noise of sirens serenading them into their sexual peace, and it lent an air of marital munificence to the proceedings. After that, simply yelling and screaming and hitting came as a let-down: it lacked what Evelyn was later to learn was *éclat*. Their normal fights, as abnormal as they were to the family and the neighborhood, seemed fairly run-of-the-mill after the one with police escort. So for a while, something quite like peace and brotherhood reigned.

Besides, on particular evenings when they did manage to get a little violence going, Evelyn had not quite gotten her plans together in her head, or her money together in her purse. Once everything was collected, her thoughts, her cash, and the train schedules, he started trying to trick her with quiet affection. It was almost as if the devious bastard knew what she was planning and was deliberately screwing it up by being nice. He spoke constantly in solemn tones of forgetting the past, and building a loving and sharing future together, the prospect of which was enough to make Evelyn shudder.

But she could not leave cold-bloodedly, without an obvious reason. Without provocation. The only problem was getting him to provoke her, which he managed to do effortlessly, just by being alive. The subtle murder of his mere existence would be difficult for her family to understand. They would have to see something a little more vivid, slightly horrendous, according to the style of art and life that seemed to be preferred by Jewish people.

So it became a waiting game, about which Walter was always singing, along with Huston's recording of "September Song."

"You see?" Grandma said, when there had been nothing broken, or even chipped, for several weeks. "You see what a wonderful marriage you children have? Sometimes it takes a while for people to get to know each other. Pappy and I didn't have such an easy time in the beginning either."

"You never hit me with *nyutin*," Pappy said. "I would have broke your head."

48

"He's bragging," said Grandma. "He wouldn't hurt a fly."

"They stay out of my way," said Pappy. "Even at the fruit stand."

Walter laughed. He put his arm expansively around Pappy, who was hunching over his soup, a little of which had dripped onto his one-piece long, cotton underwear. "I have a wonderful life, a wonderful wife, a wonderful family. And I owe it all to you and Grandma."

"Along with a little rent," said Pappy, and smiled into his spoon.

"I've been meaning to speak to you about that."

"Don't be shy," said Pappy. "I got very good ears."

"Well, business has picked up a little lately . . ."

"I could tell that from the shells," Pappy said. "There weren't so many shells in the back."

"*Sha,* Moisch," said Grandma, as Evelyn returned from the bathroom.

"So right after I treat my beautiful wife and my beautiful daughter to a vacation . . ."

"Vacation?" Evelyn sat down, fighting the sudden dizziness with a pickle, trying to quiet the buzz in her head with the crunch. Where was he going to take her, where they would be alone and the family couldn't see if something terrible happened?

"A real vacation. The three of us. Conneaut Lake. We're leaving tomorrow. I wanted to surprise you. Right after we come back from the holiday, we're going to start looking again for a place of our own. With Sadie's baby coming, and Sammy seeing the *shicksa*—"

"I'm not going to marry her," Sammy said. "She's just a very nice girl."

"Shut up," said Pappy. "I don't want to hear her name mentioned."

"He didn't mention her name," Murray said. "It's Pegeen, if you're ready for that."

"Shut up," said Pappy. "I was listening to the dentist."

"We're going to look for a place of our own, and move. Somewhere in Squirrel Hill."

"Where else?" said Pappy. "Back to Roumanian soil."

Walter smiled. "But that doesn't mean I won't still be giving you some money. No, with things the way they are, money may not yet be growing on trees, but the fillings *are* paved with gold. So to show you my gratitude for how kind you've been to us, all these years, I'm going to continue giving you six dollars a week rent money, even though we don't live here anymore."

"Six dollars a week?" Pappy put down his spoon. "Since when have you been giving—"

"What do you mean, Conneaut Lake?" Evelyn yelled just in time, her cheeks flaming against the nearness of the averted revelation. "You know my little girl isn't altogether well yet. The doctor said to be very careful about her lungs. She could go in the lake and catch a chill."

"She doesn't have to go in the water," Walter said.

"You'd do that to a child? You'd torment her with water and not let her go in? What kind of a man are you?"

"I only thought—"

"All of a sudden he wants to go to Conneaut Lake," said Evelyn. "What could be the cause of such a sudden, bountiful surprise? And why Conneaut Lake? Have you got some girl there?"

"Evelyn, for God's sake, I only wanted to give you a vacation. Like a second honeymoon."

"What second, you stingy son of a bitch? We never even had the first."

"But that was only because—"

"Don't tell me what it was only because. It was only because you're a miser. Trying to use my Chrissie as a front, so you can go and meet some whore."

"Cover your ears, Chrissie," Grandma said.

"Run in the front room," said Pappy, recognizing the signs. "Lock the door!"

"Do what your Grandpa says," said Evelyn. "Don't let your father try and use you!"

"Stay where you are, Chris," Walter said quietly. "I've done nothing or said nothing—"

"*Liar, philanderer!* Quick, Chris, run!" shouted Evelyn, as Grandma quickly cleared the glasses off the table, and Sadie helped.

Chris got up from the chair and started down the hall. Walter threw his chair over and ran to the dark-bordered doorway. "Get back in here, Chris. You'll listen to me for a change."

"And if she doesn't, what are you going to do?" Evelyn shouted. "Beat her?"

"I've never laid a hand on that child," Walter said.

"Only because you were after bigger game, you sadistic bastard. *Lock the door!*" Evelyn screamed down the hall.

"I won't have my child frightened of me." Walter started down the rose-papered corridor. "I won't have her scared."

"Then get out of our life. *Get out of our life!*" Evelyn screamed. "Get out of our lives, so none of us have to be frightened again!"

He was gone into the front room.

"You see?" Evelyn whispered to the family. "You see?" she said loudly to Grandma. "He's crazy. He's a madman. I have to save her before he does something terrible." And with that she was down the hall.

The train for Washington left at midnight. That would give her an hour and a half to clean up after the fight, an hour to pack, and three hours to pretend to be asleep.

"Go, Moisch." Grandma righted Walter's chair, sank into it, and covered her eyes. "Go, stop them."

"I'm tired of stopping them," he said, and blew his nose into his handkerchief. "Let them kill each other. I'm finished."

"But the baby," Grandma said. "Our baby."

There was a lot of banging and clattering from the end of the hall, and the noise of sliding doors being opened and shut, other doors being pushed and pulled. No splintering glass, yet. The usual screams from Evelyn, shouts from Walter, muffled through heavy wooden doors. Pappy put his head on his naked arm and belched.

"Finished," he said. "I'm through."

And then he heard the sound of the little girl crying. "They should both be put away!" he proclaimed, flinging his handkerchief onto the table, starting for the hall. "Sammy! Murray! Hymie!" he called to his junior soldiers, who were behind him but could not move as fast as he did.

The door to the bedroom was locked, so Pappy ran through the parlor, opened the sliding doors. Evelyn had hold of Chris' feet, and Walter was pulling her arms.

"You won't take this child to Conneaut Lake!" Evelyn screamed. "I won't have you using this child!"

"I'll take her anywhere she'll be safe and happy, especially away from you."

"That's right, use her for camouflage, you bastard, so you can go meet your whore."

"My God," Pappy said, and flung his fist at Walter's throat. "My God," he said, and slapped Evelyn's face. "What's the matter with the two of you? Look! Look what you're doing! Look!" Pappy shouted. "You're tearing her in half."

They stopped then, and saw him, and the child they held between them. They let her slide, weeping, onto the bed.

"Shame, shame," Pappy said, and gathered Chris into his arms. He carried her back to the dining room, where Grandma gave her chocolate pudding.

"You understand now," Evelyn said to Grandma in the kitchen, after they had cleared up the mess in the bedroom and could start on the dishes. "You understand why I have to leave him."

"Huh?" Grandma said, because Evelyn was speaking too softly, and Grandma could still hear only the racing of her own heartbeat in her ears.

"You understand why I have to go. For the child."

"I thought it wouldn't be good for her, the water in the lake."

"I don't mean Conneaut Lake. I mean somewhere else. Where he can't put his hands on her."

"Where? Where do you mean, somewhere else? Where would you go?"

"I don't know," Evelyn answered. The midnight train had a

six-hour layover in Washington, before the Silver Meteor left for Florida.

"I'll write you. Explain to Pappy. But not until tomorrow."

"You're packing a lot of summer things," Walter said, as he sat on the armchair and watched Evelyn filling the suitcase. "We're only going to be in Conneaut Lake for four days, and it gets chilly in the evenings."

"I want to look pretty for you," Evelyn said. "As long as we're going, I might as well be a fashion plate."

"You're a fashion plate naked," he said, and came up behind her, tracing the pale olive of the skin on her ear with his finger, kissing the back of her neck.

"Later," she said. "When I've finished everything I have to do."

"That's very elegant," he said. "Three suitcases. Why can't we put everything in one? I'm not taking as many clothes as you are. Or Chrissie. What does she need so many clothes for?"

"She wants to be pretty for you, too. She loves you so much."

"And I love her. I love both my girls." He kissed her again, on her ear.

"Later," Evelyn said.

"You could put my clothes in with yours. I'm not taking as much as either of you. And it's going to be a lot of carrying."

"I wouldn't want your slacks to get crushed. I know how meticulous you are. Why don't you go get your things from the bathroom? Your many things from the bathroom."

Before they went to bed, she had him put the suitcases outside the bedroom door, so they would have plenty of room for making love, in case he wanted to do anything fancy. He did, and to her surprise, she found that it really aroused her. "My life begins today," she whispered against his lips, unable to contain her excitement.

Partly she was excited about the cab coming at eleven-fifteen, and sneaking out, like two little girls in a Kill Daddy Club, off on a True Adventure. Evelyn could explain to Chris that part of the fun of the game was whispers, and silence. She could dress her in the dark—the clothes were laid out already. And if Chris wanted to say goodbye to Daddy, Evelyn could tell her that would spoil the fun, because they wanted Daddy to be surprised.

And he would be surprised, the son of a bitch, with his filthy little tricks he had picked up from his whores. One of them he was using right now, and Evelyn lay back and let herself enjoy it, in spite of how disgusting it was. Not in spite of, she thought—now that she was at the actual threshold of escape she had to be completely fair. Because of how disgusting it was, and how much she despised him, that was what made it so good. Made it wonderful.

TWO

For SONNY STERNE, God was not in the White House. But He had certainly manifested a part of Himself there. While Republicans, of whom Sonny considered himself one, spat the name of Roosevelt hatefully into the air, adding the vile label of Jew—which Sonny knew was impossible, as he was elected, not Chosen—Sonny regarded the flat-spoken gentleman as a subtle ally. To begin with, Roosevelt was the first of Them in public to act as if it was all right for them to be Jewish in private. But Roosevelt never went so far as to suggest it was so all right to be Jewish that you didn't have to feel any different.

Sonny prided himself on his heritage, because there was so little of it in actual existence, he had to struggle to remember. When memory failed him, because so many of his family were dead, and the dead cannot prod memory with anecdote, the thing Jews did best, Sonny would study the Bible.

Not that he was more interested in biblical history than he was in law and finance, which he also studied. But when everybody who belonged to you, and to whom you belonged, kept on dying around you, it gave you a terrible fear of the future. Fear of the future could only be assuaged by faith in the past. That way death became a part of history, ennobling—not an eradicating blow to those who participated, and a crash to the stomach and mind of those who were left to mourn.

The first he had mourned was his mother, although he could not remember her, no matter how often he studied her picture. He had been too young—he could not even recall how young anymore. He had to keep asking his brother Arnold how old they had been when their mother died. He remembered only the grief, which he had managed to keep alive. He would study his face in the mirror and look for signs of her in his slate-blue eyes, seek out her continuing history. But all he could see was her sorrow at not being there to help him.

The fullness of straight blond hair, the impressive immensity of his forehead and skull—these, along with the high Slavic set of his cheekbones, came directly from his mother. She had been Russian, his father told him. The part of Sonny that was most obviously German, the best possible thing to be, had come from his father, who had also died, only within living memory. Sonny remembered protestations on his father's part that Russian was thought by some to be better than German, but Sonny did not think so. He was sure that his father had not thought so either, or he would not have kept so strongly alive the news that he had come from Germany. Because who was there to dispute him? They were all dead.

Everybody died. That was a physical and historical and philosophic truth, as little sense as it made. What everybody didn't do was die when their children were children, leaving them with their whole lives ahead of them, unguided. It was a personal betrayal, people leaving Sonny like that, without consultation. He enjoyed discussion even more than reading, and if people were planning on dying, Sonny considered it only fair that they should discuss it with him. By the time he was ten years old, in 1922, the world was already too full of terrible surprises.

A part of it, Sonny supposed, came from living in Brooklyn. When a person dwelt in such Babylonian splendor, he should not be surprised when the Samson that was Fate brought the roof crashing down around his head.

The crash that he remembered most clearly in his twenties was not the one that other people considered to be a crash, which, with Roosevelt, gave the Sterne brothers their best chance. The one that struck at his soul, robbing him of all living history, had occurred when he was nine, a few years after his mother had died. (How many years? He would have to check again with his brother Arnold, as he checked all things with his brother Arnold, because there was no one else around to give evidence, a vital thing in law.)

His father had remarried. Because it was not right for two young boys to be brought up in a world without women. They needed a mother. That's what Otto Sterne told them. Nothing about a man not being able to live alone, because he needed relief, he needed release, a housekeeper was not enough, no matter how well she cooked and cleaned, because there was nothing to ease the pressure in his thing. Sex was not a topic for Otto Sterne to discuss with his boys. They were too young, even though the older one, Arnold, was already reputed to be running with *hoor*s.

"You boys need a mother," was all Otto Sterne said, going off to court the widow.

"He needs to get the pressure off his thing," Arnold said, when their father was gone.

"What thing?" Sonny asked his brother, sitting in the crystalled and antimacassared and overstuffed brown-cushioned magnificence of their dark living room. The pointy prisms that hung from the flower-painted lamps were well dusted. The doilies that lacily guarded the backs of the brown sofas and chairs were well laundered and ironed. The cushions on the furniture were finely fluffed. The dinner settling in their bellies was well cooked

5 7

and tasty. It should have been enough for any man. It was certainly enough for Sonny.

Arnold ignored his question.

"What thing?" Sonny asked again.

"You're only five," Arnold said, with the contempt of those who are thirteen. "I'll tell you when you're older."

"Do you know why this is called an antimacassar?" Sonny said, pointing to the lace doily on the sofa. He was always trying to find out obscure pieces of information, questioning everybody, in order to know what Arnold might not know, and have something to trade. It was very difficult with Arnold knowing almost everything, and being such a good trader.

"No, little brother," Arnold said, with a semblance of patience, as though he already knew. "Why is it called an antimacassar?"

"Because there was a hair oil called macassar and everybody used it on their hair once and it got on the furniture."

"I'm sure not many people know that," Arnold said.

Sonny beamed. "So what's a thing?" More than a fair trade.

"I'll tell you when you're older."

"You won't forget?" Sonny already had colossal fear of facts being lost to him. He couldn't remember his mother, his own mother. How could he be sure that Arnold would remember a *thing?*

The widow Otto Sterne was courting was a beautiful Polish immigrant with one child. After they married, she uncovered more and more children, revealing them one by one, slowly, as a magician pulled rabbits from a hat.

"The cunt is quicker than the eye," Arnold Sterne said.

"What's a cunt?"

"You're only seven. I'll tell you when you're older."

"You won't forget?"

Arnold laughed. "When I forget that, I'll be dead."

"You're not going to die?" Panic deadlocked the beating of Sonny's heart.

"Everybody dies."

"But not you, Arnold."

"I'll do my best to stay around as long as I can."

"And you'll tell me what a cunt is?"

"By the time I tell you, you'll already have found out for yourself. Or you're no brother of mine."

The widow (Sonny could not call her Mother) turned out to have six children altogether. None of them looked or thought like Sonny. It worried him terribly, the slanted suggestion that Arnold might not really be his brother. It was bad enough never having seen your grandparents, not believing that two of them at least came from Germany, not being able to remember what your mother looked like. To be without a brother who was your own flesh would be emptiness. Disaster.

So when he was eight, Sonny asked his father what a cunt was. His father smashed him once, hard, across the jaw, and went to work, to the barbershop where he shaved faces, and cut hair, and in late-night meetings did something called politics.

Sonny did not ask his stepmother what a cunt was. If it evoked such anger from his own father, who really loved him, what would it cause in a woman who had no love for him at all? She pretended affection—at least she had pretended it while she was in the process of revealing the existence of all those children, one by one. But she had no real love for him, Sonny could tell. Just as she had no real love for his father and had only used him to find safe harbor for those spindly, thin-haired rodents she called children. ("Polacks," Arnold said. "That fair-haired giant of a German has built this nest to be overrun by a load of Litvaks and Poles.") Even the baby swelling her still-young belly was no testament of love for Otto Sterne, Arnold assured Sonny.

"She is merely sealing the Concordat," Arnold said. He was an excellent student, not as good as Sonny was to be, but he loved history. It was Arnold's intention to build empires, and one could not build them without solid past examples. "She is creating another little pig of a Polack to make sure she gains heavily of his riches."

"Is he very rich?" Sonny asked.

"He is richer than any Polack," Arnold said.

The little girl that was born was known as his sister, but Sonny wasn't sure. She didn't have the great massive skull that he and Arnold had inherited, and her eyes were dark, almost black, not gray-blue like theirs. In the roundness of infant face it was impossible to decipher cheekbones. As it was too soon for her to speak, Sonny would have to wait to see if their same planning, clever brain was in her head. But she was pretty, if you liked babies.

Stepmother Sterne apparently didn't, in spite of now having seven of them. Sonny could hear her fighting with his father through the walls, more amazing for the fact that their walls were thicker than most other walls in Brooklyn, made of cement and brick, even inside the house.

"What do you want?" Otto Sterne was screaming to his wife. "What do you want from me?"

"I want nothing. Nothing! Except you should stay away from me."

"Why? What have I done?"

"Nothing. That's just what you've done. Nothing. Nothing for me and my children. Everything is your sons, your wonderful sons, the oldest who wouldn't spit on me, except in his heart."

"I married you. I gave you my home, my name, everything."

"You gave me nothing. You give me nothing. I'm your maid."

"You have your own maid."

"To clean a house that is not in my name."

"It's in my name, Hannah. A name I share with you."

"To be passed on to your sons. I saw the will. If you touch me, I might have another child. To be left nothing. Nothing."

"What will?"

"The will that you have locked up in your desk. With all the names of people who make votes. I saw. I saw. I found the key."

"That's an old will. From when my first wife died. I had a fear of death, because I thought I could die too soon, and I wanted to make sure nobody robbed my sons. But I'm fine now. I'm still young. I'm not afraid."

"I am. I am."

"Of what? I'll protect you. I'm strong."

"Don't touch me!"

"What do you want? My money? Here!" The rustling of a mattress. "Here it is. All of it. You want the house? The house is yours. I'll write another will."

"No." Softer now. "You certainly managed to save a lot of money."

The next day she was gone, taking her original six and the cash with her. She left the baby with him, and the house. Otto Sterne spent seven months trying to find her, even though she was living less than a mile away, under another name, in a crowded tenement. A needle in a haystack, someone said.

"Some haystack." Otto Sterne looked through the great, lace-curtained bay window out at Brooklyn, with its stunted houses, its endless streets. "I have to find her."

When a man is involved in politics, on no matter how lowly a scale, when a man is used to collect voters and win friends for people without accents who run for office, he is owed a lot of favors. Some good, some bad. One of the men who owed him a bad favor found her.

"She's over on Nostrand Avenue, Otto," the man said, handing him a piece of paper. "The number and the apartment are there. It's a pigsty. Eight families sharing one toilet in the hall. She must be keeping your money in paper bags. She certainly isn't spending it."

It was a very cold night in December, so in spite of the fire in his eyes, Otto went to put on his good heavy overcoat, the one he usually wore to important political meetings. Arnold helped him with the sleeves.

"What are you going to do, Pa?" Arnold said. "You going to kill her?"

"I'm going to plead with her to come back."

"Why?"

"You're a smart boy, Arnold. You learn things well in school. You're old enough to know about *hoors*. I hope it isn't too long before you learn about love."

"Jesus Christ," Arnold said, after he had shut the door behind his father. "What a potato."

Sonny was sitting huddled in the great wing armchair beside the fire, warming himself against more than cold. He had never seen his father's face so anxious, heard his breathing coming so fast.

"He wants her back," Sonny said. "After everything she did. Is that what love is?"

"That's what being a potato is." Arnold put his red knitted scarf around his neck, pulled his wool gloves up tight against the sleeves of his heavy brown coat. "Our father is a *schmuck*."

"You going to help him?"

"I'm going to get laid." Arnold paused in front of the dark-framed mirror in the entrance hall, squinting at his reflection in the dim, flickering gaslight in the fluted hanging lamp. The face that looked back at him was strong, but not as impressive as Sonny's; he lacked that buttress of chin that made the younger brother look ready for battle. But it was a good face. Intelligent, with high-angled cheekbones, emphasizing the clarity of the eyes. The eyes were exactly the same as Sonny's, except that they lacked compassion. That was what would save him. Compassionate men could not build empires.

He turned and looked at Sonny, at his own face, only with a big jaw and sadness in the eyes. "You know what getting laid is, little brother? It's when you stick your thing into a lady's cunt. Now you know it all. And that's all it is, is getting laid. There are some potatoes what call that love. Don't ever make that mistake."

"He's not a *schmuck*," Sonny said. "He's a great man."

"Any man who lets himself be diminished by a woman can never be great. You're nine years old," Arnold said, opening the front door. "What the hell do you know?"

Sonny tried to stay awake as long as he could. He wanted to see his father returning in triumph, with her loving, repentant, clinging to the hem of that great black overcoat. He wanted to see his father flushed with manly victory.

When he saw his father again, Otto Sterne was no color at all. Some friends woke the younger son and told him to come downstairs. They brought the nine-year-old boy down the winding staircase to see his father.

They had moved a great carved oaken blanket chest into the middle of the foyer and lain Otto Sterne on it like a hideous bouquet. They told Sonny Otto had died, his heart had just stopped beating, while he was pleading with the widow to come home. He lay wrapped in a coarse gray muslin winding sheet and potato sacking, candles at his head and at his feet, which were bare and very gray. There were pennies on his eyes.

Sonny had never seen death before. Only felt it, all the time. Fear clutched at him with skeleton hands, mortality clutched at his soul. He screamed, slid down the stairs, and fainted.

The intricate white-painted, carved wood latticework framing the front porch of their home, distinguishing it from the identical one- and two-family houses on their street, the clusters of plaster grapes protruding from cornices outside the building and over the fireplaces inside, grew dark in the ensuing years. Not that the boys wanted their house to fall into disrepair: there was simply not enough money to keep up the house. Arnold got a part-time job, full-time on weekends, running errands and doing things he didn't want to discuss with Sonny, for one of the politicians who had paid for Otto's funeral. The money Arnold earned was enough for the maid, so there would be someone to look after Baby, which they continued to call her, even though she was now a little girl. He had a few dollars left over for those schoolbooks he couldn't borrow from his college friends, and some second-hand clothes for himself and Sonny. The only thing they didn't have too often was food.

Neighborhood families, who knew very well the story of the Black Widow Sterne, had the boys over for dinner once in a while, rotating the hospitality according to the amount of pity they felt and how far the meals would stretch. Hot soup was ladled into oversize bowls; Mason jars filled with thick broth were sent home with them, although the boys swore they couldn't eat another thing, ever. The soup, along with the six eggs the chicken merchant who had loved their father gave them twice a week, was enough to take care of Baby and the maid for three or four days, supplemented by the milk the maid herself bought, and the fruit Sonny stole.

He kept a regular checklist of what exactly he lifted from Bernstein's cart, along with the price of the item that particular day. It was his intention to pay him back in full when he and Arnold became czars of big business, which couldn't be more than a few years away—at which point he might even be generous and build Bernstein a store that didn't walk around. Maybe somewhere on Flatbush Avenue, in between the clothing store they couldn't afford and the delicatessen that Sonny and Arnold robbed in tandem.

It was the only food they actually stole for themselves. No matter how hungry they were, Sonny saved the fruit for Baby and tried to keep his loot to a minimum, Bernstein being an independent pushcart peddler and a kind man. McCloskey, on the other hand, had a delicatessen that was warm even on the coldest day of winter, and a delivery trade that a rich man would envy, because McCloskey delivered to the people who were so rich they didn't have to go outside for a walk to a store with plate-glass windows where they would be warm and get all the good smells. He prided himself on being a pickle-barrel philosopher, and thought he could match points of history and political theory even with Arnold, who had almost finished college, and Sonny, who would one day go across the river to Columbia University, that was how smart he was, Arnold told McCloskey all the time.

"Brooklyn isn't good enough for him?" the storekeeper said. He was sweating in the heat of his too-comfortable store, beads of moisture collecting atop his totally bald head, tear-shaped pools that found each other and became erratic little waterfalls coursing leisurely into his heavy eyebrows. When the eyebrows themselves became sodden, and the wetness started to go into his eyes, McCloskey would wipe the thick inverted "v's" above his

64

eyes, the skin on his head, and then the counter, all with the same rag.

"Brooklyn is good enough for anybody," Arnold said, eyeing the roll-mops, too well protected behind glass. "I myself am finishing my matriculation at Brooklyn College, which I consider to have as fine a curriculum as any university in the world." Arnold did not speak that way, except to McCloskey, who was hypnotized by bright flashes of education, which gave Sonny a better chance at the tomato herring stacked in the corner.

"You really consider that?" McCloskey said. "What about those ward-heelers you run with. They think they can make a political hero out of a Brooklynite?"

"It is not my wish to run for political office," Arnold said. "However, with my brother's vast appreciation of history and economics, it's possible that one day—"

"He reads Karl Marx," McCloskey interrupted. "How can he be a decent American politician if he reads Karl Marx?"

"One must search out the historical errors as well as the historical successes. Marx was a clever man, you realize. It was Germany he intended the revolution for. Germany might have benefited more than Russia. It had the industry, you see. An industrial country could make much more use of communism than an agricultural one. Germany will never make a comeback from the Great War. With all the progress they've made from our loans since 1919, they will never be a power again. They might have done better to listen to Marx."

"They would never listen to a Jew."

"But he was a *German* Jew," Arnold said. "It wasn't as if he were a Pole." Arnold held his breath for a moment, studying the big, bushy-browed, sweaty face. McCloskey was always claiming to be Russian, but Arnold wasn't so sure.

"So are you buying anything?"

"Well, we were just passing by, and you know how much pleasure we get from these discussions with you, my brother and I . . ."

"Where is your brother?" McCloskey leaned over the counter, his white-aproned belly dipping slightly into the square metal pan

65

filled with potato salad. "He was right over there a minute ago."

"Right here, Mr. McCloskey," Sonny said, his arms tight against the sides of his bulging jacket.

"What were you doing?" McCloskey said. "I didn't see what you were doing. Where were you?"

"I was listening with great interest to your discussion about Karl Marx," Sonny said. "You know, the most interesting fact of all about revolutions, I think, is what Marx said about the French. That they really knew how to have a revolution, they just didn't know what to do with it once they had it." He started to point a finger in the air in a scholarly manner but heard the slight clinking under his arm of can against can. "Do you agree with that?"

"I have no use for French people," McCloskey said. "They pee in the street."

"An interesting intellectual point," Arnold said.

"What? I didn't hear you." McCloskey was listening very hard for another metallic sound from Sonny's jacket.

"I was asking you if you've ever visited Paris," Arnold said.

"I don't need to," McCloskey answered. "I nearly got killed near Campillon, and after the armistice I met my own Mademoiselle from Armentières. She told me everything about Paris, and she never washed anything but . . ." He looked at Sonny. "You know."

"No, I don't," Arnold said. "Perhaps you'd be so good as to tell me."

"Not in front of your brother."

"Sonny, why don't you go stand over there in the corner for a minute while Mr. McCloskey and I—"

"Enough standing in corners," McCloskey said. "Are you buying anything?"

"Not today, thank you," Arnold said.

"I hope you're enjoying my food."

"Pardon me?" said Arnold. The cold expression was gone from the slate-blue eyes, which were suddenly pale with angry innocence.

"The rabbi's house. Every *Shabbas* I send over, the fish, the

6 6

meat, everything. His wife won't prepare anymore, she's getting a lot of religion since she got sick. I understand you've been sharing their table."

"Only on Saturdays."

"And the daughter. How is she?"

"She's a lovely girl."

"Pretty?"

"Of course she's pretty. Why would I be seeing a girl if she wasn't pretty?"

"Why indeed?" McCloskey said. The little metal bell against the front door clanged gently, and an old woman wearing a heavy sweater and a babushka, carrying a straw bag, entered the store. "Excuse me, boys. A *paying* customer."

"We look forward to another discussion soon," Arnold said. "We'll be seeing you."

"I'm sure," said McCloskey.

The Sterne brothers walked out into the chill of early evening. A sleet-fringed wind from further up the block where the fish store was brought the smell of halibut stinging into their faces and their stomachs. They kept their heads down until they had turned the corner, where lines of bakeries and clothing stores and stationers with fine new sharp-pointed pencils gave way to pushcarts, and two- and three- and four-family gray-brick homes.

"How many did you get?" said Arnold, when nobody could hear but a group of ragged children, pitching single pennies against the cracks in building stoops.

"Ten, maybe eleven cans," Sonny said.

"All tomato herring?"

Sonny nodded.

"I wish to hell he'd change his display. I think I'd give my soul for something besides tomato herring. A sardine. Anything."

"And these," Sonny said, his face dissolving into smiles as he pulled two sour pickles from his pocket, fresh from the barrel, dripping with brine.

"You're crazy," Arnold said, as he took one and bit into it. "Your jacket will stink for a week."

"It's worth it," Sonny said, and, tasting and feeling it fall into the emptiness inside, he thought he could hear it echo. "So now you won't have to give your soul."

He chewed for a while, enjoying the crunch of it inside his head, not even feeling the cold as he walked. "You think he's on to us? I could have sworn there for a minute he knew exactly what we were doing, that he was on to us."

"Don't be ridic," Arnold said. "We're much too smart for him."

They heard the clatter of horses' hooves kicking smartly onto the icy streets, the jingle of coins the little boys were pitching, the rumble of a passing motor car, the clanging of cans of tomato herring in Sonny's jacket as they began to run. "Don't run too fast," Arnold said. "Maybe it isn't the police."

"Nobody else has horses anymore," Sonny said. "Run."

"Stop running," Arnold said, trying to keep pace. "If it is a cop, he isn't after us."

"I never trusted McCloskey," Sonny said.

"They're not after us, they can't be after us. It's only a couple of cans."

There was an ice truck parked by a private six-family house in the center of the block, its rear door hanging open. "Under or in?" Sonny said breathlessly.

"We're crazy to hide." Arnold said. "It looks guilty to hide. Under."

They slid themselves between the rear wheels and lay on the ice of the street, waiting for the horses to pass, the moment of peril to become history. "What can they do to us?" Sonny whispered.

"Nothing," said Arnold, his breath coming faster. He moved himself further under the chassis of the truck. "They're not looking for us. The only thing that makes us guilty is hiding. It's tomato herring, for Christ's sake. A couple of cans . . ."

"So it's crazy to be afraid," Sonny said.

"Crazy," said Arnold, as his body shook from the cold of the street, and fear.

They could see the hooves of the two horses moving past

them, and the foot of one of the riders. "Ask him for a match," Sonny whispered. "It's cold down here."

"Shut up," said Arnold.

The riders were gone. "They weren't even looking for us," said Arnold, as they slid back out into the street, walked to the pavement, and strolled back into freedom. "I told you it was silly to hide. McCloskey knows nothing."

"I was afraid," Sonny said. "I'm not like you. I don't want to get caught."

"Nobody wants to get caught," said Arnold. "The important thing is always to deny everything."

"With eleven cans of tomato herring in my jacket?"

"Someone must have put them there," said Arnold. "You have no idea how they got there. You're going to be a lawyer, you remember that. The most important tenet of law is to deny everything."

"Then why were we hiding under the truck?"

"Exactly," said Arnold. "That was a stupid thing to do."

"I'm sorry."

"It's all right. Stop apologizing. And don't ever be afraid of McCloskey. The man is a moron, he has no idea what's going on. Most of the people in the world have no idea what's going on, so never be afraid of them."

After the old lady left, McCloskey pulled down the shade on his front door for a few minutes so nobody would come in. He went behind the counter and took up a black and white speckled cardboard-covered notebook with ruled pages inside, which held his credit accounts. He opened it to the indexed "S" and turned to Sterne, Arnold and Abraham. The Father. What an old name for such a young boy, with that beautiful face, even with the mean jaw that belonged to a thief. No wonder they called him Sonny.

He went to the display of tomato herring and counted. Eleven cans missing. That made a total of—what?—over the past year. And how many before he had gotten wise to them? Two thousand and eleven? Three thousand and eleven? Ten, twenty cans a week for what? Three years? Four years? How long had they been robbing him?

It didn't make any difference. They'd pay up. The inventory he kept was as good as the one he didn't know Sonny kept on Bernstein, and one day they'd pay him back. Whether or not they planned on it, *he* planned on it. When he'd first found out about the stealing, he let them keep it up out of pity. By the time he started to get angry, Arnold Sterne, that clever *vonce,* was seeing the rabbi's daughter.

Pretty? "Why would I be seeing a girl if she wasn't pretty?" Why indeed? A girl whose plainness was legendary, coming from the background and riches she did. One way or the other, Arnold would pay him back. Even if he couldn't get to the money and power of the politicians across the river, Arnold Sterne would be able to stock a fine table. And then maybe he could start ordering in bulk: gefilte fish, and beef, and pastrami. To be charged, of course, to his already established account.

Sarah, the rabbi's daughter, was not only plain, she was not very bright. But bright enough to appreciate that Arnold was brilliant; that much was evident from the admiration in her eyes, which made them seem twice the size they actually were, and lent her a glow of loveliness she would not have had for Arnold if her eyes were the size they should have been and had she asked too many questions. It was enough for her that Arnold was handsome, that he seemed genuinely interested in her, and, more important, that he was continually attentive when her father spoke, which was almost constantly. She was intimidated by masculine wisdom, and by vocal strength, and that made her very appealing to Arnold.

His courtship of her was not hypocrisy, no matter what the people in the neighborhood thought: a man with no money had to make very fast tracks if he was going to catch up with bankers like the Warburgs and the Rothschilds and the Sangers. That meant he had to be carrying very little on his back. Arnold, at the age of twenty-one and a half, already had two children to raise, and if he was going to take on a wife, she should weigh less than a hundred pounds and look at him like that. When a woman looked at you like that, you didn't even have to be as smart as you were with the owner of a delicatessen.

There were no other children except Sarah in Rabbi Shimkus' family, and that suited Arnold, too. The rabbi was wealthy, but only in comparison to other rabbis from good family. Besides, Arnold did not look to him for any kind of inheritance, except for the good faith of his congregation. The "flock" that Rabbi Shimkus so enjoyed, who looked to him for spiritual and moral guidance, were fairly moneyed. It followed that they would need financial guidance when they became more sophisticated, since everybody was starting to make so much money in speculation. And what better place to seek financial guidance than from the son-in-law of the man who had led them beside the still waters spiritually?

So Arnold ate heartily at the rabbi's table, where the food was almost as good as the prospects. And he did not defile the rabbi's daughter, because he had too much respect for the dour, bearded old man. Besides, he had no real wish to touch Sarah. Her wrists were too slender, and there was a light down along the sides of her throat.

But he was fond of her, he was sure. Not fond in the Shakespearean sense, to go crazy as his father had, surrendering his manhood and eventually his life. But fond enough to contemplate a life with her, to give her a few children, and to prosper enough to take care of her and have some real women on the side.

He did not consider his attitude cynical or opportunistic. The robber barons had joined great lines of transportation together; it could not have been possible if they hadn't had dealings with those who were beneath them, and cheated on them occasionally.

Nor did he impart any of his true attitudes to Sonny. Sonny

7 1

was a romantic, you could see that already, looking for love with the same uneasy finesse with which he shoplifted. When he came to the rabbi's house for Saturday dinner once a month, along with Arnold, he would listen with great joy to the rabbi's constant dissertations, assuming that his brother was there to drink of the wisdom, as he was doing, as well as the sweet red wine, pleased that he was allowed to take in such knowledge and beneficence.

When the discussion moved too deeply into religious study, Sonny would act the biblical scholar with the reb, whoever Shimkus was being that night, taking the pressure off Arnold. Sonny asked all the right questions, and was never put off by the eclecticism of the finer points of the religion. He could discuss the Talmud as well as if he had danced at his own bar mitzvah, as if there had been money enough to continue his religious education and celebrate his becoming a man.

The dining room of Rabbi Shimkus was dark: heavy olive-green velvet curtains closed against whatever small majesty might be in the back yard. The walls were paneled with ancient wood on which hung gold-framed penciled sketches of the Great Rabbis, *taleysim* draped over their shoulders, stripes on the white material giving small relief from the heavy gloom of the bearded faces. Candles, some commemorating the Sabbath, some saving on electricity, gave dull warmth to the formal stillness, broken only by the rabbi's words of history, and Sonny's questions, and Sarah's occasional shy inquiries if Arnold wanted more to eat.

The mother never spoke. She was old, her beauty was sapped from her, and she was dying, waiting for some message from God that would come to her through her husband, or in the flashes of lightning she feared would split the sky outside the window, which was why the curtains were kept closed. It was an atmosphere of unremitting gloom, not like the Sterne dining room had been, filled with light and friends and laughter. But there were parents here, and food.

" 'Two men pick up a garment,' " Rabbi Shimkus quoted. " 'Should one say, "I found it," and the other say, "I found it," they must divide it equally.' "

Sonny nodded vigorously. This captured the rabbi's full attention, giving Arnold more time to eat.

" 'However, should one say, "It is all mine," and the other say, "It is half mine," then Rabbi Gamaliel says . . .' "

"Is that who you'd like to be?" asked Arnold. "Rabbi Gamaliel?" He was not used to challenging Sarah's father, but the chicken was a little gamey, in addition to soft, and they had discussed the same passage a month before.

"I would like to be who I am," the rabbi said. "A man with a good life, a good woman, a fine daughter, a loving congregation. I have only one regret, and that is I have no son to follow after me."

Sarah and Arnold exchanged glances, her small eyes crinkling with a shy smile. It was as good a time as any, she was signaling him. Arnold bit into the chicken and let the moment pass. If he made it too easy, there would be less money to furnish the apartment he had already located in Manhattan.

"And how would you educate your son?" Arnold asked. "I'm asking, of course, because I dream of a son, and I already have a brother who is like a son to me. I worry about him spending too much time with the Bible."

"There is no such thing as too much time with the Bible," the rabbi said.

"He's fourteen years old, and he studies the Pentateuch. There is more fornication in it than in Captain Billy's Whizbang."

"Filth can be found anywhere, Arnold."

"But you don't even have to look for the dirty passages. Joseph and Potiphar's wife, for example. When she cries out, 'Sleep with me, sleep with me.' " Arnold never read the Bible or the Pentateuch himself, but Sonny had come to him with great excitement in the midst of several stories, asking if that was what it was all about, getting laid.

"Would you like some more applesauce?" Sarah got up quickly from her chair so her father would not see the redness on her face.

"No, thank you," Arnold said. "How about it, Rabbi?"

"Joseph is a fantastic story," Sonny said. "Even forgetting the religiosity, it's better than a movie. Because you can imagine, you know what I mean? The chapters in Genesis end all up in the air, filled with suspense; there he is, *Perils of Pauline,* sold as a slave into Egypt. Then all of a sudden they break away and tell the story of Joseph's brother Judah, having a full life among non-Jews."

"There can be no full life among non-Jews," the rabbi said.

"There certainly was for Judah," Sonny ventured. "Becoming friends with 'a certain Adullamite,' getting involved with 'the daughter of a certain Canaanite . . .' Having three sons and finding a wife, Tamar, for them, and the second son is Onan . . ." He looked nervously at the rabbi. The dinner table was no place for a discussion of onanism, even if it was in Genesis.

So where was the right place? The sexuality of the Bible obsessed him. He wondered every time he saw a bunch of Yeshiva students, with their frightening *payess* and dark mournful clothes, and their hands always on some religious book, if underneath the long black coats they were playing with themselves. Surely they could not bring themselves to have relations with *shicksas* and loose women, the way his brother did.

"You must remember," the rabbi cautioned dourly, "that the story ends with Judah's never sleeping with Tamar again."

"Oh, I know that, I know that," Sonny said. "It was a mistake. He didn't realize it was his daughter-in-law. But it's still a very fascinating story. Sex aside."

"We are all capable of mistakes, and remorse. We can err, because of our humanity. It is our ability to triumph over the weakness of our humanity that brings us closer to our God. That is the message of the Bible. That is the heritage of our ancestors."

Sonny shifted uncomfortably in his chair, the sweater that had belonged to someone else's son scratching his throat. Ancestors. He did not even know what his grandparents had been like. How could he possibly connect with ancestors? God was less remote to him than forebears.

"It's still full of stupendous stories," Sonny said.

The rabbi smiled. "You have the enthusiasm of a true scholar," Shimkus said. "I have no hope for your brother."

Arnold looked up from his plate. He squinted into the semi-darkness, the apartment on Riverside Drive vanishing for the moment.

"He is a bright young man, but his sights are on the earth, and the gold that can be gotten out of it. There's nothing wrong with that . . ."

"Thank heaven for small favors," Arnold said. "I thought you were fascinated by investment banking."

"So I am, so I am," the rabbi said. "As I am fascinated by science. But that doesn't make it comprehensible or divine to me."

"Maybe because you never had to worry about money," Arnold said.

"Perhaps. But there can be no infinite riches, except the riches of God."

"Oh, I'll go along with that," Arnold said, and passed his plate to Sarah for more potatoes. The living room would be furnished in deep reds and browns.

"And that is why I should like your brother to study to be a rabbi. With me. He would be under my personal supervision. I would school him with more energy and affection than the wealthiest of Talmudic scholars receive."

Arnold looked over at Sonny. The boy had stopped eating and was looking at the rabbi with a mixture of joy and panic. The sacrifice of—who the hell was it? Arnold couldn't remember. Isaac? Was that the thing about the lamb and the burning bush? Wasn't it enough that he would throw himself between Sarah's spindly loins? Did he have to offer up his brother to this outdated old man, who might be handsome underneath the curly red beard with its constantly moving pink mouth. This relic from another age, an ancient fear, who probably had thanked God all through his youth that there were some nights, at least, when he could call his wife unclean.

"That's very kind of you, sir," Sonny said. "Kind and generous. I can't think of anyone from whom I'd rather learn."

"Then it's settled?" The rabbi's dark eyes shone, as history was augmented by future.

"Anyone, that is, except my brother." Sonny smiled, and the hard set of prominent jaw was lost in the softness of open face. "Arnold knows everything there is to know about the world of finance . . ."

"The world of finance, Sonny. It is still only the world. A man can conquer the world, but it is still only earth."

"As opposed to Heaven?" Arnold said.

"As opposed to nothing," said the rabbi. "The earth is in no contest with Heaven."

"Well somebody ought to tell Heaven that," Arnold said, "and then maybe it'd stop hitting us with earthquake, fire, and flood."

"You make jokes about things you don't understand, Arnold, so I cannot be offended by you. I forgive you your lack of understanding, your unwillingness to learn anything except what will make things *easier*. You had to be a man when you were still a boy, and you did it well. I doubt that I myself could have taken care of an orphaned family as you did, with no help from anyone except those crooked politicians . . ." He was sliding into sermon, the basso voice sonorous. ". . . . who give nothing to the synagogue because they think that the destiny of man is in man's hands, to be guided by subtle bribery and fixing. I pity these men, and I forgive them. Just as I forgive you, for thinking as you do. You have a brilliant mind, Arnold, and it is not your fault that your thinking is too narrow."

Arnold swallowed a laugh, along with a roasted potato.

"Perhaps one day when you have achieved the financial success you think is the be-all and end-all of life—"

"I don't think that. I just think success helps so you can do what you want to beyond that."

"Such as?"

"Helping people."

The rabbi nodded slowly, digesting the remembered propaganda Sarah had given him. "My daughter tells me that is your real goal. To be a philanthropist. But there is no greater help than being a teacher. A rabbi. To help your people, one by one. I know you have no interest in that particular goal, but your brother is still a boy . . ."

"His brother," Sonny said. "That's all I am."

"You're more than that," the rabbi said. "You could be brother and father to hundreds. You are family to millions."

"I can't think in terms of millions," Sonny said.

"Except in dollars," Arnold said, and laughed. "That he's going to pick up very fast."

When they were walking home in the warm spring night, along cracked sidewalks that gave lying evidence of better days where none had been, Arnold threw his arm around Sonny's shoulders. Sonny was already taller at fourteen than his brother was at twenty-one and a half, so Arnold had to reach up and over, and couldn't quite hug him. But it felt like a hug to Sonny because it was his brother's hand.

"Don't feel bad about the old man," Arnold said. "If you really want to make him happy, you can go there once a week when he's finished at *shul* and let him dump the overflow on you. After Sarah and I get married, I'll give you cabfare from Manhattan."

"It's settled then? You're marrying her?"

"It's been settled since I was sixteen and she saw me."

"But you've spoken to the rabbi, and he's given his consent?"

"His consent," Arnold said, and laughed aloud, aiming the noise in his throat at a yellow-curtained, second-story window. "He's been talking so much for so long he can't even hear that he isn't the one making decisions."

"She'd listen to him," Sonny said. "She'd have to listen to him."

"And while she was listening to him, he'd be looking at her. He may be deaf from his own voice, but he isn't blind. Who would want her?"

"You don't love her?" Sonny asked, alarmed. The Bible spoke in very simple sentences, giving whole family histories in two lines. And for all its vibrant sexuality, there was not much description of how, for example, the young virgin looked who had been brought for the old, stricken-in-years King David; only the imperative that she should stand before the king and let her cherish him, and let her lie in his bosom that "my lord the king may get heat." Sarah was young, and there was no doubt that she was a virgin, but would she give Arnold heat?

"Certainly I love her," Arnold said, and did a small peg-legged dance in and out of the gutter.

"I don't mean that way," Sonny said. "I mean the way—"

"The way they tell about it in the Bible?" Arnold smiled. "Well, if you think *that's* exciting, wait'll you set your chest on a pair of those soft little knobs. When are you going to be ready, Abe? When're you going to get your face out of those books and into some sweet pink bellybutton? Anytime you give the word—"

"I don't want to traffic with prostitutes," Sonny said.

"You don't have to traffic with them, baby brother. You can just zip in and out like the fastest Ford on the market."

"We don't have money for women."

"We don't need money. Any brother of mine gets a free ride any time he's ready. I've got this one little redhead with freckles on her toots that'd give up a weekend in the country for a big fat circumcised Sterne cock."

"I wish you wouldn't talk like that," Sonny said.

"But that's life, Abe. Life is gross, and real, and vulgar. Vulgar. That means common. It's common to all men; all men have reality in common. We're born, we fuck, we have children, we die. You can't put that in lofty language. The lowest of men can do that, so why try to give it any stature? The only thing that's ennobling is power, and what you do with it."

"Everyone can't feel that way."

"That's right, everyone doesn't, and because they don't, they can't get the most from life. They cover it all with butter to make it taste prettier, to make it sound better. When you schmaltz it up like that, it fattens up your arteries and your brain and puts a strain on your heart, and you drop dead in some bitch's bedroom, pleading with her for your life."

There was silence between them, echoing across the lamplit

7 8

night. Sonny could hear their footsteps amplified by the emptiness of the street, the emptiness of his brother's soul. Not possible. It was remembered agony, that was all. Arnold was pretending a cynicism he did not really believe. Probably from the
little he had read of Ecclesiastes.

"I think the rabbi's a very great man," Sonny said.

"You want to study with him?"

"I want to work with you. But if I didn't, I would like to study
with the rabbi. He's a great man, don't you think?"

"If you like Hebrews."

Sonny laughed. Across a vacant lot a cat meowed, sounding
equally as phony.

"All that Talmudic shit: who asked what question, and if it
had been the other way round, what would the wise man have
answered. Who cares? The Chosen People. Chosen for what? To
live in ghettos, and be feared and despised, because somebody
said don't eat pig, and let your hair grow funny. Dependent on a
set of rules not even Rabbi Gamaliel could make clear. Out of
Egypt to what? Imprisonment by self, and who even knew the
reason?"

"But they did get out of Egypt. God let them be freed and led
out of Egypt."

"Another joke," Arnold said. "Another good-natured joke for
the Jews to make out of terrible history. To try and convert
despair to dignity. What's that stuff in the Haggadah? That
singing routine that we dip from the wine, to tell how hard God
made it on the Egyptians so they'd let my people go?"

"Dom," Sonny intoned. *"Tz'far-day-a. Kee-neem . . ."*

"English," Arnold said. "I speak English."

"Blood. Frogs. Lice. Flies. Murrain. Boils. Hail. Locusts.
Darkness. Death of the firstborn."

"Right. God visited those plagues on Egypt, right? Because
the Egyptians were being hard on the slaves, the poor Jewish
slaves. So the Pharaoh freed them and let Moses lead them out of
the land."

"Exactly," said Sonny. "You can't question the Almighty
power of that."

"It makes a good story," Arnold smiled. "Now I'll tell you what really happened.

"This guy comes running into the Pharaoh, see, like the Minister of the Treasury, or Bad News. 'Pharaoh,' he cries. 'Look what's going on in this country. Ten plagues. Ten plagues in one year, in Egypt. What could cause ten plagues in such a terrific country? It's got to be the Jews.'

" 'You're right!' says the Pharaoh. 'Let's get them the hell out of here.' "

Arnold laughed harshly. Sonny strained for some sign of his brother's soul.

"Have you read Spinoza?"

"I read law and economics and history. I read everything I need to make the twists in my own fate. I'll be twenty-two in May and I graduate in June and I will have made a mark by twenty-five. I have no time for philosophy."

"Spinoza was a Jew who was rejected by Jews and then they came to accept him. He had all the ethics, without the fancy tradition, the"—the word fell dryly from his lips—"bullshit."

"He was afraid of God," Arnold said. "And how clearly can a man see when he thinks there is no such thing as absolute evil in the world? We're up to our eyeballs in it—how can a smart man not see what's in front of his eyeballs? And how smart can he be if he's afraid of a God he can't see?"

"But there's evidence everywhere."

"The boidies in the trees," Arnold said, affecting the accent he had prided himself on losing. "Why not just Natural Order?"

"You *have* read Spinoza," Sonny said, and a little of the warmth came back through the hand on his shoulder. He grinned and turned his face so his brother could see the amusement on it. "You can say all these things, because you're afraid of seeming scholarly or sentimental, but I know you. I really know you. You can't fool me."

"Then I'm in very big trouble. You can't fool a fourteen-year-old kid, how the hell are you going to make it on Wall Street?"

It wasn't easy. Right after graduation, Arnold was married to Sarah.

In spite of the fact that he could practically hear the boom echoing through the canyons of Lower Broadway, feel the excitement of capital growing as high and straight as the gray of the buildings in the crowds that rushed past early-morning-sun-tinted windows, the reality of the fantasy actually moving into action was not quite what he expected. There were other eager faces in the rippling stream of striped ties and gray suits coursing along the sidewalks, crossing over to Broad Street and Wall, which might have seemed as intelligent as his own. He would study mouths as he moved along toward the office building where he was temporarily camped, and see if any of them were set in more smug lines, look for eyes that shone in fulfillment of greater promise, wonder how many of them had been on the subway with him from Ninety-sixth and Broadway, or which of them had been dropped on the corner by Dad's limousine.

The whole charade of their pretending to scramble the way he had to, still, at twenty-five, was a pain in his butt, a giant prick in his balloon. How many of them knew there was a seat waiting for them on the Exchange, as soon as they finished acting out their apprenticeships? He had been with Whittaker and Lief since his college graduation, entertained one or two of the junior board members in the palatial apartment on Riverside Drive, had been nodded at once by the president of the firm—approvingly, he was sure. But with all his academic kudos, he had still only been hired by the *assistant* head of personnel; with all the accounts he brought to the firm from the people of Brooklyn, who were more than willing to cast in their lot and their cash with the rabbi's son-in-law, his office was still only a glassed-in cubicle, without secretary, without his name painted on the door.

"I thought it would be bigger," Sonny had said the first time he came in to see Arnold's office. "I thought it would be all paneled in wood, and there would be five or six telephones, and a lot of girls in short skirts bringing in papers for you to sign."

"You're a romantic," Arnold said, and took his brother out to a long, expensive lunch, eating instead of talking, because he had thought it would be that way, too.

After two years, he had a brass plate made with his name engraved on it, but there was no way it would stick to a glass door. When another six months had passed, and his salary had been increased again but there were no signs of an official promotion, he started an affair with the secretary of the vice-president, and had her duplicate her boss's customer file.

"What will happen, if Mr. Greenson finds out?" she said. She was a tiny girl, blonde, and covered with freckles. Arnold imagined if she shook any worse than she was already doing, the spots would all come loose and join together in a large brown puddle between her boyish breasts.

"He won't find out." The papers were spread out on the floral covering of her small single bed, a bulb in the yellow fluted hurricane lamp dappling the treasured names and figures with hazy promise. He had arranged the files alphabetically, but his mind was already reorganizing them in terms of dollars invested, monies outstanding, and net worth.

"I think you're brilliant," Nancy said, her little freckled hands on the back of his neck, her undersized bosoms pressing against his jacket. "I think you're brilliant, and wonderful, and kind, and caring."

"Well, that only shows how easily fooled you are," Arnold said. "Brilliant and wonderful, yes, but the rest of it . . ." He laughed, and turned to her, planting one fraternal kiss on the edge of her upturned nose so it wouldn't get too involved. "I'm not going to call them, you know. I'm just going to be in the right place at the right time, and make them my friends, and when the moment is right, show an extraordinary knowledge about their operations and consider how they might be better advised."

"But that's raiding. Greenson will have you fired."

"By the time he realizes he'd better fire me, I'll be long gone. With the best chunks of his customer list."

"You're going to start your own firm?"

"Why not? Unless you're related to someone at the goddamn

company, you're never going to be a partner. And I don't have enough time."

"You're a boy," she whispered. "You're only a baby."

There was still plenty of good she could do him, if he was going to be at the right place at the right time. There was no way without her that he could find out where that was. "Could a baby do this?"

"Oh, Arn . . ."

"Gather up the papers, my angel. No point fucking over my new customers, until they're really mine."

The next week she started listening in on Greenson's phone calls to and from clients, and when they mentioned where they were having lunch, or dinner, or spending the weekend, she would pass the information on to Arnold. A few of the clubs where the people ate were private, as were the homes where they spent the weekends. But when they were public places, where anyone could go—and why not Arnold, who was better than anyone—he would be there.

The private office of Edward Greenson was paneled in wood, and there were six telephones, and a lot of girls in short skirts bringing in papers for him to sign. Not, however, once he had begun his meeting with Arnold Sterne. "I want no interruptions," he said to his secretary, Nancy, who closed the door on her way out of the office.

Greenson was seated behind a large leather-covered black desk, papers neatly arranged in a two-level wooden box marked "Incoming" and "Outgoing." His small, pale-fingered hands poked out from stiffly starched white cuffs and clutched at the arms of a great red leather wing chair, oversized, diminishing him like a middle-aged bespectacled Alice after she had shrunk in Wonderland. But it was a very important chair.

"Sit down," Greenson said, his voice compatibly reedy with his small frame and the tight little stripe of his morning coat. He wore a gray velvet vest, across which dangled a thick gold chain with several small keys, one of them Phi Beta Kappa. The watch that peeked from his pocket was gold, and large, Arnold could tell from the stem alone. It had probably belonged to his grandfather, or great-grandfather, a symbol of tradition that was more important than the time it kept, which was obviously passing its wearer by.

Arnold sat down in the small wooden chair opposite the desk, his large bulk creaking the legs. A customer sitting there would have to feel less significant than the man behind the desk. When he had his office, all the furniture would be oversized, so the man with the money could feel as big as the dream. In a very important chair.

"Thank you, sir," Arnold said.

"There's no need to be too respectful, Mr. Sterne."

"Thank you, sir. In that case you can call me Arnold."

Greenson did not smile. His fingers worried the skin around his metal-framed glasses, and he cleared his throat. "How long have you been with this company?"

"Three years, sir. But I'm sure you've checked that out."

"I haven't got time to keep tabs on all the employees here . . ."

"I'm sure you're much too busy for that, sir . . ."

"But certain striking examples of initiative and accomplishment do have a tendency to catch one's eye." His own eyes were a little watery; Arnold could see that even through the glasses. "In the time that you've been with this company, between the business that you originally brought to us, and the accounts that you've managed to . . . acquire, I see that your income has moved into the six-figure class. Very impressive in such a young man."

"Well, it depends," Arnold said, "as the banks would say, on whether it was a low six-figure or a high six-figure."

"Any six figures are impressive at your age," Greenson said.

"I prefer seven," said Arnold.

"You want to be a millionaire?"

"Why not, sir, when so many people are?"

"But to be a millionaire, Sterne, one would have to have the original investment capital, wouldn't you say? Commissions are good in this office, but they would hardly lead to making a twenty-five-year-old boy a millionaire."

"I'm aware of that, sir. Unless of course he was an owner."

"You have the temerity of a wart hog," Greenson said, and slammed his hand on his desk. "It was my considered wish at the board meeting that we fire you— What kind of a fool do you think I am? You think I don't know you've been stealing my accounts? You think I haven't been aware of it all along?"

"Well, you couldn't have been aware of it all along, sir, or you might have done something to stop it. Like being a little more progressive in your thinking, and getting your customers to diversify the way I've done. Otherwise, I couldn't have gotten them away from you, could I?"

"If it were up to me, I'd throw you out of this office."

"You're free to do whatever you like, sir." Arnold got up from the rickety chair.

"Sit down." Greenson took off his glasses and wiped imaginary moisture from them with a white handkerchief. Then he wiped the bridge of his nose and his forehead. "I am not free to do what I like. I'm part of a very important company, and at the board meeting this morning it was decided—over my objections, I won't lie to you—that you be offered a higher position in the firm."

"How high?"

"Assistant vice-president," Greenson said.

"Whatever that means."

"It means a great deal. It means that your base salary will be fifty thousand dollars a year, plus commissions, which could very well lead to your being in that *high* six-figure category that you're so fond of."

"But not so fond of as seven," Arnold said.

"At twenty-five." Greenson shook his head. "When I was twenty-five . . ."

"Was a long time ago," said Arnold, "with a father and a grandfather, and a great-grandfather, and who knows who else behind you."

"All right," Greenson said. "So you've done it all on your

own. Most admirable. Whereas I come from a good family. Another argument for you to be grateful, Sterne. Everyone on this board has a minimum of . . . well, let us say, a century or two of family connection. For you to be an executive of this company would make you the first—the first—"

"Jew," Arnold said. "It's a very short word. It shouldn't stick in your throat."

"It doesn't stick in my throat," Greenson said.

"Well, it sticks in mine." Arnold got to his feet. "So this clever raider, this upstart who comes to your most reverend and clean-blooded firm with nothing to recommend him but brains and talent and close to a quarter of a million dollars in investment capital from people who have never dared to come to your far-from-welcoming doors before, this *gonif* who has taken over forty-two of your best accounts, he is to be taken into the firm. Because he is so well-spoken and beloved by all those who have never seen fit to invite him into their homes, and a vice-president who has never before this day had him into his office, his well-oiled, well-paneled office, this kike is to have the incredible privilege of being the first of his breed with a name on the door, and maybe, if he behaves himself, on the letterhead of the firm's stationery. Because of his initiative and accomplishment."

"Precisely for that last reason," Greenson said. He had gone rather pale, the tone of his skin merging with the faint outline of thinning gray hair.

"You're full of shit," Arnold said. "The board has carefully considered the situation of Jew-bastard Sterne, and rather than have him go elsewhere with his fat portfolio has offered him a lollipop."

"There's no need to resort to insult when somebody is trying to show their appreciation of your worth."

"You're right," Arnold said. "It must be my lack of breeding. That and the fact that the appreciation of my worth has come about two years too late. That and the fact that my worth is in excess of the appreciation of my worth by about a couple of million dollars."

"You're a very greedy young man," Greenson said. "Greedy and foolish. I take it you're going with another company."

"You take it wrong," Arnold said. "Another company would just give me a bigger lollipop. I want the whole candy store."

"You're starting your own firm?"

"I started it last week, when I found out you had asked for an appointment with me this morning. I've got offices two blocks from here, and now I go to look for furniture."

"You're a very foolish young man," Greenson said.

"Not that foolish." Arnold paused at the door. "I'd like you to know there's a job for you anytime at Sterne and Company. I'm really not that crazy about the way you do business, but I think I could get a little pizzazz going in your well-connected head, and it wouldn't do any harm to have a Protestant in the office."

He closed the door behind him and passed through the large reception room. Nancy was typing furiously, not even looking up.

"It's all right," Arnold said. "Nobody else is in the room."

"How did it go?"

"I was a little rough on him, but I offered him a job."

"You didn't."

"I did. And I was very serious. I'll call him in a couple of weeks and take him to lunch. Once this office is really set up, and I can talk to him dollar for dollar about what he'd be able to make, I wouldn't be at all surprised if he ends up coming with me."

Whether or not Greenson would have joined Arnold had to remain in the realm of speculation. Because by the time Arnold made the phone call, Greenson, along with a number of his well-connected friends, had gone out a window.

"Christ," Sonny said. "It's like being Michelangelo, and just when you get the big commission from the Pope, the ceiling of the Sistine Chapel collapses. I mean, before you even get a chance to start your painting."

He was in Arnold's office, where the decorating had been stopped halfway that Tuesday in October two and a half years before, when no one, including the furniture men, was sure the world would continue. A large Oriental rug nearly covered the floor of the reception room. There was a sideboard against the walnut-paneled wall in the rear, with a potted palm next to it. Two original light-framed prints hung on the wall, depicting hunters, one on horseback and one accompanied by two dogs. ("Scenes of our youth," Arnold had said, laughing, when he raised his hand at the auction.) The fourth wall was bare: of picture, paneling, and the receptionist, whose desk was empty in front of the wall: of receptionist, telephone, and chair.

There was no real need to have a receptionist, Arnold had assured Sonny; he needed all the action he could get *inside*. So two girls sat in front of adjoining typewriters, with two phones on folding tables beside each of them, right outside Arnold's office, a cubicle with the glass knocked out. He had planned on paneling, but who had time, who had time? In the smaller cubicle, to the rear of what would one day be a huge oak-and-leather complex, as soon as Arnold had a moment to concentrate on something as unimportant as decorating, an accountant sat. Arnold had knocked the glass out of his cubicle too, so he wouldn't get claustrophobia, and Arnold could keep an eye on him, so he wouldn't go to sleep. The accountant, a thin little man wearing a green dealer's eyeshade, labored over figures that were and had been, and tried to anticipate according to mathematical probability and inside information the figures that might come.

In the midst of melee, and melee it was, because if you were going to stay alive—better than stay alive, come up soaring—then it meant WAR!! Arnold stood in shirtsleeved sweaty splendor, cuffs rolled up against his enemy, Defeat, forearms bulging to scare off the fairy bastard. His shirt was tieless, open, thick tufts of red-gold hair showing above his cotton undershirt. There were little beads of perspiration just between the masculine clumps, and the throat above that no one could mistake for womanly, not with the prominence of *that* Adam's apple.

He was on two telephones at once, telling the other guy to

hold on, hold on, he'd see what he could raise, it was all speculation, see, he didn't even know if he could unload one share of that lousy food company, much less ten thousand. Then turning to the second phone, lowering the first phone to its side on the big tin desk (well, who had a second to pick out a really important thing like a desk with all he had going on?), he covered the receiver with his buttocks.

Half-sitting, and speaking in a somewhat softer voice, he would tell the person who had been holding on before the second call that he thought he knew where he might be able to get hold of a very promising up-and-coming food company, but only through terrific manipulating, they probably wouldn't be willing to let it go, how much was he willing to pay for, say, but understand it would take a lot of work on Arnold's part, ten thousand shares. Twenty-two thousand? "Not enough. I wouldn't go to him with a dollar under twenty-five. Okay. Twenty-four. You got a deal, send me a confirmation." He hung up the phone and picked up the one under his behind, and told the guy he could unload them at twenty-one. "Okay, twenty-one and a half, you got a deal, send me a confirmation." In that minute and a half, he had netted himself two thousand five hundred dollars. Plus commission.

He was not doing anything wrong. It was a charity he was running in times like these, when everyone should do their bit for the distressed. Some distressed wanted to unload, and some wanted to buy, because who knew? It could change any day now and people might start buying and selling like human beings again, and we would all be rich the way some of us were. A few fellows he knew who ran charity benefits took a straight ten percent off the top, and people still called them philanthropists; if he was running a private charity, what could they call him— *pischer?* Crook? A nicer name than apple-seller.

Not every minute and a half was marked by a gain of twenty-five hundred dollars and legitimate commission. There were days when Arnold borrowed so far above his head, a shorter, lesser man would have drowned in his own fear. But these were times when everyone was afraid, and only the Titans could kick themselves above the surface. He was a Titan, a Titan, nothing less could survive, much less triumph. He could afford to be nothing less.

"It's like being Michelangelo," Sonny said again, because whenever Arnold went off on one of his self-buoying dissertations, Sonny tried to bring it over to an artist, or a philosopher, so he could be reminded of how sensitive Arnold really was.

"What is?"

"When you were talking about the Titans, Michelangelo did them you know, the painting or the sculpture . . ."

"You're going to graduate college, you ought to be sure." Arnold sat down on the desk, pushing the telephones further apart so he could be more comfortable, and wiped his forehead. The gesture was one he had seen Greenson make with great style, so he supposed it was all right if he sweated.

"I mean, can you imagine, the chance to paint the Sistine Chapel, and the ceiling collapses before you plant your first stroke?"

"What's that got to do with me?"

"Well, here you are, the greatest artist in the world of finance, and before you get a chance to prove it, the market crashes."

"What do you mean, before I get a chance to prove it? What do you think I'm doing?" He pointed to the telephones on either side of him. "What do you think all this is?"

"Hard work on water," Sonny said. "I never saw anybody working so hard. I thought it was going to have all this style and dignity, that you'd be sitting in some plush office, smoking cigars. And here you are, lucky if you have a chance to eat a stale cheese sandwich in wax paper from down the street, and a paper cup of cold coffee. Sweating like you were McCloskey. You were in better shape when we were living off his tomato herring. It just isn't the way I thought it would be."

Arnold got up from the desk and poured himself a drink from the liquor cabinet in the corner, swallowing instead of talking, because he had thought it would be that way too. Still, there were trips he could take, eventually, to Europe, why not, very fancy. Going back in style, dignity, to the place his parents had fled with less than dignity and in terrible style. Trips were the time to be who you wanted to be all the time, when you didn't have the pressure of having to be who you didn't want to be at all. Money made for trips, and trips took you away. To places where you only sweated because you wanted to.

But meantime the journeys were as far away as the places they would take him to, and he stood in his uncompleted office sweating out other people's panic in his shirtsleeves, not exactly the picture he had of bankers. Which was what he was, it said so on the door. "Sterne and Sterne, Investment Banking."

"My brother's a banker," Sonny told the boys at Columbia. They wanted to know what bank he was with, that was how little they understood of the money business. They thought you had to be a Morgan or a Rothschild or a Rockefeller, somebody's son, or some natty pinstripe in a cage, passing bills across a counter with only vague hope of advancement. They didn't understand that an emblem could be forged out of your own guts, that one man's receivership could be another man's deliverance. They thought you had to have a building on the corner of Fifth Avenue and Forty-fourth Street, or some burglar-proof little edifice in Bayonne, New Jersey; they couldn't conceive of a bank being an independent sweatshop with a lot of the glass knocked out of the cubicles, so it wouldn't be just full of hot air.

"That's what we are, is a bank," Arnold said to Sonny, after the younger brother's graduation from college, when he came to work with Arnold full-time. Evenings he was studying law at Columbia Law School, but daytimes he was a banker, Arnold told him. "Don't ever forget it, and don't minimize. They deposit their hard cold dreams with us, and we make them into full-flush fantasies. Unless, of course, we make a bad decision, or a bad investment, and then we all go down the drain together." He laughed when he said that, a harsh, hacking laugh, somewhere between the giggle of a child and a cough, as if he couldn't quite grow into it, or get the joy up.

"But we're as good as Chase Manhattan, or First National, and don't act like we're not. Maybe we're a little better, because we know who all our customers are, and in times like these it doesn't hurt, that personal touch. I mean, you can't put the touch on people unless you know them personally, right, kid?"

The croaking laughter again, and then a slight wince of premature middle-aged pain, because the banks themselves, those big outfits with the decades of formerly gilt-edged securities, wouldn't do business with a twenty-eight-year-old renegade and his baby brother, no matter how smart they seemed to be. You couldn't count on people who had known what they were doing for generations, so how could you take a chance on a couple of upstarts?

The big banks' failure to acknowledge them stuck in Arnold's craw, like his laughter, because there had been a couple of moments in his career when he could have made a killing, a real killing, getting the paneling in place and his jacket on, if only one of the real power outfits had come through with the couple of million he needed to sew it up, really sew it up, and we'll own practically the whole of Connecticut—there's some land development that's got to skyrocket, I'm in on the ground floor with the subdivider, and we can pick it up for beans, a million and a half, two million beans. But they turned him down, the established banks, and his own customers didn't have that much in ready cash. When the issue was gone, out of his hands, out of the realm of fulfillment, he still couldn't tell the high-line presidents to go fuck themselves, because one day, when he needed them, they just might be there. A true speculator had to allow for futures.

Sometimes, at night, when Sonny was finished with his law classes, he would return to Riverside Drive, to the big, dark, partially-furnished-with-less-than-priceless-antiques apartment, to find a note saying it was urgent business he meet Arnold at the Cotton Club, or some other jazz place, stylishly featuring Negro entertainers. He would always go, no matter how tired he was, and he would always stay, even though it had nothing to do with business at all. He liked the music, and he liked the way Arnold commandeered the best ringside table. ("Headwaiters, unlike First National, recognize class when it's shoved into their palm," Arnold told him.) Sonny liked getting a little high on bootleg whiskey; it gave a certain arrogant stimulation to the proceedings, which were always gay, and decorated with big-breasted, long-legged, tartily dressed girls who fit nicely in the circle of Arnold's arm.

"I only got two hands," Arnold told him one crisp September evening, when the one on his left was Flo, or Babs, it was hard to get any of them straight. "Two hands, and look what she's got," Arnold said, butting gently at her breasts like a tender bull. "More than enough for me to take care of. Laurie Mae, she's for you."

"Laurie Mae?" Sonny looked at the girl to Arnold's right, with copper-penny hair and wide-set brown eyes, and only a little of her roots showing black.

"Ah come from the South," Laurie Mae said.

"I would hope so," Sonny said, sitting down beside her.

"Ah'm new in town," Laurie Mae said.

"Ah told her to say that," Arnold said. "Ah figured as how you'd like it better if it hadn't been around town too much."

"Wheah do you come from, Sonny honey?"

"Brooklyn."

"Not true, not true," Arnold said. "He sprang from mine own forehead like Diana from Mars."

"Huh?" Laurie Mae twisted a white lace handkerchief in her lap.

"So you see," Arnold smiled at Sonny, "you need have no premature remorse. It won't be as if you're desecrating anything holy, or even reasonably intelligent. She was created for one thing, and one thing only, and you will be befouling her creation if you don't make use of it."

"Huh?" Laurie Mae said.

"*Gleb mir,*" said Arnold.

"Ah don't understand anything your brother says."

"That is an ancient Nordic expression," Sonny said. "It means trust your brother."

"Glay-eb May-year," Laurie Mae said. "Ah certainly like the sound of that. Glay-eb May-year. It never hurts to pick up other languages, don't you think? Ah mean, a girl never knows when she might get a chance to travel. Travel is so broadening, don't you know? Ah learned so much just taking the bus up here from Mississippi."

"We set sail for Tahiti with the next full tide," Arnold said. "You play your cards right, maybe Sonny will take you with him."

"What kind of deck do you use?" Sonny asked, and moved the ice cubes around in the pale liquid the waiter had placed in the teacup in front of him. The fact that his brother slept with other women besides Sarah had ceased to bother him too much, because Arnold had explained that he had no respect for any woman except Sarah, and screwing other women helped him keep up his respect. But the thought of using anyone badly made Sonny uncomfortable, even when, as Arnold was pointing out with his eyes and his conversation and his life, the world was full of suckers longing to be used. Like Laurie Mae.

"Why don't we go back to mah place?" she whispered into his ear, when the dance orchestra had taken over and he told her he was sorry, he didn't know how to dance. "Ah could teach you."

"I don't have time to learn right now," Sonny said. "I've got some studying to do, and I've got to go to work in the morning."

"Your brother's got to go to work in the morning, and that's not going to keep him from going home with mah friend."

"I've got to study."

"Ah could teach you things besides dancing."

"I'm aware of that."

"Don't you like to have fun?"

"When I've done everything I have to do, I'll be able to start having fun."

"But, honey, it might wither and fall off by then."

"I don't think so," Sonny said. "I'm a pretty quick study."

"Well, then, you ought to be able to learn to dance in no time."

It ended up with him taking her home and learning the basics of the two-step. The rest that she offered him, he declined.

"Don't you like girls?" she said to him, naked, so quickly

94

naked that he didn't even have time to ask her what she was doing because it was already done, and she was on the green spread of the daybed, a red-headed lily on a chenille pond.

"I like them very much," he said. "I like them too much to give them less than my best, and I've got no time yet to give my best."

"Well, it isn't a contest, honey. Nobody has to win."

"Everybody has to win or it doesn't mean anything."

"You certainly haven't been talking to your brother," Laurie Mae said, and bent one knee, so he could see the flash of pink behind the other coppery clump, slightly black at the roots. "Your brother said you just wanted to get laid. Come on. Come here. It won't hurt. Your brains aren't going to fall out of there." She reached for him, but he moved away and started putting his coat on.

"Your brother said—"

"My brother said you were a consummate moron."

"Ah didn't hear him say that." Laurie Mae got up on her knees. "What's consummate mean?"

"It means what we're not going to do with this relationship, only you have to pronounce it differently."

"So, if you can teach me things, how come Ah can't teach you?"

"I don't like studying anything I can't give my full concentration."

Laurie Mae giggled. "You want it to have *meaning*," she said. "And you're not even a girl. That's absolutely adorable."

"Thank you," Sonny said, and went to the door.

"But, honey, it *would* have meaning. It would mean you weren't a virgin anymore. Doesn't that mean anything to you?"

"It means more to my brother," Sonny said. "I'll tell him you were wonderful."

"Well, mustn't overdo," Laurie Mae said. "Ah know my own limitings, and ah'm not wonderful, ah'm just good. He knows ah'm only *good*. So don't tell him ah was wonderful, or ah won't get paid."

9 5

"It's only gash," Arnold said, when Sonny got home. "I don't know why you take it so seriously."

"Her roots needed doing."

"So do yours." Arnold was seated by the open marble hearth in the red and brown living room, a small bulb in a shaded lamp casting gray shadows across the Blue List, open in his lap to the latest figures on municipal bonds.

"You're going to go blind," Sonny said.

"That's from masturbating. You're getting your myths mixed up."

"And a myth is as good as a mile."

"Not up to standard," Arnold said. "Unless you've really started talking that way. Have you? You don't have to be afraid to tell me, kid."

"Tell you what?"

"Are you a pansy?"

"Not up to standard," Sonny said.

"Theirs or mine?"

"I just don't think you should have to pay for it," Sonny said. "Especially when you say it's free."

"The best things in life are free, Abe, even when you have to pay for them."

"You're going to go blind," Sonny said. "It's not like you're Abraham Lincoln, is it? You haven't even got logs in the fireplace to read by."

"Don't get smart with me, kid," Arnold said. "I don't want to be President. I just want to get rich. You get better odds on that American dream."

Sonny turned on the overhead light, eight little bulbs dancing in a hideous arrangement of cupids and pink and blue crystals, which Sarah had picked out personally.

"You're still going to go blind."

"You sound like my mother," Arnold said.

Sonny didn't even try to remember her anymore. Arnold's wife, Sarah, was a short, affectionate presence, who cooked well enough and asked few questions, and was already starting to look old enough to be his mother. She packed them sandwiches for the office in brown paper bags, and on the few nights when Sonny had time to come home in between office and classes, the food was hot. His bed was made, and the linens were changed once a week, and his pajamas were freshly washed and ironed every third day. He did not comment on her doing it, never even questioned whether she personally had done it, or the maid. But every once in a while he would inject an abstracted "Thank you," into her day, and she would whisper, "It's my pleasure." So he supposed that was what it would have been like, having a mother, only with more hugs. And he had very little time to feel the poignant absence of hugging, between his studies and the craziness at the office.

That emptiness which occasionally gaped open in his insides, in the moments to spare on weekends, he would fill by embracing his little sister. She was turning out to be very pretty, a dark-eyed child with an alien grace about her, and none of her family's brains. But it was enough that girls were pretty, he understood that from his brother; they didn't have to be smart, or even perky, unless they were some little number with a tight ass that you wanted to punk on a dull Saturday.

Speaking of which, Arnold would add, had Sonny gotten laid yet, and if not, why not, and how about this weekend? There were two sisters stashed on Eighty-seventh Street who would be more than willing to take both brothers on. And Sonny shouldn't be embarrassed about being a virgin. Arnold would supervise. It wasn't all that different from the banking business. Assets and deficit: one puts in, the other withdraws. Double-entry system. Sonny didn't want to cloud up the beauty of the relationship by telling his brother he didn't want it to be that way, because if it was good enough for Arnold like that, it should have been good enough for him. But Sonny had dreams of soft breasts and soft hands, not always accompanied by a soft head; in a lot of his erotic imaginings, he and the woman actually had conversations, and the questions she asked were sometimes very bright. There was no point in passing that on to Arnold, who would have laughed at him, the sharp edge of his hoarse chuckle cutting off the comfort of those soft fantasies.

Sonny was a brilliant student, the best in his class. He picked up law as quickly as he had learned economics and history and the banking business. There were some moments when he wondered, taking the subway back down to Ninety-sixth Street, if he would have shone as brightly at Harvard by day as he did at Columbia by night. But there was no time to worry about that, because it was out of the question, even supposing they had accepted him, assuming he had applied and had broken through the quota. Just as it was out of the question that he could be with Milton Radnitz away from the campus.

Milton came as close to being a best friend as anyone Sonny had ever known, besides his brother. Milton was short, but there was a power he had, a connection of words with the volume and timbre of his voice and the dark flashing of his eyes, combined with a passion he was not ashamed to show even when talking of cerebral issues, that made him seem very big. Sonny had the suspicion that Milton was, in fact, brighter than Sonny but didn't want to make a show of it, because then the professors might pay too much attention to him. That was risky if you were a subversive.

"You're wasting your time on Wall Street, Abe," Milton said. They were sitting in the student canteen, in a wooden-benched booth in the corner, far away from where other people might hear, if there were anyone else left on the campus drinking coffee after midnight. "Abela, Abela." Milton reached over and touched his friend's hand, cold on the coffee mug. He had to try for affection by diminishing the name, as he was the only close friend Sonny had who hadn't known him as a boy; he had no idea there was a warmer name already extant, and Sonny wasn't about to tell him.

"The world is on its butt, with no hope of recovery. Not the way it was. People will never be fooled again, don't you understand that, even with your massive brain? When you put the ability to feed and clothe in the hands of an effete aristocracy, even if you call them bankers, collapse is inevitable. The only hope for the future is in the balls of the proletariat."

"It's all going to change now," Sonny said. "Not that I have blind faith in Roosevelt, he's a new boy. I don't think he'll come up with any complete panacea. But there will be modifications, and control, and growth—"

"You can't modify disaster," Milton said. "The only prayer is complete revolution."

"Prayer?" Sonny said.

Milton laughed, his eyes flashing as dark as his teeth were white. "Remnants of my misspent orthodox youth," Milton said. "I sit corrected."

"I think you ought to keep that ambivalence," Sonny said. "Religiosity in the midst of the atheism. It'll make you quaint, an object of study. Sort of the life of the Party."

"You're making a terrible mistake," Milton said. "I know you'll be a great banker, but what's the point of being the brightest cog in a rusted wheel? Capitalism is over."

"Then why does it represent such a threat to you, my wanting to be a capitalist? If it's over, I'll just go into those big buildings and slowly peter out."

"But why should you? You've got too much, the head is too good, the heart is too full; I can't stand to see you wasted. Especially as you'd be such a fantastic asset to the Movement. Just because we've got the only solution doesn't mean the solution can't be *improved*. Made better, because we've got the best people. We have, you know. You wouldn't believe the exchanges of plans and ideas. But your ideas, your mind could make things even better. Passion tempered with intellect. It's the political ideal. And you could rise very high, Abe. Very high indeed."

"With everybody equal?"

"Well, some of us have to be more equal than others," Milton said, and they both laughed. "Listen, Abe, I'm really serious. I've talked to some of my comrades about you, and they're so impressed, they even let me drop the number-one rule of secrecy."

"Maybe they want an infiltrator on Wall Street."

99

"They already have them, don't worry," Milton said. "And if they didn't, they wouldn't need them. Wall Street has done a very good job of destroying itself, as has this country."

"I don't believe that," Sonny said. "I don't like to listen to it, even from you."

"What the hell has this country ever done for you?" Milton said, hitting the table with his fist. "Killed your father—"

"That was love," Sonny said. "Love can kill a man anyplace."

"But she stole all his money, didn't she? He ran after her to get back his money."

"You heard the story wrong. He wanted her, not the money."

"All right, forget about that part of it. Forget about your father. Just look at yourself. Struggling to make it through night school, when any law university in the world should build a library just to have you study in it, pipe up soup to keep you going, clothe you, and comfort you."

"I never saw that offered in any curriculum."

"But it should be. Love should be a part of any academic environment, and it would be in the ideal, because in the ideal a man is appreciated by his comrades, and given sustenance in his—"

"Soul?" Sonny said.

"Oh, fuck you," said Milton. "I don't know why I even talk to you."

"Neither do I," Sonny said.

"Yes, you do. Yes, I do. Because I think you're a phenomenally gifted man. I think you could be an asset to any movement. So why attach yourself to a dying one, especially when it isn't even a movement at all? A stultified, stagnant vestige of an outdated mentality. About to be cut off, like a gangrenous arm. And why even lament its passing? What has this country ever done for you?"

"A lot more than Russia," Sonny said. "Russia drove my people out."

"But that was *before*. That was part of an arcane prejudice on the part of a tyrannous aristocracy."

"You mean they'd love to have me now," Sonny said.

"They're crazy about Jews in Russia. Now that there are no more Cossacks running around lopping off lives with swords, I might even be able to own a horse. They'd love to have me."

"We'd love to have you," Milton said quietly. "Give it a chance, Abe. You're not a bigoted man. You have no preconceived prejudice. Come to a meeting and see for yourself. Listen for yourself. The people are brilliant.

"And the women! The women are young, and excited, and free. Free from the stupidity this country's heritage has chained them with, free from the outdated concept of marriage as women's only hope. Free from all that Victorian crap that women aren't supposed to like sex.

"They love it, Abe. They'd love you. Come down and see. Just think of it as a social evening, where you might get lucky and end up in someone else's warm bed. Anything else you get from the evening is a bonus."

"Possession is nine points of the law," Sonny said. "Why do people always assume they can get it by way of your crotch?"

"You know a better way?"

"How about the head and the heart?"

"You really are an idealist," Milton said. "We could certainly use you."

Sonny never went to any of the cell meetings, and he never told anyone, including his brother, that Milton was a communist. He fervently hoped there would not be a revolution, but assumed that if ever there were, he would have a good friend in a very high place, and he, for one, would be spared.

In the meantime, there was another battle raging, besides that of the proletariat. A much more important one to Sonny. With all that Arnold had told him of the change that was inevitable, the present blessed opportunistic system which was going to give the Sterne boys their big chance, money was tight. The little cash that was in circulation was not on tap for Sterne and Sterne, and the banks—their brothers, only the banks didn't know it yet—wouldn't come through with any loans. Nor would any of the big brokerage houses, who were refusing to deal with Arnold and Sonny because big houses weren't even too sure about the established banks anymore, so how could they trust two upstarts? Arnold would sit in the darkness of the apartment, late into the night, cursing the well-known names that considered themselves too good for the unknown—except through crazy accomplishment—Sternes. Then Arnold would curse his own clients, the small investors who couldn't get it up, couldn't get the cash together to make the real killing. Because it was still there. The chance at the cash murder was there. A man could do it, even in the middle of the panic, if he had the brains and the imagination.

"And we've got them, Sonny," Arnold said in the office, waiting for the strangely silent phones to ring. "Son of a bitch, we've got the brains and the imagination. If we only had the cash."

"But it's moved from crash hysteria to depression to panic," Sonny said. "People mistrust the banks, the really big established banks. You can't be angry at the banks for not trusting us."

"Who can't?" Arnold said. "I'll kill them. I'll kill them all, those smug bastards. Something will happen and I'll knock them down like mumblety pegs. I'll have those big solid brokers and the banks on their fucking asses. I'll have this city on its ear."

Sonny did not consider the possibility that his brother was going crazy. Turning those tall buildings sideways seemed as reasonable a dream at the moment as earning a living. "How are we going to do it?" Sonny said.

"How do you bag an elephant?"

"I don't know, I've never been to Africa."

"Don't admit that to anybody," Arnold said. "Nobody else has been to Africa, either. So how are they going to know you haven't been there if you don't tell them? The first thing you have to do is get an elephant gun. Then you wait for the elephant to charge. Or else you charge the elephant. I don't think it makes any difference, as long as you kill it."

"You'd be taking on an animal you've never seen."

"Nobody knows the animal anymore." Arnold looked out the window. "The people who consider themselves hunters. Look at the excesses they created, letting the thing run wild. Bucket shops, for Christ's sake, where a man could come in and put up a thousand dollars for a thousand shares worth a thousand times a thousand shares, no margin requirements, making the whole economy a colossal gamble, so any sissy could go on safari and knock off a big one. Nobody knows the animal anymore." He turned and looked at Sonny with eyes that were a very cool blue. "It isn't a bull. It isn't a bear. Let's get an elephant gun."

Sonny assumed Arnold was talking about buying a seat on the New York Stock Exchange. It seemed the most logical money analogy. An elephant gun: the power chair. Before the market had crashed, some seats were selling for as high as six hundred and twenty-five thousand dollars. At the time Arnold had accumulated a little over a hundred thousand. Now that seats were going for as low as ninety thousand, they didn't have that much cash.

"Where do we find this gun?" Sonny asked.

"Maybe Mr. Roosevelt will give it to us." Arnold walked over and sat on the edge of the tin desk, smiling at Sonny's expression. "Well, why not? He seems determined to wipe out elephants."

In March of 1933, when Roosevelt declared a national Bank Holiday and ordered the Stock Exchange closed to try and stop the panic, an ad ran in the New York *Times,* stating that business would be conducted as usual in the offices of Sterne and Sterne.

"Well, why not?" Arnold had said, after Sonny had suggested the idea and then backed off from the audacity of it. "People will still want to trade. There will still be buying and selling. And we aren't members of the Exchange, he hasn't ordered us closed."

"But everybody else will probably close down as a courtesy."

"A courtesy to whom? The banks? The banks haven't exactly been courteous to us, have they?"

"Maybe as a courtesy to Roosevelt, to try and give him a chance to make things sane."

"I received no note from the President," Arnold said, his eyes the brightest they had been since he left Whittaker and Lief. "Did you receive any note from the President?"

"No."

"Then we'll write him one, afterwards, on proper stationery. A very polite and well-worded thank-you note, for his very kind gift of an elephant gun."

There were fourteen telephone lines in the office, because Arnold had known all along one day it would happen; when it happened, fourteen lines were not enough. The phones were jammed from eight o'clock in the morning, when Sonny and Arnold got there, hoping, until six o'clock at night, when they stopped answering the phones because it was too much to believe. There were calls from everywhere in the country, calls from all over the world, all those places that Arnold had planned on seeing sometime, and now knew he could see.

Because in midst of crash and panic and hysteria and depression, people still wanted to unload or load up on issues of Graham Paige Motors Corporation (low for the year 1, high 5⅝), Hudson and Manhattan Railway (6½–19), Bullard Company (2½–13¼), People's Gas, Light and Coke Company ("People still need their Gas, Light and Coke," Arnold grinned, and sold and bought and resold for 25 a share, 27 a share, 29 a share—the high for the year: 78). And California Packing, and Diamond Match, and Nash Motors, and Atlantic Coastline Railroad, and Brown Shoe ("People still need their Brown Shoes," Arnold grinned). On a day when no one but Arnold and Sonny Sterne of the United States of America handled any trading, they had turned over twenty-three million dollars in trade. Even taking a conservative percentage, they had to be millionaires. And they weren't exactly conservative.

They sat on the floor of their office, trying to make some sense out of the clutter of buy and sell orders. The two secretaries were on the carpet in the reception room, doing the same. Fourteen telephones were still ringing, but nobody answered. They had done more than they could do, more than most men could do in a lifetime. The accountant had fallen asleep at his desk, his green eyeshade resting on his books.

"I think maybe now," Arnold said, beaming, "I think maybe now they'll know who we are. This one I may have framed." He waved an order slip in the air. "The president of Whittaker and Lief, baby brother. Elliot Sanderson Whittaker himself, and he had to buy his National Acme through me. National Acme. Love the name. National Acme, at an all-time low, and Elliot Whittaker had to deal with me. I may have it framed."

"I sold fifty thousand shares of Real Silk Hosiery Mills to Clifton Sanger," Sonny said.

"People still need their Real Silk Hosiery."

"Clifton Sanger." Sonny shook his head. "I wonder what he looks like."

"Like an ordinary man," Arnold said. "They all look like ordinary men. Even the ones with centuries behind them, international banking families."

"Clifton Sanger couldn't look like an ordinary man."

"You'll buy him lunch," said Arnold. "You'll see how he looks like an ordinary man. He buys like an ordinary man, doesn't he? Any way he can. There are no gods in business."

"You think he'll have lunch with me?"

"I think he'll invite you to dinner."

"Clifton Sanger," Sonny said, and shook his head. "I'd really like to meet him."

"He needs to meet you, now. That's the difference."

"I don't know," Sonny said. "He sounded very reluctant to deal with me on the phone."

"Nobody broke his arm. He made the call."

"I got a hang-up, one of the calls. Somebody said we weren't gentlemen, and then he hung up."

"Not gentlemen. Imagine that. We didn't behave like gentlemen." Arnold laughed, and for the first time it came out of his throat full and free. "I guess that means we're really on our way, kid." He got up from the floor, picked up his tie from the back of a chair, and started to put it on in front of the window.

"No lights to look at," Arnold said. "All those big tall buildings, dark and empty, because nobody else had the nerve. I don't like being the only lighted window on Lower Broadway."

"Oh, yes you do," Sonny said.

"Almost twenty-nine years old, four years behind schedule. But we did it. EVERYBODY!" he shouted. The accountant woke up, and the girls came in from the reception room. "Clean up this mess and go home. Take the day off tomorrow. I got to go buy some furniture."

"Who will answer the phone?" one of the secretaries asked.

"I'll come in and get the calls," Sonny said.

"No, you won't. They'll still remember about us the day after tomorrow. They'll remember about us for a long time to come." He put his arm around Sonny's shoulders. "Tomorrow's your day to get a bar mitzvah suit. Custom-made. You got to be well dressed for the parade."

"Ticker tape for heroes? You think it'll be like that."

"I think it'll be rotten tomatoes and anything dirty they can throw. But we took the stage, Abie. That's the important thing. To take the stage. You're twenty-one years old, and you're big enough to be a hated man. How about that for a beginning?"

"I just wish there had been some other way to do it."

"Are you crazy out of your mind? Are you questioning the brilliance of my idea?"

There were veins standing out on the sides of Arnold's temples, so Sonny didn't even say that the idea had been his, and no, he didn't question the brilliance of it. "I only wondered if we did it right."

"We *did* it. To do it is to do it *right*."

"You said that we'd be hated. If you do something right, you can't be hated."

"You can if they didn't think of it. That's why they're mad. *They* didn't think of it. They didn't do it. We did. The land of opportunity, kid. But how many of us have the nerve to make our own. *Hey, you out there!*" he screamed into the dark vastness of the high concrete canyons. *"Where were you to-day . . . ?"*

He started laughing. Really a good laugh now.

Sonny went over to the small closet in the corner with the sink inside, and the mirror, and took a fresh blade out of the razor. Then he pulled his shirt out of his pants, and slashed the front of it, ripping it free.

"This is no time to go nuts," Arnold said.

"Trust me," said Sonny, and made the shirt into a folded strip of cloth. "I'm your brother."

"What the hell are you doing?" Arnold said, as Sonny wound the cloth around Arnold's forehead.

"I'm blindfolding you. Relax."

"I don't feel like being blindfolded," Arnold said. "I don't want to play games. I want to have a party."

"Trust me," Sonny said. "You've earned a surprise."

"Where are we going?"

"If I tell you, it won't be a surprise," said Sonny, and led his brother carefully toward the front door of the office, helping him on with his coat, as if he were, indeed, a blind man.

"I can see out of my nose," Arnold said. "Right here." He touched underneath his right eye. "You better get some tape or something."

"Adhesive," Sonny said to one of the secretaries. "Quick."

There was no way for Arnold to tell where he was being taken. He couldn't guess from the direction their limousine seemed to be going, the whispered instructions Sonny was giving to the driver, where they were. There were too many turns; he lost all sense of direction. He knew only that it was a very long way.

"I want to stop here for a minute," Sonny said, and the driver moved to the curb. "Don't look," he said to Arnold.

"Where's he taking me, George?" Arnold said to the driver.

"It's a surprise, sir."

"I don't like surprises."

"Sure you do," said George. "Everybody does."

"And you understand the surprise?"

"I don't understand anything," George said. "I just drive."

When they got to wherever it was, Sonny helped Arnold out of the car, clanking slightly as if he were carrying bottles. A whorehouse, Arnold thought, with only some small sense of disappointment. If it was going to be a whorehouse, it should have been Arnold who picked it out. What did Sonny know about the triumph over women? What did Sonny really understand about real triumph at all?

"Step up," Sonny said, as they reached the curb. "Step up one step, and then walk straight ahead. I'm right beside you."

"This is silly," Arnold said, and then fell silent, as a crisp, long-ago-remembered smell hit his nostrils. He heard the opening of the door, and felt his brother's hand on his arm.

"A little threshold," Sonny said. "Step over it gently."

"You sure you don't want to carry me?"

"*Oh beautiful, for spacious skies,*" Sonny sang. "*For amber waves of grain* . . . You're not singing," said Sonny.

"The blind are not patriotic," Arnold said.

"Then take off your blindfold and join in the song," said Sonny. "Now." He loosed the bandage from his brother's eyes.

They were standing in the middle of McCloskey's. Sonny held two bottles of champagne.

"Okay, McCloskey," Sonny said to the man who was standing behind the chopped liver and the pickles, an astonished grin on his face. "How much do we owe you?"

The party lasted until ten o'clock. They were drinking champagne out of little containers that were meant to hold pickles, and eating the pickles the containers were supposed to hold, along with corned beef sandwiches and fatty slices of pastrami, and anything their hearts and their bellies desired.

"To free enterprise!" Sonny said, and they all toasted, even George, who had come inside to join them in the delicatessen orgy.

"I figure with tonight," McCloskey said, consulting his books, "and the six years you robbed me, it's over three hundred dollars."

"You got it," Sonny said, and peeled off three crisp new bills.

"It's nice to see that men remember," said McCloskey.

"I remember everything," said Sonny, and kissing the delicatessen owner on his bald head, pocketed a can of tomato herring on his way out the door.

THREE

WAR IN FLORIDA! What an occasion!

It was not that Evelyn wished anyone any harm that she didn't know personally. But if there had to be a war, how lucky she had gotten to Florida in time for it to start someplace else.

She had taught herself the basics of shorthand by the time the train got to Miami, with Chris reading aloud from the Gregg Shorthand Book while Evelyn practiced symbols. They drilled every night, and during the day Evelyn got jobs. She drifted from secretarial job to secretarial job until the wonderful war was declared, and she got to go to work for someone called Colonel, who gave her files marked Top Priority and Urgent. The filing room was locked, and she had one of the keys. When everyone knew that a slip of the lip could sink a ship.

Well, she wasn't about to sink a ship, not when the country had been so kind to her, letting her become a Colonel's right arm. She was Colonel Bramford's right arm, he told her that all the time, while she organized his filing system and his social life: finding scientists, or wholesalers, or getting together delightful soirees or afternoon barbecues for the war-torn and war-weary of Miami Beach.

Giving herself to no man, preferring to remain what she was convinced was a mystery, she bobbed through the early days of the war like a buoy, signaling hope, signaling rescue, signaling the shore. Oh, not to Walter M. White, who still wrote her poems, still sent her little recordings of love made in an arcade in Kennywood Park. Poems, recordings, love. Not exactly top priority urgent.

By the peaceful tropical water of Biscayne Bay, studded with white hotels and palm trees and growing prosperity, there were quiet encampments. Death, actual death, within or without war, had no meaning to Evelyn. Distant or disliked old relatives were the only ones who died, unknown cousins in Chicago and our gallant men overseas. How could she be disturbed about gallant men? Especially as she didn't know them.

Nor was she clear on where she stood with the God business, so she couldn't take it seriously when Chris told her she was starting to believe in Jesus, from going to the convent. It had the best curriculum in the county, and they let Evelyn board Chris there. What could be wrong with it?

"Just pay attention to the lessons," Evelyn told Chris on Septuagesima Sunday. "You don't have to listen to the prayers."

Chris' hair was pulled into two stubby dark braids, and there was a little fringe of brown curls wisping around the edge of her plumping-up face. "They pray before classes in the morning and at lunchtime and at prayer time. There's a time that's just for prayers. They pray to Jesus and Mary. What am I supposed to do?"

"Don't pray," said Evelyn, and tried not to see Walter in the dark brown eyes.

"I tried that. Everybody looks at me not praying." Chris scratched her chubby upper arm.

"Just move your lips," Evelyn said, smiling past the green

bench they sat on at the rose bushes, as if they were distinguished visitors. "No one will see you're not praying."

"If God's looking He won't know I'm just moving my lips."

"He'll know," Evelyn said. "That's what makes Him God."

"They put us to bed under mosquito netting in a tent. It's like sleeping with a veil on the room." Chris kept on scratching. "The mosquitoes still get me. Sister Veronica Daniel says Jesus loves me even if I'm not Catholic. But if Jesus is in charge, he doesn't save you from mosquitoes."

"I'm sorry about that," Evelyn said. Beyond the walls where the convent ended there was a street with poinsettias and palms, and Evelyn could practically see herself on it, visualize herself striding into the future, a fine tomorrow, after the great conflagration. Buying her wardrobe: two trunkloads for a trip to Paris. When would it be? With whom?

"What's dying?" Chris said.

Evelyn adjusted her new sunglasses on the fine bridge of her sun-bronzed nose, squinting against the glare of the sunlight, letting the light rebeam from her toasted skin. Blue-gray clouds softened the afternoon. Past where the children were picnicking in clumps with their parents, she thought she could detect the sound of running water.

"Dying," she said, when there was nothing to save her from the silence, "is when living is over."

"That's not what the sisters say. The sisters say that to die is to come closer to Our Lord Jesus."

"Well that's what they believe."

"I'm starting to believe it." Small tears raged. "There's so many of them and they know more than me."

"More than *I*," Evelyn corrected.

"You're making me stay here and believe in Jesus, God's going to get mad at me!"

"You know I have work to do. Your father doesn't send me a penny, not a penny. I have to go to an office and earn money so you can eat and have clothes."

"God's going to get mad!" Chris shouted.

"You're just like your father," Evelyn said. *"Quel drame."*

"I'm not like my father. I'm like you. I'm a girl."

"So are the other children in the school. So are the sisters."

"They're not like me. I'm not like them. They're Catholic and they want to be with Jesus. I want to be with you."

So much love. Evelyn ended up having to take Chris out of the convent to live with her. Jesus Christ. There was no God.

There had been some fascination with the actual business of movies in the south of Florida at the start of World War II. Cecil B. De Mille had shot *Reap the Wild Wind* in Key West, at enormous personal peril, according to the Chamber of Commerce. Cecil B. De Mille fighting the elements, fighting the potential appearance of a submarine during the giant squid scene, aided only by his fabled courage and the presence in the cast of John Wayne.

Actually, second-unit shooting on the film had been concluded a few weeks prior to the bombing of Pearl Harbor, and by the time news of the war had filtered through Florida, Cecil B. De Mille was long gone back to Hollywood. But the Chamber of Commerce continued to issue stories about the fearless director and his fearless shooting of *Reap the Wild Wind* in Key West. It didn't hurt in those few, panicky, soon-to-be-very-rich moments at the end of 1941 to let them know up North there was no reason not to buy property down South.

The new luxury spot of the nation, no question about it, once the highways were paved and the mosquitoes were cleared away, and some of the play could be taken away from Atlantic City. And if anyone could take the play away, it was Cecil B. De Mille, even if he had finished shooting.

Evelyn had never seen the great director, but she had no wish to, any more than she wanted to go to movies. Movies had no particular glory for her; people who loved movies were trying to escape from reality. Evelyn wanted to escape into it.

Her first glimpse of it, or what she thought reality was, came at the home of Colonel Bramford, on a Saturday. The house itself was a two-story white colonial, taken over by the Army, partly for the Colonel's personal use, partly to ensconce visiting military dignitaries, partly to entertain the proud combatants of Key West and Miami Beach. This particular Saturday, early in 1942, after the emotional upheaval of Septuagesima Sunday, there was a barbecue, organized by Evelyn, where she would act as official hostess. Even before she arrived, the barbecue had a glow around it. She just felt it, yes. Sally Bramford had had a hemorrhoidectomy (poor Sally Bramford, but better her than her hero husband; Napoleon had suffered from hemorrhoids, and it was during a particularly painful attack that he had lost at Waterloo, Evelyn had read an article), so Evelyn was the hostess.

She had arisen at six, partly out of excitement, partly from the need to shore up her suntan, coppery-brown now, glistening through baby oil. The caterers had been checked and rechecked ten times, and there was nothing to worry about or grow old or wrinkled about. She would wear white sandals, with high-corked soles to add to her stature, straps to emphasize the slenderness of her ankles. And she would be brown. Rich and brown, the best possible combination to be, provided the brown was optional, and worked for.

She deposited Chris with the landlady, checked herself one last time in the mirror of the downstairs hall, smiled back at the white sparkle of her teeth, and went outside. Feeling one stab of self-doubt, she looked up at the window, where Chris verified the magnificence of Evelyn, brown, in white sharkskin. Oh yes, it was all there. Evelyn could see herself in the little girl's eyes: dark radiance, moving off toward palm-studded destiny.

The Colonel had sent his car; his aide was driving. She did not sit beside him as she usually did.

There were five pigs roasting on spits on the acre of green behind the Colonel's house. Tented tables were covered with cold Polynesian delicacies from Key West; tubs of ice chilled the fruit; a rhumba band from a leading hotel, their jackets slung over the backs of bridge chairs, sat in the shade of the red, white, and blue tent set up by the portable dance floor. The musicians looked warm and uncomfortable. Evelyn avoided their glances, even the ones filled with admiration. She had told them to be there promptly at noon, and they were. They had fulfilled their present, the best they could do for Evelyn. Their future would be limited to shaking maracas. Evelyn had no wish to share in any such life, unless it belonged to Xavier Cugat, and he wasn't in the band. She had had enough of ordinary men.

As if to sound a drum roll to thought, the young officer appeared, coming through the colonnaded porticos out onto the lawn. He was woven into the ordinary tapestry of afternoon with golden hair that matched the braid on his broad, proudly held shoulders.

"Lieutenant Granson," he said, extending his warm hand. "I hope I haven't come too early."

"I was afraid," Evelyn managed, trying not to catch the words on her suddenly dry tongue, "I was afraid you'd never come at all."

When she had been young, young enough to believe refugee myths of accomplishment, Evelyn had received a legacy of a hundred and fifteen dollars from a cousin in Chicago. She had taken a few violin lessons, but Sammy and Murray had started calling her "Yehudi," so she spent the rest of her inheritance on learning ballet. Her breasts were too full, even in early adolescence, to allow for her to become a genuine ballerina, and she worried about too much dancing putting knots in her lithe calves. When the money was gone, she did not mourn the loss of that particular career. But she had always worried about her one true windfall having been wasted.

Not so now. The one thing she had digested from her dancing lessons and put away was the ability to "spot," to whirl in circles through the dizzying confusion of life with her eye always on one particular object, so she would not experience vertigo. It served her well on this particular afternoon.

The barbecue spun around them, peppered with Army and Navy brass, wives with giddy laughs, waves of damp heat, food, and music. Evelyn fixed an even smile on her face to camouflage the erratic beating of her heart and moved through it all as if it really existed, making everyone welcome, important, although she saw nothing clearly except Johnny Granson. From Delaware. Where the DuPonts lived.

"My good right arm," said Colonel Bramford at two o'clock in the afternoon, when the spontaneous gaiety was in full, well-ordered swing. "You young jackanapes," he said to Johnny Granson, beaming old and white next to Evelyn's coppery brown. "Don't you dare distract her. This woman is my good right arm."

"As if anything could distract me from my loyalty to you," Evelyn said, distracted.

"My good right arm."

"I'll call Supply and get you an artificial one," Johnny said, and removed the Colonel's arm from Evelyn's back.

"Insubordination," said the Colonel, laughing, but not really.

"It's all right," Johnny whispered in her ear, as they danced across the emergency patio that had been set up on the grass. "He and Dad are great friends."

Dad. Imagine.

"Tell me everything," he said into the beginnings of twilight. "Tell me what you were like when you were a little girl. I want to know it all."

"There's nothing to tell," she said, mentally tearing up the pictures of Grandma and Pappy on her dresser. Sepia. Mayflower was the prefix on their telephone, not their ship. "I was very ordinary."

"You could never be ordinary." He kissed her fingertips. He really did that. "You're a princess."

She did not tell him it was true.

"I have a child," she whispered into the heavy flutter of evening, against the light flutter of his heart.

"Tell me, pretty lady, are there any more at home like you . . . ?" he sang.

"She isn't at all like me," she murmured on the beach, in the darkness, while they explored each other's faces with their lips.

"She's a lot like her father." He was touching her breast, a tender commitment. "We're separated. He isn't here."

"Where is he?"

She took a breath. "Pittsburgh." Waiting for a crackle of distaste.

"I'll need more specific information than that, if I'm going to have him killed."

"He never did anything that bad." Evelyn laughed.

"He married my girl. We'll have to get rid of him. What's his address?"

What *was* his address, that miserable son of a bitch? Was he still living at her house, hogging the single bathroom, playing the pitiful victim of a contest greater than war?

"I don't know. It's a serious separation."

"Find out," said Johnny Granson, slipping his hand between her silky thighs. "It isn't serious enough to suit me."

"You really going to kill him?" Evelyn giggled.

"One way or another."

Another was the one he decided upon. Murder, of course, was unthinkable, no matter how often or happily they joked about it. Nobody in his long family history (seven generations in the New World, which was by now Old Domain) had been guilty of a crime measurable in a court of law. Divorce, likewise, was inconceivable to Evelyn's family (she did not cite how many generations of Americans were behind that decision). It was audacity enough that she had left her husband, the first in a long line of proud traditionalists to have done so. Adultery, too, was out of the question, at least for a little while. She pleaded virtue, secretly considering that if he had her wholly, he would find out she was just like every other woman with everything in the same place, at which point he might not even help her down from her pedestal.

So they toyed with each other's clothes and things they could reach through buttons and zippers, and searched for an honorable solution to their predicament. "The Navy," he said finally.

"Not Walter," Evelyn said. "Walter would never join the Navy."

"This is war." He marked her individual eyelashes gently.

"I think he's gotten around the draft. His family is very influential."

"A commission," said Johnny. "No man is too influential to pass up a commission."

"He's very close to his family. I don't know if there's any way to get him to leave his family." Or mine, she did not add.

"You're his family now," said Johnny Granson. "We must teach him to have pride for you. We must force pride on him."

"You can't force someone to learn pride."

"A good attorney can," said Johnny. "We'll get some clever shyster Jew on him."

They went to a great many more cocktail parties than they were used to attending, looking for the man with the biggest mouth and the hungriest approach. They found Murray Rabin.

"No problem," Murray said, stuffing the hors d'oeuvres in his mouth to fill the waistcoated paunch. "The man walked out on you, right?"

"Not exactly," said Evelyn. "I had to sneak out on him. In the middle of the night. He would have killed me. He tried that all the time. And my child. I have witnesses. My parents. I'd prefer not to use them."

"The child. There's a child, yes?" Fried shrimp going down the gullet.

"My little girl."

"She'll testify?"

"I'd prefer that it doesn't come to that. She thinks he's wonderful. You know how little girls are."

"How much does he give you for child support?"

"Nothing."

"The bastard," said Johnny Granson.

"Good enough," said Murray Rabin. "A heavy suit for child support. That ought to bring him into line."

"He doesn't make very much money," Evelyn said. "He hasn't

been in practice that long." She did not say that it was a dental practice, because dentistry was the garbage can of the medical profession. She did not want Johnny to know she had wed someone from a dump.

"He doesn't make much money at all," said Evelyn.

"He'll do better in the Navy," said Johnny Granson.

The subpoena charging Walter M. White with neglect and failure to pay separate maintenance and child support was served him on March 19, 1942. He had an entire day and a sleepless night wondering how he would deal with the humiliation, where he could get the money, where he could go that the lawyer couldn't find him. On March 20th, he received an offer of a commission in the Navy. As he had never seen the Aleutians, or any islands at all, he bade a tearful farewell to Evelyn's family, and a brave one to his own. He stocked up on Dramamine, which Murray got him from the drugstore, fitted himself out in smart naval whites, and reported to Naval Headquarters for his assignment.

March 22, 1942

My darling Evelyn, my precious Chrissie.

First, little girl, Happy Birthday.

These are the times that try men's souls, and test their hearts as well. Big little girl, whatever conflicts have passed between us are minuscule in comparison to that great battle that rages in the far corners of the earth, to which I have been assigned, after joining the Navy. I leave at dawn.

My heart would be heavy, as it is from moment to moment, were it not for the fact that it is uplifted by the knowledge that I am engaging in a battle that will make the world free and safe for my girls. Sometimes the hand of Fate has gentle fingers, raising us out of the morass of ordinary problems, into a sphere where we can view our foibles and failings with true perspective, and see how paltry and meaningless are our little quarrels, when seen beside the greater issues of personal freedom, tyranny, a maniacal wish for conquest and power.

Because of my orders, which are secret, I will not be able to visit you in Florida before I set sail. But when a man's country, which has given him everything, including a beautiful wife, a precious little girl, and the opportunity to become something greater, no matter how high or lowly his beginnings, when that country calls him, he cannot fail to answer. And so I go with joy in my heart that God has given me a chance to protect you, to see that no invader shall deprive you of life, liberty, and the pursuit of happiness.

I pray that I shall return to you, with full body and full mind, that we can begin again to restore the love we shared. But if, my beloveds, something greater than anger, foolish uncontrolled emotions, should take me from you, be assured that in whatever part of myself that still exists, and it will, you know—there is no destroying the human spirit when it yearns, even if no longer contained in flesh—you will be the most precious possession any man ever had, the greatest gift that our Creator ever passed on to one frail, unfaultless human being.

Evelyn, I cannot put into words my passion. This may be the last letter I shall ever write: Such words as Puritans scoff at do not belong in the final souvenir. But remember my arms around you, my lips on yours, and all that went with it.

Chrissie, my baby poet, my little learner of all the ballads of love and romance unremembered by those ten times your age, five years old today, seek always the highest ideals, the ones the poets strived for. Look for them in life, as you heard them in poems, and remember them not just as words, but as feelings. Attain it all.

The world will little note, nor long remember what we say here. (Only you could remember all of it, when you were only two, my surprising child.) But for you I pledge the last full measure of devotion . . . that this nation, under God, shall have a new birth of freedom—and that government of the people, by the people, for the people, shall not perish from the earth.

I pray that my final resting place shall be in your arms,

my wonderful girls. But should it be otherwise, otherwhere, always remember . . .

Your loving husband,
Your loving father,

Walter

"Jesus Christ," said Evelyn, and threw the letter in the waste-basket.

Chris retrieved it after Evelyn left the house with Johnny Granson. She put it in her copy of *India's Love Lyrics,* which she kept hidden behind the toilet.

FOUR

THE OFFICES of Sterne and Sterne, Investment Banking, were not just furnished, finally; they were appointed. Not an inch, not a corner, from filing cabinet to inkwell, was anything less than custom-chosen, or designed, by Raphael Hawthorne, or so he called himself, and what did Arnold care, that was what *Town and Country* called him, too. Raphael Hawthorne ("Rafe" in summers in Southampton) thought he founded the school he labeled "eclectic Modern," which was to enjoy a revival several decades later as art deco—anything gaudy and cheap but graceful that had survived from the twenties: blonde bobbed hair little flapper ballerinas *tour-jeté*-ing across a table lamp; toilet tops which when lifted said inside, "I love my wife but oh you kid" next to a painting of a sheep.

In 1934, in Germany, Speer had staged a "cathedral of light" at Zeppelin Field (Leni Riefenstahl directing the documentary film) with one hundred and thirty search beams forming a huge wall of lights, twenty-five thousand feet high, with clouds wafting through them. Art deco, with its finned and slab-sided eagles, athletes with metallically rippling hair, horrendously classical lack of classicism, was Adolf Hitler's favorite. Some of its finest examples were pointed out to William Randolph Hearst, who brought them back to America. But Raphael Hawthorne didn't dwell on the fact that the style was Hitler's favorite any more than Arnold Sterne dwelled on Adolf Hitler. As far as Arnold was concerned, Hitler was a loud-mouthed vegetarian with some pretty good ideas, at least as far as restoring the German economy was concerned. The rest about Hitler didn't concern him. Arnold had bigger things on his mind, first among which was furnishing his offices.

Toward the end of the thirties, art deco in this country was mainly furniture that people threw out, once they could afford to refurbish. As impressed as Arnold was with the reputation and manner of "Rafe," he was not too choked up about "eclectic Modern." So they settled on a style that Hawthorne dubbed "Renaissance Primitive," encompassing anything antique that could be bought at auction, plus some African wall carvings and a pair of giant elephant tusks on brass bases. These last Sonny and Arnold placed directly in the front foyer of Sterne and Sterne, so the customers would know that the shafting, if it occurred, would be colossal.

Besides the tusks, the reception room contained two twenty-by-ten-foot gilt rococo framed mirrors which might or might not have been at the summer palace at Villefranche, but had definitely been used by the Comédie Française as far back as the eighteenth century, when people were much smaller. Arnold knew this for a fact, as Rafe had gotten the mirrors in the same lot as the costumes from *Tartuffe,* and unless it had been a special company of midgets, the people had been much smaller.

The costumes were stored away for a masked ball Arnold intended to give his son, Ellis, on his twelfth birthday. But everything else bizarre, elaborate, and expensive that had been acquired was placed on display to the best possible advantage, somewhere in the vast suite of offices. Typewriters, telephones, and ticker tape machines were cast in a variety of disguises, set in rollaway drawers of carved cabinets so that at closing hour, or at a given signal from Arnold or Sonny, everything could be concealed that was not a part of the artful past. On entering, a new customer might think himself not so much on Wall Street as onstage in an exquisite production at the Met, to which Arnold and Sonny now had a regular subscription.

Everything was the way it had been in the dream: offices, opera on Thursday, a mansion with too many rooms, even with six servants, his little boy, Ellis, and Baby (growing up, growing older, still called Baby) and Sonny still living with them. That was part of the dream, too, although Arnold never admitted it. He kept telling Sonny to get out of there and get married, he was twenty-eight years old and it was planting time. But he loved knowing Sonny was down there, at the far end of the stone corridor, which echoed Arnold's footsteps as he moved under the great vaulted ceilings ("Tarrytown Medieval," according to Raphael Hawthorne). Arnold needed Sonny there midnights when he woke up from dozing over the Blue List, having the dream blow up in his head, needing to check it was all still there: chauffeured limousines, actual friends in the South. Everything except honor.

Honor was nothing you could pick up at auction, even if you went with Raphael Hawthorne. Banks could be picked up, had been picked up, like moonstones on the beaches of Ceylon, where he would go one day, Arnold promised himself, why not, very exotic. Banks could be had in partnership with white-haired genteel men called Colonel, whether or not they had served, because they lived in the South and knew how desperate the banks were to unload their ownerships, which in the days of failing had been up for grabs like moonstones on the beaches of Ceylon. All you needed was train fare to Chapel Hill and points slightly east and west and south, and the gall to say to the owners of the bank: "Okay. I buy your stock. I'll be responsible if the bank should fail completely. Sell cheap and I'll take it all on." Those were the words, as filtered through the soft golden tongues of Southern Colonels, with Arnold and Sonny the silent partners, because they talked a cruder language. One which Southern banks might not understand, as desperate as they were for cash. Even in days of failure and fear, men could buy banks, but not honor.

Honor was not for sale: the hole in the magic carpet of free enterprise. Arnold and Sonny were the Bad Boys of Wall Street, and the respectable brokers, just getting up off their duffs, were too busy wiping off the dust of the depression to play dirty in the alleys. Alleys were the turf to which the Sterne boys were restricted, because there was no room for them on the Street. No seat was open on the New York Stock Exchange. Not to Sonny and Arnold Sterne, nosirree, not for all the tea in China, not for all the banks in Carolina, not for all the moonstones in Ceylon.

With all the suicides and natural passing and hoped-for heart attacks, there were still sons to fill the seats, or people of breeding who were allowed to buy in because they belonged. Sonny and Arnold did not belong on the field of honor, were not fit to do battle on such a field, the New York Stock Exchange. It was not a conspiracy—it was a simple fact. No one would sell them a seat on the Stock Exchange. So naturally that became the only place Arnold and Sonny wanted to sit.

That was why it was good that Sonny was still living at home, in the Big House, as they came to call the Tarrytown mansion, because they were still the prisoners of the dream. The brightest arc of the rainbow still eluded them. Honor, for the son that was born, for the sons that would be born, as soon as Sonny got his behind out of there and got married. Only there was no particular rush, Arnold was quick to tell him on those midnights when they sifted their disappointment like lumps out of their joy.

"It'll change," Arnold said. "It's six, what, seven years now, isn't it? It has to change. They'll forget."

Nobody did.

"If you can buy a seat while all around you are losing theirs and blaming it on you," Arnold proclaimed, "you'd have to be a gentile."

"What about the Rothschilds and the Sangers?" Sonny asked.

"They've been rich so long, they can no longer afford to be Jewish."

"Not Clifton Sanger," Sonny said. "He gave a hundred thousand to the new temple on Fifth Avenue last month."

"That's in case there's a God of Wrath," Arnold said. "He's hedging all bets on Jehovah."

"I tried to call him again last week," Sonny said. "I've tried speaking to him and I've tried speaking to Loeb."

"What did they say?"

"That they were out of town."

Arnold laughed his suffocated laugh. "What the hell do they want from us? A public apology for being smart? Small people. Christ, how I hate small people."

"So we'll just have to wait," said Sonny impatiently.

"We'll also have to stop announcing our intentions," Arnold said. "As far as we're concerned, from now on we have no wish for a seat on the Exchange. I'll get some of those amiable drunks in the respected houses to let us know when a seat's coming up and no big noise, okay? Silent buy."

As usual, Arnold's idea made a great deal of sense: no fuss, no noise, no publicity. Through a series of washy-eyed middlemen they found out when the next seat was coming vacant. They managed to buy it after seven years of trying for close to four hundred thousand dollars. It was all accomplished very quickly and quietly and cleanly.

Except that the seat that came vacant, quite by coincidence, was one of the oldest on the New York Stock Exchange, belonging to one of the most distinguished names among American banking families. The ancestors (they had ancestors, these people, traceable still in family Bibles) had been among the merchants and auctioneers who first met on May 17, 1792, to start trading at regular hours under the old buttonwood tree on Wall Street. Men who were buying and selling for the public in government stock, insurance companies, Alexander Hamilton's First United States Bank, the Bank of North America, the Bank of New York. They had moved indoors to the Tontine Coffee

House in 1793, and sipped their way through the quieting of financial activity during the War of 1812.

Sons had flourished with the postwar boom, adding New York State Bonds issued to pay for the Erie Canal to their dealings, expanding their powers as private business did. That family had been there for the development of each new enterprise, marine and fire insurance companies, the Delaware and Hudson Canal Company, the Merchant's Exchange, and the New York Gas Light Company, the nation's first public utility.

Sons bearing their fathers' names, with numbers, moved to the meeting room of what became 40 Wall Street, voted on the formal constitution of the Exchange. Grandchildren with heraldic signatures helped adopt, in 1863, the title "New York Stock Exchange," watched the stock tickers being installed, grumbled slightly in 1868 when memberships were made salable. But this was, after all, the United States of America, where the dream was for everyone everyplace else, where telephones were installed in 1879, where volume could exceed a million shares a day for the first time in 1886, where patriotism and free enterprise flourished in the Broad Street building, with its modern trading floor.

Chicanery might have been present, but it did not go unchecked, according to the constitution. There were fines for violation of procedure, the discontinuance of unlisted trading, in which the company had no responsibility to comply with Exchange Standards, questionnaires initiated in 1922 for periodic examination of the financial condition of member firms. And in 1933 the Deale Act was passed so the Securities and Exchange Commission could regulate and avoid the financial excesses that had led to the collapse of the market.

For Arnold Sterne, the Stock Exchange shone sweeter than the world's biggest candy emporium. All he wanted was his own shimmering stall, somewhere on that big, pretty floor.

It was right, it was fitting and ironically proper, more than exciting, that the seat that came available belonged to a family so rich in cash and tradition that it didn't have to trade anymore. It was a hell of a story, to be told to Arnold's sons, and Sonny's, but nobody else until the story became history. Unfortunately, *Newsweek* considered it a hell of a story, too. They picked up on it and ran a special insert on the changing nature of American business and how the founding fathers were making way for self-made sons.

They did not phrase it exactly that way, but they did give the names of the buyers: Arnold and Abraham Sterne. When the news hit the Street, a euphemistic translation of what Arnold said about what ensued, the Sternes were called in for countless interviews in wood-paneled rooms, with long oaken tables, at the ends of which sat men with little eyes, and notebooks they never consulted.

Sonny was the one who attended the polite inquisitions, because Arnold was afraid of losing his temper, and the seat. Sonny was the one who walked, awed, into mahogany chambers, and stared into unresponsive eyes, while members of the board of governors, or representatives of members of the Exchange, did not even pretend to be wearing velvet gloves for handling the business of the Sternes. They asked questions about the brothers' background, full details of which they already had in the notebooks in front of them which they never consulted.

"You went to school, Sterne?" a heavy-set tweedy gentleman said. He did not look up out of his bifocals, but studied his own well-manicured hands through heavy lower half-moons of glass.

"Yes, sir," said Sonny. No need to be aggressive. They had already been aggressive enough. Politeness and soft-spoken, clear answers were the order of the day, the week, the month during which he submitted to interrogations labeled interviews. Politeness and crisp clear answers were all that were needed. Anything more might make him sweat, and then they would think he had something to hide.

"Where did you attend school, Sterne?"

"Brooklyn College, sir. And Columbia Law."

"You graduated?"

"Yes, sir." Look in your notebook, Ben Franklin, you bastard.

"What made you decide to give up the law?"

"I never gave it up, sir. I observe the tenets of the law in all my business transactions."

"Which law is that, Sterne? Constitutional law, criminal law, religious law, or Gresham's law?"

"Bad money drives out good?"

"What do you think about that law, Sterne."

"I think it's outdated, sir. There's no such thing as bad money." He tried to smile, but the man would not look at him. "There's only bad management of money."

"And you'd never be guilty of that?"

"Not deliberately, sir, no. A man would have to be a fool to deliberately mismanage money."

"But anyone can make a mistake."

"Yes, sir. I suppose anyone can."

"How do you feel about fair competition?"

"Passionate, naturally."

"You'd be against unfair competition?"

"Of course."

"I suppose you and your brother have your own definition of unfair competition."

"I suppose we do," Sonny said. He could feel his shoulder starting to move underneath his jacket, and turned slightly sideways so the man at the far end of the table wouldn't see, if he bothered to look, and think there was something about which Sonny was nervous.

"Would you mind defining your idea of unfair competition, Mr. Sterne?"

"I think unfair competition is when a lot of people get a smart idea at the same time, and some of them aren't permitted to put it into action."

"For what reason?"

"Who knows?" Sonny said. "Who knows why anyone would want to block someone else from putting a smart idea into action? I mean, it is called free enterprise, isn't it? That would seem to imply a degree of liberty."

"Liberty to take advantage of other people?"

"Liberty to take advantage of your own good ideas. I don't think there's anything too hard to understand about that."

"Well, some of us may be a little slower than you are, Sterne."

"I doubt that, sir." Sonny smiled again, openly now, warmly, so the man would see there was no real ax to grind, no true enemy here. Just another young man trying to carve his way through stone canyons.

"And how does tradition fit in with this concept of yours?"

"I don't think it's my concept, sir. I think it's the original concept of this country."

"But you and your brother seem to think yourselves capable of improving on original concepts."

"I don't believe we do. I think we just know how to take advantage of making the original concepts more original."

"So you have no particular respect for tradition?"

"I didn't say that." He could feel the muscle pulling in his shoulder. He put his hand in the pocket of his pants to try and anchor the inadvertent tic. "We have a great deal of respect for tradition. Especially the tradition of being your own man."

"Then why buy a seat on the New York Stock Exchange?"

"I can't think of a better place to be your own man."

"The New York Stock Exchange is a tradition, Sterne."

"That's why we're so anxious to become a part of it."

"So you can change it? Corrupt it?"

"I don't think you're being fair, sir. There's nothing in that whole dossier you've got in front of you that hints of corruption."

"Maybe not according to such original thinkers. But for those who have true respect for tradition—"

"Why don't you ask me direct questions, sir? Why don't you make straight accusations, and if there's any area in which we've been culpable, or irresponsible—"

"This is not a court of law, Mr. Sterne. Nobody's accusing you of anything."

"I know that," Sonny said. "If you would accuse me, I might be better equipped to counter your accusations."

"You understand, we just have to touch on every possible argument against your being on the Exchange."

"I understand it now that you've explained it to me, sir."

"Not that I mean to imply anyone's against your having the seat."

"I know you don't mean to imply anything, sir. You're much too straightforward to hint."

The man looked up. His eyes seemed smaller as he gazed through the upper portion of his glasses. "Are you having fun with me, Sterne?"

"No, sir. I'm not having any fun at all."

A wise guy. They'd say he was a wise guy.

Two men earn the reputation of being wise guys, Rabbi Gamaliel might have said. Should one say, "I earned it," and the other say, "I earned it," then they must divide the reputation equally. However, should one say, "The reputation is all mine," and the other say, "It is half mine," then Rabbi Gamaliel says, what? Which half do you want, the wise or the guy?

Because it is not possible to plead youth or inexperience, hence saying, I am just a kid, a guy, and anything of blackness was my brother's fault, because that makes the brother the one who was wise, and so he deserves the entire phrase.

But he cannot afford to carry all the credit, because that would make him carry the blame, and one day he will be Senator, you dirty sons of bitches, one day he will stick it to you all, and for that it will not do that he should be considered a wise guy. Let him only be considered too smart for the rest of you. Let me be the one who was called insolent.

"You seem very amused for someone who isn't having any fun," the man at the end of the table said. "Perhaps you'd like to share the joke."

"It's a little involuted, even for someone who's an expert at finance," Sonny said.

"Well, what do you think?" Arnold said, when they were having dinner that night. "You think you're making any headway with the board?"

"That depends on what you mean by headway," Sonny said. "If by headway, you speak in the vernacular sense, meaning progress, than I say it's doubtful. But if you speak in the Navy sense, head meaning toilet, I'd say, yes, we are making our way rapidly into the toilet."

"Cut it out," Arnold said. "They're going to let us in. They're just trying to make it seem hard."

"Then they are first-rate illusionists," said Sonny.

Twenty-five years after that conversation, a man was refused a seat on the New York Exchange, and sued to find out why, and who exactly were his adversaries, demanding to confront them. He succeeded. But in 1940, when Sonny and Arnold were denied the place they had purchased, the workings of the board of governors were as shrouded in mystery as the Talmud. When the Sterne brothers were informed that they would not be allowed to take their seat, there was no way for an outsider to fight the decision, or even discover how it had been reached, or who had been instrumental in deciding. No was no.

Arnold said fuck it, and went to sleep very drunk. Sonny was also drunk, but he did not fall asleep. He lay in his oak four-poster bed, his heavy-lidded gaze fixed on the cupids that danced around the ceiling, not letting them move too fast for fear that the room and his head might start spinning. He changed them into the board of governors to give it all some order, to fix them in heavy places seated around a table, their carved navels expanding into great pot bellies, girded by expensive vests, with old watches and Phi Beta Kappa keys in the pockets. They started passing a box around the board room, and the head cupid, the fattest fool in charge, instructed everybody present to consider the application of Arnold and Abraham Sterne.

Each of the board members had two marbles in his hand: one white, one black. There was a hole at the top of the square wooden box they passed slowly, from member to member. Sonny could not see the marbles as they went into the carved-out tiny circle. He could, however, imagine who everyone voting represented. He fixed his eyes on the position their particular marble might fall into, so he could guess who it was, exactly, that black-balled them.

They finished passing the box. It sat on the table in front of the head cupid, who paused a moment, stentorian even in silence, flexing his fingers like a concert pianist about to play a particularly complicated concerto. Then he slowly slid the drawer from the bottom of the box, and held it out so everyone could see. All of the balls were black.

Arnold wanted blood. He started yelling at his servants, and fighting with headwaiters about imagined slights, a booth that was one table to the left of the one he said he had specifically reserved. He was not about to hide his light behind a zebra, he screamed out loud at El Morocco, and was asked to leave.

"I'll buy the fucking club," he said as the checkroom girl handed him his coat, which action blocked the punch he was aiming at the maitre d'. "I'll buy the fucking place and fire your ass."

"It will be very far away from here, if you are the owner, sir," the maitre d' said.

"Let me at him," Arnold shouted, as Sonny helped him on with his coat, holding hard to the sleeves to restrain his brother's arms. "I'll kill the phony bastard."

"A fate better than working for you, sir," said the maitre d', smiling. Leonard Lyons was in the corner, talking to Harry Bell and the dancer he had brought back from Florida. Harry Bell was in the column all the time, and the maitre d' hadn't made it for three and a half months. He directed his words to Arnold, but his smile and his glance toward Leonard Lyons, who didn't seem to be hearing in spite of how loud everything was. "Shall I call the bouncer?"

"You do that," Arnold said. "You call the bouncer for help, you queer."

The maitre d' snapped his fingers toward the man behind the bar, and Arnold's right hand shot out of his sleeve. Sonny pulled him back, so he struck air. "Lawsuit," he said into Arnold's ear. "You hit him, he can sue you and retire."

"I'll know the fucking judge," Arnold raged, but the iron in his arm softened.

When they were out on the sidewalk, he told Sonny to check in the morning what the price was on the place. "It's not for sale," Sonny said.

"Everybody has a price," said Arnold. "Find it out." He was breathing so hard Sonny made him lean against the building, while he studied the line of black limousines, looking for Arnold's driver.

"Clubs and restaurants are a shaky investment," Sonny said.

"You're right." The blue veins standing out in Arnold's forehead were beginning to recede. "I never even liked the fucking food. Let's just not go back there anymore."

"Let's never go back anywhere, anymore," Sonny said, as the driver held the door open for them, and they got into the car. "Let's find places and make them ours."

"Good thinking," said Arnold, and leaned back against the pale gray upholstery. "Madison Square Garden, George," he said to the chauffeur. "I want to see somebody get killed."

"No fights tonight, Mr. Sterne."

"Then stop the car and get out on the sidewalk and take your coat off."

George laughed.

"He thinks I'm kidding," Arnold said.

"Maybe we could just go home and you can beat up your wife," said Sonny.

"No, Sarah's too short and pregnant. It wouldn't be a fair fight."

"I didn't know you wanted a fair fight."

"Neither did I," Arnold said, and slumped back in the seat.

Colonel Reeling thought what the boys needed was a vacation, a good stiff whiff of Southern pace. They had been doing business with him since the day Roosevelt closed the banks, when he saw their ad and called to place an order. He said he liked their style, and the sound of their brains, and the next time he was up from Tennessee, he intended to come in and shake their hands.

He liked the way they shook hands, too, firm and hard with a real arm behind it, he said, when he came into the office. Not like some of these sissies on the Street who made you think that an introduction was an invitation to the waltz. He liked just about everything about them, including the fact that they wanted to come in on the bank-buying.

"Hell, banks today are like moonstones on the beaches of Ceylon," he said. He was wearing a light gray suit with a white stripe in it, very natty. But he had a fine physique for a gentleman in his sixties, and he carried it well. The suit, and being a gentleman, every six foot two inches of him. "Moonstones on the beaches of Ceylon. They just grow there, tossed up by the sea, tossed down by the mountains, who knows, who cares, the important thing is they're just lying there on the sand, waiting to be scooped up. They know that, the Ceylonese. Those people are no fools. The fools are the ones who don't travel to Ceylon to pick 'em, as easy as you would a flower. You boys ought to go places like Ceylon."

"What are the assets of the banks you're talking about?" Arnold asked.

"Anywhere from two to five million. But, hell, the owners are so scared saltless that the banks'll fail still farther, they'll sell them for forty, thirty, twenty thousand cash . . . there's no telling how cheap we could get them for until we try." He leaned back in the Louis Quinze armchair, the oval back of which framed him like a cameo. There he was, ivory-white, pale eyes gleaming with how much good sense it made. "Good sense," he muttered, puffing on his thin cigar, "and better dollars."

He smiled his mouth into a diamond.

It was Friday morning, and the Thursday presentation at the Metropolitan had been *Faust*. It was Sonny's first *Faust* (he had had two *Aïdas,* two *Carmens,* one *Barber of Seville,* and three *Marriages of Figaro*). He was familiar with the story, having studied Marlowe in college, and the libretto with its interpretation by Milton Cross on Wednesday evening. He had been deeply moved by the performance, as he identified completely with Faust, especially had Sonny taken one of his earlier paths and become a great scholar. He knew how alone a great scholar would have to be when he was old, and, yes, he would have traded it too, at par value: a soul for a great love.

The part of the analogy that he couldn't quite make fit was what in his life was Mephistophelean. That it might be Arnold was obvious, and wrong. Arnold underneath was the same person he was, that's why they were brothers. Kindred spirit, that's what it meant; kindred spirit in kindred flesh. They had slept together on subways, riding them back and forth all night the month the mortgage company tried to take the house away from them, before their father's political friends got it back. They had huddled in each other's arms, like father and son, the older one holding, the younger one held. They had sat like that through thirty-two nights, meeting on a corner at an appointed time each evening, stopping off at McCloskey's to steal some tomato herring, or, if he was watching, have nothing to eat but air. And all the time they had been holding on. You couldn't hold on to someone, all night for thirty-two nights, and not feel what was underneath.

There was a good man in Arnold. A good man like himself. It just had a harder face on. Sonny had totally enjoyed the entire evening, dressed in his first tuxedo, escorting Baby in her first long dress. He especially enjoyed watching Mephisto, who was particularly well sung. He had for many years been using the word "Mephistophelean" but had never seen it in person. Certainly not in Arnold.

However, looking at Colonel Reeling now, grinning so angularly at them, he wondered if that one was to be the devil part of it. He studied the Colonel's smile and saw that his mouth was rather small. So it didn't have to be evil there; it was just as wide as he could get his lips to go when he was onto a genuinely good idea.

"And how much would we be responsible for?" Sonny asked.

"The entire assets of the bank," the Colonel answered.

Arnold was standing by the window, thumb hooked into his vest, the chain in the vest pockets dangling the Phi Beta Kappa key he had bought at auction. "So if we go in and buy a two-million-dollar bank for twenty-five thousand and people want their two million, what happens?"

"We all travel to Ceylon," the Colonel said, and laughed. "Hell, that's not going to happen. The panic is over. We're on the road back, boys; this young country can survive anything. We were born in revolution and we made it through civil war and the Great War and a market crash. Childhood diseases. The best thing about childhood diseases is that once you have them, you're immunized. We can't go through any of that again."

"You don't think there's any chance of its getting worse."

"Sure there's a chance," the Colonel said. "But that's what makes it a gamble. In my opinion, a great gamble."

"I'd like to share your optimism," Arnold said.

"I'd like to share his cash," said Sonny.

The three men laughed and came together in the center of the room, to shake hands on the deal. "That's what I like," said the Colonel, as Sonny pumped the well-manicured hand. "A handshake that feels like a handshake. My son's going to some damned prep school; he shakes hands like he's got no bones. Luckily, my daughter's at Bryn Mawr, and when she shakes hands, she could take your arm off. Maybe they'll even out."

He laughed, and when he was through shaking their hands, he patted their backs. "Like you to meet them sometime. Like you to come to my home."

He had been extending the invitation regularly for eight years. Now that Arnold was openly blowing his stack at head-waiters, it was imperative that good friends get him to simmer down, lest his judgment be questioned along with his breeding. When a man played a game out of rage and despair, he reduced his own chances of winning. And as the Colonel was partners with the Sterne boys on the play, the odds against him personally might also diminish.

"Deep long whiff of Southern pace," the Colonel said. "That's what the doctor ordered."

"I have too much to do here," Arnold said. "I can't afford to take a vacation."

"You can't afford not to," the Colonel said, and leaned back in the restaurant booth, watching Arnold eat the third steak the waiter had brought him, after Arnold had bitten into two and nearly thrown them back in the waiter's face.

"Nice easy ride in Pullman elegance, genteel nigras blacking your shoes overnight and welcoming you back to fair food; I give you that, the food is only fair. But the porters greet you like you're family by the time you get to Carolina. They know how to serve. And you can watch winter fading away outside the dining car window. A day and a half and you'll be in Prosperity, Tennessee. It might not be the biggest city in the state, but you can bet it's the prettiest. And we'll bourbon-and-branch-water our way to contentment and peace, boys. That's what we manu-facture besides banks in Tennessee is bourbon and branch water and peace." He sat back and smiled his diamond smile. "A little grouse shooting early in the morning to get the anger off, and the skill up, and a little fine eating at night, grouse if we get any. Or anything your heart desires. That's what we serve. Steaks'll be rare, so you don't have to come to grief with Miz Reeling, and the nights'll be full of stars. You need some real smells in your nose, like trees and flowers that hang so heavy they like to touch the ground. Willows don't weep in Tennessee, boys, they just want to tickle the ground, make sure they're really in that fine a place."

"Sold," Sonny said.

Two weeks later, Sonny and Arnold boarded the train in the subterranean blocks of Pennsylvania Station. They had two large suitcases apiece, plus outsize toilet kits that contained hair-brushes, razors, shaving cream, some cologne, the Blue List, several copies of "The Money Market." Arnold held a copy of *Fortune* magazine rolled up in his hand, and Sonny carried *Absalom, Absalom,* so that he would know about the South by the time they got there.

He was excited about the journey, because it was the only one he had ever made further than New Jersey. It was also the first time he would be sleeping overnight with Arnold on a moving vehicle that wasn't a subway. He was sure he had brought all the wrong clothes, which was why he had packed three times as many as he needed, in varying styles so there would be some combination that would be fitting.

Arnold had gone to Hammacher Schlemmer to check out what the well-dressed country gentleman who shot grouse would be likely to wear. Having seen it, he decided in favor of taking many too many clothes in the wrong style. They each packed a tuxedo, even though the Colonel had assured them that life at the Reeling place was very casual. They had seen movies about the casually rich and in them people always dressed for dinner. Bankers who lived in Prosperity, Tennessee. Ah, yes, black tie for sure.

Two redcaps handled the luggage, as Arnold didn't want the bags to be mixed up. Arnold's suitcases were red leather, and Sonny's were brown canvas. The bags were approximately the same large size and each bore the gilded initials A.S., so Arnold could see where they might get mixed up. Besides, he wanted two redcaps.

He tipped the porter who was in charge of their car the minute they boarded the train. After determining that there were no better accommodations anywhere on board, and no more amiable porter, Arnold gave the man an extra ten dollars to make sure they had the best table in the dining car.

"Will you gentlemen want to be dining alone?" the porter asked.

"I think so," Arnold said, and yelling to the compartment next door, asked Sonny, "You feel like making friends on this trip?"

"I always feel like making friends," Sonny yelled back.

"We'll eat alone," said Arnold. "The best table, though, William."

"If you eat alone, Mr. Sterne, one of you has to eat riding backwards."

"I know that," Arnold said. "You think this is our first trip on a Pullman?"

"No, sir."

"Well, you're wrong. You'll have to be our guide, William. Is it bad riding backwards?"

"Lots of people don't like it, Mr. Sterne. I don't mind it myself, but I been working this line a lot of years."

"Then get us at a table with someone interesting."

"I'll do my best, sir," the black man said, slipping the crisp bills into the antiseptic white of his jacket pocket. "And if you want anything, I'll be right the other side of your buzzer."

"I'm sure you will," Arnold said, smiling. He hung up the dressing gown he had bought especially in the event of late-night action on the train, and left his toilet kit open for William to unpack. Then he went next door to see Sonny.

Sonny's bags were already neatly in the overhead rack. A fresh pair of pajamas lay folded on the seat beside him, as he stared out into the darkness of the station. Lighted windows flashed alongside. Shuddering glimpses of coach cars showed people eating sandwiches and drinking orangeade from waxy containers.

"How do you like it so far?" Arnold said.

"I can't get over it," Sonny said into his fist. "All these networks of tracks leading everywhere, coming out of the darkness, carrying people all over the country. Don't you think it's amazing?"

"We're still in the station, little brother. There's no reason to be anxious."

"I'm not anxious," Sonny said, and his shoulder moved slightly underneath his jacket. "I just think it's a remarkable feat of engineering. How do you suppose they keep their signals straight?"

"It's what they do for a living." Arnold sat down on the red upholstered curve-backed bench beside him. "When you do something for a living, you know how to do it, or you don't live."

"That's what worries me," Sonny said. The train moved abruptly beneath them, jolting them forward. There was a noise of steam hissing from underneath the wheels, and the slow clanking of metal as the train began to leave the station. Sonny strained his head to see the light at the end of the wide tunnel.

"You're crazy to be so calm," he said. "This thing will never leave the ground."

The dining car attendant walked through the sleeping cars with a triangle and a metal stick, trilling them into the first call for lunch. "You're in the second sitting," William said, sticking his head into the compartment. "Ask for Jefferson. He'll fix you up real nice."

"Thank you."

"Second sitting," Sonny said. "You figure that's the best sitting to be at?"

"That's the only sitting to be at," Arnold said, relaxing into being a world traveler. Moonstones on the beaches of Ceylon. It was only a matter of time.

The man seated opposite Sonny at lunch had had a great deal to drink. It was easy to tell that, because the smell of whiskey was overwhelming, and he kept telling Sonny and Arnold how much he had had to drink. "But only the finest," he said. "Joe Pape's finest black-label bourbon. If a man has the God-given privilege of manufacturing the finest, it's his God-given obligation to drink as much of it as he can." He held out his hand. "Joe Pape," he said. "Pleased to meet you."

"Abraham Sterne," Sonny said, and extended his hand. Arnold was busy talking to the young girl opposite him, so he did not join in the congeniality, although he did accept a touch in his ice water from Joe Pape's flask.

"How about some for the little lady?" Joe Pape asked the girl beside him.

"She's only seventeen," Arnold said.

"It's never too early for Joe Pape's," said Joe, and poured some into her water. "How do you like that for a motto, Sterne?" He looked at Sonny. "You're a New York fellow, aren't you? How'd you like to see that in a magazine? 'It's never too early for Joe Pape's.' "

"I think I'd like it better, 'It's never too early for Pape's.' "

"They said that at the agency," Joe said, pouring some neat whiskey into his coffee cup. "I been up meeting with some of them smart ad agency people, about maybe hiring them to make us national. But I want to keep the *Joe* in there. Gives it kind of a down-home, folksy feeling, and that's what bourbon should be, you know. Down home. Down home we have two names, and so does our bourbon."

"Where's your home?"

"Bible Hill, Tennessee. Prettiest little place for a distillery you ever seen. God's country. God's bourbon." He toasted out the window and drank from the cup.

"I thought Tennessee was dry."

"Hell, sure it's dry. It's illegal to sell and illegal to possess, but when you're in your house, it sure in hell isn't illegal to drink."

"How about to make?"

"Listen, Sterne, I started with a little still, like any other moonshiner during prohibition, and when the country went wet, Bible Hill, Tennessee, stayed dry as drought. You know what a drought is? It's when everybody gets very thirsty, including the governor and the state legislature. Now Tennessee people may be pious, but they ain't stupid, and this is the best damned bourbon in the South. It's illegal to possess in Bible Hill, but we're not possessing it, we're manufacturing it, to try and make the rest of the nation as friendly as we are."

"I hope you succeed," Sonny said, smiling.

"Christ, so do I," Joe Pape said, and rubbed a finger across the slightly swollen bridge of his nose. His face was fleshy, almost devoid of color, except for the broken rivulets of red blood vessels that ran across his nose and cheekbones. He was dressed rather shabbily in a lightweight wrinkled gray suit, and there was a big diamond stickpin in his pearly gray tie. The diamond didn't look too real to Sonny, but neither did Joe Pape.

"You meet with these fast talkers at the ad agency, hell, you'd think they'd want to carve themselves a piece of the future. Let 'em taste the fine stuff and come up with some fancy words to let the rest of the country know, you get my meaning, design a good label so it looks like what it tastes like, first rate, the best. You'd think they'd want to do that."

"Didn't they?"

"Northerners. Couldn't find a Southern kid in the place. Old doddering Northerners, what do they know about the taste of bourbon and the excitement of bringing something to life?"

"It tastes very smooth to me."

"They like the taste of dollar bills better."

"You can't blame them for wanting to get paid."

"The hell I can't. I offered them a piece of sky, and they want earth, boy. That's all the Northerners understand is earth. No offense."

"No offense," Sonny said, and meant it. He did not think himself like anyone who belonged to an organization, Northern or no.

"We're just starting to build up in Bible Hill. It's only eight years since it started being legal, except in Tennessee and the other dry states. Eight years, and it's just getting good and mellow in the cask to where it's perfect, the best I ever tasted, the best you ever drank. We didn't have no big machinery till four years ago, the distillery's just starting to bubble full force, full time, you need time for bourbon. You need time, and you need to tell the people. And they ask me for cash. I offered them a piece of sky, and they want earth."

"How much sky did you offer them?"

"A tenth. A tenth of my profits."

"That sounds like a good deal to me."

"Well, that's because you understand bourbon. They only understand Scotch, those men at ad agencies."

"To tell you the truth, I don't understand bourbon either. This is the first time I ever drank it. But it tastes very nice. Very nice." He raised his glass in minor salute. Then he studied the small card menu, and started to write his order down on the tiny ruled double-paged tablet beside his plate.

"You'll want to order the salmon," Joe Pape said. "You're a man of taste. I travel this line all the time. You'll want the salmon."

"I was thinking of ordering the steak."

"They pick up the good steaks in Washington, come in from Chicago. The ones you get out of New York are kind of stringy. Wait till dinner for the steak."

"I'll take your word for it," Sonny said, and penciled "1 boiled salmon" along the top line.

"Put down you want extra lemon. They get a little stingy with the lemon unless you ask for extra."

"Lucky for me you were on this train," Sonny said.

"I was just thinking the same thing," Joe Pape said, and poured some more bourbon in Sonny's water glass. "Not very often I meet a Northerner I can talk to."

"You ought to drink more of your bourbon, you could talk to anybody."

Joe Pape laughed. "Yeah," he said. "You're right about that. Does kind of loosen you up, don't it? I like you, Sterne. You're a really nice fellow."

"Thank you."

"You let me know your address, I'll send you a case of Joe

144

Pape's Finest. Eight years in the cask. The label isn't all that it should be yet, but you'll know from the gold letters how good it is. And the taste."

"I don't really drink bourbon."

"You will when you get used to Joe Pape's. Gimme your address."

"As a matter of fact," Sonny set down the menu, "you might send it to me where I'm visiting. We're going to see some friends in Tennessee."

"Whereabouts?"

"Prosperity."

"Prosperity! Hell, I know a couple of people in Prosperity. Not more'n sixty miles from Bible Hill, and the roads are fine when there's no flooding. I go there time to time. Who you visiting?"

"Colonel Reeling."

"The banker?"

"You know him?"

"I know about him. Not many people in Tennessee don't know about Colonel Reeling. I hear he's a fine bourbon drinker. You're not in the banking business?"

"As a matter of fact, I am. Investment banking."

"Hell, you don't strike me as a money man at all. I mean, you look rich enough, but you got a lot of thinking in your eyes. I figured maybe you were a doctor or a lawyer or something."

"I studied law."

"You finish?"

"I finished, and I passed the bar."

"And you still went into banking. Beats me. If I knew anything, I'd certainly do what I knew. I do the best I know, and the best I know is how to make bourbon. But if I hadn't a lost my chance at education, I'd sure do something educated. The best you can do with banking is an educated guess."

Sonny didn't argue with him. It would have been silly to argue, because he was right, and argument would just make conversation longer. As it was, he had no idea how he would

145

bring it to a close. The waiter took the problem out of his hands, accidentally spilling the soup that the girl opposite had ordered onto Joe Pape's lap. Joe Pape arose with a terrible roar, cursing out all incompetent niggers, cursing the railroad for having such shaky tracks, niggers to serve the soup who didn't know their blue asses from their black elbows, and various other invectives that he could call to mind through the Joe Pape's haze. He left the dining car, red-faced, and told Sonny he would see him at dinner, if the sons of bitches niggers didn't scald his balls on the way in.

"You have such a gift for making friends," Arnold said to Sonny, and continued talking to the girl.

For most of the afternoon Sonny sat by the window in his compartment, studying the land outside, cities and towns yielding to clumps of grass, fields of grain, everything but purple mountains' majesty (where was that, where were the purple mountains?). The beginning of the journey had been striped with snow, miles and miles of uninterrupted lines of blackening snow running alongside the railroad tracks. Now the snow had melted, or had never been at all. Once they were past Maryland, it looked to Sonny as though hardship and cold had moved North for the winter. Except for the falling-down shacks close to the stations they whizzed through, except for the hungry expression-less eyes of the children who stared the train by, except for the old people who sat on rickety front porches with hands clenched too tight to return his wave, it was, without doubt, a beautiful country.

Arnold changed seats for dinner, letting the girl sit by the window opposite Sonny. She had been in Arnold's compartment for the afternoon, but Sonny had been concentrating too hard on looking, and keeping the train on the track, to hear if there was anything going on. Arnold seemed especially attentive to her, opening her napkin and putting it in her lap as if she were a little girl, which she had not long ago finished being. He questioned her about her appetite with all the attention one might ask Churchill an opinion of history, and neatly penciled her order onto the pad. Sonny did not bother to study her. He knew instinctively that she would be nothing, and didn't want to come to that conclusion for fear that it might be construed as jealousy. So he gave his full wandering attention to Joe Pape, who was now seated beside him, drunker than ever, spinning the story of his life as if it warranted telling. Parts of it actually interested Sonny, as he had never known a Southern drunk before, and he had been too busy looking out the window to read Faulkner.

"My mother was a whore," Joe Pape said.

"I'm sorry."

"She wasn't. She really enjoyed it. I think that's a good thing in a woman, to know she has a real talent for something and go at it full-time. So many of 'em just lie around being useless." He was drinking straight out of the flask now, not even bothering to pour the whiskey in his cup, or offer it around. "Anyway, I always had someplace to live. That much she did for me."

"I'm sorry."

"Wish't she could've lived to see the distillery. Joe Pape's. I could've cheered her up with that. Shot herself up with morphia when I was twelve years old. Can't understand that. She looked to be having such a fine time."

By dessert he was weeping openly. He cried for his mother, and the dog he had had for a week when he was seven, and the father he had never seen or maybe he had, there was no way to tell for sure.

"Dessert?" Arnold said to the girl.

"I couldn't eat another thing."

"I could," Arnold said, and led her from the table.

Sonny started to get up and go with them. But there was a strange silence on the train, an easy tranquil rhythm of smooth wheels on well-traveled tracks, so you could still hear things. He wanted to hear Arnold making love less than he wanted to hear Joe Pape making a fool of himself. So he sat there while Joe Pape ordered loganberry pie and vanilla ice cream and talked and wept and drank from his flask.

"Don't you want some coffee?" Sonny asked.

"Coffee spoils the flavor of loganberry pie and ice cream."

"You're not eating it."

"Loganberry pie and ice cream spoils the flavor of bourbon." He blew his nose and wiped his eyes. "I guess I've been going on a bit."

"That's okay. I don't mind."

"So tell me about you, Sterne. What was your family like?"

"My mother was a ballerina. Her mother was the mistress of the czar. She was a ballerina, too. The czar covered her with so many jewels she was too weighted down to move, so she turned her tutu over to my mother. My mother danced her way into the heart of everyone, and came to America where she disappeared into the middle of the New York Ballet performance of *A Midsummer Night's Dream* and went to live with the fairies."

"No shit," Joe Pape said.

"I'll help you back to your compartment," Sonny said.

The woman who slipped into the room in the middle of the night was dressed in flowing robes, virginal. Her yellow hair hung below her waist, and it was knotted with pearls. Sonny wanted to switch on the lamp to see her better, but it wasn't necessary, as she flowed through the room lit with her own white aura, pearly, like the jewels knotted through her hair. Her breasts glowed pink through the thin silk of her robes, and before he could tell her he was saving himself for a great love, she let her garments slip to the floor and shone naked in front of him. Then she sang twelve bars of the "Jewel Song" from *Faust,* and started to suck his toes.

"This isn't the way I pictured it," he said, as she ran her tongue along his instep.

"The Pennsylvania Railroad is built on progress," she whispered, and moving her face between his thighs, took him into her mouth.

He didn't try to argue with her, because it felt good, it felt wonderful, he could never touch himself as gently as that. She bit a pearl loose from the strand woven through her hair and placed it on his scrotum, teasing it between his testicles, slowly moving it up along the increasing length of him with the pointed tip of her tongue.

"Did Arnold pay you for this?"

"Don't give him credit for everything," she murmured, and the pearl fell off and there was nothing for her to toy with but him. "This is your idea."

"I don't even know you."

"Of course you do," she said, and mounted him.

"You dance, too," Sonny said. "I thought you only sang."

"Be quiet and kiss me," she answered, and thrust her nipple into his mouth, and held him in her lap all the time she was moving on top of him. He was rocked and lulled and mounted and whipped into ecstasy all at once.

"You certainly think of everything," he managed.

"Well, we wouldn't want you to travel by bus."

And he was shattering up into her, shooting himself out of the sexual darkness at his own tip into the milky whiteness, flooding her insides with light. "Come with me, come with me, come with me," he screamed.

"But I'm right here," said Arnold, shaking his arms. "What the hell's the matter with you?"

Sonny shook himself awake and pulled the blanket tight around him. "I must have had a bad dream."

"That's what Joe Pape said," Arnold said. "Get dressed and get your bags packed and your ass to the parlor car, so we don't get involved. We'll be in Nashville in a couple of hours and I want us right off the train and into the Colonel's car. No talking to Pape, no talking to anybody."

"About what?" Sonny said.

"Joe Pape's shot one of the porters."

Above the hills glowing green in early morning, hawks soared in silent, unfluttering circle, swooping down from time to time to seize a field mouse or a rabbit. Sonny tried to keep his concentration on what was going on outside the train, so he wouldn't hear the excited talking of everyone around him in the parlor car.

". . . drunk, of course. Obvious he was a troublemaker the minute he got on the train . . ."

". . . with a shotgun, for Christ's sake. Blew the top of his head off . . ."

"Maybe he thought it was a revenuer," somebody said, and chuckled.

Sonny did not turn his head away from the window. He could feel Arnold's eyes on him, watching to see if he was paying attention to anything else besides the scenery. His shoulder moved up and down inside his jacket, and he tried to fight the dryness in his mouth with some cold water. Jokes about murder. He could not understand people. He could understand greed and lust, because they were human failings. But he couldn't fathom killing, or those who made jokes about it.

"Mr. Sterne?" the conductor said.

"Yes?" said Arnold.

"Mr. Abraham Sterne?"

"I'm Abraham Sterne."

"Would you mind coming with me?"

"What for?" said Arnold.

"There's been a shooting."

"We know that," Arnold said. "What's that got to do with us?"

"Joe Pape said Mr. Sterne is his lawyer."

"Joe Pape is full of shit," Arnold said. "We never even saw him before yesterday."

"I'd appreciate your coming, Mr. Sterne. We've signaled ahead for the sheriff to come on board at Gallatin, but that's a couple of hours yet, and he's pretty out of hand."

"So would you be if you'd committed murder," said Arnold.

"It hasn't been established that it was murder," Sonny said.

"Are you crazy?" Arnold stood up and leaned over his brother. "I told you to stay out of it. He's a white trash rummy from nowhere."

"Wrong," Sonny said, and started to get up. "He grew up in a whorehouse. That has a certain flashy pathos to it."

"Sit down," Arnold said.

"You know what a whorehouse is. It's where you have to go when you can't pick up roundheels on trains."

"That's it? You're angry with me for that girl, so you're going to get even by getting us involved in murder?"

"It hasn't been established that it's murder."

"Stop trying to sound like a lawyer. You're a businessman."

"I am a lawyer." Sonny stood up, and he was taller than Arnold. He had almost forgotten that. "It can't hurt to talk to him," he said.

"Did he say anything, Joe Pape?" he asked the conductor, as they moved through the sleeping cars.

"He's just sitting in his compartment, blubbering, can't make much sense out of what he says. We didn't have any trouble getting the gun away from him, but he put up a terrible fight about having his hands tied."

"Can you give me any details about the shooting?"

"There was an eyewitness. A minister."

"Well, if that's all the state has to base a case on . . ." Sonny said.

There was a sheet covering the body. In spite of Sonny's assurance that he did not need to see the victim, the conductor drew the top away. The porter lay, immaculate in his fresh white jacket, his early morning grin still fixed on his face, his eyes still open and shining with greeting. Only his cap was out of place, lying two feet from his body in the corridor, with the top of his head in it.

"Jesus," Sonny said.

"Dr. Ebens saw it all."

"I was on my way to the dining car," the minister said. "I heard the shot the same minute he came flying out of there. I thought maybe he had stumbled, and then I saw his head, and the blood."

"You saw Pape fire the gun?"

"I saw the bullet hit, and I ran to the door, and I saw him sitting there with the shotgun."

"Did he say anything?"

"I didn't wait to hear," said Dr. Ebens. "I went straight for the conductor."

Sonny went inside the compartment. Joe sat huddled, weeping, his bound hands clutching a pillow to his breasts. His nose was running, and there was mucus on the collar of his wrinkled gray suit. His eyes were red with lack of sleep or plenty of Joe Pape's Finest, Sonny couldn't tell which—maybe both. Sonny closed the door behind him.

"What happened?" Joe said, when he saw who it was.

"I was going to ask you the same question."

"I don't know, I swear. A bad dream. I must have had a bad dream."

"Did you know him?"

"Who?"

"The man you shot."

"Did I shoot somebody?"

"The porter."

"I don't know any porters."

"Was there a fight?"

"Why would I fight with a porter?"

"I don't know. I was hoping you'd tell me."

"I never did sleep well on trains." Joe Pape shook his head. "Don't wake me up till we get to Nashville, goddamit, I need rest."

"You're in a lot of trouble, Joe."

"You'll get me out of it, though. You're a smart man, Sterne. You're probably the smartest lawyer in the country."

"I don't practice law."

"But you could, if you wanted to, couldn't you? You're as smart as anybody."

"Nobody's smart enough to get out of a murder with an eyewitness."

"You are, Sterne, I know it. I know it as sure as I know what

Joe Pape's Finest is going to be worth. A third. I'll give you a third of the distillery. I swear by all that is holy, if you get me out of this, I'll give you a third of Joe Pape's Finest Bonded Bourbon, one third of all the profits. I swear by all that is holy."

"If you're going to swear by all that is holy, I think you better save it for the minister."

"Which minister?"

"The one that saw you shoot the porter."

"A senseless murder by an illiterate drunk, with a fucking minister for an eyewitness and you're getting us involved?" Arnold shouted. The train had made a special stop at Gallatin, the Sumner county seat, and the sheriff's men had taken Joe Pape from the train. Sonny had cautioned him to deny everything. He would have a Tennessee lawyer at the jail by late afternoon.

"A goddamn homicidal rummy," Arnold ranted, "and we're mixed up with him."

"Not we," said Sonny. "I."

They were sitting in Arnold's compartment, so Arnold would be free to yell loud. "For what reason? What possible reason could you find to get involved?"

"A third of Joe Pape's Finest. He signed an agreement."

"You'd risk whatever reputation we've managed to build for a goddamn still?"

"When did *you* get so clean?" Sonny said angrily. "Ward-heelers from Tammany. Roundheels on a train."

"I pick up a girl, so you pick up a murderer?"

"It hasn't been proven he's a murderer." Sonny smiled. "It might turn out to be a very interesting case."

"Stop trying to sound like a lawyer, goddamit, you aren't a lawyer."

"Yes, I am. And Joe Pape thinks I'm a good one. He's willing to bet a third of his distillery on it."

"He's a drunk!" Arnold shouted.

"Not everyone is a fool who admires me, Arnold. There were

those who thought I'd make as good a lawyer as anyone around. There were those who thought I might make it to judge, what with the fine sense of justice I had."

"Fine sense of justice? Where did you learn this fine sense of justice? Running around with those commies at Columbia? Milton Radnitz, for Christ's sake, that nickel-and-dime Bolshevik."

"Who told you about Milton?"

"Milton told me about Milton, you goddamn innocent. Milton tried to hit me for funds for the Party with a subtle hint of blackmail, using your name."

"I don't believe you."

"Then how would I know about Milton Radnitz?"

"I don't know," Sonny said.

"You don't have to know," Arnold spoke quietly. "I know enough for both of us."

"Not this time," said Sonny. "This time I learn on my own."

Sonny had never even considered practicing criminal law. But his mind was used to running in back alleys. So when Colonel Reeling put him in touch with a good Nashville attorney, and they went over the facts together and agreed on the hopelessness of winning the case, Sonny knew exactly what to do.

"Find out about the minister. Dr. Freyman Ebens."

Ralph Wheatley was a tall man in his fifties, scholarly-looking, easy in his speech, secure in his reputation. His specialty was corporation law. But the Colonel was a good friend of his, the victim had, after all, been a Negro, and Sonny was paying Wheatley twenty thousand dollars. "What do you find out about a minister?"

"Anything you can," said Sonny.

"He's clean," the private detective said, when he was back in Nashville in Ralph Wheatley's law offices. "He's completely clean."

"Nobody's completely clean," Ralph Wheatley said.

"I talked to his wife, and the members of the congregation. I talked to him. I got a set of his fingerprints from some papers on his desk, and I've run them. No records of arrest, nothing. Like they say, he's the pillar of the community, and unless he's having some little girl behind the pillar, we've got absolutely nothing. A town that size, it's hard to hide scandal, even a scandal that's a lie. There's nobody that doesn't love him, in the spiritual sense."

"Maybe a little boy behind the pillar?"

"Afraid not. I could stay there for a while and try to nail him, but I think you'd be wasting your money."

"Okay," Wheatley said, and wrote out a check.

The murder trial of Joe Pape took place three months after the killing. There was not much publicity about it, and the Sumner County Courthouse, small as it was, was not completely filled. Sonny had come down three days before the trial began, searching the law library for some precedent that might apply, searching the rugged terrain for some sign of wistaria, anything that might give him some mysterious clue to the South, opening the part of his mind that was not cerebral to inspiration. He hadn't found it.

Joe Pape, looking haggard and deprived, stripped of his dignity and Joe Pape's Finest, sat quietly through the trial, behind the long wooden table near the docket, a sheriff on one side, and Ralph Wheatley on the other. Sonny sat on Wheatley's left, watching the district attorney playing the jury. The D.A. seemed very comfortable, confident of getting a conviction, swaggering only slightly as he spoke in rounded tones of murder being murder, and killing being killing, and Tennessee being a place of golden justice, no matter what the color of a man's skin. The jury listened attentively, as did Joe Pape, whom Sonny had instructed to say nothing, to try and keep his hands and his face still, and his eyes looking confused and trusting.

The conductor took the stand and gave his testimony, as did one of the porters who had been in the next car. The coroner who had examined the murdered man's body ("The allegedly murdered man's body," Ralph Wheatley interrupted. "He didn't shoot the top of his own head off," the D.A. said) described full details of the porter's condition, which were medical and bloody, and all of which amounted to the fact that the man was dead. Then Dr. Freyman Ebens took the stand.

Sonny watched the jury. There was no doubt in his mind that the twelve men were God-fearing men, he could tell that from their faces in the presence of a man of God.

"Open and shut," Wheatley whispered to Sonny. "Look at the jury. I'm sorry."

Twelve men, like gangly cupids on the ceiling of the Big House bedroom, passing their vote on the application of Arnold and Abraham Sterne for a seat on the Stock Exchange. Twelve men with blackballs to throw in a box. "This is not a court of law, Mr. Sterne," the final interviewer had said. "Nobody's accusing you of anything." "I know that," Sonny had said. "If you would accuse me, I might be better equipped to counter your accusations." What had he asked Sonny? What all had he asked him, to establish his discredit?

"You're a minister, Dr. Ebens?" the district attorney said.

"Yes, sir."

"And your congregation is where?"

"Brunswick, Georgia."

"And on the morning of April 24, 1941, you were traveling from New York City back to Brunswick."

"Yes, sir. I woke up early, it was about six-thirty, and I wanted to prepare my sermon for that following Sunday."

"Objection, your honor," Ralph Wheatley said. "It has already been established that Dr. Ebens is a minister. We don't have to lard his testimony with more piety than that."

"Hold it," Sonny whispered. "Just let him talk."

The minister described the shooting in vital detail, but Sonny wasn't listening anymore. The jury was listening intensely, but Sonny wasn't hearing at all. He was back in the room on Broad Street, remembering all the questions. It had been a trial, of course, although they wouldn't acknowledge that on Wall Street. But a trial was a trial, and maybe he had been put through it because he was supposed to learn something from it, and gain something from it, like a real trial made you do.

The district attorney had concluded his examination. The jury knew that Joe Pape was a murderer.

"Open and shut," Wheatley whispered again.

"Let me take over the questioning," Sonny ventured, smiling.

"What's left?" Wheatley said.

"Just let me take over," Sonny said.

He got to his feet and moved toward the witness box. "Dr. Ebens," he said slowly. "Where exactly did you receive your religious education?"

"Pardon?"

"Objection, your honor," the D.A. said. "What does this have to do with an eyewitness testimony to a murder?"

"I am trying to establish the credibility of the witness."

"He's a minister," the D.A. said. "What more do you need to know?"

"We're dealing with an accusation of murder," Sonny said. "The jury needs to know everything it can." He smiled at them to let them know how important they were.

"Objection overruled," the judge said.

"Where did you study for the ministry, Dr. Ebens?"

"I studied religion from the time I was a boy."

"Very admirable, Dr. Ebens. At what seminary did you study?"

"Pardon?"

"You attended theological school?"

Dr. Ebens looked at his hands. "I wanted to, but there just wasn't the money, and—"

"A direct answer, *Dr.* Ebens. You attended theological school?"

"No, sir."

"Did you go to any college that conferred a theological degree? You're under oath, Dr. Ebens."

"You don't have to tell me that."

"Did you go to any college that conferred a theological degree?"

"No, sir."

"And the title of Doctor. Who conferred that title on you?"

"Nobody."

"Well, that can't be altogether true, Dr. Ebens. Somebody must have given you the title."

"I am at one with my God," Dr. Ebens said.

"You got your title from the Almighty?"

"I didn't say that."

"Then who gave it to you?" Sonny hooked a thumb inside the belt of his trousers, opening his jacket so he'd look as respectfully casual as the South.

"I studied all my life—"

"Who gave you the title of Doctor?"

"I always knew there was a congregation that needed me. I traveled this country till I found it. My congregation is one of the most loyal flocks—"

"No speeches, please. This is a murder trial. Who gave you the title?"

There was a silence. The jury was looking at the minister almost as hard as Sonny was.

"I did," Ebens said.

"So you said you were a minister, a doctor of theology."

"I am a minister."

"No further lies," said Sonny.

"Objection!"

"Excuse me, I meant to say no further questions!"

The jury was out for only thirty-four minutes. They returned a verdict of "Not Guilty."

Joe Pape waited until they were in the car to begin to dance. "I told you, Sterne, I told you," he chortled as he sat in the back seat. "The smartest lawyer in America. Hot damn! Hot damn!"

"I think you could find a better way of expressing your euphoria," Sonny said.

"That's right," said Joe Pape. "I'm going to hustle my ass back to Bible Hill and make that distillery sing. You're going to be a rich man, Sterne. You're going to be very rich. A third of Joe Pape's Finest. You're going to be as rich as anybody."

"I can't get over it," Ralph Wheatley said. "The most open and shut case I ever heard of. What made you think of that education business?"

"A hunch."

"That had to be better than a hunch," Wheatley said. "Ask me, it was divine inspiration."

"We should leave divine guidance to Dr. Ebens."

"Then what made you think of it?"

Sonny smiled. "When you run out of everything else that might degrade a man, you can always ask him where he went to school."

"I still can't get over it. And Joe never even said he didn't do it."

"Ah, yes," said Sonny. "The law works in mysterious ways."

He did not contemplate the morality of it. He thought mainly about Clarence Darrow on the trip back to New York. He thought about himself as well, and how, if he had taken a different path and given his life to law, there might have been a Scopes he could have defended, as well as a Leopold and Loeb. As a lawyer, he might have achieved Greatness.

"You're a whore," Arnold said, when Sonny got back home.

"Then I guess you must want me," Sonny said, and packed the rest of his bags.

FIVE

IT WAS THE FIRST TIME they had been naked together. And as
his hands moved downwards, so did Evelyn's. The hair on his
chest continued past his ribs, over his waist, and down into the
pubic region. She reached more hopefully for his back, only to
find it, too, covered with hair. These were not the things you
discovered furtively in cars. In cars, on beaches, where you
might be discovered by tourists or the rising sun, symphonies
were played on a wrist, concertos on a tongue.

The only part of him she had ever held completely was his
thing, which was silky and thin and regulation, excepting for the
strangeness of its tip. But she never had to do more than just
hold it in her hands, stroking it from time to time as it jutted
from his pants, which he had never taken off. Now she understood why.

Clutching for some straw of nakedness, she found hair going

down even onto his buttocks. She realized with something approaching anthropological wonder that what Johnny Granson was, besides handsome and rich and fair of face and from Delaware where the DuPonts lived, was the Missing Link, in uniform. Out of uniform now, oh my God. Had she found the legendary blond Ape of the Himalayas? Was there a legendary blond Ape of the Himalayas? How had he ever found his way to Wilmington?

"Touch me," he whispered fervently. "Touch me."

Fur in the middle of spring, in St. Augustine. Did he molt in summer?

"Please," he muttered. "Please."

"Take me," she said, with all she could manage of seeming passion. "Take me," she groaned, although she was far from ready, wanting only to avoid touching him.

"I want you to touch me."

"Take me."

"Touch me," he pleaded.

"Let's fuck, goddamit," Evelyn said. "We've waited long enough."

He made his way into her. Evelyn reached for the headboard of the hotel bed. She clutched it, pretending the movement was passion, throwing herself into the rhythm of his plunging, using the cold wood in her hands for leverage, giving him the ride of his life.

"My angel, my darling, my sweetheart," he murmured into the canyon of her throat.

My ape, thought Evelyn, and couldn't wait until he was gone. Uncircumcised dog. Gorilla. Where was the glowing bulb of yesteryear? Even the one that belonged to Walter White.

She began answering Walter's letters, via V-mail. To her surprise, he was actually making a success of the Navy, having received two promotions by the middle of 1943, when she dropped Johnny Granson. ("He's gone the way of all flesh," she wrote to Sadie. "Believe me, I'm being kind, when I use the expression flesh.") She started using cream on her eyes, and luxuriating in the lithe firmness of her own skin, which was present almost everywhere, in very good condition, unlike some people's. The hair on her head, which was where she assumed most hair should be, was still thickly dark and radiant, her smile a flash of brilliance, indicating the wit and charm that were inside. Her hopes of meeting the Origin of the Species that dwelled where the DuPonts lived were dashed into conscience-riddled oblivion. If she went to meet them, and they were wonderful, charming rich people, she might be tempted to continue cutting her way through the overbrush, and that would be wrong.

She would never marry again except out of love, she had sworn that to herself. It was bad enough when you couldn't stand them after you married them, which was inevitable. To loathe them before, and to marry, was something only bad women did.

And she was not bad. She was only a little bigoted. And that was a part of life (a part of evolution, which had skipped over Johnny Granson). She hated hairy bodies, and liked rich men who were circumcised. There was nothing wrong with any of that.

So she told Johnny Granson it was over between them ("I can't stand you" was how she phrased it exactly). And she started answering Walter White's V-mail.

"My life begins today," she said to herself in front of the mirror, when she went to work at a hotel in Miami Beach. In spite of her colossal loyalty to the Armed Forces, as she told Colonel Bramford, she was forced to make a change. She had wasted over a year of her life on the war and its seeming shining lights, and now it was time for a civilized change. "My life begins today," she repeated to her mirror, but did not tell that to Colonel Bramford.

What she told Colonel Bramford was that she owed it to her child, because that was the explanation that usually worked. "Her father sends me nothing, nothing, and the Reef needs someone to handle the guests, you know to make them comfortable, to forget about the war and Atlantic City." She went on to tell him that everything she had learned of poise and how to handle people she had learned from him, and was very, very grateful.

"But not grateful enough to stay and help," Colonel Bramford said.

"I'd stay in a minute. But I owe it to my child."

"What do you want? I can give you a raise."

"The Army's very regular about these things," Evelyn said, having gone through the files to see what was the most she could ask for. "I wouldn't want our nation overextended because of me."

"What are they offering you at this hotel?"

"A greater opportunity for my child." And two hundred dollars more a month, and hors d'oeuvres from trays at cocktail parties to be carried home that evening so she wouldn't have to worry about making Chris' lunch the next day. And a few not too bad-looking 4F's and older men who were not with women. And duties which would include, along with some light book-keeping, acting as social director for the hotel, planning activities for those who did not know how to create their own amusement, making introductions between men and women who were too shy. And if she was lucky, perhaps the best of the men, the cream of the crap, she would skim off the flashy surface of the hotel and save for herself.

But just in case she could not, she wrote to Walter. She told him how thrilled she was at his promotions, which was true, and did not add that as long as he was making more money, why didn't he send some, because the suit for child-support was still in effect, and she would get it, she would get it all. She wrote that she prayed for his safe return, and sometimes, late at night, she actually would. Because so far she had met nobody better, and you never could tell, you never could tell.

She began making friends with women, even though she had never particularly cared for them, except Grandma. Women could be won so easily. You only had to smile at them as if you were glad to see them, and tell them their slip was showing, in a very quiet voice so they thought you were trying to spare them embarrassment, instead of giving them some.

She needed women in her life because they knew men. That much they had in their favor. She had violated all the mandates of her past, throwing out dirty water before she had clean, hairy before she had smooth. To break with tradition completely and not expose herself to the matchmaker instinct of women for their friends would be foolhardy. And Evelyn was anything but a fool.

Besides, one of her new girlfriends Evelyn actually enjoyed. Wandra Kane was a spirited woman in her early thirties who openly made jokes about men, whom she didn't like at all, and children, whom she hated. She was married to Harvey Kane, a war profiteer, although that was not how he was introduced. When he met people he told them he was a manufacturer, but Evelyn knew how to read between the lines without even having to go through people's mail.

They sat together, Evelyn and Wandra, by the kidney-shaped pool of the Reef Hotel, when Evelyn wasn't having to plan Events. They spoke of life, and jewels mainly, and now and then the conversation moved to furs, which Wandra taught her could be tested best (especially mink) by running up and down the pelts to see how well they sprang back. And sometimes they spoke of Chris.

"She's a nice little girl, if you like children." Wandra made a canopy over her eyes with her hands in the glare of the sun, watching Chris in the pool practicing her flutter kick. "She always been heavy?"

"It's just baby fat," Evelyn said.

"Bullshit," said Wandra. "Fat is fat. You want her to get it off, you better start now."

"She didn't put it on until recently . . . when I left her father."

"She misses him, huh?"

"She doesn't miss him at all, she's just hungry."

"You should have let him have custody, then you'd have freer rein."

Evelyn wondered. No, no, too shocking. This woman beside her, for all her long lean blondness, thought like a man—tough, invulnerable—and such things were unbecoming to women. Evelyn leaped from the chaise, chastened and chased by guilt; she ran to the edge of the pool.

"Chrissie," Evelyn shouted softly. "Come. Kiss your mummy."

Chris swam the width of the pool and held up a smiling, wet, curly-fringed face. Evelyn leaned down a little.

"No hugs," Evelyn said. "Your hands are wet. My hair."

Nights, when there were Events, like Costume Balls and Talent Contests, Evelyn would bring home as many hors d'oeuvres as her suitcase could hold, and leave them in the refrigerator for Chris. She wondered if caviar was good for a growing girl, but eggs were eggs, and children were starving in Europe. Then she would run back to the hotel and direct the wonderful Events, introducing the lonely to the lonely, convincing herself she was not one of them.

Her life was so busy at moments it would actually seem full. She made a dutiful trip to Central Beach Elementary School, where Chris was now going, having told Evelyn she'd definitely decided at Immaculate Heart to become a nun. The principal of Central Beach Elementary assured Evelyn she had a very bright daughter. They had already skipped her a grade and a half, that was how clever she was. It was only a pity she was plagued with such ill health.

"What ill health?" Evelyn asked. The principal sent for the infirmary file and presented a series of neatly typed notes saying Chris would have to be excused on a number of afternoons as she had to see a specialist.

Evelyn recognized the typing. It had been done on the machine the Army had given her as a good-luck farewell present.

She had been sure the Colonel would have given it to her if he had thought of it; there were so many typewriters at the command base, no one would miss it, especially if Evelyn wasn't checking the inventory.

The signature was not a very good forgery of Evelyn's own. But the typing was remarkable, considering the child wasn't quite seven and Evelyn hadn't even known she could type. She felt a momentary flush of pride before the fury of having Walter's malingering genes based in her household overcame her.

"What have you been doing all those afternoons?" Evelyn screamed through the locked bathroom door. Chris had heard the clicketing heels on the pavement at the unaccustomed hour of three-thirty in the afternoon—heard from her teacher that Evelyn had visited school that morning. So it seemed a very good idea to lock herself in the bathroom.

"Open up!" cried Evelyn.

"I have diarrhea."

"Write me a note about it!" Evelyn shrieked, and pounded on the door. "Come out of there, goddamit. I have to get back to work."

Chris opened the door and darted past her, started to run around the living room, Evelyn chasing. "Will you stand still so I can hit you? I have to get back to work."

The blow when it fell was sharp, but there was only one. To Chris it was almost a pleasant surprise.

"Dammit," said Evelyn, sinking onto the couch. "You've broken my finger."

"I'm sorry," said Chris, and started to cry.

"Look what you made me do, I'm going to have a crooked pinky. Where did you learn to type?"

"I taught myself. I watched you type letters and I taught myself when you weren't home."

"There are two spaces after a period," Evelyn said, keening over her hand. "Where did you go all those afternoons?"

"To the movies."

"I'm killing myself to give you an education and you go to the movies?"

"That school is too easy. I do all the work I'm supposed to do all day in the morning. It's boring."

"You think the world is set up to stimulate you? Where did you get the money to go to the movies?"

Chris looked at the floor. "I tell them my mother is inside and I have to find her. If they look for me, I hide under the seat."

"That's cheating and lying," said Evelyn. "All those things you learned from your father. Don't they ask you why you're not in school?"

"I tell them I'm five."

"Well, it's all right to fib about your age, you're a girl. But not on a school day."

"I'm sorry. I won't do it anymore." She flung herself into her mother's lap and felt the tentative embrace.

"If you're really sorry and promise not to do it anymore . . ."

"I promise."

"Be careful of my hand," Evelyn said, and patted the curly head.

Right after that, Evelyn decided to enroll Chris in Sunday School. There was a synagogue within walking distance of their apartment. It was time the child learned something about her Jewish past, if only to give her a conscience and fill up her weekends.

There was a Purim festival, whatever that meant, and Chris was going to perform. "Right after the song about Esther speaking to the king," Chris half-sang excitedly. *"Oh today we'll merry merry be, oh today we'll merry merry be—"*

"Very nice," said Evelyn, setting her hair for the Cocktail Dansant.

"Oh today we'll merry merry be, and nosh on Hamantaschen."

"Fine," said Evelyn.

"Right after that I get to do my solo. It's 'I'm Breathless.' Do you know that song? It's got nothing to do with Purim, and it hasn't made the Hit Parade yet, but my teacher thinks it's wonderful that I can remember all the words, so she's letting me sing it, do you want to hear it?"

"I'll hear it at the festival," Evelyn said, spraying her pin-curls.

" 'If I had a dictionary/I could use the customary/Compliments and phrases/When I want to win your praises . . .' "

"Wonderful," said Evelyn. " 'But I'm apt to be in trouble,/ My adversity is double/And on top of all that,/I'm breathless.' "

"You know what all those words mean?"

"I looked them up."

"I don't know why I even asked," Evelyn said.

"You want to hear the rest of it?"

"I'll hear it at the festival."

"You're really going to come?"

"Honestly," Evelyn said, putting moisturizer on her face. "What kind of mother do you think I am?"

What kind of mother did she think she was? Evelyn didn't think about it. What else were women good for but having children and marrying the right man, hopefully not in that order. Of course, she loved her daughter, she could hear her singing, see her rehearsing her gestures, hear her singing, hear her singing, hear her singing, Oh my God would it never end, would the singing drive her CRAZY!!??

"But do you have to go out tonight, again?" Chris asked. "I want to practice my song for you."

"I'll hear it at the festival."

"Why do you have to go out?"

"He's a toy manufacturer, sweetheart. You'll have all the toys in the world."

"I don't want a lot of toys."

"Children should play with toys," Evelyn insisted. "Don't you think that I feel bad that your father, that stingy son of a bitch, sends me nothing, nothing, so I can't get you a lot of presents. Don't you think I eat my heart out when you don't have dolls to play with? How do you think it makes me feel when I see other little girls playing with so many dolls, and you have library books. You're a baby. Much too chubby but you're still just a little girl. You should be having a good time. Carefree! Happy! Dolls! It isn't normal, a child your age, playing with books, typing, even if you don't use the right fingers."

Evelyn put her watch in the drawer. "You should be having fun. I want you to have *fun*. That's why I'm going out."

He was a widower from Chicago. Evelyn thought when she first met him at the hotel he was very young to be a widower. By their fourth date she thought it likely that his wife had died of boredom.

They were in a restaurant he considered very chic, "chick" he pronounced it, when they talked about anything besides toys and Chicago, which he called "Chi."

"What time is it?" she said, making sure she had left her watch at home. Hoping he might buy her one. So far he had given her nothing but a synthetic rubber doll with synthetic dimples on the backs of its hands, and Chris didn't seem too crazy about it.

"It's a quarter to nine," he said. "A quarter to nine and here we are on a Saturday night, underneath the palm trees. They must be freezing their butts off in Chi."

"Saturday night," Evelyn said, and choked on a fishbone. "It's Saturday?" She drank some water. Ate some bread.

"Sure it's Saturday. You're my big date for Saturday night."

"Oh my God!" She wiped her mouth. "Get the check. I'm supposed to be at temple."

"I thought you weren't religious."

"Will you get the check? My daughter's in the Purim festival, and it started at seven. Oh God. Oh God. If I'd only had a watch."

"There's nothing to be upset about," he said when they were in the car, driving through the sparkling dark streets of the Miami Beach night. "So you'll be a little late, that's all."

"She's been rehearsing for weeks, oh my God, all those words. And I'm not there to hear them."

"Maybe they put her on late in the program."

"Maybe," Evelyn said, and bit her lips. "Oh dear. I hope we're not too late. What time is it? I don't own a watch."

When they got to the temple, Chris was sitting on the "Keep Off the Grass" sign in the center of the manicured lawn. She was weeping.

"Oh, honey," Evelyn said, as they ran to each other and held on, on the grass. "I missed it. I missed your song."

"You didn't miss it," Chris wailed. "They took me out of the program. They said the program was running too long, so they cut me out of the show."

"We'll see about this!" Evelyn started to stomp toward the temple doors.

"Don't, Mummy, don't. It doesn't matter. I don't want to go back there anymore."

"Oh, my poor baby." She kneeled on the sidewalk and took her daughter in her arms. "How long have you been sitting here?"

"I don't know."

"She doesn't have a watch either," Evelyn said to the fellow from Chi.

She refused to go out with him ever again, the whole episode made her feel so guilty. Especially as nothing came in the next few days but a bunch of goddamn toys.

Evelyn was starting to get a *lit-tle* tired of her job, she wrote to Sadie, writing to Grandma that she was having the best time of her life—*My life begins today!"* she wrote, but to Sadie she told the truth and that was that the men were old and fat and the women were boring, except for her friend Wandra Kane, wife of the well-known War Profiteer. And that that stingy son of a bitch Walter still hadn't sent her a penny, not a penny, and if she could just keep Murray Rabin from trying to put his hands on her, they'd be waiting at the dock with another subpoena when he returned, the sailor from the sea, had Sadie heard about his promotions, wasn't it amazing?

But meanwhile she was getting just a *lit-tle* tired of her job. But, not to worry, things would change, they just had to, how was Pappy, was he still having fits? She missed his fits. She had a few of her own, she wrote Sadie, but having only one child she lacked a big audience. How was Grandma? She missed Grandma, she missed everybody, was Sammy still seeing the *shicksa,* what was her name, Pegeen? Would Murray ever get married? God, she even missed Enid. That should give Sadie some idea, Evelyn wrote, how boring it was.

Chris was okay, getting fatter, but what could you do, that was life, she was still smart as a whip, but she missed her father, how smart could she be?

Evelyn was going to get Harvey Kane to teach her how to be a war profiteer. Then she could send for everybody, she wrote Sadie.

She wrote that to Sadie because she knew there was no way Harvey Kane would ever really admit to being a war profiteer. Few were the men who admitted profiting from war. He wouldn't teach her what she had to know. So she couldn't send for them, ever, no matter how much she wanted to, which was a great relief.

P.S. I love you, she wrote to Sadie, and I'm glad about the pregnancy if you are, and if he ever lets you out of bed, be sure and come down here.

She wrote that to Sadie because she knew there was not the remotest chance of anyone in the family's getting together enough money to come to Miami Beach. Which was why she got hives when she heard that Walter M. White had sent Pappy and Grandma a month's salary so they could go see their grandchild.

"Please," Evelyn said to Chris, "it has nothing to do with you. I just feel like being alone." She was lying on the couch swelling, till the doctor got there. "Don't you ever feel like being alone?"

"No," said Chris.

"He's sent me nothing, nothing, that son of a bitch," she muttered, as the doctor dosed her up with Pyribenzamine. "How do you like his sending me nothing, and then he sends my mother and father a whole month's salary? If it weren't for me, he wouldn't have even gotten the commission."

"Who?" the doctor asked, having never seen Evelyn before this house call.

"That bastard I'm married to," she said. "How's my eye?"

"It should be better by this evening."

"How do you like him, doing this to me? It's only to degrade me, you know, to make me look foolish at the hotel."

"What hotel?"

"Never mind," said Evelyn. There was no point in telling too much to a stranger. "Guam. Wouldn't you know he'd be on Guam. I'm working my legs off to support my child, and he ends up on a tropical island."

Spite, spite, spite, that's what he'd done it out of, she was sure, sending the family so they could remind her what she'd come from. Nice people, sure, but common and poor. They wouldn't even have anything to wear.

She had only just gotten to the point where she got her own clothes wholesale, true wholesale, three percent above cost, from the manufacturers themselves, or rather the manufacturers' wives, who adored Evelyn for not making a play for their husbands. She had just overcome her Pittsburgh accent, softening the flat A's with warm sounds vaguely redolent of the South, crisping up the ends of her sentences so statements no longer sounded like questions. She had chucked off the chains of her speech and slipped into some smart little numbers at three percent above cost, and they were going to tread their way into the middle of her dream looking like greenhorns.

It was too late to stop them, she knew that already from talking to Sammy long distance, before the rates had even changed, that was how nervous she was. They were on the train.

Oh God. She made reservations for them in eight different hotels, inconvenient to the Reef.

"You seem very edgy tonight," Wandra said, in the hotel lobby. She was dressed in sleeveless white crepe banded with silver sequins, and her midriff was bare.

Evelyn was wearing aquamarine rayon with aquamarine beading and rubbing her eye, which was still swelling, she could feel it getting bigger, under the tortoise-shell-rimmed sunglasses. "It's my eye," she said, searching the front entrance for disaster, trying to see past the pink-shaded lamps that made the women look younger, the men look at the women. The lobby was filled with the newly arrived pale, in gowns and tuxedos, the too avid sunburned with Noxema on their bare upper arms, and the ones who had had confidence and time, like Wandra, to become gently tanned, no rush, no rush. Furs shrouded the shoulders of women who really didn't need furs, because they could afford to pursue summer wherever it went.

Evelyn checked the groups of people sitting around taking after-dinner coffee, cakes; it was piggish how much they all ate, even if it was included. She tried to usher them inside for the Barn Dance, the motif for the evening. (The caller was supposedly from Kentucky, so straw hats and a piece of grass to chew on were provided for all the men, checkered gingham aprons for the women, to put on over their gowns.)

"All right, everybody." Evelyn clapped her hands, almost along with the violin and harmonica beat that was already issuing from inside the Soiree Room, redecorated for the evening in hayseed. "Let's all go into the Barn Dance, and start having *fun!*"

She managed to get most of them inside, started the caller calling, introduced the singles to the other singles who were lounging around trying to appear a part of the walls, which were peppered with paper silos and ribbon-strung pieces of straw. When she came back to the lobby, there were some diehards playing gin rummy with their straw hats on, and Wandra in a chair, drinking brandy.

"What are you nervous about?" Wandra said to Evelyn. "Anyone with your energy has no right to be nervous."

"It's just my eye," Evelyn said, rubbing it fiercely, freely now, left with no responsibilities but the door prize. "That, and I have to wait for some friends of friends who are coming."

"I never like friends of friends," Wandra said.

"Neither do I," said Evelyn. "But I still have to watch out for them."

That was what she would tell people, if anyone asked, if anyone saw, God forbid. She would say that Pappy and Grandma were friends of friends. She was not going to hide them completely, just stash them in some other hotel, and when they refused to be invisible, she would say that they were friends of friends, and everyone would admire her for being so kind to people that were obviously beneath her.

"Will you look at that," Wandra said.

Evelyn turned. Just inside the entrance to the lobby stood Pappy, in his serious blue suit, too shiny, too small. As small as he was, his white socks were showing beneath the cuffs of the trousers. On his bald head was the gray felt hat he wore whenever he was outside, even in summer, in his undershirt, at the fruit stand. Grandma was standing very close to him, in a three-piece white suit with a peplum that Evelyn had sent home when she started getting more fashionable things. Grandma's light brown hair was swept up into a little coronet of curls, obviously all the rage in Pittsburgh, sweet Jesus. She was clutching one of Evelyn's old pocketbooks, imitation green alligator, a few of its scales fallen off. And next to her, belly extended, stood Sadie in a print housedress. They looked very tired, and tiny, and confused.

"They must have got off at the wrong country," Wandra said, and giggled into her brandy snifter.

"They're my family," said Evelyn, and ran to take them in her arms.

"So where is it?" Pappy said, after she had gotten them into a room, minimum double rate with a discount and a cot for Sadie.

"Where is the tropical splendor? When do they Begin the Beguine?"

"It's almost over for tonight," Evelyn said. "You should have let me know you were coming."

"We sent you a letter," said Pappy. "Enid the Junior Scholar wrote it herself."

"I only got it this morning. You should have called me."

"Then it wouldn't have been 'a Febulous surprise.'" Pappy took off his hat and shone bald-headed into the flourescence of the hotel room. "That's what it was supposed to be, according to Walter M. White. 'A Febulous surprise.' What is it according to his happy runaway bride, Evelyn Moskowitz White?"

"Evelyn Mosk White," said Evelyn. "I changed your name too when I registered you."

"Who's changing anything?" Pappy asked. "I am not a Roumanian. I have nothing to fear from the law."

"Mosk," said Evelyn.

"The cathedral where Arabs come to worship," said Pappy, citing source. " 'Information, Please.' "

"It's just easier to remember."

"I never forgot Moskowitz," said Pappy. "My whole life I been Moskowitz, *mein* darling daughter. I forget a lot of things, but I never forget who I am."

There was no point in arguing with him, there had never been any point in arguing with him. He was much too old-world and stubborn to learn, so she let them go dancing, the Moskowitz-Mosks.

She watched them from the bar where she sat with Sadie. Pappy was wearing the suit he had come in, but had changed into a fresh white shirt and polished his shoes with a can of Griffin Grandma had packed in the corner of his valise along with ten Kleenex for spreading the wax. She had also packed his denture powder and another wad of Kleenex, and inside the actual Kleenex box Murray had given them for their adventure was the glass for Pappy to soak his plates in. Grandma had been

I 7 5

sure the hotel would give them a glass, but as she had never stayed in a hotel, she couldn't be completely sure.

Grandma had changed into Sadie's wedding gown, which was now dyed royal blue. She was following Pappy's trumped up rhumba, an aggressive little step he invented from watching the couples on the floor. He sang along with the music and his erratic movements. Grandma stayed tight in the squarish circle of his arms, laughing, and looking up at him as if he were tall.

"They're cute," Evelyn admitted to Sadie, who had her belly tucked inside a sequined cape Evelyn had loaned her.

"It's hard to be cute when you're older," said Sadie. "They're better than cute."

"How do you like him, sending money to Grandma? He hasn't sent me a penny, that stingy son of a bitch. They *are* darling. Why was I in such a hurry to leave home? Why did I ever marry him? I could have done so much better if I waited."

Sadie took a deep sip of her Cuba Libre. "Forget about it. What was, was."

Evelyn looked at her sister thoughtfully. She was not really regulation pretty, but she had something, the family smile, that was it—the family smile and a hint of Grandma's wisdom. Where did she get off being so wise? She hadn't even gone to college, except for a year.

"Who made you the family philosopher?" Evelyn said. "What was, was. What does that mean?"

"Don't count your chickens when they're dead," said Sadie.

Evelyn smiled. "You don't get to be a philosopher marrying a truck driver. What did you marry him for?"

"He had no respect for me. Everybody else I went out with had so much respect for me I thought I'd go crazy. Hymie's an animal. He raped me our second date."

"And you *married* him?"

"It felt very good after so much respect," said Sadie.

"Come," said Evelyn, when they were all regrouped in the lobby, Pappy hanging around the fringes of a card game, wishing it were pinochle. "You've had a long trip. You must be tired."

"Tired I can get when I'm working," said Pappy. "I'm on vacation."

"It's almost two o'clock," said Sadie.

"That's a nice watch," said Evelyn.

"Hymie gave it to me when I had the baby."

"Very pretty." Evelyn checked it for real gold, even though she knew better. "How's your little girl?"

"She's nice. She's a child. You wouldn't like her."

"So what's next?" Pappy asked.

"It's two o'clock in the morning," said Sadie.

"That's a really nice watch," Evelyn said. "I'm surprised he had such good taste, the rapist."

"What?" Grandma asked. "I didn't hear."

"What was, was," said Sadie.

"Right," Pappy said. "Rest you can get when you're dead."

" *'Twas on the Isle of Capri I first met him . . .*" Sadie sang while she scratched Chris' back. They were sitting by the diving board at the far end of the pool in the glare of early afternoon, away from the card players, the peppermint-striped umbrellas of the lunch bar, the professional tanners, where they would have more privacy, Evelyn assured them. Sadie lay back in her expectant-mother bathing suit, with a flap over the exposed hole for her belly, on the chaise next to the one where Chris lay face down, soaking up song and fingernails.

"Further to the right," said Chris.

"Farther to the right," Evelyn corrected.

"My arm's getting tired," Sadie said.

"I'll scratch," said Grandma, in her one-piece print dressmaker suit that had been Evelyn's favorite until she realized little skirts on swimwear were for people with bad thighs, and Evelyn's were the best that thighs came. Grandma leaned over and started scratching.

"Every night you'll hear me croon/A Russian lullaby . . ." Grandma sang and scratched.

"Honest to God, you'll spoil her rotten," said Evelyn.

"How often do we see her?" Grandma said.

"I scratch her when she's really itchy," said Evelyn. "I have a job to do."

"Evelyn!" Pappy commanded. "Move your chair over here, I'll scratch your back." He was wearing Walter White's bathing suit, the striped one he had planned on taking to Conneaut Lake and had sworn never to wear again, leaving it at the Moskowitzes when he went to war. The suit was too big for Pappy, but nobody could see that as long as he sat in the chair, which Pappy felt he was doomed to for the rest of the afternoon, as Evelyn wouldn't let them go to the peppermint place and order lunch.

"The free hors d'oeuvres start at three o'clock," she had said that morning in their room, bringing them a small coffee pot, a can of Sterno, and a half-dozen hardboiled eggs. "These will hold you till then."

"I'm on vacation," Pappy insisted. "If I want to, I order cantaloupe out of season."

"I'm not made out of money," Evelyn said.

"Don't tell me, I made you," said Pappy. "I know what you're made of: sugar and spice and everything nice and only a little stingy." He reached into the secret compartment Grandma had fashioned, making a false bottom out of the Kleenex box, and pulled out seventy dollars. "Very good produce this past season, war or no war. If I want to, I eat honeydew."

"There's no point in spending like a drunken sailor."

"I don't know no drunken sailors," Pappy said. "I only know Walter M. White and your brother Murray, who's enlisting in the Navy."

"Why?"

"The Army wants him," Pappy said. "He heard the Navy's better."

"These will hold you till three when the free hors d'oeuvres start." Evelyn cracked the shell on the white painted top of the bureau and peeled an egg for him.

Now it was only two o'clock and Pappy could hear his stomach growling. "Speak up!" he said to his belly, hanging only a little flaccid inside the band of the bathing suit. "What's news? Good evening, Mr. and Mrs. American, and all the ships at sea."

"Stop it," Evelyn said, laughing.

"Move your chair over here and I'll scratch your back."

"I'm not itchy," said Evelyn, and moved to where he could scratch her back.

"You want to sit on my lap?"

"Don't be silly," Evelyn said, and watched while Grandma scratched Chris and kept on singing.

"Just a simple little tune/When Baby starts to cry/Go to sleep my baby . . ."

"I love that song," said Evelyn. "How come you didn't sing that to me when I was little?"

"I'm sorry," said Grandma. "So many babies, and helping Pappy at the store. Don't be mad."

"I'm not mad," said Evelyn. "I'd tell you if I were mad."

"Some day there may be," Grandma sang, *"A land that's free/ For you and me . . ."*

"How come you didn't sing that to me when I was little?"

"It wasn't written when you was little," Pappy said.

"I thought it was from the Old Country," Evelyn said.

"Wrong," said Pappy. "Mr. Irving Berlin. Kay Kyser, the Kollitch of Musical Knowlitch."

"I thought it was from Russia."

"In Schventiensky we had no Russian lullabies," said Pappy. "We were not so crazy from the Russians. Eh, Tillie, how did they feel about the Russkies in Hungary?"

Grandma started to cry, the song interrupted, the scratching stopped.

"Oh, for Heaven's sake," said Evelyn. "There's nothing to cry about. If it wasn't written yet, how could you sing it to me, even if you hadn't been too busy with the other babies?"

"My beautiful sister." Grandma wept into one of Murray's Kleenexes.

"What's wrong?" asked Evelyn.

"They're killing all the Jews," said Pappy.

"An ugly rumor," said Evelyn.

"My beautiful baby sister . . ."

"They're rounding them up like pigs and putting them in sties. Concentration camps," said Pappy. "They want them to concentrate on dying."

"You don't really believe that?" Evelyn asked.

"I had a letter from my sister," wept Grandma. "They took her husband and her son to a place called Theresienstadt. She's waiting for them to come for her and the girls. My beautiful sister."

"She'll be all right," said Evelyn. "Roosevelt didn't believe it about the Jews. Otherwise we would have gotten into the war sooner. If he didn't believe it, and he's President, why should you?"

"She got a letter," Pappy said. "Maybe nobody wrote to Franklin Delano Roosevelt."

"You should have seen her," said Grandma. "Eyes like the sky on a beautiful day. I used to think my eyes were blue, till I looked at my sister."

"I'll see her." Evelyn got up and put her arms around Grandma. "I'll marry a very rich man and we'll bring her to Pittsburgh and the war will be over and we'll all live happily ever after."

"In Pittsburgh?" asked Chris.

"How come you're not asleep?" said Evelyn. "You had a lullaby."

"How can you marry a very rich man when you're already married to Daddy?"

"Take a nap, dear, and dream about Daddy getting very rich."

For a moment, with Grandma crying like that, Evelyn let her thoughts drift darkly to the potential annihilation of all the Jews in Europe. But then she saw the man.

He was an officer. He seemed to be alone. His back was toward her. A handsome back, made wider by the fine cut of white material. He looked very tall, taller even than the maitre d' of the Peppermint Patio, whom he seemed to be questioning. He was wearing an officer's cap, and his hair stopped, finely cropped, at the back of his neck, where hair should stop.

The maitre d' pointed in Evelyn's direction. Evelyn closed her eyes. Was there a god of Mercy and Romance? She sealed the hope tightly inside her head and prepared the dazzle of her smile.

"Nobody say anything," she instructed the family. "Just let me talk to him."

"Who?" asked Sadie.

"That good-looking officer coming over here," Evelyn said, and prayed, eyes shut.

"You still think that's good-looking?" Pappy said.

Evelyn opened her eyes and saw the full pleasure of the wide-open face advancing on them. "Oh my God," she said.

"Lieutenant Senior Grade Walter M. White," said Pappy, springing to his feet so fast his shorts fell to his hips, and he had to grab at them with his hands. "Isn't this a Febulous surprise!"

He had been captured and tortured and rescued by the Marines. Honest to God. He was getting the Navy Cross.

"What happened?" said Evelyn. "What happened on Guam?"

Walter averted his eyes, indicating his daughter, who was clinging to him. "I don't want to say in front of . . ."

"Go get an ice cream," said Evelyn.

"I want to hear," said Chris.

"Go get an ice cream."

Walter reached into the pocket of his uniform. "Here," he said to Chris, and handed her a dime.

"A shiny new dime," said Evelyn. "You'll spoil us."

"I want to spoil you," Walter said, and hugged Chris, who was holding hard. "I want to spoil you both."

"Go get an ice cream," Evelyn instructed Chris, who moved reluctantly away. "Okay," said Evelyn. "What happened on Guam?"

He gave them every detail of the torture, every detail. How the Japanese had captured him and taken him to an animal trough filled with water, spread-eagled his arms, forced his head forward, and drowned him. Three times they had drowned him, each time bringing him back with artificial respiration, choking, vomiting. Each time the commanding officer demanded to know what he knew, and Walter said he knew nothing. And each time the officer said (in English), "Give him ten minutes to think if he wants to go through that again, to think what he knows. If he insists he knows nothing, then drown him."

"My God," said Pappy, "they have such ways. I would have told them everything."

"I am an officer of the United States Navy. I gave them my name, rank, and serial number."

"But what actually happened?" Evelyn said.

"They kept me with the rest of the sick and wounded prisoners. My right lung is collapsed. It can never be restored."

"I understand that," said Evelyn. "I'm asking what happened. How were you captured? What happened? What were you doing? Tell me what you did."

"She wants to know so she can figure out if she could have done it better," said Pappy, and slapped his leg, laughing.

" 'It is not the critic who counts,' " Walter started to recite. " 'Not the man who points out how a strong man stumbled, or where the doers of deeds could have done better . . .' "

"Walter, I'm asking you how you were caught, exactly."

" 'The credit belongs to the man who is actually in the arena; whose face is marred by dust and sweat and blood; who strived valiantly; who errs and comes short again and again.' "

"Walter, I want to know. I'm really prepared to listen."

"A moment, dear." He waved his hand. " 'Who knows the great enthusiasms, the great devotions, and spends himself in a worthy cause; who at best knows the triumph of high achievement; and who, at the worst, if he fails, at least fails while daring greatly . . .' That's how I felt while it happened."

"While *what* happened? While *what* happened?"

Walter smiled at her. " 'So that his place shall never be with those cold and timid souls who know neither victory nor defeat.' That's Theodore Roosevelt."

"I didn't know that," said Pappy, shaking his bald head,

running some fast fingers through the little gray fringe behind his ear. "Theodore 'Roughrider' Roosevelt. That one I knew."

"Poems you write me," Evelyn murmured. "Love letters you write me. And you have an adventure like this and you don't write me?"

"It wasn't a happy experience."

"It was an adventure!" Evelyn sprang to her feet. "Why didn't you write me? Not everybody is interested in poems. Everybody likes to read an adventure!"

"I wrote you love letters," Walter said softly. "Love is the greatest adventure of them all."

"Excuse me," said Evelyn. "I have to go throw up."

"I didn't mean to upset you. I shouldn't have told you about the torture—"

"You didn't upset me," Evelyn said. "I just have to throw up."

"Sadie, run," Grandma said. "Carefully. Go hold her head."

"He could have at least bought me lunch," Evelyn said, when she came out of the toilet in the ladies' room off the lobby. She lay down on the chaise beside the big gilded mirror, a wet towel on her forehead. "I can't stand to throw up dry. The Navy Cross, for Christ's sake."

"It's incredible," Sadie said. "I didn't think he had it in him."

"He has nothing in him. If he didn't tell them anything, it was because he didn't know anything."

"Evelyn, he's an officer. He must have known things like the movement of the Fleet. Things the Japanese tried to get out of Farley Granger. Didn't you see *The Purple Heart?*"

"I didn't have to see it. I'm married to it."

"Stop it," Sadie giggled. "You're proud of him and you know it. You're proud, and you're upset. Otherwise why would you get sick?"

"How could he come so close to getting killed and still be alive?"

"You must be proud of him. He's a hero."

"How can he be a hero? He's a dentist."

"Not anymore," said Sadie. "He's an officer and a hero."

"You really believe it? You don't think he's making it up?"

"Evelyn, he's getting the Navy Cross."

"I can't believe it," said Evelyn. "I just can't believe it. I've made him into a hero."

"You've made him . . . ?"

"If it weren't for me, he wouldn't have even been in the Navy." She got up from the chaise, washed her face, and gargled with some mouthwash that was on the makeup tray. "I'm married to a hero, what do you know." She smiled at herself in the mirror. "Behind every hero who was originally a coward from Pittsburgh, there is a great woman."

"So what does this mean, exactly?" Evelyn said, when they were back at the pool. "Does it mean you'll get a promotion?"

"Well, first I must go to Washington and receive the Navy Cross from the Secretary of the Navy."

"Why the Secretary?" Pappy said. "How come not the Boss?"

"I missed you, you old codger," Walter laughed, and slapped Pappy's shoulder. "Will you come to Washington for the ceremony?"

"There's been enough spending around here," Evelyn said. "There's a war on. When did all this happen, what you couldn't write me?"

"Three months ago. I wanted to write you from the hospital, but once I knew I was alive, really alive, I thought it would be better in the flesh. Everything with you is better in the flesh," he said, hugging Chris, moving his lips into a kiss directed at Evelyn over the small curly head. "How about this?" he said, cupping his daughter's cheeks in his hands. "How's my big girl?"

"Smart as a whipper," Pappy said. "What do you know about that. A Cross from the Navy. Such a life. Everything's going to be hunky-dory, right, Evelyn?"

"I'll stay with Chrissie at the apartment tonight," Grandma said.

"Why?" asked Chris. "Isn't Daddy staying with us?"

"There's no room at the apartment," Evelyn said.

"He can sleep with me. Please, Daddy."

"Another night," Walter said. "I'm going to have plenty of time to be with both my girls. I'm being transferred to New York, to Naval Intelligence."

"Whatever for?" Evelyn didn't go on. Out of the corner of her eye she could see Wandra and Harvey Kane, oiling up.

"I want you to meet somebody," she said to Walter.

"You will come to New York." He tried to embrace her, but she was moving too fast, clomping her cork-soled sandals neatly against the pavement by the pool. "Won't you? This whole separation has been silly."

"It hasn't been silly at all," said Evelyn. "You've found yourself."

"I'm nothing without you."

Well, he had said it first. Maybe he was learning wisdom along with bravery. She would see how he handled himself with Harvey Kane. If he could come such a long way dealing with the Japs, the Lord only knew how far he could go with a war profiteer.

SIX

ALONE, Sonny took to smoking four packs of cigarettes a day. Wings when he could get them, any brand that was available when he could not. Alone, after the fight with Arnold, he'd found an efficiency apartment in a luxury hotel on Lower Fifth Avenue. Overpriced, but it still didn't make him happy. He was living alone, cramped. No space to march through late at night, no one at the other end of the long stone hall. The mind didn't stop working just because it was late at night.

He tried to avoid going home (small apartment) as late into evening as he could, asking anyone to join him for dinner, little bankers and their wives, clerks at some of the better investment houses, drunks that seemed amiable at restaurants where he went. Alone.

He did not pick up women, because he was so lonely he was

afraid he would fall in love, and he did not want it to be someone he had picked up in a bar. So he tried to collect a retinue, and when it wasn't the usual retinue, he would try to round up a new retinue, and pull it from restaurant to supper club, to one of those dingy places he was good at finding, those darkly lit after-hours clubs that owners were trying to make known as "boites." When everything was closed, he would urge his entourage back to his apartment, where they seldom joined him. It was just as well: he didn't feel the living room reflected his personality, and he really didn't mind drinking alone.

In the mornings, he would suffer for it. But that didn't matter. Hangovers made it easier for him to sit back and watch Arnold trying to run it all, making decisions Sonny never would have made. Hangovers gave you a heavy head and a heavy tongue, so you couldn't say "I told you so" too quickly. Even if you thought of it very fast.

There was never a question of their not continuing in business together. In spite of the fury of the personal rift between them, there wasn't a moment when it occurred to Sonny or Arnold to end the investment firm that bore both their names. Joe Pape's was moving up nationally to be the third most successful bourbon in the country, and profits were coming in fair share, more than fair share. Joe Pape might know how to commit murder, but he wouldn't dream of cheating, especially not the eminent counselor-at-law, had he pursued it, Abraham Sterne.

Sonny regarded the income from the bourbon with the bemused pleasure with which one might look at a mistress. He was wedded to Arnold, and he knew it. Maybe the love had gone out of the marriage, but they had to keep it together for the sake of the company.

There were no more lunches, except those they took together on rushed days at the office. No more dinners at the Big House, except on occasional Fridays when Sarah lit candles, recited the whole of the Sabbath prayers, and pleaded with him to come.

"You have to come, Sonny," she told him on the phone. "He's going crazy. He cries at night because you hate him."

"I don't hate him. He's my brother. I respect him. He has no respect for me or he couldn't have talked to me the way he did. I respect his lack of respect. I spend as little time with him as possible."

"People say things," Sarah said. "That doesn't mean they mean them."

"We see each other in the office."

"That's business."

"That's all we have between us now, is business."

"He loves you like a son."

"Then I hope to hell Ellis grows up a lot smarter than I did, or he's going to be in very big trouble with his father." Ellis was Arnold's son, almost fourteen now; the daughter, Althea, was two. (Baby had married, a very nice fellow from California, very well off, the important thing, Arnold and Sonny had agreed when they gave her hand and her wardrobe and some bonds in marriage.) Sonny was not too crazy about either Ellis or Althea, but he was gentle to them, and gave them presents, the treatment he accorded all human beings whom he felt he should like, but with whom he did not feel comfortable.

"You'll come," Sarah said. "It's Friday. You'll come."

And sometimes, when it was Friday, and all the loose people who could have been corralled seemed to have disappeared into private pens, Sonny would go to the Big House for dinner. But he never let himself enjoy it.

He was the same way with women. He had absolutely no intention of drifting into his thirties a virgin; that seemed ludicrous to him. That he had waited out of some childish aspiration was fitting, even touching, in a very young man. Such things categorized people as dreamers, and he didn't mind having an outrageous dream. But the innocent heart of his early twenties was now behind a slightly thickening chest, and aesthetes and tuberculars and Mama's boys and faggots could keep idealizing into their forties. It became them because they were wispy. But it had no place in a very tall man with a huge forehead and a much too prominent chin, whose pants size was growing a little larger, now that he could really afford pants.

So he took up with one or two ladies. They were not as foolish as the women Arnold had been with. They were twice as expensive, so that made them twice as smart, Sonny was sure. Without doubt they knew enough to keep their mouths shut and just sit there looking pretty, which was nice, really nice, especially across soup.

Soup. The staple of the depression. When there was nothing else to eat. Now that the depression was really over, with prosperity zinging through the country during the first year of the war, people didn't have to eat soup; they could afford to have something. But it looked as if you were less than spendthrift if you didn't order it, also. A suddenly very elegant thing: *potage*.

Potage. High-priced ladies looked very elegant across potage, touching their spoons to the back of their china soup cups so nothing would drip. Moving the soup spoon delicately up to the flowers of their lips. Gently pulling in the liquid. Spilling nothing.

Not even what they did for a living, to the friends of Sonny's who might stop by and say hello, which few of them ever did. That was really just as well. Those weren't the evenings he liked to stretch out. The ones he wanted to make last longer were filled with friends, not emptied by women.

The nights with women were prophylactic, preventive hedonism, to make sure all his pleasure poisons were drained. He was not tender, nor was he brutal. He touched their faces to give the illusion of gentleness, but got his business over with with as much quick force as he could. Everyone except his mother, whom he did not even try to remember anymore, could be gotten and paid for. Only in opera and erotic dreaming did they come to you willowing arias, in costume, pretty to see, exciting to listen to.

Besides drinking and high-priced whoring, which was not that much of a happy pastime, his other pleasures were chess and art. He was embarrassed about both of those, because he knew what Arnold would say if he knew Sonny really considered them pleasures. "Commie pleasures," Arnold would call them, since Sonny had learned about both at Columbia. It was true. Milton

Radnitz had taught him to play chess when they were both graduate students in law. Long philosophic discussions which Milton turned into recruiting speeches had begun behind the move given a Bishop.

Sonny had been as mesmerized by the game as he was by Milton's thought processes. Although he did not like confusing the two, the game and Milton's thinking, he was able to pay attention to both without losing the ability to concentrate on either.

Art he had learned at the elbow of Lorenzo Kornblatt, another Brooklyn boy who had studied Fine Arts at Columbia. They had moved as friends on weekends, when they went to exhibitions and galleries together. When Lorenzo became the staple intellectual among art critics, Sonny encouraged him to keep his fervor up, mild as it was.

As Sonny started to fall into fortune, Lorenzo had him buy a big canvas, six feet by twelve feet, from a painter called Jackson Pollock. Lorenzo said Pollock was a very nice guy, a little disorganized, no sense of profit, no wish to do anything but paint. But he had a big family, and would be very important one day, Lorenzo assured Sonny. But meantime Pollock didn't have money to feed the kids.

Sonny couldn't tell from the huge painting itself whether the man would ever become intelligible enough to be popular. But he did like Lorenzo, and felt sorry for hungry children. So he bought the painting for six hundred dollars, twice the price Pollock was asking at the time.

Sonny felt so good about being a patron of the arts, he even bought a painting Lorenzo had done himself, a still life of two avocadoes, an onion, a tomato, and a lemon. (Evelyn, on first seeing it, many years later, relabeled it "Guacamole.") Lorenzo wanted to give it to Sonny for nothing, but Sonny insisted on paying him. Nobody had said critics had to be talented at doing what they criticized, not even Lorenzo Kornblatt had said that. But Sonny thought he saw so much love in the confines of the painting, so much tight regret that it could not burst into itself and become something wonderful, that the picture was the critic's comment on how much he cared about art, when it was as fine as this could never be.

Sonny considered the work modest and self-effacing. Lorenzo judged it flat and uninspired. But he wanted to sell a painting very much, and liked the thought of being in the collection of a collector who collected Jackson Pollock, even if his own work hung in the maid's bathroom (which was where it ended when Evelyn got her hands on it).

So Sonny's cultural appetites, at least, were fairly sated. He read as many books as interested him, but preferred talking. There was time enough to read when there was too much time: every night, before he went to sleep, no matter how much he drank. It was incredible how educated even an educated man could become, being lonely. He wondered if Arnold was getting educated too, late at night, when there was nobody left to talk to, so he could hear himself talking. He didn't miss Sonny at all, he missed hearing himself. That was why he cried.

He really cried. It was impossible to believe that Arnold could cry about anything, even though Sarah said so. Arnold had wept at his father's funeral, sure, but he'd already cast his pronunciamento out on the air.

"Any man that lets himself be diminished by a woman is a *schmuck*." Well, you couldn't get more diminished than dead. A man that let a woman kill him was the biggest *schmuck* of all. Okay, so Arnold had wept, but his words were still hanging in the trees near the open grave. This is what you weep for: a *schmuck*. The opinion was more degrading than the grief was uplifting, especially once you were dead.

And now Arnold was crying for Sonny. What difference did it make, provided what Sarah said was true? She was being maternal, conciliatory, concerned, if that's what maternal was, trying to make it tender between them again. How could anyone ever make it tender? Arnold had called him a whore. That meant Arnold believed that Sonny would do anything for a buck. Sonny hadn't done it for money at all, he had done it for being *right*. A man had to do anything, give everything he had to, everything short of his life, maybe even that, for being *right*.

The hard part was knowing what right was, because who was there around to ask whom he knew for sure he could depend on? Well, there was a court of law, twelve men brave and true, and an incontrovertible verdict. Besides the trial, and the jury of twelve, how many opportunities were there to know for sure? Without checking with Arnold.

He could exist in a world without his brother, Sonny could. And would. He just needed to have a few more things to do. He went to the theater a great deal. There was a minor boom on Broadway because of the war. People needed to forget about the war, and ration stamps, and they did it best by enjoying the subtle luxuries of the privileged, like going to a play and never a battle.

Tickets were hard to come by. Sonny found his own broker, a man named Nick Gould, and started testing him, trying to see if Nick could come up with tickets to a hit two hours before curtain time. When Nick delivered seats in the first six rows for the fifth week in succession, Sonny invited him to accept the other ticket and accompany him. Nick was flattered, very flattered, but his wife would kill him, he said. He had to get home to New Jersey. Everybody had to get home someplace, eventually. There was no way you could be sure to keep them around.

When the call came in from Mrs. Catherine Warnecke, Sonny was coming down with a cold. Sickness was one way of avoiding loneliness: if he could get deep enough down under the covers and take enough medicine, he could lull himself off to where he believed he had comfort and security. But he didn't like getting sick as much as he enjoyed an occasional day pretending to be. So when his throat started feeling really raw, and there was an ache in his ears, and an occasional tear that had nothing to do with sadness materialized in his eye, it made Sonny angry. That was how he felt, when the call came in from Catherine Warnecke.

"A friend of who?" he said into the phone.

"Nick Gould."

"I don't know any Nick Gould."

"Your theater broker," Catherine said. "He's a cousin of mine." There was a slight catch in her voice, a breathy speech pattern. Very nice, the voice, if you were in a mood for nice voices, which Sonny wasn't; his ears were hurting.

"Yes? Well?" What did she want. Two for a matinee?

"I've run into a little trouble with some of my investments, and Nick suggested . . ." Breath. "He suggested I call you. He doesn't know the market, but he gets tickets for a number of stockbrokers, and he says out of all of them . . ." Breath. "You're the most gentlemanly."

"I never even met him."

"I know. He told me he'd only talked to you on the phone . . . But you can pick up strong hunches over the phone, don't you think?" The whispery quality again, feminine, just the slightest bit poignant. Her skin would be soft.

"Mrs. Warnecke, I'm not exactly a stockbroker. I'm an investment banker. Mutual funds. Municipal bonds. You know the difference?"

"I don't understand any of it, but I'd really appreciate your explaining it to me."

"I've got three other calls waiting. I don't mean to be rude . . ." Which was what he was being. What the hell was the matter with him?

"I didn't mean right this minute. I thought perhaps we might get together at the end of the day. Or another day, perhaps."

Of course. Soft skin and a breathy voice and a husband who bored her in the suburbs. Well, that was all right. That was exciting, even. Why shouldn't he have a little hanky-panky in his life, even if it was so full?

"I'm worried about myself," he said in front of the mirror in the wardrobe closet (Raphael Hawthorne, the Palace at Versailles via Sotheby's). He was putting on a fresh shirt for his cocktail meeting with Catherine. He had bought a new tie that afternoon because he spilled some potage on the one he was wearing at lunch, which he had not eaten with Arnold. Now Arnold was watching him preening, and in spite of the fact that Sonny didn't care about Arnold anymore, it was good to have him really looking. "Really worried," said Sonny. "I'm becoming cynical."

"It's about time," said Arnold, and went out the door.

Sonny was breathing very hard in the taxi on the way to his hotel, where he was meeting Catherine for drinks and a little explaining. He didn't feel like explaining anything, although it was one of his favorite things in the world, explaining. He was sick, he was sweating, and if she was after anything besides advice on her portfolio, he doubted he could deliver, soft skin and all. Bored lady.

He tried to put such thoughts out of his mind, because those were Arnold thoughts. Sonny closed his eyes, and tried sending himself back into the state of sweet innocence he had felt himself suspended in before the train ride, when everything still held wonder. When no murder touched on him, and nobody he loved thought him a whore. But it was too far to go, even by cab, back to innocence.

Innocence was not something that stood still there, reeking sweetly of pickles like McCloskey's Delicatessen, to be returned to when you had the time and the wish and the money to pay it back for taking good care of you. Innocence was the starry cotton of white you blew from a dandelion, when you still believed that wishes could be granted. There was no way to pick up the strands that weren't even petals and paste them back onto the stem, once you had blown them off.

By the time the taxi was halfway up Lower Broadway, he was sweating through his clothes. He took off his overcoat, opened a window, and let some biting cold hit his face. His forehead turned clammy, so he closed the window again, took his hat off, and rested his head back against the seat.

It would have to be Friday. The bastards were always away

for the weekend, the ones who had made it, the doctors who cared for the big politicos—the politicos with a lot of publicity, helping few bills pass that might aid humane causes, but who at least had had a heart attack or a seizure in public, so constituents would think they could still get worked up about something.

Those were politicians Sonny considered politicians—not the heavy-lidded round-shouldered cigar smokers of Di Bonaven's crowd, the ones Arnold considered important. Sonny didn't care about the men behind the men. He cared about the men themselves, the ones who seemed on very rare occasions to have the makings of statesmen, even if they didn't really care about the people as much as Sonny would have cared about the people, had he taken a different path and decided to become a politician with the heart of a statesman.

He cared about good politicians, and he cared about their doctors, because a doctor that kept an important politician alive had to be at the top of his profession. You didn't go shooting things into a heavyweight politico's arm without really knowing your business. If anything happened to that patient, the party could kill you.

So Sonny got his doctors out of the headlines, after they had saved a state senator's life, or the heart of a man with his eye on Capitol Hill. He would call and make an appointment with the advertised heavyweight, be impressed with the vast complex of offices, the incredibly advanced equipment, the many people waiting, the assistants who seemed to be everywhere, and the doctor who looked like he'd never show up. When all the tests had been run, and the blood drawn and the X-rays completed, the doctor himself would actually meet with Sonny for between five and seven minutes, assure him he was in fine physical condition, was only a little overweight, would give him a diet and say if he ever needed anything not to hesitate to call.

The bill would usually run between five and seven hundred dollars, so Sonny would know he was really in great shape. And whenever he felt bad, he would give the doctor a call, the way the doctor had said. If it was Friday, the service would advise that the doctor was in Easthampton for the weekend, or Washington, or Fall River, Massachusetts. Everyplace the really needed went, when they didn't need anybody.

The service would offer to contact the covering doctor, but unless Sonny was convinced he couldn't live till Monday, when he could see the regular doctor in the office, he passed. Once he had been lucky enough to fall ill on Wednesday, so Kenistrode, the heart specialist who saved Congressman Wilmott, came by to see Sonny on the way home from the office. Kenistrode seemed very annoyed, as Sonny's fever was only 102°, and he'd told Kenistrode on the phone it was 104°, to make sure he came. But now it was Friday, and Sonny could feel real sickness reaching for him by the throat, and there was nothing he could do except be very strong, all by himself, because the doctor was out of town, he would have to be. They always were.

The taxi stopped in front of the canopy. The doorman helped him out. He was sweating like a pig now, and he was freezing. He had a feeling he would fall if he didn't sit down. Ridiculous. He had absolutely no intention of being ill this particular weekend. There was a sculpture exhibition he was supposed to go to Saturday afternoon with Lorenzo, theater tickets for Saturday night, reservations afterward for El Morocco, where Sonny never had a very good time but went nonetheless because they wouldn't admit Arnold.

He even had a date with a woman he almost enjoyed. She was lovely in bed and didn't talk too much when she was upright, except to ask him quite intelligent questions, they seemed to him, as they gave him plenty of opportunity to answer. The only thing he didn't like about her was a faint conviction that she understood almost nothing of what he said. But that was all right. That was to be expected. As long as she didn't tell him she didn't understand, he could talk to her as if she did. To speak to women at all was a compromise.

Life was a compromise, if you stayed alive. The only idealists who hadn't been disappointed were those who died in their early twenties, when most of the shattered dreams were still up ahead.

He staggered through the lobby like a drunk, embarrassed at

his failing physical senses. Seasick, and he'd never been to sea. The elevator man and the doorman were standing there, waiting, salaried to be anxious about him, especially with Christmas coming.

"Can we help you upstairs, Mr. Sterne?" the elevator man asked.

"No, it's all right, Ned. I have to meet someone in the bar." He checked his hat and coat in the cloakroom of the cocktail lounge, and went inside to pick her out of the red-tinted darkness. There were candles on all the tables, candles in red hurricane lamps, little candle bulbs in the bronze sconces that dotted the red flocked-velvet of the walls. The wood of the tables and bar that ran along the far side of the room were deep, dark brown. Nothing to disturb the feeling of darkness and somber warmth except for the white-jacketed cocktail waiter, who moved busily between the bar and the various couples sitting around the tables, talking in tones to match the muted colors of the room.

And Catherine. He knew it was Catherine, because she was the only woman alone, and there was no way she could be a B-girl, not by the farthest stretch of imagination and chance. She was a little too heavy-set; her face was too open. You had to be able to hide feelings if you were a whore, which was why Sonny couldn't make it, no matter what Arnold had called him.

Catherine's eyes shone out of the paleness of her face with a transparency that convinced Sonny he could see what she was thinking. What eyes. He had never seen eyes quite that blue, and he had been looking into blue eyes all his life, between the mirror and Arnold.

To be impressed with eyes was a boy's thing, and he was thirty years old. He would not be put away by the sight of beautiful eyes. Still, he struck a match after their first drink together, held the flame close to her face to make sure they were really that blue.

"What'd you do that for?" she asked.

"I'm foolish."

"You're anything but foolish," she said. He had explained to her the basic difference between regular stocks and mutual funds and tax-free municipal bonds and long-term investments. He had rushed it because he wanted her to know, and he wanted to see how he looked in her eyes, and try to pick up how much she really understood. She had nodded throughout it all, as if she absorbed it completely, what it had taken him his whole life to learn, the part of his whole life when he didn't choose the different path to law or religion or history.

"You understood what I told you?"

"I understand I can trust you," Catherine said. "That's all that matters to me. I'd like you to take on my account."

"Why?"

"You have to trust somebody, don't you think?" She toyed with the small straw that cut through the thickness of her Brandy Alexander. "Life would be pointless if there were nobody to trust."

"Don't you trust your husband?"

"I did." She looked away.

He could not see her eyes. He couldn't remember them. The beauty in them. The pain in them. All he could see was the rest of her face, and it was not such a good setting for those eyes. The skin on her cheeks was starting to go slack, and there were lines around her mouth, the corners of her eyelids. He could not tell if they were laughter lines, or records of sorrow, or simply time making note of itself.

Without her looking at him, she was not beautiful at all. Her face was weak and tired, and maybe even, Arnold would say for sure, a little old. But what beauty must have rested there when she was truly young, with tightness of cheek, warm ash-brown hair, unsalted with gray. What a wonderful frame must have been there for those eyes. Ago. Of course. Everything perfect had to be past, or up ahead. The present was only for those who had little to dream of. Or someone to touch so they could really feel the moment.

Why didn't it ever feel the way you dreamed it would? Why didn't he reach for her and start it and have it over with? Because she would disappoint him, of course. They always did.

"Are you ill?" she said, as he wiped his forehead with a handkerchief. "You are," she said, touching his cheek. "You're burning with fever."

Eyes. Looking at him with concern. Nothing but eyes. When there were eyes like that, you didn't need to see anything else.

And then he saw nothing. Not even eyes.

When he came up out of the darkness, he was in bed, in his pajamas, and she was sitting on a chair beside the bed. "I've called my doctor," she said very soothingly. "Ned, the doorman, helped me get you upstairs."

"Thank you," he managed to say.

"He'll be over in a few minutes. Don't be afraid."

"I'm not," he said, and took her hand, because he was.

He did not remember even seeing the doctor, but believed he had actually come and was not in Nantucket or someplace where no one cared if a man was dying in New York. There were pills on the night table, and she was easing sweet liquid into his mouth. Holding his head.

"You must have to be someplace," he said.

"Is there anyone to take care of you?"

Arnold. "No," he answered.

"Then I have to be someplace with you."

He awoke for a few minutes at a time, from time to time, having lost track of it, having almost lost track of his life he was sure. But her hand would be there, cooling his forehead. Touching so gently the fingers went down in his chest, where history was, and heart. Nothing could move you that deeply unless it had history to it.

"Thank you, thank you," he managed to say, and was unconscious again. Unconscious, but feeling her breath coming warm across him, floating down from all those years away.

"How can I ever repay you?" he said on Sunday morning. He knew it was Sunday, because the New York *Times* was there, all fat and sassy and full of information he was too weak to try to digest.

"Just drink this," she said, and moved some juice to his mouth. "You caught a very tough bug, but apparently you're a very tough man."

"I'm a baby," he said. "I was afraid I was dying."

"Well, you weren't," Catherine said, smiling. "And you didn't."

"Thanks to you."

"Thanks to you," said Catherine. "I felt absolutely useful for the first time in a long time. I had no particular plans for the weekend. Your temperature's practically normal."

She saw the expression on his face and laughed. "I took it under your arm. You haven't been violated."

"I'd love to have been violated. I'd just hate to have missed it."

"You didn't miss anything."

"I don't believe you," Sonny said. "I have a feeling I've missed out on something very important, not knowing you."

"That's very romantic," she touched his cheek. "Sweet, and very romantic."

"I used to be a romantic." He took her fingertips and moved them toward his lips. She made the gesture her own and caressed them, one lip at a time, with one finger at a time.

"My people were of the Romantic Faith," Sonny said, when he could speak again. "I was a Romantic for a very long time, before I converted to Cynicism. You have the most beautiful eyes I ever saw."

"And you have to take some medicine."

"Tell me about it," she said a little later, when he was sitting up, he felt that much better. "Your conversion."

"Well, a long time ago, I decided to save myself for one great love. And then I decided I'd never find it. And here you are. So I was wrong."

"Go to sleep," she said. "You're still sick."

"I don't think so," said Sonny.

She held out her hands, and he moved her fingers inside his mouth again. She stroked the inside of his lips. Yes. That's what it was. Agonizing love. That's what it felt like, something that could make you sense exquisite things in your gums. And where else? Where else could she touch him, where nobody had ever been? What if she went away before she showed him?

"Please don't go away."

"I didn't say I was leaving."

"You didn't say you wouldn't."

"Well I won't," she said.

She brought him breakfast on a tray she had found behind some hotel dishes. He had bought the tray himself, because it had been a hopeful thought in his head that one day someone might bring him something on a tray. They had done that at Colonel Reeling's house for him. They had rapped on his bedroom door, and opened heavy printed drapes in front of the windows, and let the light stream in on him, while someone brought him breakfast on a tray.

It had thrilled him, literally thrilled him, sent juices up to his head that made him alert before he was fully awake. There had been four days like that, and every one ended with his going to bed early, because he was tired from working on the Pape case, he had said. But the truth was he wanted to go to sleep so he would be ready to enjoy the morning when it came. Morning. He had never loved morning until he got to the Reelings, and they brought him breakfast on a tray. He had never loved morning before that. Not that he could remember.

And now she was bringing morning to him, on a tray. And she was looking at him with those eyes, filled with caring and warmth and concern. Even admiration, as sick as he was. He felt almost convinced that he was remarkable, that he was intelligent and appealing and handsome and fine—all the things a man should be. He only wanted a verbal confirmation of the "buy" order before beginning the proceedings of selling his soul.

"I love you," he said.

"It's the fever."

"The fever's almost gone."

"It's the after-effects of the fever."

"It's you," said Sonny. "What are we going to do about your husband?"

"My husband's dead."

"I'm sorry."

"I'm not." She sat up, strangely prim on the chair. "He was burned in a fire in the woods where our cabin was. He and his secretary. They found them sealed together. Pretty picture. I wish he had lived and gotten over her, but I can't be sure he would have. So that's how I have to remember him. On fire with her."

"Make love to me," Sonny said. "Let me make love to you."

"Pity?"

"Are you kidding me?" said Sonny. "Have you ever felt your skin?"

"You're a sick man."

"Not anymore." Sonny smiled at her. "Come. I won't infect you. We don't have to kiss."

"Oh, yes we do," whispered Catherine, and fell into his mouth.

"I want to spend the rest of my life with you," Sonny said, against the silky roundness of her breast.

"We made love," said Catherine. "That's all we did, was make love."

"Not like any I've ever made."

"You're an innocent," she said. "That's only a beginning."

"Then I'll need all the experience I can get. I want you to marry me."

"You born romantics are all alike."

"You think I'm like everybody else you've ever known?"

"I think you're like no one else."

"Then you better marry me."

"We have time. We have time, my dear. There's plenty of time."

"Not if you're going to teach me everything I have to know to be good enough for you."

"I'm not so good. I'm a very bitter woman."

"You taste very sweet to me. I want to spend my life with you."

"So did Charley. Only he got burned to death with his secretary. It's hard to spend your life with your wife when you've been burned to death with your secretary."

"I'm going to wipe that out of your head. I'll wipe it out of your body."

"A romantic notion."

"I'm not a romantic anymore. I'm a very realistic man."

"Not so bright for someone so smart. You should learn to recognize romantic moments and let them go by without framing them forever. Snatching at them. You can't be the scourge of Wall Street and have a romantic nature, or you'll go crazy."

"That's why I'll need you to keep me sane."

"It's too late for that, you're already crazy," Catherine laughed. "Wanting to marry me."

"Are you crazy?" Arnold shouted when they were in the office Monday morning. "What do you mean, you want to marry her? How long have you known her? Three days."

"She doesn't want to marry me. She says it's too soon."

"Then she's smarter than you are."

"That's why I have to marry her," Sonny said.

"You're full of shit. You fucking greenhead. You bouncing baby boy. Don't you think I have eyes? Don't you think I can see what happened? A woman touches you right and you forget everything."

"It goes deeper than that."

"The hell it does," Arnold ranted. "Do you forget who you are, what you are, what you're going to be?"

"I'm going to be hers. I want to belong to her."

"Nobody belongs to anybody," Arnold said. "There are no more slaves."

"No conscription into slavery," Sonny said. "People can still volunteer."

"You have to be out of your head to volunteer to get killed."

"She won't kill me."

"Why don't you really start living, and then you can get all you need from different women."

"That works for you, Arnold. It doesn't work for me."

"Because you're a greenhead," Arnold shouted.

"I don't know what that means."

"It's a person whose head just got off the boat." Arnold blew some of the anger out through his nose. "I made it up."

"Don't be so angry."

"*Angry!*" Arnold threw over the umbrella stand (French, eighteenth century, Raphael Hawthorne, Parke-Bernet). "You don't want me to be angry. You're so stupid, you want to marry a woman old enough to be your mother, and on top of that you expect my blessing?"

"She's thirty-eight."

"That's closer to forty than thirty, and you're thirty and I'm almost forty, and I'm telling you she's old enough to be your mother."

"I don't remember my mother," Sonny said.

"Oh shit," said Arnold.

"But I remember Catherine. I can smell her. I can still feel her. And you, Arnold, have only seen her once."

They had had dinner at the Big House. Catherine had protested Sonny's going out so soon, but he had insisted, begged her to let him seem masterful and fearless. He had called Sarah and told her to fix something special, he was bringing home his bride-to-be. ("You're crazy," Catherine had whispered, kissing his naked back.) Sarah almost had a seizure on the telephone. But she was so glad to know Sonny was coming for dinner and it wasn't even Friday, that there was some way to ensure Arnold's staying home, she just laughed and laughed and laughed.

"I only needed to see her once," said Arnold. "She's a lovely woman, pleasant, very warm. But she's a widow, her husband died screwing another woman, she tells you that the first time she meets you at dinner, for Christ's sake, it must be eating her heart out. She'll never forgive him, and she'll never forgive you. She'll make your life a fucking hell, brother, you better believe me."

"I don't."

"But you're wrong. The whole thing is a mistake. She doesn't want to marry you, you told me that yourself; she's smart. I got to give her that. She's got a lot more sense than you do."

"I'm willing to wait. Not too long. But I'm willing to wait a little. And then I'll marry her. I'll go down on my knees and plead with her to marry me. And she will. And I don't want you angry."

"She's older than you by a lot more than years," Arnold said. "You're a goddamn baby boy where sex is concerned."

"I'm learning," Sonny said. "I'm still a very quick study."

"She'll lead you around by the nose, Sonny boy. I've seen this kind of thing happening and I don't want it happening to you. Let me introduce you to some nice young girls. No whores, Abie. Nice young girls with pretty eyes in pretty young faces on pretty young bodies."

"I think Catherine's pretty. I think she's better than pretty."

"Sure, she's pretty," Arnold conceded. "But she's old. She's as old as I am, and I feel like your father."

"She doesn't feel like my mother."

"What the hell do you know?" Arnold said. "You don't even remember your mother. Let me introduce you to some nice young girls."

"You don't know any nice young girls."

"Then I'll find them," Arnold said. "We can start looking for them together. Nights out on the town. Like the old days. New again. The Sterne brothers together, plenty of laughs, and only occasional arguments with headwaiters. Come on." Arnold hugged his brother for the first time since he had called him "whore." "Come on, come on, brother mine, the beaches of Ceylon are waiting. We'll go to Ceylon."

"What about the war?"

"What about the war? The war'll be over in a week. It's been on a year, and the economy is booming. So it's served its purpose. People are tired of it. They're bored already. It'll be over in a week, in time to get them home for Christmas. You'll see."

"How about the fact that we don't seem to be winning?"

"Ridiculous!" Arnold said. "Americans don't lose. It's against our way of life. It's overturning the Constitution. It's like having a President who's a crook or throwing a baseball game. The war'll be over in a week, and we'll go to the beaches of Ceylon. Together. Sterne and Sterne, what do you say?"

"What if it isn't over?"

"Then we'll go anyway," Arnold said. "A little thing like a World War can't interfere with our travels."

"I'm marrying her."

"She's *old*."

"She's beautiful and caring. She took beautiful care of me."

"You balloon. You big head full of air. Thank God every day of your life you're a strong man, or you would have gone to the hospital and fallen in love with your nurse."

"I'm not that much of a target."

"Not anymore. Fortunately now you're rich enough so you can have home care."

"That's right, Arnold. That's as rich as I ever want to be."

"That's *now!*" Arnold screamed. "That's *now!* A greenhead who never had it good before so his goddamn sense falls out."

"I don't want to continue the discussion."

"Then don't see her anymore."

"I'm marrying her."

"Listen," Arnold said. "I swear. I don't want to fight with you. I love you. Like a brother." He laughed. "Please, Abe, listen to me, the woman isn't for you. It's hard to listen when you think you've fallen in love. But that wonderful glow you seem to see is called paleness, Sonny, not enough blood. That's a very weak woman."

"Now who sounds like a mother?" Sonny laughed. "You're trying to play on my sense of superstition. That's the sense I lost, Arnold. I was superstitious I'd never find a woman like that, and now I know I was wrong. Somebody I can love with all my soul can love me back. All things are possible. If she's weak, I'll make her strong."

"And if she's old, will you make her young?"

"I'll try," Sonny said. "I'll break my ass trying."

"That's what you're going to do, is break your ass."

"We'll see."

"You'll see. I won't be here to see."

"Where are you going?" Afraid. Again. Just starting to grow up, and afraid again.

"I'm getting a commission in the Air Force."

"You spent most of this year trying to make sure you weren't going to get in."

"I changed my mind," Arnold said. "I ought to go and fight for this country as long as the war's going to be over in a week." He was putting on his jacket and his tie, in the middle of the day. "This country's been good to me." For the first time since he'd called Sonny "whore" he was putting on his jacket and his tie, and they were going out to lunch together. His hair was starting to get gray at the sides, he was getting a commission, and they were going out to lunch.

"What if it isn't over in a week?"

"I'll do the best I can not to get killed."

"I'm joining with you."

"Stop being so courageous," Arnold said, laughing, hugging his brother, holding him around the neck, pulling him toward him with laughter. "What am I going to do with you? How can you be so smart and act so dumb?"

"Who's dumb?" Sonny asked. "You're the one who said you'd have to be out of your head to volunteer to get killed."

"I was talking about women, not war."

"Killed is killed, Arnold. What difference does it make to the one who's dead how it happened?"

"I'm not going to get killed," Arnold said. "No war could kill me."

"I'm not going to get killed either. No woman could kill me."

"The right one could," said Arnold. "I know you."

"Maybe Catherine isn't the right one, we could always hope for that."

"Yeah," said Arnold. "I guess we could hope for that."

"Maybe I'll never find the right one. I'll marry Catherine and she'll protect me from ever finding the right one."

"Nothing can protect you from that, baby brother. If there's a dame out there that can kill you, she'll find you somehow."

"Try to have a little less confidence in me," Sonny said, and hugged his brother. "Why are you going to war?"

"Di Bonaven and the boys thought it might be a very good thing on my record, in 'forty-six. That's the first year I can run."

"What if you're hurt?"

"I'm not going to get hurt. It'll be a cushy desk job, they've promised me. Something that only looks risky and brave in the records. Anyway, the thing'll be over in a week."

"I'm joining with you."

"It isn't the foreign legion, Beau Geste. It isn't some Arabian Night. There's a war on out there, with bullets and bombs."

"I've already tried to join."

"No shit," said Arnold. "Well you can't. Your blood pressure's too high and you're overweight. And as if that weren't enough, you've got a punctured eardrum. You better have a punctured eardrum, I paid five yards to the doctor and a grand and a half to the head of your friendly draft board."

"What doctor? What draft board?"

"The one where you went to volunteer. I got friends all over this town, Sonny. You don't go in and try and join the Army without telling me and expect I'm not going to know. Stay here."

He patted Sonny's shoulder. "Somebody's got to watch the store."

"What if anything happens to you?"

"Nothing can happen to me," Arnold said, putting on his overcoat. "Let's go to lunch. The war'll be over in a week."

SEVEN

THEY WERE LIVING in an apartment between West End Avenue and Broadway, within walking distance of P.S. 9, which was wonderful for Chris. Evelyn had checked around and found it was considered the best public school in Manhattan, and the public schools in New York City were at the top of the list. It was also within walking distance of Zabar's Delicatessen, good for Walter.

He did not go to Zabar's every evening. Some he spent with Harvey and Wandra Kane at their apartment, some with his commanding officer, Admiral Foley, a cheery, white-haired, blue-eyed Irishman with a fine sense of humor, especially for a chief in the intrigue business. They called it Intelligence, but it was fast moving into intrigue, Walter could sense that. The end of the war was very close, within the year, the Admiral advised Walter very whisperly, so it was very important to line up the countries that might be pulled away in the aftermath.

"We're going to need some heavyweights in China," the Admiral told him. "Meat-eaters. Too much going on there that's divisive. They're holding together because the Japanese are their natural traditional enemies—common enemies make common friends. But historical axioms can blow sky-high when you take a giant step into the future."

"A giant step how, sir?"

"That needn't concern us, for the moment. Let's just speculate if the pattern of war, alliances, politics, if all possible past experiences we have to draw upon were suddenly cracked apart." Admiral Foley walked to the pull-down map at the back of his office, took a pointer, and aimed it at Asia. "Humpty Dumpty. All the king's men. A whole new substructure of foes." He shook his head. "Napoleon warned us that China was a sleeping dog. But how about these little puppies here?" He indicated several countries that were not to be paid attention to by the American public for six, then twenty years, when it became their turn to nearly tear the world apart, with some help from their cousins across several seas.

"Life is cheap in the Orient. They don't care if they live or die, but Americans do. That's why we'll need you to go to the Far East when it's over. You've been with these people."

"It wasn't exactly social, sir."

"I know that, White, but you've got a head start on practically everybody knowing how to deal with them."

"The Far East," Walter said softly.

"Not of course till the ending of the conflict."

"The ending of the conflict," Walter repeated thoughtfully. "I really have to go, sir. I promised my wife. I got home late last night."

"It would mean the future. Yours. Your family's. Maybe even your country's. You're not a small man, White. You can't just have your eye on the present."

"You're right, sir," Walter said, and sat down to talk with the Admiral for a while longer.

He heard about Roosevelt in the subway.

He walked, shoulders back, chest high, up the steps of the Eighty-sixth Street subway station. He marched, at sorrowful ease, to his apartment house. "Five, please," he said to the elevator operator. A full-time elevator man—no longer a reliance on the angry inconstancies of the super. Everything starting to be the way he had hoped it would be, a full-time elevator man and a full-scale career plan after the war. His only regret was that his father and Roosevelt couldn't be there to see.

"Have you heard?" he said very softly, as he opened the door with his key.

"Of course I heard." Evelyn got up and took a cigarette out of her black calfskin purse, the one Wandra Kane had helped her get wholesale. "Your daughter's been in the bedroom for an hour, sobbing and writing a poem. Sobbing and writing a poem. I thought you said you'd get home early. Do you call this early?"

"This is when I usually leave, Evelyn, I swear it."

"Over my dead body?"

He took his officer's cap and laid it upside down on the bookcase next to the door.

"I didn't dust today," Evelyn said, indicating the top of the bookcase with her eyes. "I didn't feel like dusting. What did you feel like doing?" She pinned him with her irises.

"Evelyn, for heaven's sake, I got away the minute I could."

"What exact minute was that? I called your office at three-fifteen, and you were gone. Who were you with, the Admiral?"

"Well, as a matter of fact . . ."

"How long do you think you can keep pulling this on me? Your secretary wasn't available either. Where did you take her, Casanova? Down in a submarine off the Brooklyn Navy Yard?"

"Will you stop? Will you ever stop? I *was* with Admiral Foley. He made me an incredible offer for after the war."

"The war can't end, ask your daughter. There's no room for anything but sadness. Her whole life she's known only one President, and he died on her."

"I'm sorry."

"I bet you are, you cheating son of a bitch."

"Evelyn, I was with the Admiral."

"Discussing your *deal?*" She slanted her head so she could observe him sideways.

"It isn't a deal. It's a very complex career change. The possibilities are enormous, better money than I ever hoped for, and the chance for advancement . . ."

"What exactly is it?"

"I can't tell you," he said. "It's undercover."

"I'll bet it is." She threw his mother's picture on the floor, shattering the glass, and stepped on it. Then she ran to the bathroom and locked herself in.

"Will you listen!" he shouted through the door, pounding. "I swore that I'd never tell anyone, but you've got to believe me. It'll involve some work with Chiang Kai-shek's people after the war, and I'll probably have to go as something else, not really American Armed Forces, you understand. Red Cross. Something like that."

"And who will be your date for this dance, Clara Barton?"

"I swear it! I swear it!" he pleaded against the door. He turned as he heard the click from the bedroom and saw Chris.

"Oh, hello, sweetheart. How's your poem coming?"

"Daddy!" She ran to him, sobbing. "Isn't it awful?"

"We're not really fighting," Walter said. "We're just having a discussion."

"You know about President Roosevelt?"

"Yes." Walter hugged her. "That's what happens."

"But why to him?"

"It happens to everybody."

The door to the bathroom opened behind him. Evelyn was standing there in a chartreuse belted silk bathrobe, cutting the rays behind her with the thrust of her elegant figure. "Everybody but your father," she said. "Your father gets drowned three times by the Japanese and lives to tell the tale. My luck."

"Shut up," said Walter.

"To tell the tale and get the Navy Cross." She leaned back

against the sink and started laughing. "And now," she gasped, "and now . . ." the choking laughter. "Now they want him to be a spy."

"I never said that!" Walter's cheeks were flaming. "Don't listen to her, Chrissie, it isn't true."

"You bet your ass it isn't true."

He caught Evelyn in his arms and whispered into her hair, "It's true, it's true, I swear to God, but I swore I wouldn't tell, so don't tell her, for God's sake, she's a child, she'll tell everybody. She might even be endangering her own life."

"Cut out that *crap!*" Evelyn shrieked. "They don't use fairies for spies. I read an article where a fairy can be very easily blackmailed."

"Get out of here, Chris," he said. "Get out." He threw Evelyn to the floor.

"Call the police!" Evelyn screamed, as her forehead landed on the scale.

Chris pulled at the back of her father's pants.

"Get out of here," he said, and pushed her backwards.

"The phone," groaned Evelyn.

Walter was there first, pulling the wire from the wall. "Stay out of this, Chrissie, I'm warning you. I'm telling you this for your own good."

"Don't listen to him!" screamed Evelyn from behind the bathroom door, which she had locked again. "Go call the police."

"Be quiet, Evelyn," he said with something like calm. "If you stop now, I'll let it go."

"Well, aren't you generous!" she spat at him, a tiny echo from all the tile around her. "You wouldn't even give your child a nickel to call the police, and now you're adding to your magnanimous gesture by not killing me. What more could a woman ask?"

"What do you want from me?" he pleaded.

"The truth!" she shrieked. "The truth and the money for child-support you've owed me for three years."

"Open the door," he said. "I'm going to kill you."

"You'll hurt your career as a *spy*," she sang. "Everybody will know you killed your wife, it'll be in the *Daily News*," she chanted. "That'll be a very hard 'cover' to use, don't you think, an escaped murderer? I don't think the Chinese will be too comfortable with that."

"Don't say any more."

"Wait a second," she said. "I have to put on my Malay boot. You know, the one that gets tighter and tighter while they ask me if I can give them any information about my husband, the spy." She started to laugh again, very loud.

"Here's a quarter," Walter said to Chris. "Go get some ice cream."

"Call the police!" Evelyn shouted to her daughter, and started to cry. "An officer and a gentleman and a secret agent in the foreign service. Oh, my God, how easily can people be fooled."

"Evelyn, please, don't cry, I swear it. I swear on it all."

"You're a cheat and a profiteer," she wept. "You've been cheating and profiteering from the day I married you. Why should I believe you'd stop at a little thing like lies?"

"What profiteering?" he said. "What profiteering?"

"Don't you think I know about you and Harvey Kane?"

"Go," Walter said to Chris, as he started to throw his whole weight rhythmically against the door.

When she saw that the hinges were starting to give slightly, Chris ran out of the apartment.

"She's gone now," Walter said, breathing very hard. "She's gone and I'm going to kill you if you don't tell me what you meant. *Tell me what you meant.*"

"I mean that you and Harvey Kane haven't buddied up because of a common interest in wolfhounds. That's what I mean. If you kill me, Wandra will know. She knows you have a deal with Harvey, that he's paying you off to let him have secret tips."

"That's a lie!" Walter said. "I would never give anyone information that might hurt this country."

"How about if it didn't hurt this country but helped Harvey Kane, who in turn put a few dollars in the pocket of Lieutenant-

Commander Walter M. White, D.D.S., U.S.N., S.O.B.?"

He brushed off his pants and broke the door open. She had a metal nail file in her hand.

"Put it down," he said.

"How could you think for one minute that I could believe this about you?" She pricked the tip of her finger with the nail file. "How can you believe I'd be stupid enough to buy this picture with no eyes. Walter M. White, Super Patriot. I'd be willing to bet four years of nonpayment of child-support that you might even have thrown Harvey an order, maybe directed a little business his way."

"I am an officer in the United States Navy."

"You're a Roumanian," Evelyn said. "You've got to be crooked."

When the police came, Chris was waiting in the lobby. She had spent the quarter calling them, not even stopping for change on the way to the pay phone at Whelan's, although she knew Evelyn would probably be mad at her for that later on.

"Five, please, Felix," said Chris, stepping into the elevator as if she were not accompanied by two policemen.

"Sure," Felix said, trying to seem as casual about it as she was. He wondered as he opened the grilled elevator doors if they had settled it between them again, or if she was dead. No. Nobody ever got killed in this neighborhood.

"Mama," Chris said, pounding on the door. "Mother!" She rang the doorbell frantically. *"Evelyn!"* she said, screaming.

"Ye-es," sang a voice from inside. "Who *is* it?"

"Mama, are you all right?"

"Of course, I'm all right, dear, did you lose your key?"

"I forgot it," said Chris.

"Well, you shouldn't be in such a hurry." Evelyn turned the lock inside the door, opened it slightly so the right half of her face showed. "My goodness! Policemen. What's going on here?"

"Your little girl said your husband was beating you, Mrs. White."

"She said that?" Evelyn asked with wonder, scolding Chris with the lowering of her eye. "Oh, Chrissie, I'm surprised at you. No. I don't suppose that's altogether fair. She's had a very upsetting day." Evelyn smiled at the two uniforms. "The President, you know."

The policemen lowered their eyes, understanding.

"The President, and living in this building, I suppose. Did you happen to notice the plaque on the wall outside?"

"No, we didn't," the younger officer said. "We came here in a kind of a hurry."

"Well, be sure and look at it on your way out. On this very site lived Edgar Allan Poe, and while he was living here, he composed 'The Raven.' My husband loves reading plaques and Edgar Allan Poe. You understand." She smiled. "It's bound to have some effect on her. The plaque. The President. 'The Raven.' She's a child. She writes poetry." Evelyn tilted her head up very slowly, so only the taller ones present could catch the next words she would mouth. "She's crazy," her lips went.

"I see," said one of the policemen.

"Sorry you were troubled unnecessarily," said Evelyn, as she pulled Chris inside the door and shut it. The left side of her face had a dark blue welt on it, and her eye was closed.

"Mama!"

"I told you never to call me that. I'm much too young to be anyone's mama. Why did you call the police?"

"You told me to," Chris said, and started to cry.

"Oh, honey." Evelyn hugged her tight. "You know you shouldn't listen to me when I'm in one of my moods."

The poem was not one of Chris' best efforts. She had tried for the diction of "Oh Captain, My Captain," but it was a little too lofty, she couldn't make that much of a speech in rhyme. Especially with her eyes burning with grief, and Evelyn and Walter going at it—this time with love sounds—in the bedroom. She finally settled on an invocation to the heavens, because she had just found out what invoking the heavens meant. She thought if God was there being riddled with pleas, He should keep an eye out for FDR.

She arrived at school with the poem folded neatly in hand, on a piece of lined paper, in case anybody wanted to hear a poem. Miss Burns, her teacher, a tight-lipped woman in her fifties, saw how swollen Chris' eyes were, and the paper clutched in her hand.

"I suppose you're in mourning for That Man," she said, while Chris hung her coat up in the closet to the side of the wooden-desked room. "I suppose you've been crying all night with the rest of the deluded Democrats. You have any idea what he did to this country?"

"Yes, Miss Burns," Chris said. Miss Burns was always asking Chris if she knew what plagiarism was, and did she really expect a woman of Miss Burns' years to be fooled.

Chris had, of course, looked up plagiarism in the dictionary, and presented herself back to Miss Burns, saying no, she didn't plagiarize, the words were all her own.

"And no help from your parents, I suppose," Miss Burns had said.

"No."

So Miss Burns had made her sit down and write a poem, there on the spot, in the back of the classroom, behind the desks that were wedged into runners on the floor, right underneath the American flag and the map of the world, the explorers' routes. Chris had worked for an hour and handed Miss Burns a ten-stanza ballad about tyranny, using for examples Hitler, Mussolini, Tojo, the witch in Hansel and Gretel, old sour people who did not love children, and teachers who turned to teaching not because they wanted to teach anybody anything worthwhile, but because they had nowhere else to go and so turned to tyrannizing their pupils instead of teaching them.

Miss Burns tore the eight pages into sixty-four. Chris tried to retrieve them at the end of the day, but Miss Burns had already emptied the wastepaper basket.

Since that time, Chris had not shown her poetry to Miss Burns.

The day after Roosevelt died, April 13, 1945, there was a special assembly. The rolling doors, which moved into place on their runners, dividing the whole of the third floor into classrooms, were pushed back now to convert it into a hall.

"Young lady, if you say one word," Miss Burns hissed behind her on the metal-bannistered stone stairway, "one word about That Man, if you start your sentimental heartbroken mewling over the loss of that communist . . ."

Chris held her head straight and tried to catch the eye of Joey Shapiro, with whom she was in love, but he was talking to Glenda. Glenda's uncle made Frozen Malteds, The Drink You Could Eat With A Spoon, near the Loew's 83rd Street Theater, so she had a definite edge with everyone in the class.

"I'm warning you, missy. Not a word. You hear me?"

"Are you talking to me, Miss Burns?" Chris said.

They had reached the double doors into the assembly hall, and Joey Shapiro was pushing the door open for Glenda. Chris ran so she might get in on the push and touch his arm, but he let the door go in her face. She thrust herself against it, bursting with energy to escape Miss Burns, and smiled when she saw Mrs. Schatteles, the principal, on the platform. Whenever Chris had a poem she hoped was really important, she made an appointment with Mrs. Schatteles and read it to her.

The classes moved to their different areas of the assembly hall, pledged their allegiance, and sang "The Star-Spangled Banner." Chris kept saluting all the way through the national anthem, because the poem was in her right hand and she couldn't be sure Mrs. Schatteles had had a chance to see.

When the students were seated, Mrs. Schatteles made a brief, tender speech about Roosevelt, the meaning of greatness, the tragedy of death, to which nobody in the assembly hall paid too much attention. Chris sat weeping over her piece of paper.

"Chris?" The principal was looking at her. "Have you anything to add to the program?"

"Excuse me?" she said, and looked over her shoulder in Miss Burns' direction.

"Is that a poem you have?"

Chris nodded.

"Then come up and let us hear it."

She stood and the wooden pull-down seat behind her sprung closed. She walked up the two wooden steps to the small platform, trying not to trip. She stepped to the small microphone on the speaker's stand, opened the paper, and read, and cried. She cried because Roosevelt was dead, and the words were very emotional, and Joey Shapiro loved Glenda, and Miss Burns would probably beat her up after assembly, and the poem was good for a little girl to write, but he should have had more than that, he should have had Walt Whitman, only not so excited.

"Thank you," said Mrs. Schatteles. "That's a very lovely poem."

"I don't think it's a lovely poem," Miss Burns said, keeping Chris in during recess. Down below, outside, where the black asphalt play yard was, Chris could hear some of her classmates laughing, and Joey Shapiro being in love with Glenda. "I think it's a stupid poem. He was a very stupid man."

"Stop it," Chris said, crying freely now, because she was not just in mourning and miserable in love, she was terrified.

"It is the end of this poem, you understand. Throw it away."

"No."

"What do you think you're going to do with it, lady?"

"I'm going to publish it in *The John Jasper Journal*."

"Not on your life, you're not. Not the way it is. Let me look at that poem."

"No. You'll rip it up. You'll rip it up the way you did the poem I wrote in class."

"What poem you wrote in class? You never wrote a poem in class. I don't believe you ever wrote your own poems."

"Give me a piece of paper, I'll write you one."

"Don't you start with me again." Miss Burns wheeled on her own fury. "Let me see that poem."

"What do you want to see?"

"That verse. That especially stupid verse about his being weak."

"I'll read it to you," Chris said.

> "Some people said he was not strong
> And that he couldn't help us along
> But God we know they all were wrong
> Keep him, dear God
>   Forever in Thy Kingdom."

"What do you mean, but God we *know* they were all wrong. Who do you think you are to *know?* How do you *know* you aren't the one who was mistaken? You're too young. What do you *know!* Roosevelt was a terrible man, a blight on this country."

It became an argument that raged all the way up to the principal's office by two o'clock that afternoon. The glass door to Mrs. Schatteles' office was opened by the secretary, and Chris went inside.

"Well, Chris," said Mrs. Schatteles. "I hear you're having a little misunderstanding with Miss Burns."

"It's not a misunderstanding."

"I hear the argument is over a word. She only wants you to change one word, and then she'll let you submit it to the school magazine."

"It's a very important word," Chris said. "She wants me to change it from 'God we *know* they all were wrong' to 'God we *think* they all were wrong.' If you're making a prayer for him to get into heaven, you have to be pretty sure he deserves it, you can't just *think.* She hates him. She's glad he's dead. I can't change it to 'think.' "

"Isn't there another word besides 'know' that you could use, that wouldn't spoil the poem?"

" 'Feel'?" Chris asked. "Does that sound strong enough. 'But God we *feel* they all were wrong'? *Know* sounds better."

"Not to Miss Burns," said Mrs. Schatteles. She picked up a

pencil, leaned back into the wooden captain's swivel chair, and smiled. "Chris, sometimes in life we have to compromise."

"Why?"

"Because this is the world, and we live in the world. There are a lot of people in the world. Not all of them are ever going to agree with you at one time. That means if you want to argue with all of them, you'll be arguing all the time.

"Choose your battles. Try to make sure they're very important. Save your energy for victories that count. Okay?" She took the round chin in her palm and lifted Chris' face. "I love your poem."

"Even with the change?"

"Even with the change."

EIGHT

DEPENDING on how deep a sense of irony he allowed himself to
have on different days, Arnold considered it funny sometimes
that he had been sent overseas. With all his connections, all the
people making sure that nothing real could happen to him as far
as the war was concerned, he still ended up with bombs exploding around him when he was on the ground, and shrapnel splitting the sky outside his plane.

It was a desk job all right: he was doing some public relations
for the Air Force. But they kept sending his desk all over the
place so he could talk to various generals, and find out how the
war was going.

He knew exactly how it was going. He read the papers every
day from his base in London, when they let him be based, where
the bombs kept buzzing around him, exploding on other people,
but still making him uneasy. He wrote a letter to Rosey di

Bonaven, asking him if the Party had ever gotten a Senator elected posthumously, and then explained what posthumously meant. He listened to Edward R. Murrow, and the other broadcasters brave enough to send their warnings, their accurate reports, their emotional descriptions of the horrors of war, from England. Arnold swam in the rhetoric of Winston Churchill, and knew very well how noble and complex was the quest of the Allied Forces. So he didn't really need to go flying around to see the generals, as handy as knowing the generals might come in after the war.

After the war was only good if you came back from the war. Up in the air, the way they made him be too often to suit his taste or sense of fearlessness, you made an easy target. He did not wear a parachute when he flew. If the plane was going to get hit, it meant that the charmed part of his life was over, and he didn't expect to survive any more than the charmed part.

Besides, he had managed to skip through a large part of the training at Airborne School, never really expecting to be Airborne, or Airdied. The greatest danger he had faced in training was when they tried to get him to parachute from a plane. He had seen one man Roman-candle. He had watched one young lieutenant—alive, and seemingly bright, and genuinely enthusiastic about fighting for America, and unafraid—show him what a snap it was, you just hooked up your clip, waited for the door to open, and then went zinging out of there for the jump—
WHEEEEE!!

Except that the parachute never opened. That was to say, it opened, but did not billow full. The air did not catch the silken folds, or maybe there was a slash in the chute, Arnold never found out. He just watched a young man who might have become his friend plummeting toward the earth, trailing a complex of unsupporting strands, a marionette whose puppeteer had lost interest.

Arnold wrote to the family of the lieutenant. They were from New York, potential constituents, but Arnold didn't think about that until after he mailed the letter. He tried to write about it as if it had been a heroic ending, and not just a wasted life. Not part of his job, writing letters to the newly bereaved. But he was a captain, and that made him higher up than a lieutenant, especially one who had dug a tunnel with the force of his own body twenty feet into the ground.

People did not believe they could really die; the moment of actual death was beyond their comprehension, and that was what made heroes. Arnold knew very well he could die; he intended doing nothing heroic. Nothing heroic, even by accident.

But he did write the family of the lost lieutenant that their son had died bravely, in the service of his country. He did not let himself stop to examine how brave the young man really had felt with the ground rushing up toward him, and plenty of time to feel fear. Too far away from the ears of the other trainees for them to hear the screaming.

"Your son saved my life," he wrote in the letter, because he wanted to give some stature to pointless death. After the war, he promised them, he would try and visit them if he made it back.

He did not write that the young man had saved his life demonstrating how foolish it was to be brave. The full details of the actual death were left to the commanding officer at the base. Arnold's letter was only to give them some dreams and one extra memory to hang on to, to store by the window that held the Gold Star.

So he never learned to parachute, pulled enough strings so he wouldn't have to: better the strings should be pulled than the strings should fail to hold up. That he had actually been sent to the European Theater (where was the laughter, where was the music, where were the chandeliers?) was a terrible angry joke. He intended letting it be played on him with as much grace as possible, so he could get to the punchline and enjoy it, too. Applaud at the fact that he was still alive, surviving a war he considered madness, except in terms of how much it had improved the economy. He hated being a part of someone else's notion, a pawn in a game that had shifting rules. It was only when you drew up the playing instructions yourself that you could control the moves. When the war was over, he would draw up a new set of guidelines, some excellent rules, to be broken only if he wanted them broken. Meanwhile, he got friendly with generals, sending them cases of Joe Pape's Finest, asking them how the war was going.

It was going pretty well, for a war: the Allied liberation of France was a *fait accompli*, according to the diction of the country. Arnold decided when he was due for a leave to see Paris. He heard the wine was as good as any he'd ever tasted, and the girls were the same. He loaded up on real silk stockings (it was too late to weave them into a parachute). Life was for the living. Stockings were for shapely legs that would wind themselves around him. Much too easy and infantile to regret, and stock up on Hershey bars.

Paris was still too heavy with the stench of occupation and collaboration and urine to give him the breath of spring he had heard about in the songs. He stayed at a little inn in Bougiville, twenty-five minutes from the city by jeep. There were flowers blooming in the garden outside his window, geraniums gobbling up the earth with no ashes on it. Flowers continued to grow, that was amazing. Flowers didn't know there was a war on, when even children did.

The child who lived at the inn was fifteen, and her eyes were already filled with more disappointment than Arnold's were at forty. Her father and mother had been killed on their farm in a bombing; she did not know if the plane had been German or American or British. She did not really care.

"N'importe," she said to Arnold, when he asked her, in his limited French. She struggled to learn English so she could talk to him, because there was no one she really could speak with at the inn except the grandparents who ran it, and when they talked to her they only saw her parents, and tears filled their eyes.

"You should know who was responsible for their death," Arnold said. "It helps to be sure who to be angry at."

"Je ne comprends pas," she said.

"I don't understand," instructed Arnold.

"I don't understand," she said very slowly, pink lips moving around the edges of the words.

She had long straight hair, the flax that fairy tales were made

of, and it moved in a piece when she shook her head. Her skin
had the tone of a newly ripening peach, fresh, never touched,
sitting in a gift box, framed by the curtain of her hair. Her feet
and her clothes were sometimes dirty, but her hair was always
clean.

He wondered how she kept it so shiny, if at some time, young
as she was, she had collaborated, or her grandparents had, to
reap such a wealth of soap. But these were not the questions he
could ask her within the limitations of language, the boundaries
of compassion.

So he spoke with her of simple things, and they taught each
other simple words. He told her her hair was very white, and her
eyes were very green. She told him he was a fine gentleman, very
handsome. He told her in the imperative, which he hoped was
really polite (with the aid of an Army booklet on making friends
in French), not to be afraid.

"N'ayez pas peur," he said, and saw from her smile he had
used the wrong mode of address. She was still just a child, he
should speak to her in the familiar. "Don't be afraid."

"Afraid?" she said unsurely. "Afraid *de quoi*."

"Afraid de anything," he said, and laughed and looked up the
word.

They spent the mornings exchanging language and feelings,
expressed the best they could. They walked through the countryside, and she pointed out the streams that webbed it. She washed
her feet in a brook that sang its way across rocks, and made him
take his shoes off. Took his shoes off for him.

"Relax-ay vous," she said, the way he said it, and smiled at
him. Her smile was a cluster of happy innocence, giving a bright
contradiction to whatever experience saddened her eyes.

Afternoons he went into town and found a whore. He did not
make the mistake of seeing the same woman twice, no matter
how good she was. He was not going to be stupid enough to
attach himself in any way to anyone, just because he was grateful
for being alive, happy to feel his energy juices surging into a
woman. When he was over the momentary euphoria of recon-
firming the strength between his legs, he would pay them and

give them a pair of silk stockings, not even inviting any of them to dinner, which he ate alone.

After the first three days of his leave, he stopped dining in town. The food the grandmother cooked at the inn was excellent. At the end of the third day he was eager to return there by early evening, loaded up with Hershey bars and soap, and some sweet-smelling shampoo.

"This is for you," he said, giving it all to the child. Jeanne. As in Jeanne d'Arc? he had asked her. *Oui,* Jeanne d'Arc, she had smiled at him, glowing. *Mais non,* he had said, Jeanne Light.

"*Pour vous,* Jeanne Light."

"*Pour toi,*" she corrected softly. "*Il faut que tu me dises 'toi.' *"

"*Il faut que . . . ?*"

"*Subjonctif,* you must." She had spent the afternoon with his language manual, learning it the other way around. "You must to address me in the familiar."

Of course. She was a child, and a child had to be spoken to in the familiar. That was the reason he had to speak to her so. She was a child. A child. A year younger than his son. She might have been his own daughter, without bombs falling, with fairy tale genes, palely glowing, coming from his sperm. Out of Sarah, by miracles.

"Do you want me?" she asked the next morning. They were walking in the woods. She had brought the shampoo and the one big towel that had been in Arnold's room. She wanted to wash her hair in the brook. Shampoo, shampoo, she'd never seen it before. She loved the word, she loved the way the thick jelly felt on her finger. She wanted to wait till she got to the brook to try it on her hair.

"Do you want me?" she asked him again, while he pretended not to hear her, looked at the trees, at leaves insisting that spring was actually happening. She said it very clearly, but she didn't understand what she was saying, Arnold was sure. Arnold wanted to be sure.

He had never let a principle stand in the way of something he wanted. But he never corrupted anyone innocent, not even Sonny. Sure, he had tried to lure Sonny away from too much purity, because a man could not live in the business world with his feet anchored firmly in the clouds. But he had always known Sonny wouldn't listen to him, not completely. This girl, this thin-armed beautiful girl, straw hair to be spun into gold by the right Rumpelstiltskin, would do anything Arnold said. So he said nothing.

"Do you want me?" she whispered, close to him now, bending her long graceful neck from beneath the branch of a budding tree, leaning up toward him.

"Tu as quinze ans."

"I have fifteen?" she asked proudly.

He nodded.

"Jeanne d'Arc she lead armies at fifteen."

"And died soon," Arnold translated.

"Maybe," she said, and let go of the branch, watching it snap back in place. "Maybe we everybody died soon."

"Come," he said, and took her fingertips and nothing more. "Come, I'll watch you wash your hair."

For a while he watched. For a while he sat like a boy on the warm soft green beside the brook. She knelt on the bank, stretching her neck toward the water, letting the slow moving current make curly tendrils from the straight white weave of her hair.

He closed his eyes and asked himself why. Why now, why just this minute, just this time, did he have to decide to act better than his own nature? He heard her whispering to him, calling his name, an invitation, familiar. He opened his eyes to the brilliance of life, and spring, and her. She had taken off her thin cotton dress. She was standing naked in the water. Water that came only to her ivory thighs. She bobbed down to her waist, almost shyly. Very shyly, considering what was in her eyes.

"I am not *vierge*," she said.

"Neither am I," said Arnold.

"Alors?" She was smiling at him, but the joy did not spread past the corners of her mouth. Her eyes were blazing green, transparent. There was anger behind them.

"You don't want to make love," Arnold said.

"No."

"Then why are you doing this?"

"I think," she traced a momentary tide in the stillness of water, "I think maybe you want me."

"Everybody would want you," he said. "You mustn't make love for other people. You must make it for yourself."

She looked at him, not understanding. She eased herself forward, balancing herself on her forearms, her hands resting on the bottom of the brook. Her breasts floated just beneath the surface of the water, bobbing at him like almost ripe nectarines, pink at the sucking place. She stretched her legs backwards, and kicked, very slowly, one leg, the other leg, slowly and rhythmically. Shimmering beneath the water was the Valentine curve of her buttocks. Hardly a Whitman sampler. But Arnold knew without there being a chart what all the flavors might be.

He tried to tell her about love being a selfish act. That when someone was as beautiful as she, she should choose very carefully, and very well. But he faltered, he rambled, he lost the construction, the words were too complex for him in French, the feelings too complex for him in English. He didn't know how to make his meaning understood. He didn't understand it himself.

So he went to the water's edge and reached for her hand. She kissed his fingertips.

"Why do you want to make love with me, when you don't want to make love?"

Her pale, carved shoulders cut the water: she became a part of a ripple. She dipped her face slightly forward, and let some water bubble through her open mouth, raised her chin toward the sun, and let the liquid slide from her lips.

"Do you like making love?"

"*Non.*"

"You should. Who made love to you?"

She did not answer. She seemed not to want to say.

"You want your shampoo?"

She nodded. "Yes. Please. Cham-poo."

"I'll bring it to you," said Arnold, and started to take off his clothes. Quickly. Watching her. Watching her watching him. He picked up the bottle he had purchased for such selfless reasons at the PX, and stepped into the chill of the nearly motionless current. He knelt down next to her, and turned her around, moving her gently by the outsides of her breasts. He locked her back in the easy grip of his spread thighs, so her body floated in front of him. Her beautiful body, a statue, lightened by water, floating lengthwise in front of him.

And he shampooed her hair. He massaged her scalp, and rubbed her hair, pressed it strand by strand against her skull. He worked it around the back of her neck, and moved strong fingers across the rounded top of her head, till he had her purring like a cat, a cat with soapy fur. Body straining backwards to be touched.

But he stayed with her head, her remarkable head, tracing every inch of it, palms manipulating the hair into soapily rounded circles, finger kneading the sides of her temples so easily, so lightly, and so thoroughly he thought he could feel her brain.

He used the foam to wash her body. He streaked it down the slender line of her back, sat her high in the water, held her up now by the rounded hips he gripped between his knees, stroking the shampoo lather from her hair down between her shoulder blades. He took a handful of the thick white foam, and placed it on her throat, whispered into the back of her neck to wait for him, save it for him, he'd be there soon.

He stood her up in front of him, and washed her lower back, and the outside of her hips, slowly, and the backs of her thighs. Then his hand moved between her legs, and she was bending, moaning. He turned her around and made the movement a continuous one, trailing the suds with his fingers underneath her, tracing them up toward her navel with his right hand, slipping the foam from her throat down over her breasts, spreading it over stiffening pink nipples.

She was groaning, pleading with him, without words. He stood and looked down at the half-closed eyes, the pouting lips, slack with the laziness of pleasure. When she made no move to touch him, he rubbed her hands against the lather on her belly, stroked them in circles around her breasts, stretched out her soapy palms, upwards, making them into a cup, and placed himself in her hands.

She washed him. She held him in her hands and soaped and slid suddenly gifted fingers between his legs. She kneaded the skin around it, underneath it, as carefully as he had manipulated her scalp. And all the time he kept washing her. Thoroughly, deliberately. Laughing in his eyes at the pleasure he was giving her. Laughing in his eyes, but nowhere else.

She was sighing, begging, wordless. He stopped the motion of her hands and placed his tip at the soapy triangle above her thighs. He pressed gently forward, sliding across the outside of her, the warm wet foamy outside of her, back and forth, until the noise cascading from her mouth began to sound like grief.

His hands moved to the sides of her face. He leaned down and covered her lips with the soft inside of his lips, filled up the hollow of her mouth with his tongue. Filled up the hollow between her legs, and flooded the hollow in his own heart.

When they were rinsed and cool and lying on a patch of white, wild clover, when he was doing with the towel what he had done with the foam, making sure that every inch of her was dry as it had been wet, while he traced the fine hairs, the nearly invisible white hairs on her slender forearms with his finger, she told him. She explained as best she could about the soldiers, and the force, and the supposing that it would always feel that way.

He put his head between her legs, licked fantasy into the inside of her thighs, and drank her like honey from a fragile crystal jar. He held nether lips like the flower they were becoming, and with his mouth twirled slow frenzy from her second tiny hardened tongue. Moved two fingers inside her, moved her past pleasure, past screaming, felt her shattering around him.

"That's part of how it should be," he whispered. "That should give you a *petite* idea."

He thought of that soft, tender flesh being ravaged by gluttons, by pigs who thought they knew the meaning of conquest. He turned his face so the tears could come without touching her skin, so she wouldn't know, wouldn't suspect how much he could feel, that he had never suspected he could feel.

It was good she hadn't told him before about the soldiers. It wouldn't have done to be weeping like a woman while he made love to her. It was bad enough that he had given himself to the act of love as if it were not a selfish act.

They were waiting for Arnold at the airport in New York when he finally took a flight he was glad to take, besides the many he'd made to Paris. Not to check with generals.

Sonny was there, and Sarah. Ellis and Althea, both of them grown taller. Ellis was not a boy anymore, he was beginning to be a young man. A handsome young man, Arnold was pleased to note, tall and slender, with good strong features except for a certain slackness of mouth. Althea was no longer a baby: she was a little girl. Not as good-looking as her brother, but pleasant-seeming, smiling at him as though it meant something to see him.

He scooped her up in his arms and shook his son's hand, and kissed him, and hugged Sonny, and clung to the three of them at the same time. Then he let go and put his arms around Sarah. Little Sarah. Poor little Sarah.

"I was afraid," she whispered, against the front of his officer's jacket. "Even when they said the war was over, I was still afraid."

She stared up at him. "You look taller," she said, with so much affection that for a moment she almost ceased to seem plain. "See?" She pressed her head against his chest, standing on tiptoe. "I don't come as high as your heart. I used to be able to hear your heart, and now I can't hear it."

He hugged her very hard. Now that he knew what it was to feel something gentle so strongly, he could actually find some pity for her weakness.

Di Bonaven's men, Rosey himself, had offered to come to the airport to welcome the returning hero, the next Senator from New York. But Sonny had asked them to let it be a family reunion, and Rosey had thought that, yeah, that might be a nice idea. Nothing counted more than family except for politics, which could wait an extra day.

Sonny had not put on any weight watching the fort, Arnold was glad to see. There were a few deep lines in Sonny's forehead that hadn't been there before, but the face still looked youthful, hopeful, imposing. His eyes were a little less bright, a little grayer than blue, a little sadder than they had been when Arnold went away. But that, Arnold supposed, had to come with getting older. When you got older, you saw more, and knew you'd be disappointed, so naturally your eyes had to get sadder. Arnold had not studied the mirror for a while, or he might have noticed that some of the sadness in his own eyes had actually disappeared.

He reached across Sarah and gripped Sonny's arm. "I missed you, you big tough pushover. I missed your mean face, with the dreams behind it. I went to France for you. France is the place for dreams and flowers and pushovers. So I tried to visit it for you."

"Did I have a nice time?"

"There was a war on," Arnold said. He was remembering. Even thinking about her, he could feel her, and his throat got all cluttered up so not too many words could fit in.

After Arnold gave his things to the servants and Sarah to unpack and put in order, he went with Sonny to Catherine's room. A small lamp was lit on the night table next to the big fourposter bed. The room reeked of fading flowers, and medication, and future soon to be dusty with past.

As dim as the light was, Arnold could see how pale Catherine looked. Eerily pale, as if the blue that had so impressed Sonny in her eyes had seeped down through her throat into a feeble turquoise network across the tops of her breasts. Dressed in bed-clothes, the wife of his baby brother.

"Hello, Arnold," Catherine said, a little hazily, holding out a blue-veined hand. "How are you?"

"I'm fine." He clasped her fingers. Cold, premature remnants of the grave. "How are you?"

"Never been better," Catherine said, smiling. "I'm sorry I couldn't come to the airport."

"That's okay."

"Not that there's really anything wrong. I just had a bit of a cold, so the doctor thought I should rest."

"Of course," said Arnold.

"I'm lying to you. Everybody in this house feels they have to lie to you about themselves to make you feel better."

"Stop it, please, Catherine," Sonny said.

"We'll move out at the beginning of the week," said Catherine. "As soon as I feel up to packing, we'll move into town, you can arrange that, can't you, Sonny? We can stay in a hotel till I find a suitable apartment."

"You'll stay here," Arnold said.

"That was for the duration. The duration is over. You look handsome, Arnold. Good in uniform. Taller, slimmer, I don't know what all. But there's a nicer look in your eye. Like you were happier. Glad to be alive."

"I met your son," Arnold said. "Fine boy. Fine boy."

"He's very bright," said Catherine. "Quiet. But I suppose that comes from so many people hushing him. You know, the whispers in the corridors of invalids. 'Shhh. Don't wake your mother.' When he talks to you, you'll see he's very bright."

"I'm sure he is."

She sat up slightly, flesh hanging heavy around the hollows of her face. "So what do you think? You think it balances out? The little while of love, the boy with his bad eyes but very lively brain. What do you think, Arnold? Should he have listened to you?"

"I don't know what you're talking about."

"You warned Sonny not to marry me. You told him I was old, that I'd get sick on him."

"I never said any such thing," said Arnold. "You know how Sonny lies when he's losing an argument."

"We weren't arguing." Catherine looked away. "We were laughing because you were so wrong, because this could never happen. The first tenet of law, as taught by Arnold Sterne. Deny everything."

"You're going to be fine," Arnold said.

"Please don't try to take away my self-pity," Catherine said. "I have so little left."

"She's going to be fine," Arnold said, when he was alone with Sonny in the library. Paneled in wood, arched gently at the top, to appear medieval. Rafe Hawthorne had helped by placing four armor-plated statues on stands in the corners of the room, red velvet hangings to separate fifteenth-century tapestries. The chairs, however, were chosen for comfort. Wide, red leather wingbacks faced the fireplace, a fireplace that servants still filled with wood, and lit and stoked. That part of the dream, at least, was still being burned, alive. "She's going to be fine."

"This isn't law," Sonny said. "It's medicine. It doesn't do any good to deny everything."

"Nobody's telling you to deny. Insist."

"How can I insist on believing my own lie?"

"What the hell are you asking me for?" Arnold said. "You know you're smarter than I am."

Sonny laughed and pulled a handkerchief from his pocket, blew his nose. "I was wondering how long you'd take to admit it." He laughed again, and slumped back in the chair, looking into the fire.

"How's everything at the store?"

"Up and down. Some days we're very rich. Some days we're only a little rich."

"There's no such thing as a little rich."

236

"Sure there is. A little rich is when people think you can pay your bills, so you're not under too much pressure to pay them."

"How come we're only a little rich?" Arnold asked. "Unprecedented prosperity, that's what we're coming into. Even the man from Missouri seems to be convinced of that. You know how hard it is to prove things to someone from Missouri. I'm easier. Convince me how we can only be a little rich."

"Simple," said Sonny. "We owe Central and Southwestern Railroad a little under five million. But that'll be okay. I have a bank that's going to lend us a little under five million because they don't know we owe it to the railroad. So all we have to worry about is that someone from the railroad doesn't talk to someone from the bank. And then we're home free, as soon as we find someone to lend us a little under five million who doesn't know we owe it to the bank."

"We that fucked up?"

"We're not fucked up at all," Sonny said. "It's part of the shell game, you know that. I like a little pressure. Keeps me on my toes." His shoulder moved under his jacket. "I don't know how fast I'd run without someone chasing me."

"How about your little nest-egg of bourbon?"

"Joe Pape's is climbing all the time. Joe Pape calls me about twice a year and tells me how it's climbing all the time. I don't pay too much attention to it. It's nice to know that it's there if we ever really need it. For a thirsty day."

"If *you* ever really need it," Arnold said.

"What's mine is ours," said Sonny. "You know that. If you ever need to be sullied by Joe Pape's dirty money, it's there for the sullying, Arnold."

"You look tired," Arnold said. "You ought to slow down. Enjoy life."

"I'm not enough like you to live for pleasure."

"I don't live for pleasure," Arnold said. "I live for power." He tried to laugh, but he was remembering her, and aching. "I'd live for pleasure but I haven't got the guts."

"Hey," Sonny said, a little while later when there was nothing to look for in the fire, when all the dancing shadows had smouldered to rest, "Catherine got flowers from Clifton Sanger. Mrs. Clifton Sanger, but it's the same thing, don't you think? She wouldn't send flowers to a business acquaintance's wife without checking with her husband, do you think?"

"I don't know how those work, the minds of the Clifton Sangers."

"I'm starting to think he doesn't really exist. They just keep the news of his name alive so the banking empire won't collapse. He's probably been dead for fifteen years. Anyway, she sent flowers. I thought that was nice. She knows Catherine from some charity thing Catherine was working on before . . . before she got ill. So she sent flowers. Do you figure Sanger knew?"

"Not if he's dead."

"He's too rich to be dead."

"The great international banking families," Arnold contemplated. "Something inspiring about that. Many nations. Many years of cash behind you. Inspirational. People have more faith when you've got that much atmosphere."

"How was it really, soldier boy, being in the war?"

"A matter of life and death. I liked the life part better. They wanted me to continue behind my civilian disguise, the be-very-secretive types. Skulky O.S.S.-ers, trying to round up talent for peacetime war. Trying to intrigue you with intrigue, and the offer of protection. They can protect you from just about anything, I'd imagine. Almost makes you tempted to throw in with them. To be that safe from any enemy would be a form of power."

"So why didn't you do it?"

"My future is politics. To join with them and go into politics would be like shitting where you eat."

About four in the morning, after they'd both drunk a great deal of Scotch, they decided they were going to become Clifton Sanger (constructing a family tree that stretched back two centuries, with money blossoming on its branches, that was the part they would skip). The rest they'd do, sure they'd be able to do it. The house in Southampton, formerly restricted. The children at Harvard and Yale (to which Ellis had been accepted, wait-listed at Harvard). The flat unbroken speech of men with no accents behind them. Being boring at dinner. Why not? Why not indeed?

They could hardly keep their heads up, they were so tired and sedated by drink and the security of each other's company. "I just want you to know I'm glad I married her," Sonny managed to say, not too thickly.

"Then so am I."

"It's a real bitch, Arnold. Aching to hold a woman you can't have."

"Yeah, I can imagine."

"She wants me to have other women, but how can I have other women when I love her?"

Arnold did not answer. There was silence again for a while, broken by the clanking of crystal decanters against glasses.

"The F.B.I.," Sonny chortled over the edge of his glass. "J. Arnold Sterne of the F.B.I."

"Nothing to do with the F.B.I. They consider the F.B.I. cops."

"What do they consider themselves?"

"It's too hush-hush for them to even consider. They'll probably take over the country. I was really tempted to join, I got to tell you. But I like politics better. You can do everything shifty out in the open, as long as you don't get caught. If they make it to total power I'll really be sorry."

"Secrecy and conspiracy can't make it in this country," Sonny ventured. "Americans are too indiscreet. We like to gossip too much. You can't have a really secret organization except in a fascist country."

"Fascist countries aren't too bad. It depends on the fascist."

239

"I wish I could be like you. I wish I could learn not to care about anything. Not a criticism, Arnold. It just must be much easier, not really caring."

"You got it, kid."

They helped each other up the stairs. "I'm sorry, pal," said Sonny.

"You got nothing to be sorry about. You've just had too much to drink."

"I'm sorry you don't really care about anything. You can feel your guts, you can feel what's inside your belly, even if it's a little too fat, when you care about something."

"That's one I'll have to miss."

"I love you, Arnold. I'm a sloppy drunk, so I get sentimental. Forget it in the morning, will you?"

"It's all right for you to love me. It isn't sloppy. I consider it neat. I even love you."

They kissed each other and hugged. "No tongues," said Arnold.

"I'm just so sorry you don't really care," Sonny started to cry. "It aches but it feels good, to feel that hard. I think you're missing something."

"Not me," said Arnold. "I'm sure about the way I live. You're the one who's missing something. Confidence. If you were so sure you were right about things, you'd have more confidence. I don't mean ego, I mean confidence, like Clifton Sanger."

"I'll never be like him. *He* probably isn't even like him."

"What we need is an international aura," said Arnold. "That'll give you the confidence of Clifton Sanger, make other people have that much confidence in you."

"Right," said Sonny. "Terrific idea. We'll float some mutual funds overseas."

"Maybe," said Arnold. "Something like that. Or maybe we can get someone working in the office who's European."

Sonny remembered so little of the conversation, Arnold was able to convince him it had been Sonny's idea, getting a customer representative trainee from France. It was so seldom Arnold gave him sole credit for what was his own, he gladly accepted something that was Arnold's.

"But why France?" Sonny wondered aloud, the next night at dinner.

Sarah had been cooking for three days, chopping pike and whitefish and onion for gefilte fish, boiling it, letting it sit in its own bony juice in the refrigerator, so it would have a fine clear gel, the way Arnold liked. Making pot roast with garlic and paprika and just a little bit of tomato sauce for a half-hour at the end, the way Arnold liked. Making chocolate mousse, with the recipe she had clipped from the *Ladies' Home Journal,* melting chocolate into sauce, bringing it in with whipped cream even though God was watching, because that was how Arnold liked it. And Arnold wasn't eating.

"What could I have been thinking of when I said France?" Sonny pondered. "France is economically off the face of the earth. The French don't get their hysteria going, coming back from war. Germany will build itself back up to full economic strength before France does."

"God forbid," said Sarah. "Not those terrible people."

"You can't condemn them all," said Arnold.

"All right," Sarah said.

"That was Hitler's mistake. His one mistake."

"Six million people," said Sarah.

"You mustn't take it personally," said Arnold. He saw the expression on her face. "Still, you're right, Sonny. It shouldn't be someone German, even if they weren't a Nazi. You're right to have decided on someone from France."

It took Arnold eleven and a half months to bring Jeanne from Europe, to cut through the red tape and pull multicolored strings.

With all he had taught her of English and business, with the training he made sure she would get, being schooled by one of the top economists in Europe, with all he had arranged of making certain her ability would be unique, deliberately unique, Immigration still toughened the soft road he set up to bring her in as an employee. For a year of his life he almost went crazy, almost forgot personal ambition. Almost.

McCarthy's Steak House on Second Avenue had long been a favorite with the press. It was the wood that did it, as well as the steaks, which were starting to be as good as the times when there hadn't been ration stamps. Reporters liked huddling around near wood, hunched over in leather booths, because they spent so much time on display in glass cubicles, or no cubicles at all.

Arnold knew the feeling of too much space around when you'd been hoping for wood-paneled walls. Journalists were intermittent dreamers. Along with the Pulitzers, and incredible scoops, and the praise of their peers, and a break like Louella got which gave her the goods on Hearst and a wide syndication, and the novel they would write as soon as they had the time and could figure out how to fictionalize, they also hoped for a door they could close.

Arnold had been shocked, the one time he went to visit his friends at the New York *Sun*. Joe McCreery was as brilliant an economics analyst as anyone writing in the newspapers, a positive influence in financial circles. Brokers would discuss his column at lunch, in private men's clubs. If the question was bigger than anyone's personal experience, the smart men on the Street, when asked what they thought, would say: "Have you read McCreery?"

That was his stature, and his influence, from the bad days of the thirties to the good days when the war started making things right on the money. When Arnold had gone to pick him up for a long-awaited lunch one day early in 1942, and stepped out from the elevator onto Joe McCreery's floor, he'd been stunned. Stunned by the noise. Stunned at the sight of the army of worker ants, in shirtsleeves, fifteen desks across, twenty desks deep, clattering away at ancient typewriters, talking into old-fashioned telephones, buried alive in noise.

"How can you think?" he asked Joe McCreery when they were on their way down in the elevator. Arnold considered Joe a poet, if you thought there could be a poet of economic opinion, and Arnold did. A genius, at the top of his profession, two miles ahead of his own brain, and they made him sit in the midst of endless clatter and confusion.

"You get used to it," Joe said. "You learn how to shut it out."

"Bullshit," said Arnold. "I'm going to get you an office. We can't have Wall Street hanging on the words of a man who is being systematically driven insane."

"It doesn't bother me," Joe insisted.

"It bothers me," said Arnold.

They ordered sidecars, and restructured the world over lunch. One of the first things Arnold would do was rent Joe an office close to the New York Public Library, so there would be even more spacious silence to run to. Joe appreciated the offer but thought it was dangerous. People might think he was in Arnold's pocket, and neither of them could afford that.

"No favors in exchange," Arnold said. "Strictly friendship and good business. I value your opinion, so I need to make sure you're not berserk. No favors in exchange."

"Nobody would believe it."

"On my oath, I want nothing but your brain to stay clear, with no machines tap-dancing on your cerebellum."

"A gift of silence," Joe McCreery said. "You're a generous man."

"I'm selfish."

"That's why nobody would believe you did it out of altruistic motives."

"So let's not tell them."

"I make a hundred and ten dollars a week," McCreery said. "I have a wife and three children in Montclair. Once a week during the academic year I lecture at Rutgers, so when those boys take off for summer vacation I can put my own family in Ocean City so they won't sweat and my kids can learn about tides.

"Once a year the Sanger Foundation gifts me with a trip abroad that lasts six weeks, second-class hotel accommodations, so I can meet with fine European money thinkers." He drank deeply of his sidecar, and sat back in the booth. His eyebrows were thick and very shaggy, hanging gray-white over the outside corners of his lids.

"I guess that part of it is over now, until after the war. Oh, yes. I left out the cases of Scotch. Many cases of Scotch, my friend, at Christmas. But not so many as go to writers of gossip, you understand? The only kind of bribe I can accept with dignity."

"This wouldn't be a bribe," Arnold insisted.

"No way they'd believe that. No way they wouldn't know. You don't make a hundred and ten a week, after steadily increasing taxes, and have an office on Madison Avenue. But thank you. Thank you for thinking of me. Thank you for thinking. Hell, that's gift enough from any man."

"How about a job? Junior membership in the firm. I'd make you a partner, but my brother doesn't really know you. It's a family thing, you understand, he's very gung-ho on family. We never had any. What do you say? I'll start you at a hundred thousand."

"I'd get gout," said Joe McCreery. "Too rich for my blood."

"Pretend it's only a hundred and ten a week. You're a brilliant man, Joe. You ought to get paid what you're worth."

"I get the salary of a newspaperman. That's all I am. I don't think I'd see things as clearly if I had a stake in them."

"Integrity," said Arnold, shaking his head. "Beats hell out of me."

"Me too," said Joe McCreery.

When he came back from the War to End All Wars just this one last time, again, Arnold was glad Joe McCreery hadn't accepted his offer. It was much more important to a politician to have a friend on a paper than a payroll. He felt unaccustomedly clean that he didn't have both.

He was starting to worry about his future a little. He'd wasted so much time thinking about Jeanne, he hadn't been putting enough pressure on Rosey di Bonaven. They had to get organized. The election was only ten months away, and the campaign staff wasn't even completely selected.

He'd taken Rosey to the opera a couple of times. When he saw how bored Rosey was with the women singing ("Those are chorus girls?" Rosey had asked him), how unexcited he seemed at the sight of those stuffed shirts in full dressing, he took Rosey instead to Harry Bell's new club ("Where the beauty flows like wine, and the girls kick as high as you get to feel," according to Harry Bell's own slogan).

Arnold didn't know the little promoter himself. But he tipped enough at the club so the headwaiter would come over with a bottle of champagne and say it was compliments of Harry Bell. Rosey di Bonaven was probably very impressed, but it was hard to tell for sure, he was so busy watching the girls. So Arnold tipped enough that when girls were willing to come over, they were more than willing to come over Arnold and Rosey.

It was very hard on evenings like those to get the conversation back to political business. A good idea then, an excellent idea, Arnold thought, was to take Rosey to lunch at McCarthy's Steak House. The wood walled you in; there was no way the talk could get other than serious. Unless some reporters got drunk and felt too amiable, glad to be coffined up with friends instead of buried alive in noise.

"Two steaks," Arnold said to the waiter. "Sirloin. One very rare, one . . ." He paused and fingered the red-checked tablecloth. "How do you take yours, Rosey?"

"Over twenty-one."

"Medium-rare?"

Rosey nodded.

"Medium-rare," said Arnold to the waiter. "Okay." He moved a little closer to the portly, thin-haired man, lowering his voice as he lifted his Scotch. "Let's get down to it."

"How come there's just men at this place?" said Rosey. "My whole life I spend with men, mealtimes I like a restaurant with pretty girls."

"We can go to Harry Bell's tonight."

"I been to Harry Bell's. No point in getting your juices started that late. How come they don't have pretty girls here at lunch?"

"It's mainly for reporters."

"Aren't there girl reporters? I thought there were plenty of dopey girl reporters. Jesus, it shakes your faith in Brenda Starr."

"I'd like to talk with you seriously about next year."

"What about next year?" Rosey bit on a roll. "Isn't that Joe McCreery?" He chewed, pointing toward the bar.

"Yes."

"He's older than his picture. The picture they run with his column, he looks about twenty-five, all full of beans."

"He's full of better than beans."

"But he's no damned twenty-five." Rosey scooped a little butter up with his bread. "He's sixty if he's a day."

"He's forty-six," said Arnold. "A personal year for every year of this century."

"He must be a heavy juicer. You don't get that old from thinking."

"Maybe you do if you think hard enough."

"Then I count myself smart to think easy." Rosey ate an olive. "That's how you stay young and alive. No overworking the brain, no overworking the heart, no overworking the possibilities."

"Very good thinking, Rosey."

"You bet it is. I'd like to meet McCreery. You know him?"

"I know him," said Arnold, less than enthusiastically. He'd been trying to set up a quiet lunch for weeks. He could talk to Joe McCreery anytime. He didn't feel like sharing him with Rosey, or vice versa.

"Get him over here."

"He likes to relax at lunchtime."

"So do I," said Rosey. "Get him over here."

Joe saw Arnold coming and opened his arms, splashing a part of his drink into the welcome. "Old friend," he said. "Old buddy," he grinned. "Old renegade bear-trapper, how the hell have you been?" He hugged Arnold around the shoulders. "I'd introduce you to the rest of the boys, but I have no idea who you are."

"Can you come over and join us for a minute?"

"Not to that table," said Joe. "I've been avoiding that table for over twenty years."

"Come on. Do it for me."

"Why him?" Joe moved Arnold over to a quiet corner of the bar. "Christ, Arn, I know how badly you want to win, but what are you going to win with him on your shoulder? He isn't worth your left testicle, and that's what he'll take out of you, friend, that's what you're going to owe."

"So I'll welch."

"No you won't. You'll even make good on corruption. I know you too well to think you won't. What do you need him for?"

"He's an expert. I need experts."

"You need experts on the right way. Not a graft-oiled machine."

"Come over and just say hello, as a favor to me."

"Hello," said Joe McCreery.

"Well," Rosey stood, extending his hand. "This is a very great pleasure which I have looked forward to for a very great time. Won't you join us?"

"No," said Joe McCreery.

"Oh, come on," said Rosey. "It can't hurt you to talk to me."

"How do you know? You ever listened to yourself?"

"You're trying to insult me."

"And they say he's insensitive," Joe said to Arnold. "How wrong can people be?"

"I'd like you to sit down," said Rosey.

"And I'd like all the children of the world to have French toast for breakfast."

"I heard he drank," said Rosey. "But I didn't realize he was a communist."

Joe McCreery laughed out loud, a very good laugh, and signaled the waiter for a refill on the glass in his hand. "Okay, I'll sit for a minute, deluded buddy," he said to Arnold. "I want to see how stupid he really is." His eyebrows had gotten thicker, heavier with the ensuing years, so he looked like John L. Lewis, around the eyes at least, which should have made Di Bonaven more comfortable.

"I've admired you greatly for a very long time," said Rosey.

"I wish I could say the same."

"Okay, Sterne. Get him out of here. The man is a drunk and a fool."

"Coming from you," Joe said, "I regard that as the ultimate compliment. Ultimate means last, as far as you can go."

"I'll call you," said Arnold.

"Come on." Joe reached for the glass the waiter was carrying on a tray. "You asked me to come over here, Arn. As a favor to you. So let me do you a favor."

"Get out of here, Joe," Arnold said softly. "Please."

"So tell me, Rosey," Joe asked, sipping, "is it true that every street's a boulevard on old Broadway?"

"I'm not sure about that," said Rosey, sitting up so tall his matte suit surface looked shiny. "But I have heard that the power of the press is on the wane, you know what wane means, I'm sure. That's when the moon goes down. Yeah, I heard that, a couple of places. That the power of the press is draining, the newspaper business is losing blood with the war being over."

"You really hear that, huh?" Joe said with interest. "Maybe you're right. Maybe people have had enough news. So tell me, is it true there's a broken heart for every light?"

"No, but there's a heavy run on bubble gum," Arnold said quickly. "Now that they've got ingredients to make it expand again—"

"Shut up, Sterne," said Rosey. "To bring it down to even more personal information, McCreery, something that should do your heart good, I've heard that the first one to fail will be the New York *Sun.*"

"You've frightened me nearly to death."

"I sincerely hope not," said Rosey. "The setting for that should be not this pretty."

"Threats. Isn't he cute, friend Arnold? He really makes threats."

"Get him out of here," said Rosey.

"Come." Arnold pulled Joe's arm. "I'm pleading with you, Joe."

"You don't plead with me. I'm your friend. Friends you don't have to plead with. You only have to plead with a filthy son-of-a-bitch, up-for-graft, gerrymandering—"

"Get him out."

When Arnold returned to the table, after putting Joe in a cab, Rosey was gone. Arnold went to Rosey's office, and the club, and his home, where the butler said nobody was in except Mrs. Di Bonaven, who was under sedation. Arnold moved through all the bars where the boys spent their easy afternoons, but Rosey was nowhere. For six weeks Rosey ducked Arnold, in person and on the telephone. When Arnold finally managed to catch up with him again, it was in the apartment of a hooker whom Arnold had tracked through some of the girls.

It hadn't been easy tracking. He let it out that he would give five hundred dollars to the one who could inform him first when Rosey had an apolitical appointment somewhere. So the girl called, greedier for the five than she was afraid of Rosey Di Bonaven.

Arnold could see why, when he went into her apartment. There was a mirror on the ceiling in the small living room, and a floor covered with pillows. No other furniture. A bed in the wall, ready for sliding down. Hide-a-bed. Hide-a-profession. Not the way she looked.

"You want anything while you're waiting?"

"No thank you," Arnold said.

"He won't be here for fifteen minutes. I could give you a blow job."

"Thanks anyway."

"I'm really good. Nobody gets past ten minutes."

"Sounds great, but I'll pass."

"Oh." She pulled her white satin bathrobe closed, retying the belt at the waist. "Then would you like a magazine?"

Rosey was less than pleased to see him. He was ready to leave right away. But in front of Rosey, Arnold gave the girl two thousand in cash and told her she could take care of Mr. Di Bonaven for as long and as much and however he wanted. When the two thousand was used up, she should call his office and bill him. He handed her his card. Embossed.

"Okay," Rosey said. "I'll talk to you." He looked at the girl. "You got someplace we could sit down and talk, Vera?"

"The bathroom."

"Come on," Rosey said. "There's a bar on the corner."

They sat at a table in the rear, far away from the bar where the Four Roses drunks were, so there was no chance of anyone overhearing. "Okay," said Arnold. "Now what about the seat."

"What seat?"

"Don't do this to me, Rosey. We've been together on this for sixteen years. Sixteen years you've been on the take against that day, against the day you delivered the nomination. I'm a smart man. I'm a good talker. I'm a good thinker, and my record is clean. My record is spotless except for the part of the payroll that's been going to you for insurance."

"Insurance for what? Not for the seat. No one can guarantee the seat. All we can make sure of is the nomination."

"Then we're straight on that?"

"Didn't I give you my word?" Rosey asked.

Arnold nodded, relieved. "I'm sorry. Excuse me for getting nervous."

"No need to be nervous. There's plenty of time. A little over six years."

"Two stingers," said the waitress, and slapped the glasses on the table. "That'll be a dollar and ten cents."

"Six years!" Arnold said, when she was gone. "What the hell does that mean, goddamit? Six years."

"You can't run this year," Rosey said. "The line is too

crowded. We're going to have to bring you along more slowly."

"Who'd you promise it to? Who paid you off?"

"I can't be bought," said Rosey, smiling his yellow-brown smile. "You know I can't be bought. No matter what anybody gives me, I never make a deal. I promise nothing except I'll do the best I can. The best I can do for you is nineteen fifty-two."

"You bastard."

"Wrong. You're wrong to curse me. To think I'm not acting in your best interests. You need a whole campaign to make them know who you are. Right now there isn't one sure bet except Tom Dewey. There's not enough time for you for 'forty-six, believe me. You have to believe me, I'm your friend."

"Cocksucker."

"Names can never harm me. And I wouldn't want to harm you either, I'm your friend. Friends don't hurt you." Rosey took a long swallow of his drink. "So you're just going to have to watch how you pick your friends."

"You're right about that, Rosey." Arnold pushed his chair away from the table with his legs. "You're really smart to say that. You know who I know, for example, someone who really can do me good?"

"Who's that?"

"Dr. Marvin. Good plastic surgeon. Very expensive. Takes care of the inner man along with the outer one, you know what I mean?"

"No. I'm not sure that I do."

"Well, for instance," Arnold stood up. He reached across the table and grabbed Rosey by his white-on-white silk tie. "For instance, if I busted your face open, he could put it back together again, and at the same time make sure there were no hurt feelings inside."

"Let go of me."

"For example, if I wore a ring like you wore on your hand . . ." He pulled the big star sapphire set in gold that Rosey had on his pinky, tugged it off the sweaty fat hand. He put it on his own little finger and held it out for Rosey's perusal. "If I wore a ring like this, and I happened to hit you across the face . . ." He slapped his hand backwards across Rosey's cheek. "If it cut your skin . . ." He slapped the other way, holding tight to Rosey's tie.

"You son of a bitch!" Rosey struggled to free himself, short arms flailing ineffectively.

"Names can never harm me," Arnold said, and slapped again.

"I'll have you killed," Rosey hollered.

"Not friendly," Arnold said, and slapped backwards again. "Not friendly at all." He grabbed the wet collar of the white-on-white shirt and pulled Rosey's face toward his own, so he was spitting the words into Rosey's eyes.

"You lied to me, you crooked bastard. You promised me something I deserved, goddamit. You lied to me." He punched him once, hard, in the belly. It felt like Jello under his fist. He let go and watched in distaste as Rosey slid to the floor.

"I'll have you killed for this, Sterne, I swear to Christ."

"You'll have nothing done to me." Arnold lifted Rosey to a sitting position, propping him against the wooden leg of the table. "I could beat you to death, right here, right now, and nobody would stop me. But you're not worth going to jail for, Rosey. You're not even worth the murder. So you'll let me live. It's an exchange. I'm going to let you live."

"Bully," Rosey whimpered, wiping his hand across his mouth. "Oh my God, I'm bleeding." He started crawling backwards, under the table, on his buttocks.

"He who fights and crawls under a table lives to crawl under another table," said Arnold. "But only if he lives. These are derelicts here. They wouldn't make a move to stop me. They probably wouldn't even call the police. You should pick your pussy from better neighborhoods."

"I swear to you, Sterne . . ."

"Any vows you make, Rosey, are based on the assumption that you're going to live. Your ring." He handed it to Rosey. "I don't like jewelry on men."

"Go fuck yourself."

"I'd say offhand you've already done that for me."

"Okay," Rosey wheezed. He looked at the few men clinging to

the bar. They hadn't even turned around. They were paying attention to nothing but drinking. "Okay. You make it right for me financially, I'll try to forget about this. You'll get it in 'fifty-two."

"You promised me 'forty-six."

"I made a mistake."

"How do I know you won't make the same mistake again?"

"Help me up," said Rosey. "You got my word of honor."

They both laughed together at that one.

In the end, they made their peace, in the form of a pact that Arnold had Sonny draw up, to ensure the legality. It also ensured that everybody involved would receive anywhere from five to ten, Sonny cautioned Arnold. Concerning as it did the payment of monies to Rosey di Bonaven, in return for his guarantee of the Party's nomination in '52, considering that there was now, on record, proof that a D.A. wouldn't have to forage for, that there was without question a political machine, and that Sonny had drawn up a document which, when signed, certified the workings of the machinery. Taking all that under advisement, Arnold agreed that the papers if ever made public could blow New York City out of the water.

"Yeah, but you're working on the assumption that somebody's going to cheat," Arnold reassured Sonny. "Di Bonaven can't afford to cheat, and I'm an honest man."

Sonny smiled.

"Well I am," said Arnold. "Just because I'm smart doesn't make me dishonest. This paper is only for my peace of mind. I don't want them fucking me up. But it is my firm and honest intention"—he raised a finger in oratory—"to go out and do good, and become a man of the people."

"You can't become a man of the people."

" 'Fifty-two," said Arnold, with only slightly sagging shoulders. "Why the hell did I waste the time in the Army?" And then he remembered her, so hard he thought it might show. "What do you mean, I can't become a man of the people?"

"This is a free country, Sonny. You have to remember that. A country where an honest man can go only so far with the help of criminals."

So Arnold had love. Love he had never believed in, to fill his unquiet days. When money wasn't enough, making it wasn't enough, and spending it was less, so much less than enough, he wrote Jeanne letters he knew he was mad to write, bursting with details of passion that could ruin him, telling her to burn all correspondence, knowing she would save it. He wrote how his hand felt on her breast, how empty it was holding only a pen. He reached out with words to touch her, begged to touch her flesh soon, any way she wanted, anywhere she wanted. He described every inch of her pale pink whiteness to her, and himself, and said that he would give up everything to be inside her.

He built her arrival in the States like a master architect, trying to plan it to seem superb coincidence, sending a European affiliate to the teacher who trained her, having him ask for applications from all qualified candidates. Arnold sorted through the files as if there were truly a contest for who would be chosen. He put pressure on Immigration, and told Sarah in one desperate moment that he thought it might be a good idea to get Althea a proper governess, maybe somebody French. He covered his tracks with every bit of shrewdness he possessed, and made mistakes an idiot could catch.

He sweated out drunkenness at the Luxor Steam Baths, and explained to Sonny that he was still upset about Di Bonaven's cross, and that was why he was drinking too much. Part of it was true. Part of everything he said was true.

Finally, he stood on the pier, holding roses like a high-school suitor, carrying thorny bouquets that bloodied his palms, he was gripping so hard. The gangplank was moved into place. He studied the faces of those disembarking, finding them empty, uninteresting, wrong. Then he saw her. The full, pale, grown-taller boldness of her.

They did not run to each other. He greeted her stiffly, holding out the roses, her sponsor, a thoughtful new employer. He offered them very formally, a page at the opera, uncertain about the talent of the diva. She thanked him and was silent. She moved through Immigration and Customs. His chauffeur carried her suitcases to Arnold's limousine.

He was angry at himself all the way to her hotel. It seemed to him she was not as beautiful as he remembered. He studied her profile, her white china profile, the curve of her chin, the droop of her lower lip, the flaxen curtain of hair.

He thought he had really been crazy to ever even consider such a scheme. He wondered how soon he could get rid of her, send her back to France where she belonged, making babies with some peasant, some strong stocky boy who would ruin her body, stretch the flat white belly and streak it with pale blue, so Arnold wouldn't want her anymore. Not ever.

He was ashamed of himself, disappointed in her. She had made him vulnerable and foolish. Having acted as though love really existed, he wished that he could have lost enough of personal ambition to forgive her for weakening him. He tried to convince himself even as he looked at her that it didn't matter, her sapping him of some of his drive, of the terrible ruthless thrust that he should have shown. But it did matter. It mattered very much.

Until they were in her hotel room and he touched her. Then, it didn't matter at all.

NINE

He was back from China. He'd been there for two and a half years, and he thought MacArthur a hundred percent right. Evelyn spent one weekend with Walter and told him the marriage was over. She would have told him on Friday night, but his head was still in a different time zone; what he thought was tomorrow had been yesterday.

He took it very well, considering. Some of the hardship he had seen in Asia had had its effect on him, and he realized how lucky he was to be a young man in a free world, with hope of betterment. The failure of a marriage, no matter how painful, could not be equated with the fall of an entire political system, the rise of tyranny and godlessness. So he agreed they should go their separate ways.

But he was tired of traveling. Evelyn, however, had just gotten to the point where all that she needed could be obtained wholesale, including shoes, and she fancied some of them had wings on their heels. She visualized herself dancing through mysterious nights, dappled with stars, and people who found her wonderful.

When she and Walter could sit down and discuss it sensibly, when they agreed that rage and violence were pointless, they went to Stark's on Broadway and Ninetieth Street, and put relish on their hamburgers. She had raw onion, he did not, and everything was perfectly clear. She would be the one to leave. She would get a job, and institute divorce proceedings.

"Does it have to be divorce?"

"We've tried separation," said Evelyn. "It isn't enough."

"There's never been a divorce in our family."

"Ours either. These things have to start somewhere." She poured some extra ketchup, smoothed it with her bun. "It's better than people living together and hating each other."

"I never hated you."

"Well, you're a better person than I am, Walter. That's why you'll be so much happier with someone more like yourself."

By that she did not mean Chris, although they agreed that the girl should stay with him, at least till Evelyn got settled. It was, after all, the middle of the school year, and school to Chris was more important than life and love, it seemed to Evelyn.

Chris had been one of sixty children admitted to the Hunter School for the Gifted, or the Blind, or the Criminally Insane, Evelyn couldn't remember. Something very exceptional when you were ten. But because Chris loved her principal, she had decided to stay in P.S. 9.

The workings of her daughter's mind were very confusing to Evelyn, so she was loath to ask Chris anything. Most of the time it was unnecessary, as Chris would speak without any provocation. She would also recite her latest poem, eyes down, in case Evelyn didn't like it, and she had added to her annoying accomplishments a sudden love for music. Words came to her now in a blanket of song. So she moved through the small apartment singing.

She did not sing with her mouth full, but she sang in the bathroom and sang in the street, and sang when she was home sick, over the sound of the radio. Late at night, when Evelyn had despaired of there being enough cotton in the world to block her ears, she would go inside the small cubicle they had fashioned out of silk Walter had brought home from Thailand. It made Chris' part of the living room like a private rectangular tent, and Evelyn thought that was fine, very comforting. Some of the happiest days of Chris' life had been spent in the convent under mosquito netting, as Evelyn remembered.

"What are you doing?" Evelyn whispered, trying to cut gently into the quivering falsetto.

"I'm writing a song."

"Do you want a pencil and paper."

"No. I'll remember it. I just have to keep singing it over and over."

"Oh my God," Evelyn would murmur as she went back into the bedroom. "She's crazy as a bedbug."

Walter was fast asleep. He seemed to find the incantations pleasant, or was mercifully going deaf. So Evelyn would go to the window and look up at the sky, the one piece of moonlit sky visible above the dark-bordered white brick of the building. "What am I going to do?" she would say. "She's crazy as a bedbug." And what was there for answer but more song.

"Sweetheart," she finally whispered, into the folds of silk. "It's all very wonderful, writing and singing. But why don't you wait until tomorrow. I'm sure the songs will be just as good if you write them during the day."

"Now's when they're coming," said Chris. "I can't make myself stop thinking."

"Sure you can." Evelyn sat by her daughter's side, on the small single bed pushed against the wall, on which was Scotch-taped a picture of Evelyn, glittering black and very white by the side of the pool at the Reef. Below that blown-up snapshot, Lieutenant Walter M. White was receiving the Navy Cross, with Roosevelt watching. Although Evelyn's picture was in a much more prominent place, it looked less shiny than Walter's, as if it had been touched a great deal.

Evelyn pulled the cord on the second bulb in the lamp, and

brightened up the tent and her daughter's face. "Look, I think it's wonderful that you do all these things. Mrs. Schatteles thinks you're a very gifted little girl."

"Do you like her?"

"Well, I believe her." As a matter of fact, Mrs. Schatteles told Evelyn that Chris was more than exceptional. But the principal was middle-aged and plain and dressed very dowdily, so Evelyn thought she had better check it for herself. She took Chris to N.Y.U. and had her tested, and there it was, *that* I.Q., coming out of Evelyn; it couldn't have been Walter's genes.

"But it's very narrow, isn't it?" Evelyn said to the man who tested. "I read an article that the line is very thin between genius and insanity."

"We only do I.Q. testing," the man said. "She seems like a normal little girl."

"She sings herself to sleep," Evelyn said. "Her own songs."

"That sounds very creative."

"That's because you don't have to listen to it," Evelyn said, ending the interview.

Now she sat beside her daughter, holding the hand that was growing all the time, where had they gone to, the years? Where was the black-eyed baby, lost behind the more than chubby, overly eager face. Where was Evelyn's youth?

It seemed to be still in her own eyes, in her face, still miraculously free of wrinkles, a combination of judicious facial exercises collected from various magazines, different creams applied at night, and a minute and a half of total tranquillity daily, from a condensation of a yoga book in *Reader's Digest* magazine. She studied the picture of herself on the wall. Her body was still exactly the same, maybe even better, because she'd been doing calisthenics, and had learned to stand with head high, shoulders back and down, and one foot at a right angle to the other. Of course she looked better tan as she was in the picture, but that was simply a matter of clime.

Had anything else changed? Would anyone know from looking at her that she had a daughter of eleven? Impossible, especially if the daughter weren't with her.

A shameful thought. She blazed it out of her mind and gave it to Wandra Kane.

"I used to think all the time," Evelyn said to Chris, sitting beside her now in the tent. "I used to think every minute of the day, and even during dinner, and you know how wonderful Grandma's cooking tastes. And then one day, I realized it was hurting me, all that thinking."

"Really?"

"Well not actually hurting my body. But maybe being a little hard on my brain. You see, if you think all the time, you're bound to develop illusions, and if you have illusions, you'll lose them. I wouldn't want you disillusioned at eleven. Besides, a growing girl needs her sleep. Okay? You'll go to sleep?"

"I just have one more number to do, for the finale."

"For the what?"

"I'm writing a musical for eighth-grade graduation next term."

"Oh my God." Evelyn sprang from the bed. "She's crazy as a bedbug," she muttered to herself, because Walter was asleep and obviously God wasn't listening. She went to the bathroom and washed her face with cold water, looked carefully at the face studying back at her from the mirror.

No. It wasn't gone. If anything, she looked better. Vague ovals of hollows had kindly invaded her cheeks, giving her the edge only Hungarians had, the thrust of high cheekbones that served as a pedestal for the eye. Her skin still felt like a baby's skin, like Grandma's skin, which was softer than a baby's. Her elbows were smooth. There was nothing about her that had changed, except her attitude. She was tired of being a dreamer.

"Look, I have to tell you something," she said to Chris, the day after she and Walter had decided to end it. Yes, it made sense, once and for all. Chris was in the bedroom, sick again with a cold, lying in bed, breathing in the croup kettle, listening to "Our Gal Sunday."

Having accepted Evelyn's dictum that too much thinking was bad for her, Chris welcomed the radio. Her particular favorite was "Our Gal Sunday," because she came from a little mining town, and that could have been Pittsburgh. But Sunday was fast losing ground to "Mary Noble, Backstage Wife."

"Turn it off," Evelyn said.

Chris did. She sat up, looking suddenly very vulnerable, even if she was a half-size, Evelyn noted, resolving to be kind.

"You know, Chrissie . . ." Evelyn reached for a renegade strand of too-curly hair. "Sometimes people get married and they find out they've made a mistake."

"Are we leaving again?"

"Your daddy and I are getting a divorce."

Chris started crying.

"Please don't start acting like Margaret O'Brien. You're much too fat to have freckles."

A sob. A wail. Oh, for God's sake. She didn't mean to hurt anyone's feelings. Facts were facts. Fat was fat. Wandra Kane had said so, and look how well she was doing, she was divorcing Harvey and getting an enormous settlement; she really knew how to handle herself. Getting the goods on Harvey, whatever they were.

"I'm sorry, dear." Evelyn hugged her daughter to her. "I just want you to be pretty. And happy. Gay! You've got to learn to be gay! It's hard to be gay when you're pudgy."

"I'll go on a diet," Chris said, blowing her nose. "When we leave Daddy I won't eat anything. Ever again."

"Well, there's the rub," said Evelyn. "That's something else I've got to explain."

She told her as best she could that she had to go to Florida alone. Divorces were easier to get there. And Chris knew she didn't like Florida, Evelyn reminded her. The schools weren't good enough. She didn't want to take Chris out of P.S. 9 before graduation. "That makes sense, doesn't it? It's all right to think right now. Doesn't it make sense?"

"I guess so," said Chris. "They're putting on my musical as part of the graduation ceremony. Will you come back for graduation?"

"You know I'll be here, if I possibly can," said Evelyn. "I certainly hope the program doesn't run too long."

The night before she left the site on which Edgar Allan Poe had once written "The Raven," Evelyn spent the night with her daughter, while Walter slept on the single bed outside, in the tent. "I'm going to miss you," Evelyn said to Chris, hugging her. "You're going to be eleven the next time I see you, so a lot of things are going to change. If you have any questions to ask me, you can call me any time, after the rates change. But don't be afraid to talk to your father. He wanted to be a poet. So in his own way, he does understand things. Good night, honey." She kissed her. "You want to sing me something?"

"No."

"Then good night, dear."

"I have a question."

"Can it wait till morning?"

"I don't want Daddy to hear. What's 'fuck' mean?"

So it had come to that. The time in Evelyn's life when her daughter could hear dirty words from strangers. Inevitable, Evelyn supposed; inevitable but sad.

"It's a corruption," Evelyn said. "Not the act, the word. It comes from the abbreviation of 'For Unlawful Carnal Knowledge.' I think it goes back to Middle English, Chaucer and all those people. They did things like that all the time, and I guess the medieval police didn't have the patience to write it out in full."

"What's carnal knowledge?"

Evelyn supplied some minor cleanly clinical details about the actual process of making love. "It's a wonderful thing when it's done right, and for the right reasons, and with the right man. You mustn't be confused because people with dirty minds put it in dirty language, because they haven't the patience to say things properly.

"For example, *lay*. That's a transitive verb. I *lay* the book down. I have *laid* the book down. I have been *laid*. That's not a transitive verb, that's a euphemism."

"What's a euphemism?"

"A pretty word for something that's not so pretty. I've been laid, a prettier expression than I've been fucked. But the nicest way is calling it making love, and only fools and impatient people corrupt it."

At that moment, Evelyn really impressed herself. She might have been a good mother, perhaps even a wonderful mother, if she'd only had the time.

Well, maybe one day she'd find the time. Who knew what the future would bring? Who knew, who knew, and if someone knew, why didn't they tell her? It embarrassed her, reading her horoscope on her knees in the hallway, leafing through the paper on the mat in front of Apartment 5B, because she didn't believe in any of that, and it certainly wasn't worth spending a nickel.

"So good night, dear," she said, and kissed her daughter.

"Good night, Mummy." Embraces. "I really love you."

"I really love you, too," said Evelyn, and meant it. In her own way.

Her own way that year ran through Pittsburgh, with three big suitcases and some clothes for Grandma and Sadie that Evelyn wasn't wearing anymore. If they didn't like them, they could give them to Sammy's wife, the *shicksa*, or Murray's, if he ever got married.

Pittsburgh geographically was out of her way, taking thirteen hours round-trip in actual railroad track time from her life. But she loved her family, she really did, and every time she did something to upset them, she liked to be able to explain, and give them a few old clothes.

Murray drove Evelyn to Sadie's house during his lunch break, borrowing the official delivery car from the drugstore. Being in the Navy had made him a little less naïve, but he still looked at the world through soft eyes. On the way to Braddock, Evelyn made a brief effort at straightening him out, telling him he was, after all, still a very nice-looking young man, and a pharmacist, thanks to the Navy. Women were desperate, especially in Pittsburgh, Evelyn said. Why didn't he find a rich one and bail the family out?

"I haven't met the girl of my dreams," said Murray. He was a very steady driver in addition to being kind. Evelyn admired that quality in a man, as she had a tendency to career when the wheel was in her hands, and had had many near collisions with parked cars because her mind was somewhere else.

"The girl of your dreams is Grandma," Evelyn said. "I read an article."

"She's too short for me," Murray said, laughing. "I like tall women."

"Rich is tall," said Evelyn.

"Yoo hoo," Murray shouted, as he pushed open the screen door to Sadie's front porch. "We're here. It's us. Murray of the Navy and the Dragon Lady."

"Oh my God." Sadie ran out of the kitchen, a dish towel in her hands. The towel was gray-white, as all things were that dried in the Smoky City, in spite of the fact that Oxydol had added bleach. "I didn't know you were coming. I didn't even clean."

In Sadie's house, it was still the middle of the depression. Cotton wadding sprung like little buds from the seams of the sofa. The floor was hardwood, not checkered with fashionable parquet, but laid with straight narrow planks of red-tinted browns, as in the waiting rooms of railroad stations, where people slept on benches till their trains came or their luck changed.

There was one large square imitation Oriental rug in front of the sofa, between it and the black iron fireplace. The twins were climbing to get out of Chris' old wooden playpen, placed in the center of the rug as if it were a decoration. Dead diapers hung between the wooden bars, like propped up soldiers in the niches of Fort Zindeneuf. To frighten off what enemy, Evelyn wondered: even an Arab wouldn't invade Braddock.

Braddock. A rented house. A worse place to be than Centre Avenue, but Evelyn didn't say so. She hadn't told Sadie she was coming, deliberately. Sadie wouldn't have had time to make the place presentable. Not to Evelyn, who inspected poverty as if it were the ranks of a defeated army.

"Twins," Evelyn said. "You certainly are a glutton for punishment. They're cute, but why'd you have to have two of them?"

Sadie laughed.

"I don't know what you think is so funny. How you let him push you around."

"He doesn't push me around. He's masterful." Sadie didn't look any older. Her hair was still dark blond, ungrayed, even by twins and a seven-year-old daughter. Her eyes were still laughing—at what, Evelyn couldn't imagine.

"Masterful?" Evelyn said. "He's a truck driver."

The twins were actually appealing, Evelyn couldn't help noticing, caged up as they were, harmless. They had curly light hair that gave them a cherubic look from the eyes up, and stocky little arms, so they looked like small editions of Pappy when he still had his hair. Boys. An amazing accomplishment, especially coming from Sadie.

"I should have married Johnny Granson," Evelyn said, looking at the wall above the fireplace mantel, where the cream-colored paint was peeling, revealing the fading gray of past undercoats. "I should have divorced Walter a long time ago and married the Hairy Ape and gone to Delaware and then I could have taken care of you and Grandma and everybody, and not almost ruined my life."

"We're fine," Sadie said. "Believe me, I'm happy."

"Ignorance is bliss," said Evelyn. "I should have married Johnny Granson. You can get used to anything, even a man in fur."

"What was, was," said Sadie.

"Another county heard from," Murray said. "I have to go

2 6 5

back to work. What do you want me to do, leave you here, or drive you back to Grandma's, or you want to go downtown?"

"Why are you giving me so many alternatives?" Evelyn said. "You know I can't make decisions."

"Stay here," Sadie said. "Be with me a while. Hymie can take you where you want to go."

"Who?"

"My husband," Sadie said. "The truck driver."

Grandma spent most of the two days Evelyn stayed in Pittsburgh standing in the kitchen. She made stuffed cabbage, cooking it for three hours, letting it sit in the refrigerator overnight so all the spices would blend and the fierce flavor of paprika and tomato could assault the cabbage leaves, taking the blandness away. Pappy had been doing well at the stand, so Grandma put in a nice piece of *pflanken,* even though it wasn't the weekend. And, because Evelyn was her eldest daughter, and Grandma loved her, she made gefilte fish, baked after it was boiled; chopped liver with mayonnaise rather than chicken fat, and a golden crusted round bread with raisins and nuts and grapes with the seeds still inside, so there was crunching inside the soft sweetness. All Evelyn's favorites, even though it wasn't exactly a celebration, a daughter getting divorced.

There were some things that were too complex for Grandma, but she accepted. Nothing was all that clear anymore. Her sister had died in an oven, and her second daughter wanted a place of her own, with no one to help her with the twins. Life was changing and death did not come from natural causes.

All Grandma could do was chop and prepare, to put her mind at ease until the moment when they could sit and eat, and she could see pleasure on beloved faces. Pleasure on beloved faces, that she understood exactly.

Once in the two days she cheated a little and went to the bakery for a marble cake, because she was nervous, with Evelyn having lived in New York, that her own recipe might not be good enough. Evelyn had brought them some Danish from Cake Masters on Broadway. Although it hadn't tasted as good as Grandma's own, she had studied the box for a half hour. Cake Masters. How could she possibly be as good as that?

They sat in the kitchen, the mother and the daughter she didn't understand at all, eating the marble cake from the bakery, stretching it out with coffee, stretching the coffee out with cream, filling the time with food because Grandma didn't know where to begin the conversation. That was no problem for Evelyn, however. She talked about the fact that Walter was unexciting to her in bed. She had read an article someplace ("Let's Explore Your Mind"?) that children should be made to feel free to discuss sex with their parents.

Grandma did nothing to shut her up, besides offering her more cake? more coffee? more cream? which she did every ten minutes. Evelyn wondered aloud what was going to become of her. She asked Grandma why she had forced her to want to get married so early, not waiting for an answer, reviewing the might-have-been suitors, reminiscing over the stockbrokers she had met in the early days of her marriage who might have been tempted to leave their wives. And what was going to become of Murray, he was a very nice-looking man in his own mild way, why didn't he find a nice rich Jewish girl with a generous father who'd see that they'd all be taken care of? As a matter of fact, if the father was rich enough, maybe Evelyn could take him on and they'd make it a double wedding.

Grandma sat there, just listening, not answering even the things that seemed to be questions. And every once in a while she'd say, "But why a divorce?"

She stared at her daughter through eyes salted with confusion and far-away memories she couldn't clarify. She watched the mouth going, and saw how beautiful the teeth were, how full the lips and charming the smile, when it flashed by before Evelyn pulled it back into a moue of regret. Grandma was aware of what extraordinary neatness of feature Evelyn had, the intelligence in her eyes, the energy in her small, pretty body. And good-hearted, yes, there was nothing she wouldn't do for the people she loved if she had extra.

But the rest eluded Grandma. The words she understood, every one of them. What she couldn't understand were the feelings behind the words: How could a woman just pick up and leave a husband, a very nice man, a little slow in the beginning of the marriage to do everything he should for a wife who wanted a castle, but a very nice man, Grandma really liked him; it was a shame they punched each other. And to leave a daughter, a girl, alone with a man even if he was her father?

"How is my Chrissie?" Grandma asked finally, when there was no more cake to fill the silence on her part.

"She's fat," Evelyn said.

"It's baby fat."

"She's eleven years old."

"That's still a baby."

"She writes songs now," Evelyn said, drinking some coffee. "In her sleep."

"You must be very proud."

"Really?" said Evelyn.

Pappy came home at three o'clock in the afternoon while Sammy and Pegeen took over for him at the stand. "Eh, Tillie," he said, when he came into the kitchen. "How come you're sitting down?"

"It's all cooked for tonight, I prepared." She went to the icebox to get him his lunch.

"Thirty-six years, and I finally caught her sitting." Pappy reached over and took Evelyn's hand. "Okay, *mein* darling daughter. Speak to your Pappy like a friend."

The table they sat at was an oversized chopping block from Gribbiner, the butcher, who went crazy and stabbed his helper in 1929. Every once in a while Grandma thought she could see blood in one of the cracks on the lightwood table. Pappy said it was from a cut-up cow, not Gribbiner's assistant. Still, Grandma wiped it scrupulously with a sponge every evening. Once a week she scoured it with cleanser, then rinsed it with lemon and water so it would smell fresh.

"Speak," he said, as he bit into the cold pot roast sandwich on white bread that Grandma had out in front of him. He didn't like white bread, his tongue felt longings for rye. But it was the middle of the day, and there was no time to soak in gravy, and the crust on the rye was too hard for him. So he ate white bread and tried to understand what the Gentiles thought was so tasty about it. "Come. I'm waiting. I ran home special."

"I told you everything last night."

"You told the family everything last night," Pappy said. "Last night was dinner for everyone. Now is lunchtime with me. I want the truth."

"About what?"

"About everything. About how a girl is raised by people with respect and she runs off like a *wilda hyer* to Miami Beach in search of fame and fortune and a *divorce*."

"It's happening all the time now, divorce."

"Not in this family," Pappy said, and drank some Hires Root Beer from the bottle.

"Sammy married a *shicksa*," Evelyn said.

"She's a nice girl," said Pappy, and belched. "She drinks beer and her brothers have red noses, but she works very hard for a *goy*. Your brother Sammy is not exactly a regular ball of fire. She helps him. They help me."

"How is Sammy?" Evelyn asked, somewhat reluctantly. One of the few joys she had had in New York City, even with Walter in China, was learning comparison shopping down to its finest detail. She had mastered completely clothing, and food, dry cleaning, laundry, and shoe repair, the basic necessities of life. So she had expanded into the field of surgery.

By 1946 she had read enough articles and magazines to know that the family was not merely hard of hearing but leaned to otosclerosis. So when doctors began experimenting with the fenestration operation (from the French, throw them out the window) on people's ears, she had naturally sent for Sammy.

"It's a very simple operation," she said as she took him to the

269

hospital. "They give you twilight sleep, it's a very pleasant anesthetic, and cut a window in your eardrum, and then you can hear as well as a regular person."

Sammy was very nervous about it, as no one in the family had undergone surgery before, except Evelyn who had had a small cyst removed from her breast. There was nothing to be nervous about, Evelyn assured Sammy. She had comparison-shopped ear specialists, visiting twelve of them before committing, and she knew this doctor was as fine as any that practiced in New York or Philadelphia, and two hundred dollars less. The operation was quick and successful. Sammy came home to the apartment only slightly shaken, the right half of his head bandaged.

"You'll rest for a few days," Evelyn said.

"Not so loud," said Sammy.

She assumed that, like herself, Sammy would be too restless to just sit still and recuperate. So she drew up a list of free attractions that New York City offered besides the museums.

There was an open-air exhibition in Central Park of the field munitions of World War Two. She sent Sammy there with Chris, all in a lovely afternoon. While he was there, they shot off a cannon behind him.

"Sammy's fine," said Pappy, eating his sandwich. "Deaf. But fine. He helps me."

"Is that what you want me to do, is come and help out at the stand? Should I hang my college degree on the green flap behind the oranges, and start hosing off cucumbers?"

Pappy set down his sandwich and looked at his hands. They were small hands, but they were very strong, calloused on the palms, dark beneath the fingernails in spite of constant scrubbing with Lava, and pure 20 Mule Team Borax scraped on a brush.

"I know you're too good for this family," Pappy said. "I just want to know how come you're too good for your own."

"Oh, Pappy, please, stop it. Some things I can't explain."

"To a father?"

"Here, Moisch," Grandma said. "A pickle."

"I don't want a pickle! I want to know what there is in the

world that a girl can't tell a man who was there from the minute she was born who might not be as smart as she is, but maybe has lived a little longer, you will believe *that?* I've been alive a little longer than you, *mein* darling. I have sixty-four years to your thirty-four."

"Twenty-eight," said Evelyn.

"What is she saying, Tillie? Wasn't I there? Wasn't it thirty-four years ago?"

"She's saying she's twenty-eight," said Grandma. "It's all right. They do that now."

"Who's *they?*" Pappy shouted. "The A.F.L.-C.I.O. for fency women?"

Evelyn stood up angrily. "I never should have come here. I only did it to try and be a good daughter. But you're too old-fashioned to understand anything."

"Teach me! I'm a very good listener for a refugee with a *bummarkeh* for a daughter."

"Go to hell!" Evelyn said, and ran from the room.

"I made cabbage!" Grandma yelled. "You can't leave."

"Pack her a carton!" Pappy screamed. "Give her a box for war relief. Stuffed cabbage for the Princess of Schventiensky, to go!"

"*Sha*, Moisch," Grandma said, placing a warm hand on his shoulder. "There are things you don't understand."

"Like what, for example?"

Grandma shrugged, and her little round cheeks reddened. "She doesn't have a good time in bed."

"She told you this?" He made a fist and hit it on the light wood of the table. "She spoke like this to you? *Evelyn!!*"

"They do that now. They read books. They read articles. They talk."

"Not in *my* house! *Evelyn!!*"

She came back to the kitchen, girded for battle but holding her tongue. They were her parents, and respect was respect. She would stay for dinner. Grandma had worked so hard. Besides, there was no train till midnight, not with direct connections.

271

"I'm understanding," Pappy said, "that the Roumanian by way of Squirrel Hill and China doesn't please you. When is your appointment with Mr. Errol Flynn?"

"Stop it, Moisch."

"Or maybe Mr. Errol Flynn isn't good enough for her. Have you tried him yet?"

"I won't be subjected to this," said Evelyn, and sat back down at the table.

"Here," Pappy said, and reached into the pocket of his white apron that he wore all the time he worked, and Grandma soaked in bleach and washed and ironed every evening so it would be fresh the next day. "The afternoon paper. Read all about it."

"All about what?"

"People who are not happy to live like people. Women who leave their husbands and children and get shot."

"Somebody got shot?" Grandma said anxiously.

"Somebody's always getting shot when they think they're too smart."

Evelyn took the paper from him and started reading hungrily, as she always did when there was a crime that hinted of perversion or terrible violence. Not since the Lindbergh case had something fully captured her attention, including the life she lived. She had been fond, in a vengeful way, of Bruno Hauptmann, and several times after Chris' birth she had fantasized that that was who Walter really was, and as soon as he was finished screwing her, he would get his ladder together and kidnap the baby.

She had been too young to get involved in the excitement about Sacco and Vanzetti, but even in retrospect the case didn't interest her. Shoe factory robberies, unless performed with hatchets for weapons, were not her style, nor was any kind of political injustice, so she paid no attention to it.

She had been captured for a few weeks by the murder of Starr Faithful (how could anyone think it was suicide?)—with Veronal in her stomach, Veronal according to the toxicologist who cut her open—how dreadful to even think about it! And sand in her trachea—it was almost too much for Evelyn to bear.

She followed the story only to find out if they'd ever lay the crime at the dirty appendage of the politician who had seduced Starr Faithful in her early teens (a Bostonian, initials A.J.P.). Of course the suicide notes were forged, and was he naked when he drowned her in Long Beach, that dirty old influential man? And why wasn't there anybody like that in Pittsburgh?

Arnold Rothstein's shooting she had considered unimaginative, as she did all gang warfare. And once they found no trace of semen inside the white girls, Victoria Price and Ruby Bates, the trial of the Scottsboro boys ceased to interest her, as did the South.

The murder case she hated to read about most often was the horrible tale of Albert Fish, who said he was taking a ten-year-old girl to a birthday party and had instead cooked her up in a stew with potatoes and onions and eaten her. The twenty-seven needles the psychiatrists found in his testicles, self-administered, seemed to Evelyn to be appropriate punishment, if he had eaten the fifteen children they thought. The death penalty was too quick, too lacking in readable details.

She despised Albert Fish as much as if she had known him personally, which was why she had taken the book about him from the library cart in the Army hospital when she had worked as a Gray Lady in New York. It hadn't been fair to Our Boys in Bed to expose them to such grizzly aspects of the American scene. Bad enough they had to kill foreigners and enemies, and had been wounded, mutilated by them. It was wrong to expose them to a man who ate children. As it was she could hardly handle it herself, more than once a year.

She studied wrath in newspapers like a connoisseur of wine, tasting, evaluating, dismissing all but the very best vintage. In the main, she liked crime best (except for the acid-bath variety, stemming mainly from the tubs of France, which prevented her from feeling any sense of national connection) when it was clean and finished and American, put away, like they had done with the Lindbergh baby, poor little thing, and that dreadful Bruno Hauptmann. Unless he hadn't been guilty, of course, that Bund-meeting Nazi, but who had time to think about that.

The murder in Pappy's Pittsburgh *Post Gazette* that day was hardly worthy then of her discriminating attention. It was a simple case of a man shooting his wife and her lover, with a pistol, not even a shotgun, in a diner, not even *in flagrante*. There was no doubt he did it, and no details about the wounds. So Evelyn opened the paper to the society pages.

"How about this?" Evelyn said. "There's a dinner dance this evening at William Penn, honoring Clifton Sanger. Imagine his coming to Pittsburgh."

"Who's Clifton Sanger?" asked Grandma.

"Only one of the richest men in America," Evelyn said.

"For shame, Tillie," Pappy said. "Not to know such a thing."

"He's probably in visiting the Mellons," Evelyn mused.

"Cantaloupe or honeydew?" said Pappy, beating himself on the knees to accompany his laughter.

"He's Jewish," said Evelyn.

"And you still think he's interesting?" asked Pappy. "How do you think that will go over with the Irisher movie star?"

"Oh, shut up," Evelyn managed, just before he was all the way around the length of the butcher's block, so fast on his feet that she didn't even have time to flinch before his hand was across her face. She sat back and up, tall in her chair, head held proudly so he could see the red mark on her face.

"My husband hits me harder than that."

"And you still want to leave him?" Pappy asked.

"Clifton Sanger." Evelyn's brain started dancing with possibilities.

"Stop changing the subject!" Pappy was back down at his end of the table, waving the last piece of his sandwich like a flag. "I want to talk about Life. The Facts of Life. Eh, Tillie? You think she's old enough now? How old did you say she was?"

"Twenty-eight," said Grandma.

"Well, you've certainly packed a lot of life into twenty-eight years." Pappy swallowed some more root beer. "Not only is she a scholar, she's a magician."

"Don't tease her, Moisch."

"I was just being amazed, I wasn't teasing. Twenty-eight years she's been alive, the Princess of Schventiensky, and she still doesn't know the Facts of Life. I'm going to tell her. Leave the kitchen, Tillie."

"Is it all right?"

"You don't ask a daughter's permission to leave the kitchen when I tell you to leave the kitchen." Pappy got up and escorted his wife to the door. "Don't worry, I'll tell her right."

Grandma smiled unsurely from the other side of the threshold. She pulled the wooden door closed.

"Okay," said Pappy. "Here it comes. Are you Ready for Freddie?"

"Yes."

"A person is born from between a woman's legs, covered with blood. The world got fancier since I came out, so you weren't born in a ditch, in a field. There was a faucet to wash you off, instead of a river. And when you had your baby, they had, what you call it, very fancy, so you wouldn't feel the pain."

"Anesthesia," Evelyn said. "I still felt plenty."

"Tish tish," Pappy said. "You still felt plenty of pain. In a way, I guess, we should all be grateful for that. You still felt plenty of pain."

He took a swallow of soda and belched. "So you know how life begins. It begins in pain. Do you know how it ends? It ends in pain.

"Do you think they go quiet in their sleep, the people where you read in the papers they went quiet in their sleep? No one goes quiet. There is a great boom in the heart, *mein* darling, a big explosion of crying, that God hears. Nobody wants to die. Not even the ones who kill themselves want to die. They want to live better and they can't, that's why they kill themselves. No one goes quiet."

"I'm getting a divorce, not dying," Evelyn said.

"Shut up when I'm speaking to you about *Life!* I can see life from sixty-four years' worth. I know! I know! I'm not an educated man, but there are some things I know. I know what it

275

means to work and work and how does it end, it ends, it's over. You're shoveling coal or running an elevator. Roosevelt's running an elevator, Adolf Hitler's shoveling coal.

"But what about the men who are not so important as Presidents and Führers. What does it mean for them, *Life,* what is there left behind but your children, and what if they disappoint you?"

"I'm sorry if I disappointed you," Evelyn said. "I really am."

"You never disappointed me," said Pappy. "Never. I could kill you sometimes, but you never disappointed me."

"Then what are you talking about?"

"I'm talking about *Life,* Princess. The way you see it when you get older and wonder why you were born to live it how you did. In America, where Jews can stay alive. All these years and there's nobody coming to kill us. Nobody coming to hug us, but nobody coming to kill. You're missing that in your life, looking over your shoulder for Cossacks."

"I'm missing nothing," said Evelyn. "I had Walter."

"Don't get smart with me when I'm talking Truth. I got to get back to the stand. When you're born in a place where nobody wants you to die, you don't have to look over your shoulder. So you can look ahead. I didn't know that. I didn't know about looking ahead until I was already looking back from time. So it was too late to change anything."

"Don't apologize for yourself to me," said Evelyn. "I think you're wonderful."

"I'm poor."

"That doesn't make any difference."

"It does to you. Live with that. Learn from that. Learn from me, scholar, I think I know. I know a little bit why we're here." He paused and gave the words great emphasis. *"No explanation!"* He pounded his fist once on Gribbiner's butcher block and raised his hand with one finger pointing toward God, or the people upstairs.

"A reason!" He was pointing at her now. "A reason, but no explanation. That means we have to make sense out of it, you understand. Live, but don't live foolishly. *Make sense out of it!"*

"I'll try to, Dad," she said.

"Oy, mein Gott." Pappy held his bald temples with both his hands, as if his brains were about to fall out. "Dad? Where did I get to be Dad? In New York or Miami Beach, Florida? Why am I here? To learn something. To leave something if I can. I have nothing to leave you but words. At least listen!"

"I'm listening," Evelyn said. "I swear to God."

"Du hörst?" Pappy said to the ceiling. "She admits You're around. That ought to make us both feel better."

"Stop it," Evelyn giggled. "Tell me what you want from me."

"I want you to *build!"*

"I'll try to send you money from Florida."

"You're not listening. I'm not asking for myself. I'm begging for *you.* I want you to take a brick and make it into a house like the third little piggy. Do you tell stories to your child? Do you hold her on your lap and tell her how the *Great . . ."* he paused. *"Big . . ."* he waited. *"Hungry . . ."* he poised, claws bared, dentures suddenly fanged, and sprang at her. *"Bear!* is coming to eat her in the woods and how you will save her?"

"That's your story. You tell it well. You enjoy frightening people."

"Only if I can *rescue* them at the end! What do you think stories are about? What do you think Life is about?"

"I don't try to tell your stories."

"It's your story now," Pappy said. "I can't save her. The Roumanian can't save her. He'd like to, but Roumanians don't know how to save, they know how to steal."

"You're being too hard on him," said Evelyn. "He's done very well for someone from Pittsburgh."

"Then why are you leaving him? Why are you leaving her?"

"I'll get her back in a little while. After the divorce."

"Divorce," Pappy said, and shook his head. "Divorce."

"It isn't such a terrible thing."

"Maybe not to the people who are dining and dancing to the

277

honor of Clifton Sanger at the William Penn Hotel. To the Moskowitzes of the produce-stand Moskowitzes, it's a disgrace, an ugliness, a scar!"

"You want me to stay with him till he kills me?"

"I want you to learn how to keep your mouth shut, and then no one will try to kill you. I want you to learn to keep your mouth shut and not run after Errol Flynn, because he chases around worse than any Roumanian. I want you to learn to keep your mouth shut in front of my wife and not speak filth to her.

"Who are you to talk to your mother about being in bed with a man? What do you know about it from your twenty-eight years? I know! I know." His bald head was shiny with perspiration, although it was cold in the kitchen. Cold, with only the smell of food to warm it.

"Tell me, then. What you know?"

"I know nothing," Pappy said. *"Nyutin.* That's as much as you can know. You can think, and you can plan and hope, and lie on the warm body of a woman and have comfort, and give some comfort to her. And you can have good meals and hard work and children that surprise you. And if you're lucky, you end up running an elevator. But while we're here, there's no guarantees. The people who know everything know nothing. That I can guarantee. Because nothing lasts. A minute. That's all we have is a minute."

"Then why won't you let me enjoy it?"

"I want you to enjoy it," Pappy said. "I just don't want you to waste it."

"Oh, Pappy," she said, and ran to him. She knelt by the table, her head on the stained white apron, crying onto the scraped-off green of unshelled peas and string beans. "What should I do?"

He patted her head for a moment, and then held her gruffly by the hair at the back of her neck. "What are you asking me for? I'm a peddler."

On the train she spoke to no one. There was not a man in the world traveling coach who interested her. Leaving Washington, she laid claim to a seat facing south, and turned the double seat opposite around so she could put up her legs. When the train stopped, before people boarded, she would lay one small suitcase on the seat in front of her, cover the suitcase with a coat, put a wig that Wandra had given her just underneath the collar of the coat so it looked like a cuddled up child asleep there. Then she would close her own eyes, so when anybody asked, "Is this seat taken?" she wouldn't have to answer, and they'd move on.

There were a couple of Okie farmers (she could tell from their speech, even with closed eyes) who sat down beside her anyway when they received no answer. But Evelyn opened her eyes when they were settled in and fixed them with a gaze at once so proud and contemptuous that they decided they might be comfortable a little further forward in the train.

During the safe hours, when people were going to the dining car, and the conductor wasn't walking through punching tickets, and the train was far from annoying stops and peasants hailing the sandwich cart, with its cellophane-wrapped ham, ham and cheese, or plain cheese on white bread, made miraculously even less palatable by some secret process restricted to those who supplied the Pennsylvania Railroad, Evelyn stretched her legs to the bench opposite and made of her thighs a desk. From her office in motion, she typed communiqués to those who were interested in her whereabouts, and anyone who might be. She still had the typewriter the Army had given her, and about forty sheets of V-mail that she supposed the government would honor even in time of peace.

Her typing was still excellent, and in between thoughts and experiences she was communicating to Chris ("Love to your dad," she added kindly), and Wandra Kane, and Pappy and Grandma and Sadie ("They're all your type on this train"), and Murray Rabin, the Florida attorney she thought she'd use for the divorce if he were still at the same place and still a little devious, she reviewed shorthand in her head. But she wouldn't go back to being a secretary, not unless she was desperate, which she didn't think she would be except once every few hours when she noticed the scenery outside the train, and the people in her car.

There was no way you could meet anyone on trains, not unless you could smuggle yourself into the Pullman section and get some Rudy Vallee playing a millionaire type to go along with the joke. No, romance on trains was out of the question. And even though some of the better people, she understood from Wandra, were flying tourist class, there was hardly enough time to make a real impression before the destination was reached. No matter how quickly people spotted her charm, a man would have to be as smart as she to know what a bargain she was between two stops. So, planes, too, were out.

Boats. People were trapped on boats, but in peacetime not by sinking. A life-and-death situation always inspired love. In her own experience nothing like sinking had spoiled the seas near Miami Beach, except for one submarine in 1943, and that affecting only Navy personnel. But being on board a boat was a life-and-death situation, even though there were no more torpedoes. Boredom lurked. Boredom lurked everywhere. People were even more desperate in times when they might not get killed predictably.

Avoiding death was at least an activity. Battles were exciting. But what if someone lived, and nothing happened?

She knew little about boats, not even that the bigger ones were called "ships," and suspected only vaguely that there was such a thing as a cruise. Even Wandra and Harvey Kane, who took constant and long vacations before she got the goods on him and could finally go somewhere alone, had never been on a cruise. At the time Evelyn was sorting out information from the strainer of her memory, she had no knowledge of Cunard or Princess or any other line. By the time she'd been in Miami for an hour, she knew it all.

She stopped into a travel agency two hundred yards from the railroad station and told the girl behind the desk she was thinking of taking a cruise. She did not smile as enticingly as she would have had the travel agency representative been a man, because there was no way to win the girl, and she didn't want to antagonize her by being too pretty. It was hard enough trying to seem as though she'd come from the sleeping car section, and just hadn't managed to find a redcap to carry her bags.

The girl behind the desk did have certain information. What vessels sailed from where, for how long, and for how much. Evelyn gathered the brochures in her arms like a gift of pirate's treasure, and said she would call for a reservation as soon as she had come to some decision.

All the way on the bus to Miami Beach, she studied and dreamed. Not so much of faraway places as unknown cavaliers strolling midnight decks of loneliness, waiting for her.

When she arrived at her destination, she had a neat little outline on her V-mail stationery of each important ship, its port of origin, and the address of the main office of the parent company. All that was missing was the names of the directors of the lines. Surely there were people in Miami Beach who would know.

It was the New World finally. Connections were made, not born.

Coconut palms no longer glittered for her. They appeared dry at the base, and uninspiring, stripped of romantic connotation by the fact that almost anybody could afford to go to Florida now. She checked in at the Reef and got an excellent rate from the manager, who was sorry her marriage hadn't worked out, and sorry the hotel had a good social director, but what could you expect when you left your husband mid-season?

She had dinner the next night with Murray Rabin, the shyster. He pinched her twice on the buttocks, agreed to handle the divorce and the suit for back child-support, since he still had the files. He was stopped from putting his hand down Evelyn's cleavage by a lobster fork, with which she stabbed him playfully.

"You haven't changed at all," said Murray, sucking his wrist.

"How would you know?" Evelyn said. "You never really knew me."

"I'd like to really get to know you."

There were two violinists in the small restaurant, wandering from table to table playing "Zigeuner" every fourth song. Evelyn allowed herself a few minutes of actual pleasure, pretending she liked gypsies, before dessert came.

"Listening to music becomes you," Murray Rabin said. "For a woman with beautiful eyes, you look even more lovely with them closed."

Evelyn smiled noncommittally, humming along with the music, swaying with bare shoulders that would, by the next evening, be brown, tonguing a piece of the melody at the front of her very white teeth, filling the air, and Murray Rabin, with promises. He was no dummy, even though he was not her type: he understood she was there for a divorce and back payment of child-support. After he had accomplished that for her, they could speak of other things.

In the meanwhile she got a job at the hotel not of her premier choice, as social director. The clientele was nothing to write home about, even though she did, mainly to Grandma and Sadie, glorifying those who were passing through. To Chris she wrote only that she was working to be able to buy her a wonderful graduation present ("Love to Dad"). And to the heads of all the steamship lines, whose names she had managed to find out, she sent long, clever, amusing resumes of her history as social director, her unique qualifications ("I really enjoy the company of other people more than my own"), enclosing a photograph of herself, as if she were applying to graduate school, which in a way she was. There was always the chance that one of the directors might have a boring day, like so many of her own, and read their personal mail.

Just in case they did not, she found out the names of their secretaries, by calling long distance on the hotel switchboard, which she offered to take over from the operator, as a favor, once in a while. She bought each secretary a little gift at the Army PX, to which she still had an identification card, covering the expiration date with her thumb, and a smile to the soldier at the door. She sent the gifts along with a warm personal note, air mail special delivery, paying full rate, as fair was fair, and she didn't know the Postmaster General.

One day, of course, there was the gay possibility that she would know everyone, Postmaster General included. Because it was America. Her whole life was ahead of her.

"My life begins today," she said every morning. Ahead of her, like Pappy said, why not, why not, why not? She was free and white and she looked twenty-one. What a world of possibilities, what a country of improbables. What difference did it make that she was Jewish and thirty-four when she didn't look either?

The years of bloom blazed radiant in front of her, like Pappy's polished apples, row on row, promising succulence on a crisp day. There was nothing she couldn't do, if she were clever about it. Nineteen Forty-eight. What a good time to be a clever woman. A clever woman could get anybody.

She looked in the mirror sometimes to compare, and there she was, as pretty as the ones who got away with murder. Women so far above suspicion they were above reproach, because they had married well. How admirable they were. How glittering.

Like the future.

America. Now that she was emotionally maturing and physically so brilliantly well preserved, Evelyn was sure the country that put such a premium on youth, and still acted the stickler for experience, was ready for her at last.

BOOK
TWO

ONE

Form No. ST-1

RCA
RADIOGRAM
RADIOMARINE CORPORATION OF AMERICA
A SERVICE OF RADIO CORPORATION OF AMERICA

FAST

ACCURATE

Prefix **P**

Sent No. **12**

Words **30** Radio

Sent to **WCC** by **SP**

Time Sent **9 AM**

CHARGES		
Coast		75
Ship	2	40
Landline	1	65
Govt. Tax		
Total	7	80

SHORE TO SHIP   **SHIP TO SHIP**   **SHIP TO SHORE**

Office of origin __SS PRINCESS OF THE ISLES__ Date filed __3/22/49__ Coastal station via __WCC__ Time filed __9:00__

Send the following Radiogram *Via* **RCA** subject to terms on back hereof, which are hereby agreed to

WHITE
285 W85THSTREET
NEWYORKNY

MY CHRISSIE
TWELVE YEARS OLD HOW COULD YOU DO THIS TO ME?
HAPPY BIRTHDAY MY DARLING LITTLE GIRL AND IF
ANYBODY ASKS YOU YOU'RE FIVE

INSIST UPON RECEIPT, WHICH MUST BE PRODUCED WITH ANY COMPLAINT REGARDING THIS RADIOGRAM

GEORGE V PARIS	SAVOY LONDON	WALDORF-ASTORIA NE YO

S/S __PRINCESS OF THE ISLES__   __3/22__ 1949

RADIOMARINE CORPORATION OF AMERICA
A SERVICE OF RADIO CORPORATION OF AMERICA
75 VARICK STREET, NEW YORK CITY

RECEIVED FROM __EVELYN WHITE__

ADDRESS __C/O TRAPPIS LINES__

DOLLARS __7.80__ FOR __RADIOGRAM__ WORDS __30__

ADDRESSED TO __WHITE 185 W. 85 ST NYC__

_____
RADIO OFFICER

Princess of the Isles
Trappis Lines

sunsailsunsailsunsailsunsailsunsail

Sweetheart,

Hope you got my birthday wire (well over the minimum rate! Nothing's too good for you)—had a wonderful day, gay, etc. Only regretted I couldn't be with you to celebrate. Trust you did something fun. Did he give you any presents?

Am bringing all mine—it makes no sense to pay postage from Aruba, our last stop. Can't tell you how much I'd love to have you with me. Appreciate your offer to run away from New York and hide on board, but know it would break your father's heart.

Of course you miss me, how do you think I feel? There's not one child on board. I'd let you come in a minute, share my cabin, but it isn't even as big as your tent—we'd trample each other before we got to Cartegena, Colombia, our next stop (picture postcards follow).

Am enclosing three snapshots (don't let your father find them) of me with Curley Harrington (he's the bald one, but very rich, you may have heard of him, he plays polo) and Rosey di Bonaven, who has something to do with politics or movies, I'm not sure which—very influential. Those are their wives in white shorts with the wattled thighs.

Twelve! I can hardly believe it! Have you lost any weight? I don't mean to pick on you, darling, but you would be so pretty if you took off a few pounds, once you got rid of your braces. Is he paying the orthodontist?

Speaking of which, has he said anything to you about my child-support? Divorce settlement finally arrived (a year overdue) but have detected no evidence of the $10.50

a week he owes me from period we were separated (Sept. '41–April '44). How could I ever have gone back to him, why didn't you stop me? That's 121 weeks @ $10.50/wk = $1270.50. Need it desperately. Can you drop a hint?

Enjoyed essay you wrote for school, rec'd March 15, but don't know why you included that quotation, *"Radioactive poisoning of the atmosphere and hence annihilation of any life on earth has been brought within the range of technical possibilities . . . in the end there beckons more and more clearly general annihilation."* Sweetheart, why do you dwell on these things? Of course he's a genius, but Albert Einstein is a very old man, and the old tend to be negative. It's only air, darling, it'll blow away. Stop worrying about little things like that and use your good brain to get your father to send me what he owes.

There are some lovely people here whose three teen-agers attend a boarding school that specializes in extraordinary children. Wish I could afford something like that. Would so love to give you everything a bright little girl should have. Wait'll you see the presents I'm bringing. Would send them from the Virgin Islands (our next to last stop) but I'll probably be in New York before they are. (We land April 6, 4:30 P.M.)

Dashing—2 minutes till shuffleboard tournament. You'd hate it here.

I love you so,
BMD
Beautiful Mother Darling

On shipboard, it was easy for Evelyn to learn about love, the lost legend of the Incas, all over again, and afresh. The moon shone on black velvet water, crystal glistened on white linen tablecloths, restoring splendor to a plastic world. Missing was only a partner, someone wonderful she could stand for more than eight days.

She was careful to have no romantic involvement with any employee, although the captain grew giddy in her presence, and the ship's surgeon (could he do ears? restore Sammy?) blushed every time he saw her the first day out to sea when he was dispensing suppositories. They were both handsome in a top-of-the-morning, top-of-the-bridge kind of way, but she knew too well the mistake of being impressed with uniforms.

She met middle-aged manufacturers from Milwaukee, someone who knew the fellow from Chi, and a host of unacceptables. Melancholy sweetened her evenings like nightshade. Evenings were made more poignant by the presence of all the trappings—wind, sea, and stars—and the absence of acceptable trappers. Rosey di Bonaven tried to slip her a few hundred dollars a number of times, but she explained she wasn't that kind of girl.

"What kind of girl are you?" Rosey wheezed, trapping her in the corridor outside her cabin, where he had been waiting. "That's what I'm dying to find out."

"A girl after my own heart," she managed, giggled, and slipped away from under his arm.

And went up onto the deck to sit with Daisy di Bonaven, Rosey's wife, which would keep him at better lengths than Evelyn could. "Daisy, Daisy," Evelyn sparkled, half in song, like the champagne served at five o'clock along with petits fours and bouillon for the infirm, and reformed alcoholics. "How are you this brilliant afternoon?"

Daisy di Bonaven was a woman who had, purportedly, once been very beautiful. Now she wore her bleached yellow hair in a tight upsweep, pulling the sides of her face upwards with two tortoise shell combs, locked at the crown, with bangs hiding the wrinkles that had mapped out her life on her forehead, and dark, white-framed harlequin Minnie Mouse glasses hiding her eyes. She was usually on some form of medication and seemed in a semi-stupor. Still, she managed to get her energy up when she saw Evelyn.

"Pretty thing," Daisy muttered from her deck chair. "Come sit down with me, pretty thing."

Daisy's closest friend, she had once told Evelyn, on a day when Rosey forgot to give her her medication, was Roxy Stinson Brast, a key figure in the Teapot Dome Scandal. Like all those who lived through the legends of their friends, Daisy would tell stories even Roxy hadn't told, and according to the records of the

Senate Committee, Roxy had told plenty. Roxy's ex-husband, Jess Smith, had been key flunky to Harry Daugherty, "Mr. Republican," as he had been known in Ohio, the Attorney General in Harding's Cabinet. Jess had been found dead in 1923, of a gunshot wound, and his death had been ruled a suicide. But Roxy had always maintained Jess had been murdered because of what he knew.

"What did he know?" Evelyn asked Daisy.

"I can't begin to tell you, I'm not allowed," Daisy said, and told.

At the time, Evelyn hadn't paid too much attention, because her eyes were still searching the decks for some renegade stroller she might have missed on board. Now, though, she had time to talk, as she had checked and rechecked the passenger list, and knew she had missed no one. He was not on board this trip. So she sat in the deck chair next to Daisy, trying not to seem intolerant of the fact that Daisy was wearing a white halter sundress, with those arms.

"You look so pretty," Evelyn said.

Daisy lifted heavy lids and attempted to focus her eyes. She touched Evelyn's little khaki short-sleeved military jacket matching the very tight shorts. "Wonderful," Daisy said. "So young, and lively and thin."

"I'd trade it all for a little of your wisdom." Evelyn lay back and let the sun warm her face.

"I'm not so smart," Daisy mumbled. "Rosey takes me on these cruises once a year to make up."

"You fight a lot?"

"I don't fight." Daisy closed her eyes. "I let him run. I don't mind. Never takes me to dinner with his important friends because of what I might say."

"Like what?"

"It isn't over just because it came out once," Daisy said, eyes open, sitting up. She was suddenly alive and fierce. "What do you think happened to those suitcases, the ones with the cash and stock certificates that got traded in those hotel rooms in Washington? Don't even think about luggage loaded with bottles of whiskey, smack in the middle of Prohibition. That part of it is nothing, nothing.

"But what about the wiretapping, what do you think about that, plugging in on somebody's phone and listening, like it was a party line? Spying in politics, and it isn't the last of it just because it came out once. The story of the Harding Administration was never fully told, espionage and all, and it won't be, I'll tell you that, until it happens again, and it's going to, believe me, only next time it won't come out so easy. You have to meet my friend, Roxy Stinson Brast."

"I'd like that," Evelyn said.

"It'll have to be for lunch," Daisy said. "Rosey doesn't let me out for dinner because of what I might say."

"Like what?"

In the end, Evelyn probably knew more than anybody outside Washington, or possibly in it, about some unrevealed scandals behind the scandals of the Teapot Dome. But as nothing was to be gained, except politically, and she had no use for politics, she made no attempt to lock the information away in her head.

"You're not going to tell anything I told you?" Daisy reached over and touched Evelyn's hand with brightly manicured nails.

"Of course not," Evelyn said, having already forgotten most of it.

"I've never discussed this with anyone except members of the press, and they won't believe me. Rosey and his friends get it going about once a year that I'm crazy, so the reporters won't print anything. I'm not crazy, you know. I'm just a little low on energy. Rosey gives me vitamins to build me up. But I'm not crazy."

"Of course not," Evelyn said.

"Roxy will confirm it all, everything I've told you. She won't talk about it in front of strangers, but you'll be her friend in no time. She'll like your pizzazz. I used to have pizzazz. Maybe I'll get it again from the vitamins."

"I think I'd better be getting aft to organize the Cocktail Dansant." Evelyn stretched her sun-browned legs.

"Oh don't go, yet. Please. It's so seldom I really get a chance to talk with someone. Rosey usually stays right with me to shut me up. I wonder why he isn't coming over?"

The faltering head turned, white harlequin pointy glasses shifted to the right. She seemed to be observing Rosey, who was standing in the glassed-in portion of the solarium, dripping an ash from his cigar, eyeing them over the black-ridged, white-lettered bulletin board on the easel, which gave the day's schedule.

"He really loves me," Daisy said. "You know that, Evelyn? He's crazy about me, that's why he doesn't want me to say too much. Rosey knows where a lot of the bodies are buried, and he doesn't want one of them to be mine."

"How lucky you are," said Evelyn.

"That's the only reason he tells people I'm crazy. If I was really crazy they'd have to put me away, and they can't do that, because psychiatrists are smart, how many of them can you put on the payroll, they're coming out of the shadows and they're not afraid to tell the truth or recognize it when they hear it. They'd know I wasn't lying. How many souls are asleep in the deep, and how about that shit hitting the fan?"

"Bouillon?" asked Evelyn, as the white-jacketed, black-capped steward offered a tray.

"I don't think I should," Daisy said. "I'm a little worried about my weight. Rosey's doctor gives me something to keep it down."

"What'd she tell you, what'd she tell you?" Rosey muttered in Evelyn's ear that evening, as they fox-trotted across the mirrored floor in the Salon Dansant.

"Why didn't you come over and talk to us?" Evelyn smiled.

"It makes me nervous when women start cackling together." He danced her backwards. "What'd she tell you, what'd she tell you?"

"How much you loved her. I thought under the circumstances I shouldn't mention your chasing me around the ship."

"It's true." His small brown eyes fixed her with his honest glance, practiced daily in front of the mirror to make sure it hadn't gone shifty. "I loved her once. We were kids when we got married. You know how it was in those days. Nice girls didn't fool around."

"And now you think they do?"

"They do if they want to know every biggie in New York."

"I don't want that from you."

"What do you want?" Rosey said hoarsely.

"I want to keep your friendship. Daisy said you loved her."

"A long time ago. It's like having a sick old dog around throwing up all over the house, and you try to remember how cute it was when it was a puppy."

"A certain gift for poesy," Evelyn said. "I'll have to introduce you to my ex-husband, perhaps you've heard of him? Lieutenant-Commander Walter M. White, he got the Navy Cross?"

"I bet Army. When can I see you alone?"

"I couldn't trust myself with you." Evelyn lowered her eyes. "You're too dynamic."

Rosey waltzed within the circle of his fox trot.

"I just don't understand it." She leaned her head slightly back, so red-black waves whisked against the edge of gray cotton, pin-striped with silver lame, Jonathan Logan. "How women can stay friendly with their ex-husbands is beyond me. I would've thought she'd be glad when Jess Smith got shot, whether or not it was murder."

Rosey stopped dancing. "She told you about Jess Smith? And Roxy?"

"Only a little. I have no head for details." Evelyn laughed. There was no way he would believe her, he was smart enough to see how clever she was, he would introduce her to *everybody*.

"You know, she's crazy."

"I haven't met Roxy."

"I mean my wife. She's nuts. She's out of her head. I only take her on these cruises to give her an airing. I can't let her out of the house otherwise. They'd put her away. The mind is gone."

"Well, maybe the vitamins will restore it."

"She told you about the vitamins?"

"I think it's sweet that you're trying to build her up," said

Evelyn. "And that the doctor is giving her pills to bring her weight down."

"She told you about the pills?"

"She's really a nice woman." Evelyn applauded as the orchestra finished the set, and the bandleader poised for the samba. "Why don't you go over and ask her to dance?"

"Daisy?"

"In the absence of what's-her-name," said Evelyn, "the one who testified for the Senate Committee?"

"Roxy Stinson Brast." There was sweat on his forehead.

"You have such a good head for names and detail." Evelyn pinched a dimple into his cheek. "I can't remember anything."

For the remainder of the cruise, she determined to stay out of his way, flashing him only occasional glances, hints that she knew more than she said, which she did, she just wasn't trying to remember. Her smile implied that she might be willing to part with more than she had offered, although she wouldn't. Still, it was a good exercise, teasing.

She figured she'd have him out of his head with lust by Haiti, where there were open sewers running alongside the colorful natives, carrying laundry on their heads. If she had had more time to work on him, and a dishonest inclination, if they hadn't stuck her with mid-morning championship bridge and canasta and gin tournaments, she could probably have won him by a duty-free port, where the jewelry shone even brighter because of no tax. Not that they ever gave jewelry, these crooked politicians (Starr Faithful had left those forged suicide notes, but no jewelry, so Evelyn knew about crooked politicians). Jewels could be traced; crooked politicians only dealt in cash. And nice girls didn't take cash, especially when they could get jewelry.

She was finished thinking about Di Bonaven, at least until they returned to New York where he'd introduce her to *everybody*, what choice did he have? She did her job and wrote her letters and concentrated her leftover charm on the Manny Kurzmanns, since Daisy was no longer allowed out of her cabin. ("She didn't feel well," Rosey explained. "The doctor had to give her a shot.")

The Manny Kurzmanns were pleasant people. The wife, Dolores, was the same age as Evelyn, and didn't look it either. They were extremely well-off financially, or very extravagant, Evelyn didn't know which. But she observed them having French champagne every night at dinner, and wine was not included, except on the night of the captain's ball, and then only burgundy or chablis. Champagne at dinner, every night. Lovely people.

Sun speckled the afternoons of Evelyn's semi-great expectations. Twice daily she completed a circular tour of the ship, boat deck at six-thirty in the morning, when no one could interrupt the purity of her striding exercise, upper deck at four-thirty in the afternoon, when everyone could interrupt, longing for her smile, a Ping-Pong game, anything to break the spell of waiting, the illusion that something exciting might happen. She practiced standing at the rail, looking out over quiet green-blue waters as if she were interested in scenery, as if she were searching for peace.

And always she was aware of men's eyes on her small, proudly held body. She'd let her hair grow a little longer, so it could blow in the wind. She stayed out of the wind as much as possible, except when she stood by the railing. She looked at the sun's rays touching the water, forging emeralds from the waves, and saw what glories there were in nature, for twenty-two minutes a day. What a wonderful place the world was, when you could afford to get away from it.

"How long have you and Manny been married?" she asked Dolores Kurzmann on the next to last day of the trip. The winds had grown cold again, men were back in jackets, even the vainest of women on board had stopped sunbathing and wore woolen slack suits under their furs.

"Eleven years," Dolores said. She was a brightly pretty woman, exactly as tall-tiny as Evelyn, lacking Evelyn's grace, which made Evelyn like her even more. Dolores had shrouded herself in a blanket, even as the ship was nearing Jamaica, sunning only her face. The coat she huddled in now was finest broadtail, a fur so newly fashionable it was hard for Evelyn to believe Dolores had been born in the Bronx. Dolores also had very bright blue eyes, and a smile that spoke of warm intelligence, and a husband who adored her, that much was obvious— why else would he still be plying her with champagne, when it was extra?

"And you're still so crazy about him," Evelyn said. "Eleven years. He must be a wonderful man."

"Yes," said Dolores. "Sure," said Dolores.

That afternoon Evelyn had tea with them. Dolores' tone had signaled potential divorce. So Evelyn wanted a chance to re-appraise Manny.

He did not raise his little finger when he sipped. He slurped in the liquid from the cup. As few things about Walter as had pleased Evelyn, he had spoiled her for table manners.

"What business are you in?" Evelyn asked, wishing to restore a little of the glow she thought he had had.

"Men's clothing," he said, and shrank to where he wasn't even tall.

That evening was the costume ball. The motif was The Princess and The Pirate. Each man had been provided with a colorful bandanna and a black eye patch, each woman with a long rope of not too well simulated pearls. There were to be two prizes; one for beauty, one for originality.

The main dining room, as large as any in the big hotels Evelyn had thus far visited in her life (which began that day), was decorated with papier-mâché masts, flying the skull and crossbones. Parrots in cages squawked above the noise of the orchestra. And in the chandelier, which had been redone temporarily as a crow's nest, Olmedo, the smallest busboy on board, peered out through a spyglass, nervously playing lookout.

There had been some question about the wisdom of putting him up there, as nobody knew how strong the chandelier was. But the effect was so good if anybody looked up that it was worth the risk of his falling down, Evelyn thought. So she had talked

him into it, promising him an extra ten dollars from her own
pocket, requisitioning the purser for twenty-five. She waved to
him gaily. Olmedo smiled out of the corner of his mouth, not
wanting to move too much.

"Isn't it beautiful?" she marveled to no one in particular,
making her way through crepe-paper streamers of red and white
and black. The tables were covered in bright red linen cloths,
bowls of heavily blossomed white poppies set in the middle of
each, and in the center of those waved a smaller paper version of
the pirate flags that fluttered above.

That, Evelyn could not help thinking, had been an inspired
touch, setting a large electric fan in each of the corners of the
ceiling so the flags could wave skull and crossbones into the
interior breeze. To the side of the black and white harlequined
linoleum dance floor sat a great treasure chest, dripping fake
riches: pearls and great chunky red and blue and yellow and
other middle-class stones.

Diamonds were there in force, authentic, strung around the
necks and wrists and fingers of the women passengers. Cold brilliance fighting its way out of folds of wrinkled skin, struggling to
sparkle on bony hands.

She stared at the stones, and the women. How commonplace
they would seem divested of jewels. That's what jewels were,
decorations to convert an ordinary life into a celebration, like
streamers of red and white and black in a room that would otherwise be drab. Except that jewels remained. No one could tear
them down and make them debris, just because the party was
actually over.

She had chosen her own unbejeweled, unbedecked costume
carefully, knowing what the decor would be, having planned it to
go with the gown. She had dyed a white off-the-shoulder taffeta
from last trip's costume ball (Antebellum, Après Moi Le
Deluge) bright red. Not a color she wore ordinarily, but few were
the passengers who could support tight-fitting red without seeming vulgar. She had tanned herself to that exact color where the
brown of her skin was even all over, and there was still a high

Indian glow on the sharp angle of her cheekbones. She had also saved one last bottle of Chen Yu nail polish that matched the dress exactly, and found a lipstick of that same nearly forgotten shade.

She entered the ball in slippers that felt like crystal, knowing there was no midnight that could ever change her back. She waltzed with the captain and looked into his eyes as if she were listening to what he was saying; why shouldn't she be generous, when life had been so good to her? So good. Only so good. Not good enough. Not yet. When would they send the miracle that would let her take part in the ship's pool, and not merely run it.

The menu was color-coordinated to the decorations. White creamy vichyssoise, steaks charbroiled so their outsides were black, broiled tomatoes with black olive garniture, white potatoes, boiled, everything served on silver-plated trays by waiters in tuxedoes, patches over one eye. The orchestra was fully costumed, and in place of the straight chairs with violin backs they usually sat on were wooden kegs. Taking a break once an hour, they signaled their departure with a chorus of "Yo Ho Ho and a Bottle of Rum."

There was a Treasure Hunt scheduled for ten-thirty, and Evelyn had divided the passenger list up into teams, which were posted on the bulletin board on pieces of paper driven in with daggers. Daisy di Bonaven seemed a little confused about what she was supposed to be looking for, but Evelyn told her not to worry, she'd give her some hints. Rosey had let her out of the cabin for the party.

"Isn't he sweet to let me come?" Daisy almost wept to Evelyn. "I got down on my knees, I swear I feel better, I'm just a little low on energy, so they gave me something to perk me up."

"You look very perky," said Evelyn, although it seemed to her that Daisy's eyes were a little crossed.

Daisy stumbled toward her table, while Rosey helped her and Evelyn held her other arm. "I'm sure you'll have a wonderful evening," Evelyn said.

"Evening?" Daisy narrowed her eyes. "Is it evening?"

During the dinner and dancing, Evelyn did not light for more than an instant. Except to share a little of Manny and Dolores' champagne.

"I can't tell you how glad I am to have met you two," Evelyn toasted. "To ships that don't pass in the night."

"I'll drink to that," said Manny, his patch raised to his forehead like a squadron leader's goggles after a battle.

"Don't you think you've had enough?" said Dolores.

"Only of you," said Manny. "Only of you."

"Excuse me." Dolores started to slide back her chair.

She looked very lovely, Evelyn had to admit, in a tight white seed-pearl bodice, a floor-length white satin skirt. On her head was a tiara, very small stones, possibly real. The bracelets she wore, two circular wrist-tight bands of platinum held together with a large diamond and ruby clip demonstrated her taste, even if she was married to someone from the garment district.

Manny had explained to Evelyn he owned a chain of men's clothing stores throughout New Jersey, West Virginia, and Maryland. But for the rest of her life, Evelyn was to consider everyone who had anything to do with clothes as being from the garment district, with the exception of Norman Norell.

"I'm sorry," Dolores whispered to Evelyn, getting up, tears in her bright blue eyes. "I'll see you tomorrow."

"You move your ass back on that chair, bitch," Manny recommended.

"I love your bracelet," Evelyn said to Dolores.

"Thank you. It was my mother's."

"I suppose now you're going to start crying because your goddamn mother is finally dead."

Dolores reached over and picked up her champagne glass, and flung the golden sparkling liquid across Manny's face. He sat for a moment, staring. Then he reached into the silver bucket for the bottle, refilled his glass, toasted Evelyn, took a sip, and threw the rest of it at Dolores. She stood, picked up the bowl of flowers, and dumped it in Manny's lap.

"You wet your pants," Dolores said. "Shame shame, and your mother thought you were all grown up."

"*Spoiled bitch!*" Manny shouted.

"Spoiled with what? Your good manners? Your charm?" Dolores was on her feet, moving away from the table.

Evelyn stared, fascinated. Their cabin was the best on board, three thousand dollars for the twelve days (she had checked it with the purser), plus the champagne every night and heavy tipping of the stewards. To be able to afford all that and still make a scene.

At that exact moment, the ship gave a colossal heave toward the port side, and tables, busboys, waiters, chairs with people still in them started sliding across the dance floor. Women screamed, as did some men, and Olmedo, who swung from the chandelier, hanging like a murderous pendulum parallel to the floor.

Dolores was thrown on her buttocks. Manny pitched forward onto Evelyn's chest, butting her backwards. They owed her a lot for that one, Evelyn thought, mentally calculating how much he would have sued the line for had he fallen on his face.

"Now there's no cause for panic!" the captain was yelling into the microphone, which was at right angles to the stage. He was gripping the permanently anchored podium. "We've just hit a little unexpected bad weather. Nothing's going to happen. But the dining room isn't rigged for a storm. I suggest you make your way slowly and carefully back to your cabins and just sit it out till this lets up."

"They're trying to kill me!" Daisy di Bonaven screamed to Rosey. "You said you'd protect me, and you're letting them kill me."

"Be quiet and pray," said Rosey.

So she bowed her head and read her pearls like rosary beads. In the chandelier, Olmedo did the same with a link of chain.

Evelyn moved Manny off her and started crawling toward the stage. Water pitchers slid across the floor, along with plates and people. The captain was still advising everyone to stay calm. But as the ship had started to heave in the opposite direction, the women's screams were drowning him out.

"What'll I play?" the bass player yelled from the floor of the stage to Evelyn. " 'Nearer My God To Thee'?"

"Very funny," Evelyn said. "Help me to the microphone."

"Wheeee!" Evelyn trilled over the loudspeaker, when they'd managed to get her up there and on her feet, and she was holding on to the podium. *"Wheeee,"* she said, along with the next great swell. "For a minute there, I was almost afraid.

"Ladies and gentlemen, ladies and gentlemen," she said, over the screaming. "Forget the gentlemen, *ladies!!* No cause for panic. Cause for joy! For those of you who were disappointed at losing the ship's pool, we're going to have another one, courtesy of the Trappis Line. *A five-carat diamond! Pear-shaped!"*

There was silence, except for the noise of the dining room falling apart. "For the woman who comes closest to estimating the time this little storm will last. Go carefully back to your cabins, and place your bets with your night steward. When this is over, we'll assemble in the Tout Le Soir Lounge for champagne and the name of the winner."

Slowly, with order, they filed from the dining room.

"Now somebody get a ladder," she said, "and help get down the Cuban."

She sat out the storm for two of its three hours, watching the sea wreak havoc with her decorations, the splendid crystal, splintered by a fickle mistress, she supposed Walter would say. The papier-mâché mast had fallen, along with the streamers once hung so gaily and well. Nothing left of frivolity in the evening. The ocean was starting to irritate her.

She had been to sea like Walter. She had acted with courage and intelligence, averting what could have been a civilian disaster. But James Forrestal couldn't cite her. No wonder men in high places went mad, having to give rewards to all the wrong people.

She would be rewarded, she knew it, she just had to be. But what if she did not live to get her just desserts? Cherries flambé, the fruits of the earth, on fire in the air. They hadn't even been able to serve it because of the sea. Rolling, churning, battering the ship, insensitive to her being on board.

"How much longer is this going to last?" she asked the captain on the phone.

"We're clear to the north of Hatteras," he said. "You were magnificent before. I want to commend you."

"Thank you. Is that all?" Roger, over, and out, is that where it ended?

"As a matter of fact," said the captain, "I'm afraid I'll need your help again. There's a passenger in the furnace room, and she's going crazy or something. The doctor's with some injured passengers, and I can't leave the bridge right now. Could you go down and see if you can talk to her?"

Through corridors rigged now with thick lengths of hemp to cling to, around staircases, their banisters paralled with rope, Evelyn made her way. She hadn't been below decks that often, except with potentials who turned out to be scratches, but instinct led her by the crew's quarters, down past the less than glistening doors, to actual sailors, who took her to the furnace room.

There were two large roaring furnaces, each manned by two stokers, who stood naked to the waist, shoveling coal. And between the two furnaces quietly raged Dolores Kurzmann, still dressed all in white, her outfit streaked with black like the stokers' bare chests. At her feet was a pile of trousers. Her eyes burned red as she rushed forward and threw the pants into the flames, pair by pair.

"Dolores?" Evelyn said, as Dolores immolated a pleated pair, with checks.

"Please, lady, cut it out," said one of the stokers.

"Dolores?" Evelyn said again.

Dolores looked up at her. "I'll be finished soon," she said, and threw in a beige pair of trousers, with cuffs.

It was the calmest performance of fury Evelyn had ever witnessed. Fifteen pairs that Evelyn observed extinguished. And each time she moved toward the furnace, Dolores would hold the pants up neatly, line up their creases so they would be perfectly tailored for the flames.

"Okay," Dolores said, when there was nothing left but fire licking at the last of glen plaid. "I can leave now."

"I don't understand," said Evelyn, when they were safely in

the cocktail lounge where the chairs were welded to the floor.

"It's very simple," Dolores said. "I hate him."

"Why didn't you just throw them overboard?"

"I wanted to see them burn," said Dolores, sipping her brandy. "Can you understand that?"

"I certainly can," said Evelyn, and knew she had found a true friend. There was no question, it was a gift she had, making friends. An extravagant gift, in her opinion, since friends were something a really secure girl didn't need.

All the same, she admired Dolores' style, not leaving him even the wet pair of trousers he'd worn at dinner, whipping them from the bed while he was in the bathroom. The steward had had to lend Manny a pair of white work pants so he could get to Evelyn's room, where he was spending the night. Evelyn was sleeping in with Dolores.

"You sure you don't want to make up with him? Walter and I had a rule we'd never go to bed angry unless it was with each other."

"I'm finished with him," Dolores said. "It's over. Like the pants."

Who said there was no such thing as generous coincidence, no god of mercy, even for Walter M. White? By the time the ship docked, Evelyn had appraised Dolores detail by detail. The face was dark and pretty like Evelyn's own, only less spectacular, the body was good, so she wouldn't fall apart. She said she liked children, and Evelyn knew she burned trousers.

"My darling!" Walter rushed toward Evelyn with three dozen red roses. "My dark angel." He covered her face with kisses and tears that stung in the cold of the badly sheltered pier. "I've thought it all over and I know I need you more than love itself."

"Come." Evelyn pulled her face away. "Come, I want to introduce you to somebody."

305

She did not attend the wedding. She sent Walter and Dolores a warm note of congratulations in a basket of flowers delivered by a process server. It was as clever a way of hitting someone with a summons as Murray Rabin had ever heard. In addition to the back payment of child-support Walter owed her, she had added to the costs plus interest, $4900, two and a half years' tuition, plus room and board, plus expenses at Coventry Hall, the boarding school Evelyn had heard about on the Princess of the Isles.

At first, of course, Chris had been reluctant to go away to school. But Evelyn explained that they would be able to spend most of Chris' holidays together, and that, if Chris stayed at Hunter High, she'd have to live with Walter and Dolores, who was a very nice woman, but had once burned all her husband's trousers.

"Besides," Evelyn had said, with faintly perfumed arms hugging around the fat little waist, not so little anymore, Evelyn tried not to say, as they sat on Evelyn's bed in the Belmont Plaza. "You know how your daddy is. Even though I got official custody of you in the divorce, he'll try and get you to go with him, just to spite me. If you go to Coventry Hall, you'll have all those wonderful advantages, the country and teachers and a tennis court and a dining hall."

"I thought you couldn't afford that."

"Well, I can't, sweetheart, but you know how I overextend myself for you. And they gave me a thousand-dollar bonus for saving the ship." Evelyn smiled. Actually it was five thousand dollars, but there was only so far Evelyn could trust her daughter. "Don't tell your father I got it, or he'll never pay me back. So it's settled then. You'll drive up there with me Saturday."

"In the middle of the semester?"

"It's all right, Chrissie, you can make up a year in a few months, you know how clever you are. Especially for a twelve-year-old."

"I'm thirteen," said Chris.

"Here. This is my best dress." She held out the ball gown, still on its wooden hanger, painted with the legend "S.S. Princess of the Isles." "I've only worn it once. It's a little grown-up for you, but you'll look very beautiful in it, once you take off forty or fifty pounds. Are you sure you're thirteen?"

So Chris, away at boarding school, had the dress, and Walter, out of her life at last, had Dolores. Evelyn could never fail, on breaking someone's heart, to give them something personal she didn't really need.

"I really appreciate all the help you've been," Evelyn said to Rosey di Bonaven as they sat at the table in Bruno's Pen and Pencil, furnished in red leather, giving the sanctity of an English hunt breakfast to a New York dinner, it said in the advertisement. "Getting Chris into that school at such short notice."

"Well, you have to thank Curley for that, he's the bigwig with education. Me, I'm small potatoes with schools. What are you going to have, the sirloin, or the filet?"

"Whatever you think." Evelyn toyed with her spoon.

"Two big sirloins," he said to the waiter. "Medium-rare okay with you, beauty?"

"Medium rare is fine."

"And two baked potatoes scooped and the shell rebaked, and lots of sour cream and chives, and no gristle on the steak or it's throwed on the floor, got it?"

"Yes, Mr. Di Bonaven."

Evelyn supposed it was all part of the political game, being tough and crude, but wished it had been more of an act that Rosey put on. Instead of ingrained, as demonstrated by his grammar. Throwed on the floor. Really. A man with true strength and any class would have thrown it on the floor without announcing it wrong.

"Ahoy!" yelled Curley Harrington from the front of the restaurant, where he was handing his coat to the checkroom attendant. "Shipmate's reunion!"

"The two of you are so sweet to take me out to dinner."

"No, we're not," Rosey said. "We both think you're a hell of a broad, unanimously." He put his hand on her knee, underneath the table.

She moved it back onto his lap. "Tell me, Curley, tell me about Coventry Hall, is it really as good as they say?" They who had said had been Curley.

"I got three kids there." He snapped the fingers of one hand for the waiter, moving his other hand onto her knee under the table. "Didn't you see for yourself when I sent you up there in my car?"

Evelyn moved his hand onto his lap. "Well, it's very pretty," Evelyn said, remembering green and white and clean buildings, magnolia trees in early bloom, the wall by Chris' double-decker bed, where Chris had started immediately taping up pictures of Evelyn. She also remembered the room outside the dean's office, where she waited while Chris was tested, a mere formality, the dean assured her, since Chris' record was excellent, and she had Mr. Harrington's personal recommendation.

But most of all, Evelyn remembered the inside of the telephone booth in the front hall of Tara, from which she had tried to call Walter collect every half hour, to tell him how wonderful the place was, and wouldn't he change his mind and pay? From the telephone booth, unfortunately, she could see the students. In dungarees and flannel shirts, even the girls.

"They certainly are a motley crew," said Evelyn now, to Curley. "Those children. Hardly young men. Hardly young ladies."

"Well, all kids are like that today," said Curley. "Rebellious and difficult. It's the threat of war in Asia."

"Oh. What war is that?" Evelyn bit the cherry from her Manhattan, enjoying the flavor, not hearing his answer.

By the time salad was served, both men were pressing so hard on her kneecaps, she changed her seat and moved the tablecloth in front of her legs, so everyone in the restaurant could see their hands, should they wander. "I'm really so grateful to both of you."

"Yeah, I can tell," said Rosey.

"Nobody's ever gone out of their way for my daughter like that."

"You know, you're pretty enough to be in pictures," Curley said. "If I was taking an active interest in the studio, instead of just buying it for an investment, I'd see you had a screen test."

"Flatterer."

"What about me?" Rosey asked. "Don't I get any points?"

"You're in politics," Evelyn said. "Mustn't offer too much."

"What do you want? The key to the city? I got it in my pocket." He handed her a key to Suite 405-407 at the St. Regis.

"You're sweet," she said, smiling, and pushed the key away. "I wish I didn't find you so irresistible. Stop being so hard on me."

"Hard on you," muttered Rosey, shaking his head. "Hard on you."

"I know how difficult it must be to be an important politician. Just as it must be hard to be in the movie business." She included them both in her admiring, helpless glance. "It's so funny how I got you both mixed up in the beginning. I didn't know if you were in politics or movies. They're both so glamorous."

"Yeah, well maybe we should get together, and glamour it up, huh, Curley? Everybody else is merging. Maybe we should merge. What do you think, politics and the movie business, who could resist that combination?"

They all laughed at the ludicrousness of the idea.

She could manage them, she knew that now. There was no man alive she couldn't manage, singly, or in troops. No man who wouldn't plunge bravely into the fray, carrying her standard, which was getting higher all the time.

"Who's that fellow by the bar watching us?" Evelyn tried to say casually. He was tall, blond, and handsome, not too tall, and not too handsome, and actually, more gray than blond. But finer-looking than the men who sat with her at the table, finer-looking than most of the men she had ever seen. His smile, as he looked at them, was tinged ever so slightly with contempt. He had to be really something, or someone, to sneer at Rosey di Bonaven.

"You know how much I like you?" Rosey said to Evelyn. "I

like you so much, I'm really going to spread you around. But you better not give him more than you give me, chickie."

Chickie. Really.

"Come here, come here," Rosey shouted at the bar, pulling the man toward him with a wave of his arm. "Come on, I want you to meet somebody."

The man did not move. He did not even nod. He stood there, one foot on the rail, smiling slightly. Ever so slightly.

"Come on," Rosey said to Evelyn. "We better go over to him."

"I don't go over to men."

"You'll make an exception," said Rosey, and helped her to her feet. "This one is worth it. You ought to know him. Open a lot of doors." They moved past curious glances. "Evelyn White," Rosey presented formally, "I want you to meet my pal, the next Senator from New York, Arnold Sterne."

"How do you do," said Arnold.

TWO

At first, Arnold had been nervous about setting Jeanne up in a New York apartment. She made so stunning an impression, even on landlords and elevator men, that he was afraid any hope of anonymity was foolhardy. For a while they had looked at furnished places in Newark, a twenty-minute ride from Pennsylvania Station. But even twenty minutes away began to seem too far, if it had to be coordinated to train schedules. In the end they found a quiet walkup in the Village, a block from Washington Square, so she could take a stroll through an imposing arch if she grew homesick, walk on streets lined with occasional trees, which gave a hint of country, if not shade. And in the absence of a brook that they could bathe in, privately, Arnold had her bathroom reconstructed from the skylight down, so it hung heavy with foliage, became an arboretum, with a sunken marble tub in the midst of living green. The bathroom cost him eleven thousand dollars, which he paid in cash borrowed from Sonny, so there would be no records of the missing money when the accountants went over their books, no checks to the decorator, nothing at all that could link him with Jeanne, except the look in his eyes.

To Sonny he explained that the eleven thousand was a payoff for a political favor, although Sonny never asked for an explanation. Nor did Sonny ever mention that twenty-five thousand a year seemed a little exorbitant for a consultant's salary, especially a woman consultant who came into the office only two or three times a week to review the international monetary situation with Arnold, to lunch with an infrequent European client. Sonny questioned Arnold about nothing of a personal nature, because he suspected nothing, Arnold was sure.

How could Sonny know, when he was so worn out from trying to enact into reality his own stubborn dreams? In Sonny's eyes, his son would be tall, his wife would get better with the aid of specialists, his fortune would continue to rise, in spite of slightly shifting tides.

Joe Pape's Finest had become the number-two bourbon on the market, so Sonny's personal fortune was expanding daily. But he wouldn't touch it, wouldn't pay attention to it, said he was saving it for a thirsty day.

The offices of the Sternes were in a constant state of monied confusion, because now the boys (men, goddamit, thought Sonny, how did that happen?) knew everybody they needed to know, everybody trusted them, except for the big banks and heavy funds like those of the Clifton Sanger Investment Corporation, Inc., managed by pedestrians. But what difference did it make that conservatives could only fly so high? So high. No higher.

Arnold had seen what the world looked like from thirty thousand feet, with shrapnel exploding around him. Living through death, nothing could get him, because he had it all: daring, and his own private rink, polished wood. Ball bearings, you bet your ball bearings, gliding on polished wood, that was Arnold Sterne, loose on the world, roller-skating. Holding hands with the ones who were too timid to make it around the steep banking. And only two years to wait till he was Senator.

"How do you do?" said Arnold when Rosey introduced him to the small dark woman at the Pen and Pencil. He did not really look at her. He was too busy searching the entrance for Jeanne. Rosey di Bonaven, for Christ's sake, of all people to run into. The worm that could turn anything against you.

Where was she, and why had he made the date here, where people could see them together? Why hadn't he just slapped her around like a man should do when she started to cry, whimpering? His baby. Weeping about how lonely she felt every moment she wasn't with him, about how tired she was of eating in small, dark, out-of-the-way, out-of-the-stomach restaurants. Tired of ordering in, no matter how good or how expensive the food was.

"Why don't you go out to dinner with friends?" he had shouted.

"What friends?" Jeanne had whispered. "What friends do I have? The only people I meet, I meet through your business. You told me not to be too personal. My life is unpersonal. Your office. This apartment. I am empty when I am not with you. Who should I talk to? You told me to trust no one."

"I mean for you to trust no one," Arnold said. "That doesn't say you can't have friends."

She had beaten him, relentlessly, the only way she could beat him: appealing to the emotions he didn't have, begging the compassion that wasn't a part of his makeup, pandering to all those aspects of human nature he despised, those weakening womanly traits like pity and love which were nowhere in him except when he was with her, goddamit. She beat him. He should have beaten her. He should have sent her spinning across the room, bruising her alabaster skin, cracking the perfect jaw, knocking the shit out of her instead of comforting, holding, promising to change, coming to this restaurant, so Rosey di Bonaven would have ammunition to kill him.

"A Senator!" Evelyn said. "I'm so impressed. I've never met anyone in politics before, except Rosey, of course, and that's not the same, is it? Rosey, have you ever been elected to public office?"

"Do I look like I enjoy self-sacrificing?"

"Really?" Evelyn said. "Is it truly all that noble, Senator? I read an article that a lot of the people in politics are selfish, in the true sense of the word. They're trying to get a public image, because they have no personal image of self."

"You don't say," said Rosey.

"Of course, the article was by a psychiatrist, and I don't really approve of psychiatrists. If you ask me, they have no self-image, or they wouldn't be giving Rorschachs. That's one of the things that worried me about Coventry Hall, the dean who interviewed my Chrissie said they have their own school psychiatrist. Can you imagine? Do you think they have many disturbed children there, Rosey?"

"Curley's the one whose kids go there."

"Have you met them? Do they seem disturbed? Oh, forgive me, how rude, we've hardly met and here I am, Senator Sterne, discussing other people's children."

"Of course," said Arnold, looking past her where he might catch Jeanne while there was time, while they could get out alive, without Rosey finding out, getting him again, past deals, past elections, into personal blackmail; he'd be able to grab him by the short hairs of his life. Arnold got up and snapped his fingers for the check.

"Oh." Evelyn studied eyes that didn't see her. "Was it anything I said, Senator?"

Arnold glanced at her briefly. "Excuse me?"

"I hope it wasn't what I said about psychiatrists and politicians. I personally don't agree with the article. I really don't trust psychiatrists, that's why I'm a little worried about Coventry Hall, the boarding school where my little girl goes. Did I offend you, Senator?"

"I'm not a Senator yet," Arnold said. "And it wasn't anything you said."

" 'Fifty-two," said Rosey. "That's the big year, 'fifty-two."

"If I'm living in New York, I'll vote for you, you can count on that. Imagine. Such a young man to be Senator."

"He ain't so young," said Rosey. "He's only a couple of years younger'n me."

"How do you do it, Mr. Sterne? What's the secret to your youthful appearance? I understand it in women, but in men . . ."

If he made a bolt past her, he could catch Jeanne outside. But here she was, chattering up at him, and there was Rosey, slavering over her, eyes hanging out like his tongue was almost doing. If he ran, Rosey would get insulted, fuck him, he was on the payroll, there was a contract. But what did any of it mean, if Rosey changed his mind? What was Arnold going to do, sue him? Why not take the contract straight to the D.A.?

He focused his eyes on her tanned tiny darkness, and tried to seem interested in what she was saying. Her smile was fantastic, and she was using it for all it was worth, which to Arnold was not very much, but he could see where it might mean a lot to some man.

"You must be very relaxed, very wise, to stay so young," she was saying.

"I'm afraid I'm neither relaxed nor wise. Won't you have a drink?"

"Thank you," she said, and perched charmingly on the stool beside him. "I mean, I thought I looked young, but you look young enough to be less than ten years older than I, and I have an eight-year-old daughter."

"Can you believe that, Arn?" Rosey shook his head. "A girl that looks like this, with an eight-year-old daughter."

"I thought you said she was going to Coventry Hall," Arnold said.

"I did."

"That's a high school."

"Well, she's very bright," said Evelyn. "She'll probably graduate when she's ten. A Manhattan, with two extra cherries," she said to the bartender.

"I'll have the same. Give my cherry to her." Rosey laughed coarsely.

Evelyn's mouth twisted slightly; she looked up at Arnold. "Do you believe in private school education, as opposed to public school? I'm in such a quandary about what to do, being so recently divorced." She looked down, and away, so her glance was pluperfect: regret for the past, hope for the future, and still a little tense.

"Yes," Arnold said.

"I . . ." Evelyn hesitated, and looked at him. She seemed almost to click her eyes, lenses that caught her subject once, forever, clearly. He wasn't paying attention. To Evelyn. "Under the bamboo tree?" she asked, to verify.

"Most of the time," said Arnold.

She sat back and waited for whatever he was waiting for, that kept him from seeing her. "Do you have children?"

"Yes," he said, and hearing the silence, added, "I beg your pardon?"

"Children," Evelyn said. There had to be some way to capture him.

"A boy twenty-two and a girl ten."

"Impossible." She pointed a well-manicured finger. "And yet . . . There'll be another before the year is out, if I don't miss my guess."

"You miss your guess."

"A man like you breeds courage into this country. You can't stop making children, Mr. Sterne. Not while you're still in your prime."

"What did you say your name was?"

"Evelyn White." Aha!

"Listen, maybe you can help me, Miss White . . ."

"Mrs. White. But I'm divorced."

"I'm in sort of a bind, Mrs. White. I have to meet a friend of my brother's, and much as I'm enjoying this conversation, I'd really like to have it another time. Would you call me at my office? Oh, there she is, Miss—uh—" He tried flagging Jeanne back out the door, taking a card from his pocket with the other hand. "Come down and have a drink with me at the office, you and Rosey, of course."

"Of course," said Evelyn, snapping the card he had handed her shut inside her purse.

"I can't tell you—" he threw a twenty on the bar—"how much I've enjoyed meeting you."

"You don't have to," said Evelyn.

"Why don't you and the lady stay and have a drink with us?" Rosey suggested.

"I would, but I hardly even know her, she's a friend of Sonny's. You know how he is, always getting himself in little binds." He held out a check for his hat, moving past them.

"Are you a Republican or a Democrat?" Evelyn asked.

"Yes," said Arnold. "Soon." He waved. He was out of the restaurant, pulling the blond girl with him so quickly they only had a moment to see the carven profile, the elegant length of her. A moment had been enough. A moment was almost more than Evelyn could stand.

"How long has she been his mistress?" she asked Rosey.

"Don't be dumb. He ain't. A man would have to be a moron to bring a mistress here. And he is about as far as you can get from being a moron."

Evelyn opened her purse and looked at the card. "Sterne and Sterne. Who's the 'and Sterne'?"

"His brother. A real sweet guy. Night and day from Arnold. Hard to believe a guy like Sonny would cheat on a dying wife."

"All men cheat."

"I don't cheat," said Rosey. "I'm dying to cheat, but you won't give me a chance. When are you going to give me a chance, kid? I'm crazy about you." His arms were around her, and the back of her dress was bare.

She could feel the sweat of his palms on her shoulder blades. "Daisy is a friend of mine."

"She's a friend of mine too," said Rosey. "I don't fuck my friends."

She looked at him with a gaze so cold and even that he knew the exact level of contempt, and that he was beneath it.

"Tell me about the brother. Sonny."

"What do you need to know about him, he's taken twice. Listen to me, Evelyn. What can I give you? What can I offer you?"

She had been thinking exactly that. "Tell me about Sonny Sterne."

"A very nice man, devoted to his wife, he doesn't fool around, and when he does, you saw who he fools around with."

"Investment banking." She looked at the card. "The money business."

"You're a very pretty woman, Evelyn, beautiful. But you saw her for yourself."

"Sonny isn't seeing her, she's Arnold's mistress."

"I know Arnold twenty-seven years," Rosey said. "I know his type. He feels the same way about broads that I do. Screw 'em and forget 'em."

"That's redundant," said Evelyn, as if he would know what *that* meant.

"Except in your case, sweetheart." He did a little two-step against her crossed legs. "For you I would make promises."

"Oh, don't do that," said Evelyn, pushing him away. "How sick exactly is the wife?"

All that night, before she went to sleep, she studied the card, felt the embossing. The money business. That would be something to write home about. Especially to Pappy. The money business he could understand as well as tomatoes.

"You're a fool!" Arnold screamed, as he threw her on the bed. "You're a goddamn fool. Not the biggest in the world, because that's reserved for me, I listened to you."

Jeanne moved against the pillow, tears on her cheeks. "I just wanted—"

"Don't tell me again." He sat on the chaise longue beside her

3 1 8

bed, looked at it, yellow-and-white-striped satin, feeling like he had invaded the nineteenth century. What was he doing here in a beautiful woman's salon, for Christ's sake, to ward off cold, when he didn't need warmth, that was the last thing he needed. "We can't go out together. Around here, sure, dumps, little places in Jersey. But not the restaurants, you see how crazy it is."

"Crazy." She slipped out of her pale pink satin-lined coat and unzipped the back of her pink linen dress. "Yes. Of course. Crazy. To want to go out and walk on the street with a beloved, to pass the afternoon, to eat dinner. Crazy. I am not rational to want such things."

"We both want them."

"You want me here." She turned on him, raging, whiteness gone from her face, anger blazing it red. "You want me here, hidden and alone. So no one can see me! You have so little trust in me, you think I could meet somebody else? Love somebody else? Is that why you want me hidden?"

"I want you on a goddamn float!" Arnold screamed. "I want you to be in the Rose Bowl Parade, the Queen of the May, the window display in Tiffany's. It eats my guts out that I can't show you to *everybody,* the whole goddamn world. Look what I've got that I can't say is mine."

She wiped her eyes with a blue-flowered handkerchief she kept, fresh, by the bed. "You know I am yours."

"But I can't tell anybody."

"Yes you can." She whirled on him. "If you want to as much as you say, you can."

"I'm running for Senator. A divorce doesn't go over too well in politics."

"This is America," she said. "You all believe in love . . ." She sang the word scornfully. "Brotherly love, motherly love. Everything but passionate love. Passionate love loses votes, yes? Passionate love is for perverts, criminals, foreigners."

"You're overstating your case. But in excellent language," Arnold said, smiling. "You continue to surprise me."

"I have nothing but time. To read *English*. To learn *English*. But I am not an American girl. Flattering does not make me forgive."

"I thought *I* was angry at you," Arnold said, reaching for her.

She turned her back to him. "We must end it."

A woman could frighten him. A woman could actually make his hands tremble. He was sick at himself, but not as sick as he'd be if she were gone.

"Stop saying stupid things."

"It makes sense," she whispered. "You are a very important man, you have a wife, you have children, it's an old story."

"Not to me," Arnold said, and put his arms around her, feeling the smoothness of velvet skin contrasted to the linen. "To me it's a very new story, because I didn't know it could happen." He hugged the outside of her breasts with his palms. "Get out of your clothes."

"My beautiful clothes," she said, and hung the coat and dress up in the closet. "Look at them," she said, indicating the double racks of gowns and cocktail dresses and casual wear, couturier, all of it, the best in the world, the best Sonny's money could buy, because it might not look good in any of Arnold's personal records. A payoff to an insider in the Mitsaki bank, who fed them information, that's what Sonny thought that money was for.

"Look at those lovely things, and I can wear them nowhere, except to greet you at the door, and have you say, 'Get out of your clothes.' "

"You're bored with making love with me."

"So bored," she said, and flashed into nakedness, pulling him by the belt on his suit pants, opening his trousers with one hand and easing his jacket off his shoulders with the other, all the time covering him with her mouth.

"Let me help you with that," he said, and hurriedly started undressing himself.

"Enough." She pushed him gently backwards on the bed. "The rest is mine."

She eased his undershorts down over his hips with her mouth, helping it only a little with guiding fingers, pacing the motion, slowly, with her lips.

"My God," he whispered, as her tongue lashed briefly across his hip bone.

"You mustn't say that. Blasphemy. When you feel this . . ." she traced the tip of her tongue across his stiffening penis, "you could think there was a God. In the flesh, not just the spirit. Not good for the election."

He pulled her up to his mouth and kissed her, held her with arms grown gently protective, insisting, surging, comforting, strangling, trying to make her part of him, an extension of him.

"No," she whispered. "Not yet."

She slithered down between his legs, and lifted his knees into the air with her elbows, pressing her breasts against his testicles, slowly, rhythmically, insisting her soft roundness onto his buttocks. She swooped like a gentle bird, and took the length of him into her mouth, nipping with gentle teeth, swirling around him slowly with her tongue.

"Stop," he said. He moved her on top of him, sitting her back, stretching her legs out over his shoulders, turning his head to lick her instep, moving inside her. He placed his hands on her hips and urged her toward him with the power in his hands. Power. Power. He would give it all for the surge that was going through him now, that was coursing out of him into her. "Come," he murmured, "come."

"I love you," she moaned into his mouth. "I love you."

"I love you too," he said softly, when he could breathe again.

She brought him some champagne, in a chilled crystal goblet, and toasted him with a glass of her own. "Cheers," she said. "*Santé*."

"And so it will stay like this, yes?" She held her champagne with one hand, massaging his testes with the other, to relax him, she said. "I will wait for you here for the rest of my life. I will put on my clothes and go nowhere."

"Not anymore," said Arnold. "I haven't been exactly fair."

Four days later he had lunch with Roan Anderson, a very

presentable young man who had left his father's investment firm to go out on his own. Roan Anderson was a little Waspy for Arnold's taste, but he was clean, and bright, and seemed pleasant enough. Handsome, but not too handsome, his hair a little too orangey red, his laugh too close to a snicker to make you think there was true passion there, no index of inner joy.

"I may have a proposition for you," Arnold said, when they had finished eating and he was offering Roan a cigar.

Roan had spent the meal telling Arnold how well he was doing. Arnold had run a Dun and Bradstreet and made a few calls and knew better.

"What's your availability?"

"Well, if it's a job with Sterne and Sterne . . ."

"Better than that," said Arnold. "I've been thinking of buying an oil leasing company. One of those franchise deals, drilling, renting labor, equipment, part tax shelter, part potential boom for everyone involved. The assets are impressive, but not as impressive as they would be if a real businessman supervised the operation."

"I don't know very much about oil."

"You don't have to know about oil. They have serfs getting it out of the ground. Serfs and machines. The same thing. What you'd be doing is checking on the various bases, making sure the foremen and accountants aren't bleeding us, goldbricking, or oilbricking." He smiled. "Base salary sixty-five thousand. Stock options in the company."

"Sounds great," Roan said. "No complaints. But why me?"

"I just have a hunch you've got all the qualifications," said Arnold. He looked up and saw her waiting by the maitre d's desk, palely beautiful in orange silk, a captured firefly. "Over here," he signaled, and smiled formally as he got to his feet. "We have a special overseas consultant with the office," he said to Roan. "I want you to meet her. You'll be working with her a lot."

He saw that they were together for the rest of the afternoon. He made them go out and have a drink together after he had laid out all the information about the leasing company to Roan. He saw that they sat close to each other in the office, and he saw that Roan Anderson had never seen anything like her in his life.

"He's asked me out to dinner," she said to Arnold on the phone. "What should I do?"

"Are you hungry?"

"I don't understand."

"Sure you do. Hungry is hungry. Let him take you someplace nice where you can be seen. You're a very beautiful woman, you ought to be seen." He hung up the phone.

"I think that's very wise," said Sonny from the desk opposite, covering the phone over which he was confirming the sell order.

"You think what's very wise?"

"Getting rid of her," Sonny said. "It's too close. The election's too close, and it's getting dangerous."

"I have no idea what you're talking about," Arnold said, and started going through the papers on his desk.

"I still think it's very wise."

She was waiting for Arnold in a negligee when he got to her apartment at eleven, after phoning ahead to make sure Roan wasn't there. "How could you even ask me if he was here?" she said angrily, closing the door behind him. "Why would I let him come here?"

"Didn't he want to?"

"Of course he wanted to. Why would I let him?"

"Because I say so."

"I don't understand."

"I want you to go to bed with him."

She looked at him with eyes as pale as the green chiffon she wore. As pale, as soft, as yielding. "Don't make jokes."

"Why shouldn't you? He's clean. He's dependable." He did not add that Roan was boring, because any man would be boring after him.

"Don't play with me, Arnold." She reached for his lips with her fingers.

"I'm not playing. I've never been more serious in my life. I

want you to go to bed with him, and see if you can stand it.
When can you meet with him again?"

"I won't."

"When has he asked to see you?"

"Tomorrow."

"I want you to go to bed with him, or I can't see you anymore."

"You make me a whore!"

"Life makes us all whores," Arnold said. "Do it. Just do it for
me."

He had a big party the following evening, taking Sarah and
Sonny and Ellis, who was in from law school, inviting Catherine,
who was not well enough to go to a dinner, at Twenty-One. He
tipped the headwaiter twenty-five dollars and still was seated in
the wrong room. But he didn't fight about it. It was a celebration.
A family party, riddled with decency, appropriate for the next
Senator from New York.

"How was it?" he said when he was with her again, five
o'clock the next evening, not even having the patience to go
through the charade of cocktails with Sonny, he was in that
much of a hurry. He sat down on the overstuffed fluffy white
couch patting the cushion beside him.

She did not move. She stood by the antique French desk and
fingered a small carved ivory elephant on top of it. She couldn't
stand the smell of herself. She had douched three times, and
bathed, and she could still smell Roan Anderson's come.

Arnold plumped up the cushion beside him. "Sit here."

"Come into the bedroom," she whispered. "I am to be treated
like a dog, I will not sit by you like a dog."

She took off all his clothes. She dipped him into Vaseline,
plunged his penis into the wide-mouthed jar, feeling the top of it
stiffen, watching it grow. And then she stroked the jelly-like
substance slowly up and down the length of him, moving it
across the tip. Around and around and around.

"Does it feel like shampoo?" she said.

"Why are you doing this?" As if it mattered.

"I think it is more fitting we make love like dogs. If I am to be a dog, then I must make love as a dog." She turned her back to him, and climbed on the bed, and bared her buttocks. "Now," she said.

"I don't want to hurt you."

She laughed.

"Bitch!" He lunged into her, too fast, too hard, too full. She screamed, and fell back against him, reaching, her lips turned for his mouth, arms outstretched backwards for his pity. And then he started again. Gently now. Gently and slowly until he had her screaming in a different way. Oh, yes. A different way.

And then they were plunging together, he thrusting, she driving backwards, moaning into her own breasts, reaching for his hand with her arm. And his fingers were around her hips and into her, and her hand was rubbing the tip of the tunnel, and he was loving it, loving it, not really wanting to hurt her of course, oh no, it just felt so good he didn't give a fuck if he killed her.

And neither did she.

"Are you all right?" he said, when he had gentled her back to the girl she had been, caressing her nipples and the rest, and they were lying in each other's arms, like people. "I didn't hurt you?"

"Only in the beginning," she said. "Everything of love always hurts only in the beginning. Like the soldiers. After a while you begin to enjoy it. Then it ends. Then you become a whore. Then you turn into a dog."

"You wanted me to do it."

"Oh, yes. Of course. I wanted you to do it."

"Did you let him make love to you?"

"Of course. You don't expect a dog to have discretion."

"How was it with him?"

"You want to know detail by detail. How he touched me? Where he touched me? You want me to call him again and we do it in front of you?"

"I only want to know if he was gentle with you."

"He was gentle with me."

"Did you enjoy it?"

"I love you," she whispered. "I wanted to be with you."

"But he didn't disgust you."

"He didn't disgust me. I disgust myself."

"I want you to marry him."

She started to cry. Very softly at first.

"I want you to marry him," Arnold said, and turned to hold her face with tender fingers. "Because I love you with all my heart, and I never knew I had one. I can't afford to have a heart. I'm building an empire, Jeanne. Partly I suppose now, I'm building it for you." He touched the white-gold hair, brushed it from the burning face. "So marry him. Marry him, please, for me. It's the only way I'll be able to take care of you. The care I want to take of you. Let me take care of you."

He had rehearsed the speech for three days. Honest words, said not in anger, came slowly to him.

The oil leasing company had a small office in Bayonne, New Jersey. But all its branches were in faraway places. Jungle stops in Central America, South America. Seventy-two hours—five, six days with bad transportation breaks away. Roan Anderson would be home maybe twenty, maybe thirty days a year.

And he would be very wealthy. Wealthy enough to buy her jewels. All the jewels Arnold couldn't parade around her throat. Nothing could hang suspended on that pink-ivory bosom and look fake. Observers would know that the stones were more than imitation. People might find out that Arnold Sterne insisted on being real.

It would never do.

He helped her from the bed, glided her rose-tinted paleness to the bench in front of the dressing table mirror, and proceeded to drape her splendid nakedness with imaginary jewels, soon to be real. "Consider them from me." He covered her pink-white breasts with pearls, a halter of pearls, a pearl at a time. "When he puts them around your throat," he touched her throat, "when he cloaks this thin white loving cup with oyster tributes from the sea, consider them from me." She sat up straight; her face and her love and her breasts were young, and strong. "When he hangs emeralds from your ears," he touched the outside of her temples as she gazed in the mirror, "to try and match the color of your eyes . . ." He leaned down and kissed the flaming cheeks. "When he starts searching the Indies for cabochon rubies, to match your lips"—he swept against her mouth—"consider them from me."

Libraries were no place to meet the man, as fine as they were for unexpected encounters: Anyone worthy of Evelyn should at least be browsing in Scribner's, ordering sets of books, leather-bound, if possible. She did not look at faces in the subway when she traveled downtown; as far as she was concerned, she was traveling incognito. It couldn't really be Evelyn, with all she deserved, traveling by subway. How could he possibly recognize her, as if he would ride the subway. Why even bother to look: the poor were all incognito.

The floor of the Stock Exchange to her dismay was closed to the public. She could have found him there, of course, her swash-buckling money pirate, some twentieth-century Robin Hood, robbing the rich to give to the rich. But she didn't want to be with the observers. Action was what she needed, to be in the middle of action, adventure, and life. Right there in the center of that frenzied floor, with all those poor men, twenty-two percent of whom needed a shoulder to cry on (she had read an article).

Twenty-two percent of the men who worked on the New York Stock Exchange were unmarried. Of the twenty-two, she supposed five percent at least were fairies, ten percent Mama's boys (a monied Murray, could such a thing be possible?), and another five percent under twenty-four. She didn't like boys that young, even if they did look too old for her. So where were they, the scattered two percent, the ones who were really available?

She studied their movements, clustery ants, carrying paper bread crumbs to the center of the anthill, and figured, and counted, and thought. What about the other seventy-eight percent, the ones who were taken, but longing to get out of it? No. Forget about them. No point in getting involved with married men. Not unless their wives were dying.

She zipped open her brown leather bag, into which she had switched the contents of her move-around life: mascara, a tortoise-shell compact, six different lipsticks for changing moods, an alligator wallet containing eleven dollars in cash, and a hundred and twenty dollars hidden in the fold behind the eleven singles, her address book, her bank deposit book, a calendar with room for jotting down possible contacts and appointments, a bag of coins holding forty-seven dimes, eight quarters, five nickels, and she never counted how many pennies, a few pieces of stationery from the Waldorf-Astoria (the lobby of which she had strolled through the evening before) in case she got a moment to write to the family, a pen that the desk clerk at the Belmont Plaza had given her (sort of), a half-used book of airmail stamps, eight books of matches, a small picture of Chris holding a badminton racquet, when she was three, in a little ridged plastic envelope to preserve it, on the opposite side of which was a picture of Evelyn in her ballet slippers, at twelve. And oyez, oyez, a card so heavily embossed she could feel the lettering just by looking at it, emotion made it Braille. Leaping out at her, the very rich grain of Sterne and Sterne, probably down on the floor, or just around the corner. Yes, that was where the address was. Just around the corner. Oh no, too brazen, and not nearly clever enough. "Hello, I'd like to invest a few thousand dollars." Flutter, flutter, flutter. She could do better than that.

Besides, Arnold Sterne was no dummy, blond mistress or no blond mistress. Arnold Sterne would think she was on the make.

She found their building, looked at the impressive directory in the marbleized lobby, studied the important-sounding firm names, biting on a Goldenberg's Peanut Chew she'd bought from the newsstand in the corner, along with the New York *Times*. She'd opened it to the stock market listings, folded it back to the financial pages, so she wouldn't look too conspicuous, standing there. Sterne and Sterne. Suites 1000–1009. Better and better.

She took the subway back uptown, spraying her trim black suit with light eau de cologne as she came up into the daylight, so she wouldn't smell working-class. She took a bus crosstown and walked to the Chambord, where she was lunching with Wandra

Kane. Evelyn had seen advertisements for the restaurant in *The New Yorker* magazine, which her dentist had given her, sort of. She'd been anxious to eat there, but assumed it was too expensive. When Wandra suggested it, Evelyn had been delighted.

Crisp duck at noon, how elegant! Crisp duck and crisp Wandra. Why shouldn't she be crisp, unruffled, almost totally poised. Still collecting alimony from Harvey, because she had caught him with goods as splendid as adultery in New York. Better even. Wandra had uncovered several of Harvey's most secret documents, signed letters of agreement between him and "persons in high places," as Wandra put it, dated during the war, in which Harvey promised to pay them in return for certain services, Wandra didn't have to enumerate, and wouldn't no matter how often Evelyn begged her.

"An oath is an oath," Wandra said. "Once I got the million, and three thousand a month, the only decent thing to do was give my word."

"Who were the letters to?" Evelyn asked Wandra again, as she always did, hoping finally to get an answer. She was looking around the restaurant as she waited, pausing long enough to note that the decorations were understated and lovely, and most of the men were fags.

"Privileged information. It's like I'm with the government, or the church."

"Were any of them to Walter?"

"Privileged information. I wouldn't tell you if they were, and I wouldn't tell you if they weren't. Just as I couldn't say if any of them were to the Red Cross in China."

"Were they?" Evelyn asked with not quite so much interest.

"I wouldn't tell you if they were, and I wouldn't tell you if they weren't."

Being divorced became Wandra, Evelyn couldn't help noting. Not drinking so much. Her hair wasn't bleached to that too-yellow shade, she was ashier blond now, subtly made up. But there were terrible lines starting.

Evelyn gulped a little of her Brandy Alexander. Wandra was—what?—thirty-eight, and Evelyn thirty-six, even if she looked twenty-three and it was hard to believe she had a daughter seven. When would she herself start to go?

"Don't you want to get married again?" Evelyn asked.

"Why? I've started my own cosmetics firm. I'm busy. I'm happy. Why would I want to get married?"

"To be married."

Wandra shrugged. "I have everything I need."

"You haven't got a husband. Doesn't that make you uncomfortable?"

"I was more uncomfortable with Harvey."

"Get another one."

"You get another one," said Wandra.

"I haven't met anyone I could care for," said Evelyn, and reviewed for Wandra Rosey di Bonaven, Curley Harrington, the man in Scribner's who had looked quite interesting, well-dressed, literate (he was browsing through the nonfiction books), who had seemed worth considering until Evelyn realized he was shoplifting, and Arnold Sterne, the next Senator from New York, only he had a mistress and a brother whose wife was dying.

"Yes," said Wandra. "I know Sonny and Catherine."

"You do? What's the wife like? What's he like?"

"I don't know them well. I just met them. At a hotel Harvey took me to one summer when he was making a reach for class."

"Could I have some more water?" Evelyn asked the waiter, and drank what was left in her glass so the words wouldn't come out too fast. "What hotel?" she said.

The black Packard limousine pulled through the great stone gates, crunching pebbles into the silence of the pine-treed New Hampshire summer afternoon. No winds fluttered the flags of all nations, hanging in miniature array from the second-story terrace of the Shushoni Inne. Like a great many of the camps the children of the patrons attended, the name of the hotel, although it sounded Indian in origin, was, in fact, a combination of the owners' names: Shumann, for the aging father who had founded the resort chain, and the son who now ran it; Shonzeit, for the wife who had married the son, trailing her family's number-two in the nation toilet paper industry; and Niki, their daughter, who had already had her nose fixed at thirteen and had it broken by an infield fly during a softball game at Trahatchapee, a nearby summer camp for girls.

The Shushoni Inne covered a thousand acres of the finest land in the country, and included, outside the main hotel with its seventy-five bedrooms with bath, huge dining room, lobby, game room for children, and ballroom for important affairs, a natural lake with canoes and rowboats and swimming only within the boundaries of the ropes strung between the landing and the raft a hundred yards out. There were two rock-decked swimming pools, one fresh water, one heated mineral spring water, golf course, a horseback riding trail, stables, and thirty-six guest bungalows, each of which was made up of two bedrooms, a servant's room, a large living room-lounge, a kitchenette with no stove, only a miniature refrigerator, so all real drinking and eating would be done in the main house of the hotel itself, encouraging a more convivial atmosphere and buying drinks at one of the hotel's four cocktail lounges.

The bungalows cost a hundred and twenty-five dollars a day, and were usually reserved a summer in advance. The clientele of the Shushoni Inne were like family, Mr. Shumann said, and family liked to know they had a place waiting for them, which they certainly did at a hundred and twenty-five dollars a day.

Meals were included for a couple, at that rate. Children were ten dollars extra apiece, a very fair price considering the food was better than any served at places specifically for children, and the fact that they ate together an hour before the main sitting, sparing the parents mealtimes at least. They were supervised by the Kiddie Hostess, who adored little people and expected a tip of a dollar a day per child at the end of their stay. Servants who came with the guests were offered the advantages of a snack bar near the stables, or a diner a half-mile from the hotel, especially if they were colored, and could drive.

The servant who drove Sonny's limousine into the driveway of the Shushoni Inne was a German in his late fifties, carrying with him all the elegance of a Prussian in uniform. He piloted the car like the general's aide he might have become, coldly, a martinet's care in his handling. Never too fast, never too slow, because the roads were always changing, not like the Autobahns, no matter how good and straight they looked on the map.

With it all, Heinz' efficiency, Heinz' caution, Sonny still steered in his head during the drive, braking the car on curves with his jaw, fending off oncoming headlights with his eyes, never daring to rest except during stopovers. In the back seat, while he and Heinz drove the car, Sonny played chess on a miniature magnetized board, letting his glance leave the road for only a split second to figure his next move and mark Norman's progress. Remarkable. The boy had a fiercely logical brain behind the curious eyes and the oversized spectacles.

His free hand Sonny used to stroke Catherine's back, touching her velvet skin, soothing her into sleep to save her the perils of the highway, trying to suspend her in time so she would be preserved for the happy part. The glorious part, the place where the sun was, and the trees, the rest that was conscious rest, with fresh air moving through her lungs, and eyes open to beauty.

"Here we are, darling," he said, when the car pulled up to the main entrance of the hotel. "Put the chess pieces in the kit, Norman."

"I have one move left to checkmate," Norman said.

"I don't see it."

"Here," said Norman. "Checkmate."

"Son of a gun. I didn't even see that coming!" Sonny grinned, even though he had.

Three bellhops helped them, with dollies for the steamer trunk, the four valises. One assisted Heinz in taking the wheelchair from the front of the car, opening it, easing Catherine into it. Heinz wheeled her through the lobby, while Sonny registered, meeting them at the French door leading out to the rock-studded patio behind the hotel. Cocktail hour, under yellow and white umbrellas, was in progress. White-coated waiters carried gaily fruited drinks, collinses and whiskey sours dotted with cherries and slices of orange, adding bright colors to the disappearing day. Friends from previous summers raised brown arms in greeting, flashed smiles at them, and invitations.

"Later," Sonny said to them. "After we're settled. You want to go straight to the bungalow, don't you, Catherine?"

"It's all right," she said softly. "I just want to freshen up. You stay here with your friends."

"I'll see you're settled." He helped Heinz move the chair down two stone steps leading to the lawn and the path to the bungalow. On a large square of well-manicured green, four children played croquet with brightly painted mallets, shining wickets, brilliantly colored balls. "You want to play croquet?" Sonny asked Norman.

"There was one other move I could have made." Norman clutched his father's jacket, holding the portable chess set with his other hand. "Bishop to Queen Three. I'll show you in the room."

"I believe you," said Sonny. "Why don't you play croquet?"

"I want to be with you," said Norman. "Don't make me be with the children. Can I have dinner with you?"

"Will you want to have dinner in the dining room?" Sonny asked Catherine.

"I'll try."

"I ought to butter the maitre d', make sure we get the table you like by the window."

"That would be nice."

"I'll wait till you get settled."

They were halfway across the lawn, when they heard the woman calling: "Mr. Sterne! Mr. Sterne!" She was not quite running, but her movements were so quick, on small firm legs ending in little sneakers that matched the shocking pink of her shorts, she seemed to be a tropical bird in flight.

"Hello," she said, with prettily flushed cheeks, holding out a sun-browned hand to Catherine. "You must be Mrs. Sterne. I've been so looking forward to meeting you."

"Aren't you nice," said Catherine, smiling in response to the welcoming smile, taking the well-manicured hand. "And you are . . . ?"

"Evelyn White," said Evelyn White. "I'm the new social director."

From the front porch of the hotel she had watched the arrival, supervising the tea and cakes served to the older guests, while the livelier ones had cocktails on the rear veranda. Watching, all the time she was talking gaily to the aging, she tried not to be overwhelmed at the size of the car, the size of the man, tall, fair, smiling, too young by a lifetime for the woman he helped into the wheelchair. Powerful-looking, that was what he was, that and noble, too strong by half to be father to that spindly child with oversized glasses and frightened face. A head taller at least than his brother, the next Senator from New York, with a gentle expression on his face, gentle and actually loving as he wheeled the middle-aged woman into the hotel.

Evelyn had waited outside while he was registering, trying to get her voice back into her chest where it belonged, out of her throat where it was jumping around. She did a deep-breathing exercise between the front porch and the French doors at the rear of the lobby, so she would be relaxed, calm, in command.

"We're having Beef Wellington for dinner," she said to Catherine Sterne. "I'm going to speak to the chef especially, and see that he saves the best one for you." She focused the full energy of her charm on the woman in the wheelchair, not even looking at Sonny. She didn't have to look at him. She had known there was luck when he got out of the limousine, easing himself from the back seat to the driveway, gripping a gray velvet strap that hung beside the window, not even having to fumble, he was so used to limousines. And he was handsome. Truly handsome. That part of it she hadn't even counted on, hoped for.

Love of the kind she had read about in *Collier's*, which she couldn't quite swallow but still had subscribed to, started to play with the top of her head, began to dance in her heart, shooting blood to the back of her skull, and holes in her composure. She was almost stuttering, she was so excited. She hoped he would attribute her unease to youth and inexperience, even though she wasn't looking at him to see if he was appraising her. She gave all her attention to Catherine, who was saying she didn't know if she was up to eating in the dining room after such a long trip; perhaps just a little something in the bungalow might be better.

"Your first night," said Evelyn, trying to pass some of the warmth she hoped to convey through her hand into the fingers that clutched at the wheelchair, into the eyes that were empty of hope; that poor husband, so much to put up with—how could he look so vibrant and young?

"Please," Evelyn said. "Let me speak to the chef. Come down to dinner."

"You're very kind," said Catherine.

"No, I'm not," Evelyn insisted. "I'm just new here. I hardly know anyone, and everyone seems so happy to see you."

"Thank you," said Catherine, and smiled. Smiled at the compact energy that seemed to be bobbing in front of her, a buoy, a sentinel, a signal to life. "Maybe I will." She reached up over her shoulder and touched Sonny's hand. "Maybe I'll change into something fresh and come back in a while for dinner. Will you join us?"

"Oh, how sweet of you," said Evelyn. "Maybe I can."

She could, she could, she could, and she did. He was witty, My God, with all that, he was witty, witty and caring for Catherine, that sick old lady and that horror of a son.

"What a wonderful family you are," she said to Catherine, as Norman spilled his soup. "I always wanted to be part of a wonderful family. Thank you for letting me eat with you."

"You're more than welcome," Catherine said. "It's nice to see such a cheerful face. You must dine with us often."

"Oh, I couldn't do that," said Evelyn. But she could, she could and she would. She would be so endearing that the woman would love her—who was there for a friend for an invalid like that? Who was there to go shopping, for linens and silver that Evelyn would get for her wholesale, even though they could afford retail? Outsize clothes brought straight to the Park Avenue apartment (she had checked the address in the reservation) to make Catherine lovely, for as long as she lived, the poor thing.

Mrs. Abraham Sterne. A little heavy and Talmudic. But it did have a certain ring to it. And bracelets. And necklaces.

In a way, it would be like playing the stock market, speculative. But the risk was slight, the odds were good: a long-term investment, with capital gains.

How long exactly if you didn't think Murder. *Out* of her head, she didn't even *glimpse* the thought. She had never in her life broken a major commandment: Honor Thy Father, she had done that one—it didn't say anything about honoring children.

But she'd never really committed a genuine sin. So she couldn't kill Catherine, wouldn't consider it *fleetingly,* although poison would probably be easy and uninvestigated in a woman that sickly, and the world was full of cliffs from which wheelchairs could be pushed. But no murder, no sirreebob, she wished no one any real harm.

Besides, the poor woman, how long could she last? Something like pity washed over Evelyn. She trembled. How sad to have to leave a man like that. How terrible to exit a life like Catherine's could have been, if it weren't for the pain and getting old. How could she stand the pain? Evelyn couldn't imagine. She couldn't imagine, and she really didn't want to know.

She was practically totally virtuous, practically worthy. With certain failings, perhaps, but she was trying to learn. She looked at the woman beside her, and felt genuinely sorry.

My life begins today, she thought. Poor Catherine.

THREE

<hr>

"AND THIS IS a Jackson Pollock," Sonny said to Chris, pointing to the enormous canvas in the foyer of his apartment. "I bought it when I was about twenty-three, twenty-four years old. Nobody thought very much of his work then, except my friend Lorenzo Kornblatt, the art critic, do you know him?"

"I've read some of his reviews in *The New Yorker*," Chris said, trying to stand tall enough to examine the top of the painting. "But I've never seen a Pollock before."

The foyer was overwhelming, floored in marble, actual marble. Deep and wide an entrance hall as was the subterranean recreation room at school where Lionel Lindenbaum had never met Chris after lights out, even though he promised. The murky blue of the painting itself, clouded with black, with only a trace of aluminum-colored oils arcing through the darkness, reminded her of passion, obscured, drowning, not being able to surface. It was a very romantic painting, of that she was sure, filled with a struggle against decadence, surging with hope to blot out despair.

"He was trying to capture a feeling of motion," Sonny explained. "From riding on railroad trains. Pollock spent a lot of his early years on boxcars, traveling the country hiding underneath freight trains, riding on his back when they were looking to catch him, hanging by his hands and feet underneath the cars, a little above the rails. This is America in motion, that's what he was trying to show."

"I thought it was passion," Chris said.

"Maybe that's what America in motion is," said Sonny, and smiled.

Dinner was served in the formal dining room, again, to Chris, the size of a hall. The table, the part that was visible beneath the vast stretch of finest embroidered linen, had carved fluted walnut legs, the same style as the grand piano in the huge living room, Louis Quinze, Sonny had labeled it, so much more graceful than Louis Seize, Evelyn had agreed.

Catherine, in a dressing gown that Evelyn had bought her wholesale, had insisted on leaving her wheelchair, and sat in the Louis Quinze blue velvet-backed chair at the foot of the table, smiling and kind, asking as many questions of Chris as she did of Norman. Norman sat opposite Chris, next to Evelyn, who smiled a great deal but avoided looking at Norman. He scraped his bread crust methodically against the hard little flower of butter shaped from a scoop, softening it after a while with his index finger.

The plates were white Minton china, rimmed in royal blue, leafed with gold. The silver was what, Evelyn asked, oh of course, Royal Danish, her favorite pattern in Jensen, she just hadn't remembered until Catherine reminded her.

The butler served sliced steak and small roast new potatoes on a large silver tray; the maid followed him with two silver serving dishes, heavy with vegetables. Chris watched Evelyn to see how to take food from the tray, trying to do it properly, studying Evelyn studying Catherine. Only Norman seemed unconcerned about the right way to serve himself, moving the food as quickly as he could with serving utensils from tray to plate, dropping some carrots and peas on the tablecloth.

"You must be very thrilled, having such a brilliant son," Evelyn said to Catherine, as one of Norman's potatoes rolled onto the floor. "When we went into his room this afternoon Norman was reading two books at once. Imagine."

"What books are you reading?" Chris asked him.

"*Tarzan of the Apes* and *1984*."

"Imagine," Evelyn said. "Isn't that incredible? He can read two books at once, and he's only eight years old. And I thought Chris was bright. But even she can't read two books at once, and she has an I.Q. of—"

"We're not supposed to know our I.Q.'s," Chris interrupted. "Dr. Mann thinks it's harmful to know your I.Q."

"Well just because you know it doesn't mean you have to use it," said Evelyn, and took some broccoli.

"You must be really looking forward to getting back to school," Catherine said to Chris.

"I am. I think."

"Aren't you sure?" asked Sonny.

"I think I'm sure," said Chris. "But then, how can a Benjamin know?"

"A Benjamin?"

Evelyn drank a little red wine. "Chris has this housemother about whom she's very sensitive, who called her a Benjamin. They get very extravagant comments on their report cards. When I was in school they only gave us grades."

"Mrs. Kornfeld's a Nazi," said Chris. "She called me the 'Benjamin' of the group."

Sonny smiled. "Not such a terrible thing to be."

"It isn't?"

"The youngest son of Jacob." Sonny read the information

from inside his eyelids. "The last child of Rachel. Tagalong. Left out in the beginning. But ultimately the founder of one of the twelve tribes of Israel."

"Frank Haskins had the Bible out," said Chris. "I didn't know."

"A very good book," said Sonny. "You should make it a point to read it."

"I will when I have the time. The Nazi wants me to study German. She'll probably gas me if I read the Bible instead of Heinrich Heine. Benjamin."

"It's important to know what names mean before you bristle at being called one of them." Sonny patted the tablecloth reassuringly, Chris' hand being twenty feet away.

"When I first got there she called me Alyosha. The innocent one. From *The Brothers Karamazov*."

"I read that last week," said Norman.

"Then I wouldn't stay away from her Unteroffizier, Lionel Lindenbaum. So she made me a Benjamin."

"St. Paul was of that tribe," said Sonny. "He was very proud of it. You should be, too."

"I don't think she meant it as a compliment."

"Then make it into one," Sonny laughed. "I do that all the time."

"So what do you think of him?" Evelyn said, when they were in the guest room allotted to Chris, and Chris was changing into pajamas. "Isn't he nice? Isn't he smart, and kind? Look at this. Television right in your bedroom."

"I don't care for wrestling," Chris said.

"Who put your nose so high up in the air?" Evelyn asked angrily. "Nobody's ever gone out of their way for us like these people have."

"They have fourteen rooms and three servants," said Chris. "Do you know what's going on in India?"

"I don't give a good goddamn about India. I live in the real world!"

"You think this is the real world?" Chris said contemptuously.

"It's the realest world I've ever been in," Evelyn murmured. "You act like a brat and spoil it for me, I'll never forgive you, never." The voice started getting louder, higher. "Who the hell do you think you are?"

"One of the founders of the twelve tribes of Israel."

"And you see how well they've done! My God, it's a dream, it's a beautiful dream. Look at this room! Look at these paintings!"

"Look at the television," Chris said. "If that's how you want to spend your life."

"Go back to your father!!"

Chris started to cry.

"Oh honey," said Evelyn, sort of embracing. "I don't really mean it. You know I love you. Want the best for you. And this is the best. Don't spoil it. It's your future I'm thinking about. Try to remember that, and keep your mouth shut."

For the remainder of her stay at the Sternes, Chris was almost totally silent. On the ride to Coventry Hall, in the great black limousine, she slunk very low back against the gray upholstery, so in case a radical saw them passing he would know she wanted no part of it, and would not aim his bullets at her.

Sonny and Evelyn, however, seemed very merry during the ride (Catherine had felt too ill to come). They spoke in admiring tones of the scenery outside the car's windows, the wonder of autumn, rainbowing earth colors onto the leaves of trees, all different shades of orange and russet, a very fine painter indeed was nature, Sonny said. Rivaling Jackson Pollock. Rivaling any mortal brush.

They also spoke of their youths, which in Sonny's case had been poverty-stricken, riddled with fear of the future, seemingly impossible dreams. Evelyn's, on the other hand, as she told of it to Sonny, had been carefree and amusing and not much to write home about.

When the limousine pulled in through the great stone-bordered iron gates of Coventry Hall, Chris asked Sonny if they couldn't park on the street. "They don't really like the cars to pull all the way up to Tara, that's the girls' dorm. It gets very congested if the parents don't park down the road."

"I see," said Sonny, and his shoulders moved slightly inside his jacket. He pressed a button lowering the window that separated them from Heinz. "Stop anywhere along here," he said. "See if you can stay near some bushes or behind a tree." He looked at Chris. "Can he carry your bags to the dorm, or would you rather pretend you'd hitchhiked?"

Chris looked at Evelyn, pursing her lips, swallowing her words. She told Sonny that would be fine, Heinz carrying her bags.

"And can we come with you if I rub some dirt on my clothes?" Sonny asked. "I'd like to see where you live."

Chris could hear the pebbles crunching underfoot. She could see Lionel dangling his long lean legs over the railing of the front porch of Tara, peering through the trees at the big black Packard with impossibly pale blue eyes. He did not smile at her in greeting, but instead pulled on a rope. The other end was tied around the ankle of Frenchy Swackholm, who was on the roof playing chess by the chimney with Frazier Peters.

"Capitalist approaching," said Frenchy, picking up his binoculars, focusing them on Chris who was forty feet away. With a chauffeur in uniform carrying her suitcases.

When Chris was settled, and Evelyn was leaving, after pleading with Chris to learn tolerance, which worked both ways, it wasn't enough just to love the oppressed, Mrs. Kornfeld came into the room. "I want you to know I have great affection for your daughter."

"I appreciate that," said Evelyn.

"We'd just like her emotional development to keep pace with intellectual achievement."

"I appreciate that," said Evelyn.

"When you're finished unpacking," said Mrs. Kornfeld to Chris, "why don't you come to my room? I have some fine pfeffernuesse, all these months before Christmas. I found some beautiful pfeffernuesse in a bakery on Eighty-sixth Street. You'll have some, yes?"

"You've got me mixed up with Hansel and Gretel," said Chris, and put her hairbrush away.

"Your daughter's certainly angry for thirteen," Sonny said as they walked down the stairs.

"But not for fifteen and sixteen, that's a very rebellious time, and most of her classmates are fifteen and sixteen. And she has her feelings hurt so easily. Anybody can hurt her feelings. She has to learn to be more selective," said Evelyn.

The front door of Tara opened, and an older couple, rather shoddily dressed, ushered their daughter into the hall. The man was wearing a gray herringbone tweed coat, worn at the elbows, and the woman with him was worn at the eyes. The gangling girl between them looked to be fifteen or sixteen, and she walked in unpolished shoes, literally down at the heels. With Evelyn's luck, this one was probably Chris's roommate, someone she could learn finesse from. Ha!

"Milton?" Sonny said very softly to the man. "Milton, is it you?"

The man stepped back slightly, and peered through his glasses. "Abe?" he said. "Abe? Abela! Abela!"

"Milton!"

Embraces. Like children. How very affecting, Evelyn thought.

"This is Milton Radnitz!" Sonny actually beamed. "My best friend from law school. Milton Radnitz, brilliant attorney, Evelyn White, a ray of sunshine."

"How do you do?" said Milton. "My wife Naomi. My daughter Paula."

"How lovely to meet you all," Evelyn said.

Once they settled the daughter in (thank God, she wasn't Chris' roommate), Milton and Naomi joined Evelyn and Sonny for coffee in a diner down the road. Sonny had wanted to take them to dinner, but Milton had to be in court next morning. Coffee was all they had time for; coffee was all they had.

"How could we lose touch, how could we lose touch?" Sonny kept saying, reaching across the table to clutch Milton's hand. They had filled in the vital statistics of all the missing years, Milton's meeting with Naomi, having a daughter, Sonny's marrying Catherine, having Norman, leaving out Evelyn, consigning her to being a friend of the family, whose daughter attended Coventry Hall. No further warming details about her, once he'd called her a ray of sunshine, nothing to match with the blazing career of Milton Radnitz, practitioner of law; what was so special about Milton Radnitz?

"You made me find my friend Milton Radnitz," Sonny said, hugging her, holding her close to his powerful face, planting a sweet lusty kiss on her cheek, touching her for the first time, besides shaking hands. "If it weren't for you I wouldn't have found my friend Milton."

She was crazy about Milton Radnitz. Now that she really listened, she could tell that Milton Radnitz was terribly bright, as bright as any man she'd listened to, except for Sonny, who dazzled Milton Radnitz, brilliant as he was.

"Still wasting it on the ones who don't need it," Milton said.

Sonny grinned. "Still wasting it on the ones who do."

The two men sat clutching hands like boys. But Evelyn could understand Sonny's affection, Milton was such a cheerful forceful fellow, in spite of the dour expression on his face, the downcast angle of his eyes, the bags underneath them. A lot of restless nights, tallied up, souvenired. Difficult to believe he was the same age as Sonny.

344

"Your daughter goes to Coventry Hall!" Sonny said, and started to chuckle. "I begin to understand better Evelyn's kid."

"What about her?" Evelyn asked.

"Well, if she's hanging around with the spawn of Milton Radnitz, no wonder she tried to make herself invisible in the limousine."

"A limousine, *dorten,*" said Milton.

"Nu, wo denn?" said Sonny.

"L'Shana Haba B' Park Avenue," Milton quoted. Both of them laughed. "Next year on Park Avenue, Naomi," Milton translated. "A part of the Passover prayer. Next year in Israel. Abe changed it to Next year on Park Avenue."

Evelyn laughed as heartily as if she attended services. "Isn't it lucky your finding each other again. What did you mean about Chris trying to make herself invisible?"

"An old law school joke," Sonny winked at Milton. "Are you taking the train? Can't we drive you back to the city?"

"We have a car, thank you."

"It better be a Chevrolet or I'm turning you in."

"It's a Nash," said Milton. "The kind you can make into a bed, in case you have to leave town in a hurry."

"Even better," Sonny said, and laughed.

"What did you mean about the limousine and Chrissie?" Evelyn asked again.

"Her attitude in the car."

"She's overemotional," Evelyn said. "Just a little overemotional. She's a thirteen-year-old entering her junior year. What would you expect her to be?"

"A communist," said Sonny.

Milton laughed.

"Some of my best friends used to be communists," said Sonny.

"Chris tried to join the A.D.A. once," said Evelyn. "But she had too big a mouth."

"Come on," said Milton Radnitz. "That's not a subversive organization."

"Well don't tell that to Chris," said Evelyn. "She'd be very hurt."

The two men said they would see each other in the city, but when he and Evelyn were back in the limousine, Sonny said they wouldn't. That was the sad part of living, Sonny told her: not seeing the people who made your ears ring, and your blood get hotter so you knew you were alive.

"Which reminds me," he said, his gray suede gloves on the seat beside him, her leather pair beside his; palm to naked palm they were, for the first time. "We can't let you go."

"I don't understand," said Evelyn, hoping she did.

"Catherine and I. We've both decided. We talked it over and figured it out and we're not going to let you leave. Taking Norman to museums and afternoon concerts—"

"Well, he's fun to go with, he's so interested in everything." At concerts, Norman read a book and listened to the music and picked his nose all at the same time.

"And what you've done for Catherine . . ."

"What she's done for me . . ."

"I won't even discuss my feelings in this matter," Sonny said, looking away, letting go of her hand. "I'm all mixed up." He pressed a button and raised the window between them and the chauffeur. He took out an outsized white linen handkerchief and blew his nose.

"Catherine knows I'm all mixed up." He set his gray hat a little further back on his head and stared out the window. "We've talked about it. She's been telling me for years it would be natural, totally understandable. She's encouraged me to see other women. Told me to have affairs."

"She must be a saint," said Evelyn.

"She is that. Only I'm not a saint. And I want you. And it's all right with Catherine."

"Well it's not all right with me. What do you think I am? A *concubine?*"

"I'm sorry. I put it wrong."

"You put it right. I'm just not interested. I don't fool around

346

with married men. Not that I don't find you attractive. But Catherine is my dearest friend."

"Then will you stay as her companion?"

"She doesn't need a companion."

"She does." Sonny grasped her arm. "Please. Whatever you make at that hotel a year, I'll give it to you."

"I couldn't take money from you."

"Then I'll make long-term investments, with tax-free yields equal to your salary, and you can live with us, on expenses. Think in terms of the future. For your child."

"My child," mused Evelyn.

She had torpedoed a marriage for the sake of her child. Stayed home from China (what adventures had she missed there?) for the sake of her child. She had sailed great oceans, traveled many train tracks, and found the bum Dolores for the sake of her child. It wouldn't hurt to take a few investments.

And while she was there, maybe God would be merciful and take Catherine from her pain, and Norman's finger out of his nose, and let her redo the library in Louis Quinze or Seize (just one more time at Parke-Bernet and she'd be absolutely sure of the difference) and bring love and affection that strengthened the bond of devotion that dwelt within the home. That part of the service she remembered, the prayer for the Sabbath, that Sonny read aloud every Friday night.

"Come," he had read from the prayer book, after Evelyn lit the candles because Catherine couldn't stand. "Let us welcome the Sabbath."

> Like a Bride
> Radiant and Joyous
> Comes the Sabbath.

Oh yes, that part she remembered.

> Like a Bride
> Radiant and Joyous

Once again now:

> Like a Bride.

And another part of the prayer, yes, that Evelyn could also remember, the part about workday thoughts and cares being put aside. Not that she didn't love work, she was happiest working. Working at helping Catherine learn all the best prices, there was a new career. And a humane one in the bargain, poor sweet Catherine. How lovely she was, how thoughtful and generous, wanting him to wander from their bedroom where he hadn't slept for years.

She looked at Sonny with eyes only slightly guarded, guile vanished, guise over, this was who she was meant to be: a woman loved by an important man. Her throat began to fill, as did her eyes.

"I don't know what to say." She reached for his handkerchief. "I know what I'd like to do. I'd like to stay with you." She was really crying. Her life was beginning today, as all real life began, accompanied by tears.

"Then you'll do it? You'll let us have the privilege?"

"I wish that I could," Evelyn wept, "but I can't."

But she did.

FOUR

"Now this is the Delta," Roan Anderson said, spreading the map out on Arnold's desk. The door to the office was closed. Roan had insisted on absolute privacy, by which he meant secrecy. Arnold knew how to translate from the language of striped ties. Although the walls of the office were so thick as to be almost soundproof, Arnold strained his ears for some indication of the action going on next door in Sonny's office, because the drawling Princetonian drone was driving him nuts. As was the spiel Roan Anderson was giving, Roan lacking the proper background to give a truly interesting spiel. Besides which, like all good Ivy Leaguers, Roan wanted to draw things out to the full fifty-five minutes of an undergraduate lecture, before giving the punch line at five minutes to the hour. What was the punch line, what was the purpose? No wonder he was driving Jeanne crazy, no wonder she'd started drinking so much, even though Roan was away most of the time. Some of the time he was home, and that would have driven anyone to drink, even Arnold, even if he didn't have to touch him.

"From here," Roan pointed on the map, "to here is where we can buy. Private deed from the government. Two hundred miles, by forty miles. Including six major towns, with all their real estate. Publicly unrecorded. It'll be like owning our own country."

"Yeah, you told me all that," said Arnold. "What's so great about owning your own country in South America?"

Roan let his yellow-gray eyes move to the antique wall clock: it was six minutes to the hour. "Diamonds," he said, letting go of the map so it flew back into cylindrical form. "A mother vein of diamonds."

Arnold laughed. "Twinkle, twinkle, little fantasy."

"Don't laugh at me." Roan's cheeks reddened, a flush moving up to the roots of his orange hair. "I haven't just been playing your stooge on these expeditions. I've been learning. Finding my way around. I've had three geologists from the oil leasing company checking the outcroppings, getting the lay of the land. You understand the lay of the land, don't you?" His eyes were almost yellow.

"There's a strong possibility of diamonds. The geologists verified it. And I know it in my bones. I feel it. I can smell them. He's in town the day after tomorrow, Ortega, and he's bringing the papers and the deeds and the guarantees with him. I have to meet him at the Pierre Wednesday afternoon with fifteen million in cash."

"You got jungle fever," said Arnold and started to get up.

"Sit down," Roan said, his voice heavier than Arnold had ever heard it. "You'll get me the fifteen and anything extra I need to mine it. You'll get me fifteen in cash and a promissory note for whatever else I need."

"You got to be crazy."

"I don't even 'got to be' stupid," said Roan Anderson. "You do it, or if this deal passes me, if I don't get one chance to ride my own wings, goddamit," his mouth braced into a snarl, "if I don't get this last chance to bust out all over hell, sky-high with no handout from any of you, not my father, not my wife's lover, then I'll kill your goddamn baby, Sterne, I swear it. I'll kill him."

"What are you talking about?" said Arnold, sitting down. "You've really gone nuts."

"Well how would you be, you mover of men? You think I'm a complete fool, a moron, not to figure it out. Sixty-five thousand for starters, a bonanza from the sky. How often does a thing like that materialize? And in this case, why?

"I see how you don't look at her. I see how you don't visit and see the baby, when you've kissed every goddamn stranger's baby in sixteen countries, duly recorded by the *Daily News*.

"So if I were as stupid as you think, would you guess I was also blind? I see the small face, Arnold Sterne, I see your face Arnold Sterne, I see a three-month-old face with you stamped on it. You come through with this for me, or I kill the baby."

"You'll kill no one," said Arnold, springing around the desk, thrusting his hands toward Roan Anderson's freckled throat. "I'll kill you."

"There are letters," Roan gasped. "I'm not so dumb."

"What kind of letters?" He eased his grip slightly.

"Naming dates and places. I had a detective on you. You and Jeanne, my own sweet *belle amie*. And I had a doctor friend of mine run a blood test on the baby. Not my type. No type I could produce. You have a rare blood type, rare man among men. Sixteen months before an election. Records of a few political payoffs. Photostats from your locked-up files, master builder. Plus the books on the loss of several millions in pensioners' funds."

"That was an honest mistake. Anyone can make an honest mistake."

"Not you, Arnold Sterne. You're too smart to make an honest mistake. Not as I'd tell it to Joe McCreery. Not combined with these other things."

"Joe wouldn't print shit like this."

"Then I'll tell it to Winchell." Roan brushed himself off and straightened his tie. "What do you say? It's only fifteen million. We'll be partners. What do you care about money? You're going to be Senator. A noble man. Just think. It's only sixteen months before the election, and you've got it practically sewn up."

"You could fall down an elevator shaft in this building. Another item in the *Wall Street Journal*. Another freckle-faced drunk, maybe accident, maybe despair at the fact that he couldn't make it."

"Don't try to make me hate you more," Roan said.

"There are no degrees of hatred." Arnold ran his hand through his thick silver hair, and sat back down behind the desk. "Where am I supposed to get fifteen million in cash?"

"Don't make me laugh."

"Every penny we have is tied up. You know that much about the business."

"Untie it," said Roan. "You have till Wednesday."

When Arnold told Sonny he needed fifteen million, liquid, Sonny laughed aloud.

It was good to be able to laugh, to get rid of a part of the intestinal strangulation he was sure was reaching his brain. Strangulation of the mind, trying to know what to do. (Maybe two days or two weeks, Catherine's doctor had said, no more. The end of March, had said Evelyn's doctor. Unless we take it by Caesarian, that'll be two weeks before.)

"So what should I do?" Sonny had almost asked Arnold. "Divorce her while she's dying, so the child will seem legitimate? Bring a rabbi into the bedroom to tear up the *Ketubah* I signed with Catherine, draw up another for me to sign with Evelyn? Marry me to her with Norman as ring-bearer? Pallbearer?"

"In cash," Arnold said. "By Wednesday."

Sonny threw back his head so the laugh could boom up to the paneled ceiling, come back down and slap him with how funny it all was. "Jesus Christ," said Sonny. "How lucky I am to have you for a brother! You sure know how to help a guy stop thinking about nebulous things."

"I'm serious," Arnold said. "He's got to have it in hand by Wednesday, or I'm over."

"What's he got on you?"

"Only everything that would look wrong." Arnold sat in the winged leather armchair to the side of Sonny's desk, and put his head in his hands. "Photostats of our bad transactions. Personal blackmail with Jeanne. All the business stuff that might smack of unconscionable gains."

"Look, we talked about this many times, Arn." The movement of Sonny's shoulder pulled at the thin white striped cotton of his shirt. "To know about something before anyone else does, and buy where you know there's a market in front, that isn't unconscionable, it's smart."

"To us it's smart. The SEC doesn't have our scope and imagination. You don't know the half. I got tipped very big, and bought it all, and the whole goddamn turnpike went straight down the tubes."

"So that happens every day."

"To the Non-Sectarian Fund for the Aged?"

"Well." Sonny took a big folded white linen handkerchief from the drawer of his desk, and wiped his forehead. "I'm afraid that was not very good judgment on my part, making that investment."

"You didn't even know about it."

"I'm not running for Senator." He put the handkerchief in his pants pocket and sat back and studied the air. "So what else is new, or can I get back to work, righting my wrongs, filling the coffers of the Yiddisher old?"

"You make a terrific victim," Arnold said. "But I don't think you'd make such a good martyr. I can't let you do it."

"The mistakes of the firm are mine, every single one of them. You're much too involved in becoming a man of the people to concern yourself with what goes on in this business. You haven't paid any real attention in years. As a matter of fact, it's starting to get on my nerves, your having half the company and me doing all the real work. I've been considering splitting up the partnership. Retroactive to . . ." Sonny looked at his calendar. "Oh, retroactive to 'forty-eight. That's when you stopped really paying attention. You ought to stick to politics, Arn. That's your field.

Money-management is mine. You've been leaving the investing to me since that time, if anybody asks. You been too busy lining up votes. Any mistakes in investing are mine. Have been all along."

"I can't let you do it."

"We are no longer partners," Sonny said. "I'm calling my lawyers. I can't have my name linked with someone who's so busy lining up votes he hasn't really been in the office for nearly three years."

"No good," Arnold said, and got to his feet. "Too good, but no good. You're taking no rap for me."

"What rap? I'm at my best in a court of law. Sit down. Relax. We'll have a drink to celebrate splitting up the firm, retroactive."

"I won't let you do it."

"You're older than me, but I'm bigger than you. Don't make me beat you up."

"You son of a bitch," Arnold said, and hugged him.

"Get your hands off me," Sonny said. "They probably got a camera in here and they'll add homosexuality to the allegations. So it's settled, okay? The errors in judgment were mine. What else do you need?"

"Fifteen million in cash."

"It's a joke," Sonny said. "He's got to be kidding. Whatever he had on you, however he got it . . ." Sonny paused. "How the hell did he get photostats of our records?"

"He probably got a key to the office." Stolen from Jeanne. One of the places they met on Thursday night was the office. One of its rooms furnished in cream, to match her.

"So whatever he had on you, he's got on me. And I regret I have only one business to give for my country. The worst he can do—"

"Is kill my son," said Arnold.

"Ellis?" he said. "Why would anyone hurt Ellis? He goes to Harvard Law."

Arnold lowered his chin into his chest. Sonny could see none of his features. Only the shrugged despair in the shoulders, the violence in hands clenched into fists, the silver thickness of hair suddenly gone limp. Where was his young older brother, the man who feared no one, nothing, he even had ferocious *hair?*

"He thinks that Jeanne's baby is mine . . . He's going to . . ." The quickness of breath coming between the words counterpointed the slow disbelief with which he spoke. "He's going to kill him if I don't come through."

"He's bluffing."

"I can't take the chance," Arnold said. "I got to get the fifteen. He's crazy."

"I guess that's the mistake we make," Sonny said, pulling the phone towards him. "You never expect that from someone who went to Princeton."

He started phoning his lawyers, phoning accountants, phoning banks, phoning Colonel Reeling in Tennessee, telling him he needed cash, to unload his shares, telling them all to liquidate all short-term holdings, start shaking loose long term positions, in his name, and Catherine's and Norman's. Easier ending than beginning.

Arnold watched it all. Arnold watched it all and listened and wept.

"Cut it out," Sonny said. "I can't stand to see a grown Senatorial candidate crying."

"How can I let you get rid of Norman's holdings?"

"You'll make it up to him after you're elected." Sonny covered the phone. "You can slip me some advance info on highways and turnpikes and dams and make me a rich man. And they'll claim undue governmental influence, and they'll be right. But we'll deny everything."

He put in a call to Joe Pape, and told him he wanted to sell out his shares in Joe Pape's Finest. Yes, he knew it would get even better and finer and bigger all the time, but this was the moment he wanted to sell, so Joe should run down to the still and see what was brewing and stick his hand in the till and see how much he could come up with, and call Sonny back with an offer. In cash. Cheers. He hung up the phone.

"Christ," Arnold said. "What am I doing to you?"

"You're keeping me from my work," Sonny said. "I already

wasted three hours. Get out of here. Go out and get a sandwich or something, you look sick."

"Sonny . . ." Arnold reached out but didn't touch him.

"The best part was always the struggle," said Sonny. "That's what gives you strength in your chest to cheer at the victory."

"What can I say?"

"Forget it." Sonny got to his feet. "From the way you acted when you came in here I thought you were going to ask for something important."

Arnold was afraid to call her. Afraid the crazy man might be tapping the line. Why should he stop at that? Why should he stop at anything? What difference would a phone call make?

"Is he home?" he asked Jeanne.

"He's having drinks with Winchell."

"He said he'd wait till Wednesday."

"He isn't telling him anything. Just buttering him up, as you say, inviting him to the races with promise of scandal. You know Roan. He's such a tease."

"That son of a bitch."

"Your choice," she said coldly, a little thickly. "Your choice to be my groom."

"I want you out of there," said Arnold. "Pack a bag for you and the baby, get the hell out of there, and call me from a pay phone. I'll tell you where I've made the reservation and under what name."

They met at the Dorset Hotel on Fifty-fourth Street. He wore the collar of his jacket up and his hat down almost to his nose, like a goddamn gangster. Like a goddamn gangster: he saw himself in a shadow tinted window, and went to call Sonny from a phone booth so Sonny could check her in.

Sonny couldn't even come to the phone, they were taking Catherine to the hospital. Was there anything Evelyn could do,

Evelyn asked. Where was Arnold calling from? Should she try and get Sonny to call back?

"Forget it." Arnold hung up. He checked Jeanne in under the name of Genevieve Hale, praying that desk clerks couldn't connect faces with names until after they were elected.

When Jeanne was settled in the suite, when the housekeeper had promised she'd be back in a jiffy with crib and linens, there wasn't a thing to worry about, they even had a sterilizer in the supply room, Jeanne and Arnold sat down together. Looking at each other directly for the first time that day.

They touched only fingertips. The baby was lying on the rug, on his back, trying to focus his eyes up at them.

"When he gets home and I'm not there, he'll tell everything," Jeanne said.

"Forget about telling. He says he'll kill the baby. I'll meet all his terms and hate his guts, but I won't take that chance."

"You care about the boy?"

"Don't ask that," said Arnold. "Don't even ask that." He got up and went to the small moving lump on the floor, got on his knees, lifted it, squeezed it, held it in front of his face. "Belated greetings," he whispered, against the soft skin. "Hello. Welcome. You smell like me."

Behind him, Jeanne started to cry.

"I'll get him the money. I'll get the papers back. I'll give him his goddamn property, his diamond mines, his big dumb dream. I'll get it in spades for him, but he's not going to hurt you, you fat little son of a Sterne." He nestled his nose in the baby's neck. "You smell like me."

"And what about me?" Jeanne said. "What about protecting me?"

"We'll get you a divorce. I'll have him killed. I'll do something."

"But you won't marry me?"

"You always knew what this was," Arnold said, getting up from the floor, carrying the baby, setting it on his lap, as he sat beside her, and fingered and fondled the small face. "How could

3 5 7

he say you look like me?" he asked the baby. "You look like every other fat-faced little pink baby in the world. Except for the intelligence in the eyes. Oh yes. The intelligence is obviously Sterne intelligence. And you smell like me."

"We won't be married?" said Jeanne.

"You're the love of my life," Arnold said, turning to her. "I didn't expect you. I didn't plan on you."

"Plans can be changed."

"Not mine," said Arnold.

"I gave him the papers," said Jeanne.

"I don't think I heard you."

"I had photostats made of your private papers. Exchanges with you and some councilmen. The deal with Di Bonaven. The records of the fund for . . ."

"Enough," Arnold said. "Be quiet."

"And it was I who had the blood test done on the baby. To offer greater proof that this is your son. I who gave him places and times we had been together. There was no detective. I told him everything. I signed an affidavit."

"Be quiet," Arnold said. "Be quiet before I forget who I am and kill you like that bastard wants to kill my son."

"Your son!" she screamed. "Your son, at last, your son. Don't tell me, tell the world. I want you to marry me!"

"You got a really good case, lady."

"I want you to marry me!" she shouted. "I want you ruined!"

He put the baby down, and went for his coat. "You certainly know how to put your wishes in action."

"Don't leave me!" She ran to his arms. "Don't you see, it was meant to free you! It was meant to help us be together. I love you."

"Your story is breaking my heart," Arnold said, putting on his coat. "And the evidence you collected is breaking my balls."

"I thought it would force you to withdraw, and you would divorce Sarah . . ."

"Don't say any more." Arnold turned away from her. "I'm trying very hard to remember who you were."

"I did it for *us*. For *us!*"

"There is no us. He'll get everything he asked for. And so will you."

"Don't leave me."

"I'm already gone," said Arnold. "Don't try to call me. Don't try to contact me. And if anything happens to that baby, I'll see that it happens to you."

"I'll get you the papers back." She had her back against the door, held the knob with both her hands.

"Get out of my way," said Arnold.

"I'll get you the papers back. I'll burn them. I'll tell him everything about us was a lie."

"It was," said Arnold. "It is."

"I love you."

"Actions speak louder than photostats," said Arnold. "Get out of my way before I break your face."

"Go ahead," she flared at him. "Go ahead. Go ahead."

"The love of my life," he whispered hoarsely. "I knew it wasn't meant to happen. There couldn't be a love of my life. What a wasted war."

After he was gone, she sat shaking in the darkening light of the hotel room. She went to the phone after a while, and called her home. Roan wasn't there yet. No, she told the nurse, she'd call him back, she had no wish to tell him where she was

She put in a call to Joe McCreery; he'd left the office for the day. She gave the switchboard operator an urgent message for him to call Genevieve Hale at the Dorset, it was really urgent. Then she flashed the hotel switchboard and asked if there had been any calls, and if Joe McCreery called his call was to be put straight through, and Arnold Sterne, if he called, hadn't he called, hadn't he left a message in the lobby, hadn't there been some mistake, would she check with the desk clerk?

Then she called Sonny at home, but Sonny wasn't there, he was at the hospital. Could Evelyn give him a message? Who was this calling? Evelyn asked. Jeanne hung up the phone.

She got a bottle of Scotch from the bellboy, and filled a water glass with whiskey, and drank it down, and called Arnold's home. When the butler said he wasn't there, Jeanne asked to speak to Sarah.

"Hello?" Sarah said.

"This is Jeanne Anderson. Roan Anderson's wife. I used to work for your husband. I met him in France. He brought me to this country so he could use me. We've been lovers for seven years. We have a son."

There was silence on the other end of the phone.

"Hello?" Jeanne said. "Did you hear me, Mrs. Sterne?"

"It would have been hard not to hear you."

"It gives me no pleasure to tell you this, but your husband's in a great deal of trouble. You could save yourself and your family much embarrassment by agreeing to give him a divorce."

"You could save yourself a dime by not making phone calls," Sarah said, and hung up.

Jeanne called Joe McCreery again at the paper, and asked if she could reach him at home, it was truly urgent. The switchboard operator asked who was calling Mr. McCreery. Jeanne said it was Genevieve Hale at the Dorset, but not really, and if McCreery knew what was good for him and his friend Arnold Sterne, he'd better call her back right away.

Then she called Sonny.

"I told you he was at the hospital," Evelyn said. "Who is this calling?"

"This is Genevieve Hale at the Dorset. He must call me right away."

"I said he was at the hospital," Evelyn insisted. "What is this in reference to?"

"None of your goddamned business. Tell him he better call me." She hung up the phone and picked up the baby, rocked him, and threw him into the crib, where he lay crying. She went to the window. Five stories to the street. Far enough. Maybe not. Maybe not far enough.

The phone rang. "Arnold?"

"This is Joe McCreery. Are you Genevieve Hale?"

"I'm Arnold Sterne's mistress. I have records of transactions.

Photostats of private papers. He's a thief, Mr. McCreery. A liar and a thief."

A moment's silence. "And not too good about picking out women."

"These are facts," Jeanne said coldly. "You're a reporter."

"I'm an economics analyst."

"Then analyze these transactions. I'll have them waiting for you at the hotel. I'm in Suite Five-oh-six. With the papers, and his child."

"I don't deal in scandal."

"These are truths, Mr. McCreery."

"I'm not interested," said Joe.

"Oh yes you are."

When McCreery hadn't come by seven, Jeanne sent the bellboy out for baby food, fed the baby, and put him to sleep. Then she contacted the hotel doctor, who was on his way out to dinner.

"I'm sure I'll be fine in the morning," Jeanne said, holding her mouth while she spoke into the phone, so her trembling lips wouldn't shake the words. "If you could just get me a few sleeping pills . . ."

The bellboy delivered them. Two. Only two. She gave him twenty dollars.

"Can you get me some more?"

"The pharmacy's closed and the doctor's gone out for the evening."

"A bottle of Scotch," she said, and saw him looking at the bottle of Scotch that stood half empty on the desk. She brushed her fingers casually through her white-gold hair. "I'm expecting a few people."

Joe McCreery sat in the dark bar of the Carlyle Hotel. Very dark, very somber, the places chic lovers chose, Joe observed, finishing a dish of peanuts, nursing his drink, letting it get watery, waiting for Arnold.

"Okay," he said, when Arnold got there. "You want to tell me."

"There were mistakes," Arnold said. "Honest mistakes. And a couple of deals that could look shady if the wrong person wanted to make something out of them."

"It seems to me that the wrong person does. She threatened turning it over to the Senatorial Investigating Committee, Kefauver, if I didn't use it. If you didn't call her."

"I'm a *schmuck,*" Arnold said. "A potato. I'm no better than my father. But I won't go on my knees. I won't go pleading on my knees. I won't let her get me."

"What are you going to do?"

"I'm not sure. Sonny's trying to bail me out with the husband. A little easily resolved blackmail. For a pittance in cash." Arnold laughed. "They got me six ways up the ass."

"Forget about five of them," Joe said, and looked at his friend. "Let's just talk about the papers she claims that she has."

"They'd look bad."

"So they'd look bad. Are they bad?"

"I've never done anything criminal. I wish I had it in me. If I did I could kill her." He gulped his drink. "Diminished by a woman. Potato. Potato."

"You don't look like a potato to me," said Joe McCreery. "You don't even look like a fool."

"What do I look like?"

"A man who's made some mistakes. Nothing I care to write about."

"Thank you," said Arnold.

"Maybe you ought to tell Di Bonaven what's going on. He hasn't got your soft heart."

"Yeah," said Arnold. "That's all I need. To level with Rosey. He'd have me by the balls."

"What does Sonny think you ought to do?"

"Sonny can't think about anything. Catherine's dying. Shit,"

Arnold said, and pounded the table. "Shit, Joe. Is this what it is? Life? Ambition? A way to get killed?"

"Talk to her," Joe said. "Maybe she'll be reasonable."

"She's a woman," said Arnold. "And I loved her. I really loved her. That makes me crazier than she is."

"Tell her that. The part where you loved her."

"I tell her nothing. I tell her nothing. Never again."

When Arnold hadn't called by nine, Jeanne proceeded to get drunk. She wrote a suicide note, and a love letter to Arnold, and a note of apology to Sarah, and a confession, in French, to her priest in Bougiville, and a letter to the financial editor of the New York *Times*. Then she put them all in a wastebasket and set them on fire, which she tried to put out with a little Scotch when the flames got too high. The basket caught fire and she carried it into the bathroom, throwing it in the bathtub, burning her hands. She drank some more Scotch, and ate some baby food, and put some baby lotion on her blisters. Then she called Arnold again. He was not home, the butler said. Mrs. Sterne was also out. There had been a death in the family.

"Stop lying," she screamed into the phone. "They're there. I know they're there. Let me talk to him. Let me talk to somebody."

"I'm sorry," said the butler. "There's nobody here."

She tried Sonny again, and Evelyn answered. "You tell him he better call me. It's Jeanne. I'm registered as Genevieve Hale."

"What do you want with him?" Evelyn said. "Who are you anyway?"

"He knows."

"I don't know," Evelyn said. "You better tell me."

"I don't have to tell you anything. I know all about you. You vulture."

"You're crazy," said Evelyn. "Whoever you are."

When she couldn't reach anybody else, when the friends she thought she had made being married to Roan couldn't talk to her anymore—because she sounded like she needed sleep, the politest of them said, because she was drunk, said the rudest—she telephoned her husband.

"Where the hell are you?" said Roan.

"I can't tell you. He's going to get you all the money. He doesn't want you to hurt the baby. The goddamn baby."

"You better come home."

"I can't. I'm too drunk. And I took pills."

"Then tell me where you are, and I'll come get you."

"I can't," she said.

"Pull yourself together and play this one out with me," Roan said. "We're going to the races tomorrow with Winchell. I'm not planning to tell him anything till Wednesday, but you know he likes looking at you. I'm playing it out like it's friendly, and you better be there to make it look friendly, or I might be tempted to tell him tomorrow. Where are the papers?"

"I have them. Or I burned them. I don't know."

"You better know."

"I didn't burn them. I burned myself."

"You sure you have them?"

"I'm sure. I want him humiliated as much as you do."

They made plans to meet at the races. She called the switchboard to try and get a sitter. The operator told her it was two o'clock in the morning, there was no one she could call.

"For tomorrow, you idiot," Jeanne said. "For noon tomorrow. Call a nursing service or something. What kind of a hotel is this?" She hung up the phone.

She finished the rest of the bottle. And started on the second, so angry she stayed conscious. Conscious and alive, with no one to call. She woke up the baby and tried to love him. She wanted to bite him, she wanted to ravish him, she wanted to throw him out the window. She put him back to sleep, and remembered Arnold had a sister. Baby. Who was she married to? Yes, she remembered. Where were they living? California. It was three hours earlier in California. Maybe there were still some helpful words adrift.

She reached Baby on the phone after trying two other George Heyers in Los Angeles. "Baby?" she said. "This is Jeanne, in New York. You probably don't remember me, I started to work for your brother Arnold after the war, oh Christ, please, you've got to help me. I'm going to die. I'm going to die. Call him. Make him call me. I'm sorry. I love him. You've got to tell him. Make him call me." She was sobbing, and her stomach was heaving. She was going to throw up, right there, with Baby listening on the phone. Baby would think she was drunk.

"I have to hang up," she wept. "Make him call me. He loves you. He'll listen to you, won't he?" She hung up the phone and made it to the window in time to vomit down on Fifty-fourth Street. There was a brief, soundless time between the heaves and the noise of the splattering down below. Would she fall faster than that? Was it far enough?

"Put him on the phone, goddamit!" she screamed to Evelyn. "I've got to talk to Sonny so he'll make Arnold call me. Put him on the phone. Put him on the phone."

"His wife just died," said Evelyn. "I don't think he should be bothered by the hysterical ravings of a drunk."

"Let me speak to him, let me speak to him."

"He'll call you in the morning if he can," Evelyn said. "Genevieve Hale, isn't that who you said it was?"

"Tell them I'll give back the papers. I'll give back the papers."

"What papers?"

"Ha!" Jeanne said. "Wouldn't you like to know."

At one point, Evelyn certainly would have. At the point in her life when secrets were important, after files marked Essential had been neatly organized by her, documents marked Confidential, to Lieutenant-Commander Walter M. White, had passed steamed through her hands, opened by teapot, studied for intrigue, corruption, Evelyn would have given almost anything to be let in on other people's papers. Her friendship with Wandra Kane had cooled considerably mainly because Wandra never told her what was in the letters of Harvey's she found. At one point the very word *secret* set a flutter loose in Evelyn's throat.

But that was before she matured, found there were dreams that stayed true in the daylight, that there was love, that there was touching a skin softer even than her own, that she could be driven straight up to the top of her skull by the movements of his body on hers, in hers, hands squeezing joy from her breasts where nothing had ever been before, except milk for a child, how much sweeter, love juice for his lips, his wonderful lips, what did she care about papers. What papers?

"Sweetheart," she said, opening the door to Catherine's room, where he sat by the bed, staring at the fourpostered emptiness. "Honey, I hate to bother you with anything now."

"It's okay," he whispered, his shoulder moving in his jacket. "It's not like it's a surprise, is it?" He reached for her without looking at her, and she stepped into the circle of his arm. "You know it's coming, you know it's coming, why is it still such a terrible surprise?"

"I should have been at the hospital."

"She knew you were with Norman. She was grateful that you were with Norman. She was grateful that you were with me." He started to cry. "She told me to thank you. She told me to thank you, and make you promise to take care of me."

"She made me make that promise to her," Evelyn said. Incredible woman. Terrible shame, really. Sort of.

"She said to be happy. Do you think we can?"

"I know we can," said Evelyn, and sat down with him, against him, on him, and still he looked at the bed.

"I've been trying to remember how it was when we first met, she took care of me, you know, I got sick, and she nursed me like a baby." He smiled. "My God, she was beautiful."

"I wouldn't bother you, not at a time like this, but some terrible woman's been calling all night."

"Jeanne?"

"Once she said Jeanne. Dorset Hotel. But she kept leaving the name Genevieve Hale, only she pronounced it the French way. Is she French? She was very drunk, I couldn't really tell."

"What does she want?"

"Something about Arnold. Something about papers. She was

ranting. It was awful. I wasn't going to tell you. Not at a time like this."

"It's okay," Sonny said, and held her for a moment, and then got up to go toward the phone.

"Why don't you use the phone in your room?"

"You're right," said Sonny. "I shouldn't spend too much time in here."

She would have it redone as a music room. He liked music. Chris liked music. Norman liked music. Even Evelyn would have liked music if she had the time to listen. It would make a wonderful music room; he would spend no time in Catherine's room at all. Not that she didn't love Catherine herself, she had never known anyone like her, such sweet generosity. But there was no point in adding to his pain with memory.

She walked him down the hall, feet strong under the weight of his arm on her shoulders. She leaned her head over and pressed her face to his chest as they walked, and he wept.

"Enough," he said, and blew his nose. "You better go to sleep."

"In your room?"

"Not tonight. A couple of weeks, maybe less. We couldn't wait the traditional year if we wanted to. But for Norman's sake, I think we ought to wait as long as we can, huh? A month, maybe six weeks."

"Whatever you say."

"Listen." He took her face into his hands and studied it by the dim light of candle bulbs in sconces on the wall. "I want to thank you, too. You brought life into my house when there was death in it. We all saw that. Besides that I love you, and Catherine loved you too, and I'm all fucked up because she wouldn't let me feel guilty, and now I do—besides those things I want you to know that I'm grateful to you. For Norman. For Catherine. For me."

"Thank you," she said, longing to hug him, beg him to take her with him, not leave her alone, not on the night when her best friend had died.

"Thank you," he whispered, and kissed her once, lightly,

367

lovingly on the mouth. "But we better stay out of each other's beds until we can make it official. You know. With Norman upset. Sometimes when he's upset he walks in his sleep."

That, too.

Whatever she got, she would earn. But what difference did it make if she had trouble with Norman? She loved Sonny. She loved him. She loved him. Even with funeral arrangements to be made, she wanted to waltz in the hall.

"So a month, six weeks, we'll make it official. And then we can be together. Always. What do you think?"

"You're the wise one," Evelyn said.

"But I got to be fair with you. When I marry you, I'll be as good as broke."

How funny he was, how tender, how handsome, how charming. "I can take it if you can," Evelyn said, willing as always to go along with a joke.

The two men sat down in the booth of the coffee shop. "I'm sorry," said Arnold again. They had held each other in the hospital waiting room, when Sarah pushed them together so they could cry. But now Arnold didn't touch him. Now Arnold couldn't touch him because touching was emotional and they both had to be cold and clear.

"I'm sorry that on top of everything you had to be bothered with this shit."

"Stop apologizing," Sonny said. "Let's just try to figure out what you're going to do. She says she'll give back the papers if you see her."

"I won't see her."

"She says if you don't see her, she'll give the papers to Winchell."

"I won't see her."

"Why, for Christ's sake. Just once. One more time. To save your career."

"For my funeral? Can you put my career in a coffin?"

"Don't talk like that." Sonny looked away.

"I won't drop dead."

"You're not going to drop dead."

"I refuse to die pleading with a cunt. I won't go like our father."

Silence. With all that was going on in Sonny's head, there was still room for that picture. Instant recognition. Otto Sterne, draped in potato sacking, a winding sheet, skin drained of life, pennies on his eyes. No. He didn't want Arnold to go to Jeanne, no matter how much sense it made. Arnold stretched out. That picture there was no room for. Not in Sonny's lifetime.

"Okay, don't see her. That would only be part of it anyway. I can't start negotiating. Not today. I can't *hondle* on prices. I put the call in to Colonel Reeling, and Pape. See what they'll deliver on banks and bourbon. Find out what my profit position is. The lawyers won't know the whole picture till this afternoon, so you get the picture, and get what you can. Whatever you can. I can't think about money. Take whatever you can get. But take care of it for me."

"I'll take care of it," Arnold said. "I'll liquidate my stuff with yours."

"That would look too fishy, your dumping everything all at once. Me, I'm unpredictable. A nut on the Street. You're the conservative. People would wonder about your getting out."

"Why? I'm going partners on my own personal country in South America."

"Imperialism." Sonny tried to smile. "Evelyn's daughter would have your head."

"What are you going to do about Evelyn?"

"What are you going to do about Jeanne?"

"I told you. I won't see her."

"I'm going to marry Evelyn."

"You got to be kidding."

"Not a word," Sonny said. "Not even one word. We don't have the same taste in women."

They were silent while the waitress brought coffee. "Here's a letter to Chase," said Sonny. "Turning my shares in Joe Pape's Finest over to you. He promised to make a bid sometime today. The bank'll handle the cash transaction. Here's the shares in Joe Pape's, endorsed."

"I can't," said Arnold. "I can't take that."

"Why? Take it. It's notarized. I got my notary out of bed at six-thirty this morning. You better take it or he'll be madder than hell."

"I'll think of something," said Arnold.

"Yeah, you do that. I got to go home, Norman'll be up by now. I should be there." Sonny put on his coat, and shook his brother's hand. "Take care of yourself."

"I owe you my life," Arnold said.

"Don't pay me! Keep it! I like people alive." He cleared his throat. "Stay alive for me, Arnold. We got to get to the beaches of Ceylon."

"Yeah, we ought to do that sometime. That would be a nice trip. Moonstones. See you," said Arnold.

"See you," Sonny waved. "Take care!"

"We'll do it." Arnold raised his coffee cup in toast. "The beaches of Ceylon."

Jeanne was gay, absolutely gay at the races, hung over, but gay, very gay. She had taken two baths, letting herself drift back into the water, taking the stench out of her hair. She had powdered herself with the baby's powder, and brushed her hair sleekly and tied it into a knot. And phoned the switchboard to ask if an Arnold Sterne had called, and if he did would they put him through right away, and also Sonny Sterne, and had they gotten her a nurse? She dressed in a pale green suit, the color of her eyes, and practiced how she would smile at Walter Winchell.

And now she was smiling at Walter Winchell, who was watching the horses, but only because they were nearing the finish line in the seventh race. The rest of the time he had been watching her, she knew it, all through lunch in the clubhouse and the unimportant races.

"You were very kind to ask me," he had said to Roan Anderson. "I love the races. I don't get here as often as I'd like."

"Do you ever get down to Wall Street?" Jeanne said, slightly drunk again, slightly repaired with a vodka collins, yes please, I would like another one, well I know it's early, but it's a celebration, yes? I've never had lunch with Walter Winchell.

"Wall Street?" Winchell said. "They got runners on Wall Street. Anything that I need from Wall Street comes to me. Cheers, little lady." He lifted his glass. *"A votre* beautiful *santé."*

"Santé," said Jeanne, and downed her second vodka collins. And yes, please, she would like another—how often did she have lunch with Walter Winchell?

"Well that's something we'll have to remedy," Walter Winchell said.

She waited it out till Roan went to the men's room. "I may want to see you alone," she said to Winchell.

"You're a married woman. You don't suppose I'd mess around with that." He was smiling.

"This is strictly business," she said. "Would you like to have some information about Arnold Sterne?"

"What kind of information?"

"The kind you can use."

"Doesn't he own the company your husband works for?"

"He doesn't own anything of my husband's," she said, and made her anger clear with her eyes.

"Here's my private number," Winchell said, and handed her his card. "If I'm not there they always know how to reach me. Call me anytime."

"It'll be tomorrow."

"Lovers' quarrel?" Winchell asked.

"Somebody lovers with Arnold Sterne? You must not know him at all."

They did not discuss Arnold the rest of the afternoon. They drove back to the city, with Winchell asking only the politest of questions, telling anecdotes, talking of a new singer he was going to make into a star, studying Jeanne from under the brim of his hat. They dropped him off at his midtown office and he shook hands with Roan, and squeezed hers, pressed it a message.

"We'll do it again, soon, you'll call me, you know how to reach me?"

"We know how to reach you," said Roan, and drove away. "I'm taking you home," he told his wife.

"No you're not," said Jeanne, feeling good, absolutely good. "Let me off at the subway, and if you try to follow me, if you try to find out where I am, you won't get your money from him, or your papers from me."

"You're the coldest woman I've ever known in my life."

"Perhaps you haven't known many women. Perhaps that's the trouble."

"If you're going to start that over again . . ."

"I start nothing. It's over. I'm glad that it's out. Not to have to touch you—"

"You hate me that much?"

"I don't hate you at all. I love him."

"Then I suppose I should be happy you don't love me. Very happy. I can do without that kind of love. You love him so much, you gave me all that information. You love him so much."

She stared out the car windshield at the gray of the sidewalks, the drab glitter of towering buildings, the overhanging black branches of lamp posts. No sight of sky.

"That's right. I love him."

"That's why you want to ruin him? That's why you want to leave him nothing at all?"

She bit on her words. "Nothing. I want him in the gutter. Naked. Crawling. With me."

She felt fine, absolutely fine when she got to the hotel, even though there were no messages from Arnold and the baby had thrown up. She had the nurse stay and give the baby dinner. She ran out and bought another bottle of Scotch. She bribed the bellboy to get her two Seconal, four if he could manage it, a whole bottle if he could manage it, there was nothing to worry about, did she look the type who would harm herself?

372

She called Arnold's home four times. The last time Sarah took the phone away from the butler and said if Jeanne didn't stop calling, she'd come to the hotel and kill her herself.

Jeanne called Sonny. Evelyn told her to go to hell, did she have no sense of decency at all?

She called Baby in Los Angeles, but she was on her way East for the funeral, and a girl in San Francisco who'd been in financial school with her in Paris, only she'd gotten married, she didn't live in San Francisco anymore.

"I just kept her old number, and they relisted it under her name," said the girl who answered the phone. "I'm not even sure of her married name. Is it important?"

"I don't suppose so. What's your name?"

"Annette."

"That sounds French. Are you French?"

"No."

"I'm French. I came here from France just to be with him. Oh, Annette, I love him so. What'll I do? I still love him so."

She took the four pills the bellboy had brought her, and finished off the last of the Scotch. She stumbled to the bed and sobbed wantonly, brokenly. After an hour she went to the bathroom and vomited, after which she burned her suicide note. Then she sat down and started composing a telegram to Arnold, trying to make concise the grief of a drowning soul.

WESTERN UNION
SENDING BLANK

```
NA152 — New York New York
ARNOLD STERNE
STERNE AND STERNE
42 WALL STREET
CITY


        ANYTHING.


                        JEANNE
```

PLEASE TYPE OR WRITE PLAINLY WITHIN BORDER—DO NOT FOLD

WESTERN UNION

```
NA153 — New York New York
GENEVIEVE HALE
ROOM 506 DORSET HOTEL
30 W. 54 STREET


YOUR TELEGRAM JULY 2 ARNOLD STERNE 42 WALL
NEW YORK NY IS UNDELIVERED PARTY HAS NOT BEEN
AT OFFICE SINCE YOU SENT TELEGRAM


        WESTERN UNION SERVICE BUREAU
```

Dorset Hotel

30 WEST 54TH STREET
NEW YORK CITY, NEW YORK

Oh Arnold,

I shall wash your feet and drink the water from which they're cleansed.

I will make it all up to you—haven't I made it all up to you, you voluptuous bastard—haven't I given you every inch of my body—haven't I taken every inch of yours—invaded you like an army of love—why won't you love me again. No one ever loved you as I did—touched you as I have—as I will—oh my darling I hurt from not seeing you —my eyes have developed sores inside—I can feel them through my eyes—my eyes—oh my angel—when will you heal them with the sight of you—

When will you touch me? I have streaks of pain on my arms—on my breasts—between my thighs—everywhere—inside me—behind me—come and heal me—Heal me or come here and kill me—I cannot endure life without seeing you once.

And I will eat you like caviar—egg—by egg—by egg—the whole great black lump of you—I will make it all up to you—I will lick your ass—I will stick my tongue into you—I will wash your feet and drink the water and make it up to you—why do I have to make it up to you—you miserable bastard—not in your wildest dreams could you have found the "lays" I've given you—not with all your millions could you buy the "lays" I've offered you—not for a million a "lay"—not for all your hopes of power could you command the "lays" I've given you—the love I've given you which you could never have for money or power—

Be careful with Roan that *he doesn't tell Sarah*—Protect yourself darling I'm waiting patiently—please call—Please be there, Arnold.

375

Dear "Sonny"

I am sorry for your grief and I must intrude but I'm
leaving this hotel unless I hear from you or Arnold tonight
—*Arnold will suffer result.*

I spoke to Clint Raddock one of Di Bonaven's men who
saw me with Winchell at the "track"—he tells me Winchell
will tell all—knows everything—Winchell said he heard a
story about Arnold Sterne divorcing Sarah to marry me—
and the reason I severed relationship with Arnold was
because Sarah would expose Arnold in Senate investigation
and had goods on Arnold—but Clint told me he convinced
Walter it was only a lovers' quarrel—

Winchell called me at this hotel—he must have had me
followed—but was told I was "not registered"—but he told
Clint Raddock he knew "all"—that Sterne would be called
in on Senate investigations and *his records at hands*—*He
also knows of Arnold's connection with city officials and of
friends of O'Dwyer's investing with Sterne and of Rosey
di Bonaven's connections thereof.*

Arnold's in a hell of a situation—Please make him see
me, help me and if he doesn't I shall try to make myself
destroy him as he has me in the eyes of everyone including
my husband—if he can do it to me I will give him his reward for being such a "son of a bitch."

Winchell will listen to anything I say—including if I tie
Arnold in with Frank Costello—and Kefauver would love
that as much as Winchell would—

I don't intend to face the world now— The only reason I've not done away with myself (and I could have—I

have courage enough to do that) is that I live in the hope
of seeing Arnold once more—

Sincerely yours,
Jeanne B. Anderson.

P.S. BE SURE TO READ THIS FIRST. I have to have
Clint stop Winchell before midnight tonight— He can do
it but why should I let him if I don't hear from Arnold—
Don't let Evelyn know about this—I know what she is from
Arnold—if you have to lock yourself in the bathroom to
read it—Please "Sonny" I don't want to hurt myself or
Arnold anymore—"Sonny" return it to me, or keep it under
lock and key until this mess is over—
P.S. Leave the house and call me from a phone booth so
Evelyn doesn't find out what's happening—you know you
can't trust her—Arnold loves you and he doesn't think you
can trust her—Arnold loves you—you are all he loves—
Don't return this letter to me, if you do I shall send it directly to Winchell—if he thinks he knows "all"—wait till
he hears what I could tell him—
Help me.

"Jesus Christ," Evelyn said, putting down the letter, which
had been hand-delivered, marked Very Personal and Urgent,
and which she had opened by mistake, sort of.

"Now what's this shit about your brother selling out his shares
of Joe Pape's Finest," Joe Pape said. He was in Arnold's office
where Arnold was in to nobody, not Western Union, not registered mail, return receipt requested, undeliverable, all things
undeliverable, refused, the addressee was out, Arnold told his
secretary, tell everybody he was out, except for the investment
houses and lawyers, and Colonel Reeling, and all right, as long
as he had come all this way, Arnold would see Joe Pape.

"First thing in my mind," Joe Pape said, "was to buy him out
myself. But he saved my life. The man saved my life. I can't
cheat him out of his share of the finest bourbon to come from the

377

South, and it would be cheating, even at fair price, 'cause the damned stuff is zooming, I tell you it's going to be bigger than Scotch, and the man saved my life. He's got to be in a hell of a bind to want to sell out his Joe Pape's. So I come up on the train from Tennessee to help him personal."

"Anything exciting happen on the trip?" Arnold said.

Joe Pape's watery eyes narrowed, and he chewed on his cigar. "I never liked you, Sterne, not from the very first minute. But you're his brother, and the man saved my life. I come to return the favor, and not let him sell."

"What do you figure his share is worth?"

"That isn't your business," Joe Pape said.

"Oh yes it is," said Arnold. He handed him Sonny's letter to the bank, the endorsed shares, and his authorization to turn the proceeds over to Arnold. Joe Pape studied the paper for a moment, and then relit his cigar.

"Well it doesn't surprise me a man like that, putting his future on the line for his brother. I guess I shouldn't be surprised, the concern he had for a stranger."

"How much is it worth?" said Arnold.

"I could let him have eleven-five in cash," Joe Pape said. "But I'd be cheating him at fair price. The state's got rumbles of going wet, and when that thing happens the distillery output could maybe quadruple, maybe more. It's a goddamn annuity, Joe Pape's is, and I'm damned if I'm going to let him give it up. The man saved my life."

"You told me that," Arnold said. "I'll take the eleven-five."

"How much does he need?" Joe Pape got up, his suit as rumpled as the one he had slept in on the long-ago faraway train ride. "I'm prepared to lend him as high as five, on the strength of his word. Abraham Sterne's word is as good as law to me. Better," Joe said, and smiled through his darkening teeth.

"He doesn't want any favors from you."

"That's too bad. I'm prepared to do him a favor. You think I got no conscience at all?"

Arnold started to laugh, but he held it in, took it back, and swallowed it. The seedy old man with the colorless eyes, only their whites holding traces of red-veined pink, was sincere for a murderer, Arnold could tell that, even though it was hard to tell much else, with a madwoman loose, and his world almost toppled, and selling his ass and Sonny's to save, what? The day? Not the day, the lifetime. All of his lifetime caught in one day, with Roan Anderson due in at three.

Colonel Reeling had come through, like the good honest cohort he was, with an offer of eight for their shares of the banks. The negotiable bonds came to a little under two, and the stocks were still being traded. So they were well over ten, that much he was sure of, even though he was sure of nothing anymore. How could he be sure of anything?

"Rosey di Bonaven on line one," his secretary buzzed him.

"Yeah, Rosey, I'm right in the middle of a meeting."

"Your ass is in the middle of a meeting," Rosey said. "I been talking to Clint and he said some woman called him, hysterical, and it's going to hit the fan, all of the stuff with my guys and some of O'Dwyer's, she even threatened to link you with Costello, what the hell's going on?"

"I'm in the middle of a meeting," Arnold said, and hung up the phone.

"You'll lend him five?" said Arnold to Joe Pape.

"That's what I said."

"Promissory note?"

"I'll do better than that," Joe Pape said. "I got a cashier's check with me." He reached in his pocket. "All I want back is his word."

"He's in the middle of arranging his wife's funeral," Arnold said. "Not exactly a time when a man can do business."

"I'm sorry to hear that," said Joe. "I'm genuinely sorry. She must have been a fine woman to be married to Abraham Sterne. But the offer still stands. Here's the check. I only want his word."

"You'll have to take mine," said Arnold.

"I don't know about your word, Sterne. For me, your word isn't good as law."

"Here's the paper," Arnold said, taking it back. "I'm the owner of all of his shares in your Finest. I'll give you a promissory note—"

"Based on how long a period?"

"I'll pay you as soon as I can. If not, you have your collateral. My share in your brewery."

"Breweries are beer," Joe said contemptuously. "And the shares don't belong to you."

"They do now," said Arnold. "Will you lend him the five?"

"I'll lend it," said Joe. "An offer to an honest man is one you can't take back."

"Get the notary in here," Arnold said over the intercom.

"Mr. Di Bonaven on two."

"Oh shit," said Arnold, and picked up the phone.

"Nobody hangs up on me," Rosey said.

"I'm happy to hear that," Arnold said, and hung up the phone. The notary drew up the promissory note, and Arnold signed it, had it notarized, and gave it to Joe. "I'd sure like to see your brother," Joe said. "Pay my respects."

"I'm sure he'd be grateful for your good wishes and your help, but he can't see anybody."

"What about the check?" Joe Pape said. "He has to endorse it. Can't I see him for a coupla minutes just while he endorses it?"

"I'll endorse it," said Arnold. "I have his power of attorney."

"No shit," said Joe Pape. "He must really trust you. Then I guess I'll have to trust you, too."

"Thank you," said Arnold, getting up, shaking hands, easing his anguish into the confines of politeness. Five million dollars deserved some respect.

"You'll give him my best?"

"Your finest," said Arnold, and almost slapped Joe on the back.

So they were over the mark, over the line, over the moon into diamonds and Senator land, marred only slightly by blackmail, and madness, scarred just a little by love.

"She's in the office," the secretary said. "She says she knows you're here, and she'll kill herself if you don't see her."

"Show her the window," said Arnold.

"She told me to give you these," said Miss Livermann, and handed him an envelope, full of photostats, riddled with the iniquities of his life. "She said to give you these and tell you there are no other copies, and no one knows anything. She's very hysterical, Mr. Sterne, what should I do?"

"Tell her I died," said Arnold, studying the papers. All of them there. For my sins. "Get the building policeman to get her out if you have to. Just get her out."

He bolted the door. Alone, he burned the papers, photostats, moved the originals into another safe, where no one had the combination. Burned the combination. Resealed the safe.

"Forgive me," he whispered to Sarah, through the black-holed silence of the telephone receiver.

"I forgive you," said Sarah. "You're a man. What's to forgive?"

"The rabbi's daughter," said Arnold to himself, and dialed Rosey di Bonaven.

"I'm in the middle of a meeting," said Rosey, and hung up the phone.

"Look, I was scared, I was in a bind," Arnold said, when he got Rosey back on the line. "Forgive me if I sounded impolite."

"Impolite? Aristocrats," said Rosey. "You have your own language."

"It's settled," said Arnold. "Everything's fine."

"Except for a broad who's going to spill everything to Winchell. Show papers to Winchell."

"There aren't any papers."

"For sure?"

"For sure," said Arnold, watching the ashes smoulder.

"How about your wife?"

"She knows. She forgives me."

"She forgives you," said Rosey. "The *Journal American*, you think that can forgive you?"

"Do something," said Arnold. "Unless you want me to withdraw."

"Withdraw?" Rosey said, and his voice choked with laughter. "After what we put in? So you're a fuckaround, and you got an extra baby, and you been playing footsie with friends and enemies alike. O'Dwyer's guys, huh?"

"There aren't any papers."

"Graft and corruption and scandal and a broad," Rosey said, and chuckled. "As far as I'm concerned, you're a shoe-in."

"You got it," said Arnold to Roan Anderson, handing him a check.

"This is only for ten."

"They're South Americans. They'll take wholesale."

"You son of a bitch."

"I want you out of the country. I want you very long gone. I want you to take her with you. She's at the Dorset. Registered under Genevieve Hale. Get an ambulance if you have to. Get a straitjacket. There are no more papers. You've got nothing to hang on."

"Winchell?"

"He's dealt with. Now deal with her. Deal with her. Take her with you. Get her out of the country. And if anything happens to the kid, I'll find you. I'll find you and kill you. *Gleb mir.*"

"I don't understand."

"You don't have to understand," said Arnold. "You just have to believe."

"Why would you give me the money if there aren't any papers?"

"I'm an investor," said Arnold. "I consider it good business. Ten million to get rid of the two of you, that's my idea of a bargain. And if I ever see your face again, I'll run my heel through it. *Gleb mir.*"

"I believe you."

382

"You got a good ear. You'll do well in South America. Diamonds!" he said, and raised his Scotch in a salute. "I wish you nothing but diamonds."

"In a way," Roan said, "I guess I should be grateful."

"Diamonds aren't it. Moonstones," said Arnold. "I didn't wish you those. There's a dream in moonstones. I only wish you diamonds. *A votre santé.*"

Joe Pape's loan he would deal with. Joe Pape's loan he could hang on to, never negotiate, return. The important thing was he was out of it, clean, clear, and he could protect Sonny. As far as Sonny was concerned, Joe Pape's Finest was gone. When the right time came, when Evelyn was out of Sonny's life, as all women who looked with too much love from fierce energetic eyes had to be out of the life of a noble man, when that time came, he would give the share of Joe Pape's back to Sonny. In the meantime he signed the shares over to his son, who was growing wise and was graduating Harvard Law School, and would give the bonanza back when the time was ready, when Arnold told him. Protecting Sonny from himself, protecting him from Evelyn, that was the least that Arnold could do. Until the time was ripe.

Ripe as the grave was rotten. Such a quiet funeral. Except for Evelyn's eyes, watching Arnold with such bright curiosity, across the lowering coffin, as she wondered what it was that could inspire passion like that, madness like that, in a woman.

FIVE

HE WAS MARRYING HER, he was marrying her, he was marrying
her. There was no music this time, but who needed music? Who
needed more than the judge standing in front of them, a personal
friend of Sonny and Arnold's. Her life began today. Somebody
take a picture of her life beginning! But nobody in the chambers
had the crassness to carry a camera, there was no one from
Pittsburgh among the guests.

That gave her a momentary turn: she really missed the family.
But she could take care of them now, she could take care of
everybody. She could retire Pappy, and Grandma could get a
cleaning woman, and a better apartment, someplace in Squirrel
Hill, modern, gleaming, without Grandma having to make it
shine from effort and love. She could help out Sadie and Hymie,
the rapist, and their daughter and the twins, see that they got an
education, maybe they had brains after all if they were related to

the woman who married Abraham Sterne, the financier. She could even do something for Sammy, and Pegeen the *shicksa,* and even that bitch Enid, and Murray, would he ever get married? And she could take care of Chris: she could send her almost anywhere. Evelyn could do something now for everyone she cared for; that was the reason she was marrying him, marrying him!

That was a lie. She loved him. She really loved him. How did that happen? Wasn't that wonderful.

No matter that Norman was witness at the wedding. They would not all be moving in with the family. Sonny was taking her on a honeymoon. A true honeymoon. To a castle. Like a princess. They were going to the castle of William Randolph Hearst.

Sonny was going to talk to him about an idea for a magazine that dealt with nothing but finance. People were so interested in money, it had to be a success.

Not Evelyn anymore. Evelyn didn't care about high finance: she was being joined to the stock market pages. She would never have to study them again. She could read the wedding announcements (hers). Birth announcements (hers, her son's). It had to be a son. Men were so wonderful. And he'd love her as much as he'd loved Catherine, who'd given him an heir.

Who was picking his nose. Little matter. She was going to the castle of William Randolph Hearst.

On a sleeping car. Pullman. Cross-country. First class, heavy tipping. How wide were the beds?

What love she would make to him, that handsome, strong genius. What a good idea, a magazine about money. Joe Mc-Creery was interested in editing it, and being a chief contributor. With him at the helm, and Sonny in the driver's seat, and Hearst in his castle, how could it fail?

How could anything fail, ever again. Life was beginning. In a castle. After a sleeping car. Where she could be alone with him at last, her wonderful arrogant love.

"Listen," he said, as they walked down the steps on the way to the waiting limousine. "I hope you don't get angry."

Nothing he did could possibly make her angry.

"Norman's coming with us."

Evelyn closed her eyes. This part was the dream. The wedding, that had been true, but now she was dreaming.

So there they all were, going cross-country, because the Dauphin had wept in the morning, frightened to be alone, and as a wonderful surprise Sonny had had Norman's bags packed. And had turned down her tight-lipped suggestion that they fly, because they had too much luggage, he said. Because he was afraid to fly, it turned out. Her hero.

Oh what the hell, she was crazy about him, and into each life some rain had to fall, even inside the compartment. The countryside flowed past their windows, flaunting space and grandeur and mountains and trees, and renegade couples strolling arm in arm. The Great Out There, it seemed to Evelyn, idyllic for the absence of Norman.

She would fling her thoughts into the wind outside the train, searching the air for contemplative feelings, finding none, feeling only the terrible oppression of imprisonment with a nonbeloved. So she threw her mind into the contents of her suitcases, four of them, filled with the outfits he had bought her at Bonwit's, which she had returned and replaced with the exact same ones from Loehmann's for a quarter of the price. Beautiful clothes. It had been worth the ride on the subway for what she had saved. That's what this was, was a subway ride, a brief perdition on the way to ecstasy, the price she had to pay for a great consummation of a noble love.

Alone, at last, sometimes, finally, she sucked on Sonny's eyebrows and licked his lashes and fingered the massive forehead as if she could make love to his brain, all the while she was riding him, gathering him into her, trying to whip him into the frenzy she felt. He was moaning and his fingers were moving down along her belly, nearly touching her, yes, they were touching her, so they could do it together, shatter each other, just another moment more . . .

And a knock on the door. Norman.

She was ready to kill him by Chicago, and herself by Denver, and Sonny by Los Angeles, Hearst Castle or no Hearst Castle. But she said nothing, at least she said little, she controlled her temper, her distaste, her wanting to scream, which was reasonable for a change. For a change. It was all going to change. It was meant to be monumental, this love. Delayed gratification might be fitting after all: appropriate, her first married orgasm in a castle. When would they get there? Would Hearst still be alive? Would she?

In the dining car, she stared at the man who had finally made her princess consort. She had been stupid about Walter, she finally understood that now, overestimating him completely, imagining his ambition to be as great as hers, thinking the solution would be living in Squirrel Hill. Squirrel Hill could never have contained her. All of Pennsylvania couldn't contain her. She had traveled the whole country with the most wonderful man she had ever met, and she still couldn't contain herself.

Norman spilled his milk on her lap.

Evelyn stared at Sonny.

Sonny stared back at Evelyn.

When they were back in the compartment, getting ready to pull into Union Station in Los Angeles, she looked at Sonny, and spoke through lips held very tight. "I don't know if I'll ever forgive you for this," she said. "To make my honeymoon an insult, a humiliation."

"I didn't mean it to be that way," he said. "I'll make it up to you somehow."

Somehow. Not good enough. Not all the perfumes of Arabia. Well, perhaps most of them. She looked at Sonny with wizened eyes, lids grown heavy with Pullman car skepticism. Here she was, pregnant Queen for a Day, for a lifetime—what if it was the wrong life? What if the solution weren't in a man but in herself? Impossible.

"Mr. Sterne?" the chauffeur said, waiting by the passenger loading zone.

"Yes?"

"Mr. Hearst has sent one of his limousines for you. Just down this way."

One of his limousines. Ah yes. Better and better.

"Happy honeymoon," Evelyn said to Sonny, kissing him on the cheek as he helped her inside the back of the car. "I've forgotten everything till now," she told him. "My life begins today."

She began to feel better, in spite of the rain-soaked torpor of Los Angeles. She felt actually happy and excited as they settled into the lush, upholstered seats, even though Norman sat in the middle, a magnetized chess board on his lap, so he and Sonny could immediately start playing chess. Leaving her out of it.

Once they were on the open highway, however, Sonny did not devote his attention exclusively to Norman. A good part of it was given to the chauffeur, and his driving, and leaning over to try and see the speedometer.

"Excuse me," Sonny said. "How fast are you going, Freedom?"

"Forty-five miles an hour, sir."

"It feels like more than that." Sonny's shoulder moved inside his jacket.

"That's because of the rain, sir."

"Yeah, well maybe you should take it a little easier."

"I've driven through heavier rains than this," Freedom said.

"Well I haven't," said Sonny. "Take it easy."

Outside the car windows, the air was being drowned. No room for breath beneath those suffocating blankets of water. Evelyn could see no further than the side of the road, not a building, just a continuous wallpapered gray. Like a terrible shield had been built around them, catching them forever inside that car.

"You're right to be frightened," she told Sonny. "I've never seen rain like this, and I've lived through hurricanes."

"I'm not frightened. I'm just cautious. And a liar."

"But of course, in those circumstances, I was with friends."

"I'm sorry." Sonny reached for her hand. "Are we leaving you out?"

"You certainly are." Evelyn stretched her trim little navy blue

Traina Norell to attention. She spoke to him with all the wonder of honest eyes, and told him in hazel how much she loved him.

"We'll stop right after this game," Sonny said, reaching across Norman again, squeezing her fingers, warming her palm. "Right after this game, I promise."

"I figure that'll be a minimum of ten moves," Norman said.

"I don't know why I even try to play with him," Sonny said, grinning with parental smug.

If they had been alone, the two of them, she could have lowered the curtains suspended above the windows, pulled down the shade that would separate them from the chauffeur, making them into a couple closing out the world. Instead of the world closing them in, as it was doing again. With only a brief flash of sun to illuminate how ugly it was.

"Where are we now, Freedom?"

"Gaviota."

"How attractive," Evelyn said, looking at the side of the road. The puddles were orange, against sienna clay. "Muddy water." As if she had not wasted enough of her life noticing the Allegheny River. She needed to go to a castle to see muddy water.

"Are we really meeting William Randolph Hearst?" she asked Sonny. Or was it all a rained-on joke, a funeral for dreams.

"We certainly are." Sonny leaned back in the car, held on to the strap, and beamed. "He hasn't been active for years. But there's hope in getting out of hopeless debt. It's hard to explain."

"I think I can try and understand," Evelyn said, biting her lower lip.

"Hell if you can beat the reversal of fortunes, maybe you can believe that life can continue. A little longer anyway. He talks to almost no one these days—his voice is almost gone. But the brain's still there. And he really likes McCreery. He trusts Joe McCreery. So maybe we can swing it. Goddamn. A legend, and we're meeting him. Isn't it great that we're here in time."

"How much farther is it?"

"A couple hours," Freedom said. "More or less."

Naturally it was more. Norman had to pee. Norman had to throw up. Norman had to be along.

"He doesn't even come up to the castle anymore," Sonny said. "He spends all his time at his nurse's house in Beverly Hills." He shifted his eyes, made contact with hers, so she'd know that they both understood who the nurse was, and that it was too early for Norman to find out about sex and gossip. "They came up especially, I mean there are other guests, but this is a very unusual weekend for him."

"Not to mention me," said Evelyn.

Sonny looked at her with warmth in his eyes, vision to see through her growing fury. "Smile at him," he whispered, stroking her hand, across Norman's lap. "Smile at him with your two-and-a-half-million-dollar smile, and I've got the magazine on the stands. If his brain's still there, so are his eyes."

"Flatterer."

"It's true. I only lie around every fifty statements."

Her faith was restored. Her love was restored. Her sanity was saved.

"BUELLTON!" shrieked Norman, pointing out the window at a road sign. "The home of Anderson's Split Pea Soup! The home of Anderson's Split Pea Soup! We're here! We're in Buellton."

"What the hell is Buellton?"

"It's the home of Anderson's Split Pea Soup," said Norman. "Its fame is worldwide. That's what it says on the can. Can we stop here?"

"What's the story with Buellton, Freedom?" Sonny asked.

"They have an excellent split pea soup, sir, and the washrooms are very clean."

"I could use a cup of pea soup," said Sonny to Evelyn. "Couldn't you?"

"We had breakfast and lunch on the train," Evelyn said. "And dessert and coffee."

"What are you angry about?"

"I'm not angry," said Evelyn, looking away.

They were stopping to eat. They were on their way to a castle five miles above the sea, looking down at the sea, touching chairs, maybe even elbows with William Randolph Hearst and his nurse and maybe Cary Grant, Errol Flynn, weren't they all close friends? Being right there, in the middle of a fable. And they were stopping to eat.

Again, they stopped on the fog-shrouded highway. For a pastry in San Luis Obispo. The world's best pastry, Norman informed them: Danish influence, American cream.

At last they were on the final stretch of coast highway. Behold the roaring ocean, some faded Walter M. White memory whispered to Evelyn. Behold the roaring ocean, and find peace in yourself. You cannot possibly hope to compete with that rage.

Gray. The waves were a terrible rush of white and gray. Not even a living color.

"This is the most beautiful coast in the country," Freedom said.

"When you can see it," said Evelyn.

"We're almost there," said Freedom, coming to the gate. "It's just up the hill."

Five miles up the hill, in the leaden rain. Terrible, twisting climbing curves.

"There's some of Mr. Hearst's zebras on the left," said Freedom. "You can just about make them out."

"How far could we fall?" asked Sonny, peering toward the right.

"All the foliage from here on up was brought in by Mr. Hearst, except for the California live oaks."

"Where?" asked Evelyn.

"And the bay and the laurel."

"Where?"

"The topsoil was carted up just the same as the cypress and the Mexican fan palms, and the thousands of varieties of flowers. Most of this work was done by Eye-talians. They have a way with the earth."

"I heard they were lousy farmers," said Sonny.

"Well, they don't eat too good, but they got beautiful flowers. Anyhow, from here on up almost all the natural wonders you will see are planted."

"Where?" asked Evelyn. "Where? Where? Where?"

For a moment, just as if there were something bigger than William Randolph Hearst, one dying beam of sunlight cut through the fog, beneath the rain, setting the whole vista behind alive with color, giving her a glimpse of a perfect day. The hills as they had been forever, green, and sloping, with gnarled little oak trees arguing back at the sky. The sky as it was meant to be, actual sky blue, the raging gray surf turned pastel green by that one brief ray of sun.

A beautiful day, for one quick ray of insistent sunlight. She would be like that. She would radiate darkness for him. The rains started again, plunging them into night.

Freedom turned up the headlights.

"What time is it?"

"A little past eight-oh-four," said Norman.

"Oh my God," said Evelyn. "How much time do we have to get dressed for dinner? Are we getting here late?"

"In the old days," Freedom said, "he preferred guests to come late at night. Very late at night, you know, two, three in the morning, so he could have the place fully illuminated. You should see this place fully illuminated. It's really something."

"I wouldn't mind seeing it not fully illuminated," said Evelyn. "What time is dinner?"

"In the old days they'd meet in the assembly room at eight, and dinner would be at nine. And there'd be a newsreel after dinner in Mr. Hearst's viewing room."

"I'm not interested in the old days. I'm interested in tonight. What time is dinner?"

"Well, we can't say for sure. He's not feeling up to par."

"*Jesus Christ!*" Sonny shouted. There was a lion in the road in front of them. Giant-maned, staring with yellow eyes, fangs bared, one giant paw with its claws raised toward the car.

"Lion in the road!" Norman shouted gleefully. "Lion in the road!"

Freedom drew to an abrupt stop. He switched off the headlights.

"Are you crazy?" Sonny screamed in the darkness.

"Headlights make them blind," Freedom said.

"You son of a bitch! Why did you stop like that? We could have been killed, we could have gone off the road. Why the hell did you stop like that?"

"Animals have the right of way here," Freedom said, turning the headlights back on. "That's the rule Mr. Hearst laid down. That's why we have so many beautiful animals still roving free in his zoo."

They were driven up to the Esplanade, to their room in the Casa del Sol. "Called that," said Freedom, "because no matter how high or how low the sunset is, you'll always see the setting sun."

Evelyn laughed into the darkness, the rain-soaked darkness. Well, as long as you could always see the sun, except if it was shrouded in fog, and too late, and raining, there was no point in not being merry. She had survived her own suffocation in the car. She was at the castle.

Norman took the larger room of the two-room suite, and she let him, she wanted him to: he'd probably like being goldleafed, massive fourpostered. And it was time he got a little phallic symbolism in his head.

Besides, the other bed was smaller, bringing them closer, wouldn't it? Nothing was between them and heaven but gold-painted plaster of Paris flower-budded ceilings, two gold flags hanging on opposite sides of a brass-button-rimmed mirror, brass sconces with eagles on, round bulbs in a shade with a yellow fringe, sick Pittsburgh yellow, her first marriage window blind yellow, a pom pom hanging fifteen inches below, a sanctuary lamp, and eagles on the bedpost. Nothing between them and heaven but that.

"What are you going to wear for dinner?" she asked Sonny, starting to unpack, while Freedom went up to the Casa Grande to find out when dinner was.

"I imagine a tux," Sonny said.

"I imagine a gown," said Evelyn. Of course a gown. A lace Dior of individually joined linen daisies ($3079.50 at Bonwit's,

$600 at Loehmann's), body-fitting. A warm demure lady with a terrific frame, that's who she should be for this portion of the dream.

Norman had requested a sandwich in his room. For the first time she could see where she might grow to love him.

They were steaming out Sonny's tux in one of the two adjoining bathrooms, when Freedom returned. "I'm sorry," he said. "I'm afraid you've missed dinner. He wasn't feeling well, so they dined at seven."

"We had to stop for pea soup." Evelyn clutched the sink.

"We didn't stop that long."

"We had to stop for pea soup. We had to stop for pastry."

"He's looking forward to seeing you tomorrow night at dinner," Freedom said. "And in the meantime, there's a tray of cold meats in the morning room, and you might be interested in a game of pool, Mr. Sterne."

"I don't play pool."

"He was too busy stealing tomato herring to hang around poolrooms," Evelyn breathed.

"You shut up!"

"We had to stop for pea soup," she panted.

"I'd like some pea soup," said Norman, appearing in the doorway.

"Oh my God," said Evelyn. "Oh my God. Oh my God."

She could not fall to the floor beating her fists, because the lace daisies were antique linen and might fall apart, and the Persian carpet was so short-napped, so unyielding. Like men. And the elements. And the goddamn castle. All of it shutting her inside, inside, when out in the world was what she wanted to be. Not caught in some terrible tapestry, a leaf on an overembroidered wind, hanging on someone else's wall.

Millefleurs. Some Hollywood phony who probably called Parke-Bernet "Parke-Bernay" stood telling her that the tapestry on the wall of the poolroom was *millefleurs.* As if she couldn't see for herself that there were a thousand flowers in between the thousand leaves in between everything else that could possibly be shoved in.

"Is that what it is?" said Evelyn, nodding at the Hollywood phony. He was, after all, trying to be nice. "The tapestry, Sonny," she said archly. "The one behind the pool table. That's a fourteenth-century *millefleurs* design. Depicting the hunt. That's where we should have gone. On a hunt. My brave, strong adventurer."

"You looking for a fight?"

"Looking?" she said. "I've had it shoved in my face."

He turned away for a moment. Then he seized Evelyn's arm and pulled her into the morning room, kissing her under one of the sanctuary lamps. She didn't kiss him back.

"You really haven't seen the most interesting feature of the poolroom," the Hollywood phony said, coming through the doorway, finding them.

"I'm a little busy." Sonny was still trying to kiss her, to soften the unyielding mouth.

"Sterne? Is it Sterne?"

"It's Sterne," Sonny said, letting go of her. "This is my wife, Evelyn."

"Charley Nestor . . ." He offered his hand. "Look, I don't mean to interfere, Sterne, but Mr. Hearst prefers that kind of thing in the bedrooms. That's why he built so many of them."

"He objects to a kiss?" Sonny smiled. "I find that hard to believe."

"Well he's getting older. What business are you in?"

"Investment banking."

"I'm retired," said Charley Nestor.

"Is *she* coming out?" Evelyn asked.

"They've gone to bed."

"I would've loved to see how she dresses," said Evelyn. "I'm crazy about her taste in plumes."

"Yes, I'm retired," said Charley. "Anaconda Copper, you know."

"I wish." Sonny smiled.

"You ever go to the races, Sterne?" Charley said.

"Are there any—uh—film luminaries expected?" Evelyn asked. Clark Gable. Errol Flynn. Cary Grant.

"Arthur Lake may be coming."

Arthur Lake: Dagwood Bumstead. "I have to go lie down," said Evelyn.

"Not until I've shown you the best feature of the poolroom," said Charley, a hand on each of their backs, propelling them past the two pool tables, over to the door, opening it, staring out into the torrent. "Look at that," he said. "That wild oak tree. If you ever get out to the races, you come to Santa Anita. I have a box there."

"That's the best feature of the poolroom?" Evelyn said.

"I raise horses," said Charley.

Evelyn looked at him with interest, watching him grow younger, handsomer, his chin becoming stronger. He smiled at her and whinnied.

Evelyn laughed because she thought he was kidding. Sonny laughed because she wasn't frowning anymore. Relief flooded that portion of the garden as heavily as rain did.

"How about that tree?" said Charley, clearing his throat, holding his bourbon tight to his vest, clearing his throat again, and whinnying. "I don't see what's so funny about it. He got that big giant of a wild oak out of the way so he could build the poolroom, he moved it to there, and look at the size of it. Still alive. A remarkable man."

"Moving mountains and trees," said Evelyn. "Why can't he do something about the weather?"

"Well he's getting older," said Charley, as Evelyn darted back inside the protection of the room.

"Excuse me," Sonny said, and turned to follow Evelyn. She was leaning over a lamp. Her hair was wet and dark, and he could smell her skin from ten feet away.

"Look at this lamp," said Evelyn, studying the tap-dancing girl on the base. A tap dancer with little red shoes, her hands crossed like feathers, her skirt flaring red and orange and green arrows, her hat a futuristic crown, an arrow dividing a spreading field of copper wings.

"Look at me," Sonny said.

"Look at the shade. It's even worse than the lamp."

"Look at me." His fingers were under her chin, and he was pulling her face toward his chest, roughly but not too roughly.

"Yes?"

He kissed her. From the corner came a whinny, and they laughed into each other's mouths. They embraced until they were finished laughing.

"You two interested in a movie?" Charley Nestor said. "There's a projectionist on duty and we got the whole screening room to ourselves. And two really good newsreels."

"Newsreels?" said Evelyn.

"That's the Chief's favorite kind of movie, newsreels. They're not making as many nowadays. But we got a couple of good ones."

"That's exactly what I feel like is a good newsreel," said Evelyn.

"Come on," said Sonny, urging her with his hand.

"That's *all* I feel like," said Evelyn.

She would drive him crazy in the darkness, if the decor didn't do it before.

Wooden goddesses stretched toward the ceiling along the walls. Gross-featured, button-eyed, gold-painted goddesses, holding out lights like an offering, along with some copper twigs and brass leaves and tulips. They sat down on big yellow-backed velvet chairs. A theater. The place was a theater. Loew's 83rd Street. She remembered the blue-bordered red feathers on the chairs of Loew's 83rd. Not as sumptuous as this, but nothing was as sumptuous or outrageous as this. Orson Welles was a genius of understatement.

Even the ceiling, the part that wasn't blue velvet and wood, was painted with gold. Gold. Gold even framing the natural wooden beams, lest they seem too rested plain.

She put her hand in Sonny's crotch once the projectionist dimmed the lights. She unzipped his fly at the invasion of South Korea. By the time the war got serious, she had him so hard he was sweating.

"I think Mr. Hearst would prefer that we confine these outbursts to our room," Sonny whispered. "Let's go to our room."

"There's a good clip coming up of one of my horses running in the Florida derby," said Charley Nestor, and whinnied.

"Would you excuse us, please?" said Evelyn. "This is sort of our honeymoon."

"Hell yes," said Charley. "But I'm sorry you're leaving. You might be missing some really good news."

"Let me do that for you," Sonny said, reaching for the back of her dress, holding the shoulders underneath. "Let me do everything for you." He kissed the back of her neck.

"I don't want you to touch me," she said. "Not after the day I went through. The last thing I feel like is making love."

"I'm sorry," he said.

He turned and moved slowly towards the doorway. "I'll sleep in with Norman."

"You can sleep here," she said. "You can sleep here," she pleaded. "I only said I didn't want to make love."

"Take a look in the mirror. How could I be next to that and not make love?"

"You son of a bitch," she whispered, and kissed him.

He opened the snaps on the rest of the lace, and lowered the zipper of the flesh-colored lining, and slid the dress carefully back over her shoulders and helped her step out of it. He moved his lips past her throat, tearing at her underwear with impatient hands, caressing her swollen breasts, and he was licking at her slightly-rounded-with-baby belly, ever so slightly rounded, ever so gently licking, he was on his knees, mouthing her pelvis and hips, and she was holding the thick silvery yellow hair in both her hands, and tearing at his neck, and his mouth moved further downwards, and Norman walked in.

There was nowhere to go but up the wall, except she couldn't find one with room for her. All the next day, from the moment they woke—silent, angry, disappointed—and dressed, and dolefully brushed their teeth in quiet shifts, indicated that the other could use the toilet, all that day, in between rain, and hoping for a glimpse of sun, or an unexpected drop-in from Winston Churchill, they saw the features of the castle. Freedom took them on an umbrellaed tour because Norman wanted to go, even if it was raining. They walked along terraces covered with Persian carpets. Persian carpets laid in stone. And everywhere sat and swam white statues carved with so little attention to anything but perfection, so lacking in character and design as to seem they could melt in the rain, which Evelyn wished they would.

She wished it would all disappear in the rain. The Cathedral of Ronda (Fleming?) with its white overscoring, overturreted, like an overstated wedding cake. A wedding cake. That's what they should have had. A regular wedding with music and a wedding cake, and the family—what was so great about the judge's chambers? They were impersonal, they were cold, so was the judge, like the Statue of Sekhmet, the Goddess of Everything Bad, Freedom was telling them. Of course there had only been one judge, and here were two Sekhmets, naturally, one atop the other—why get one lion-faced Egyptian statue when you could afford two, so you could really have a corner on Everything Bad? Why didn't it melt in the rain, and they could start all over, and she could bring him home to Pittsburgh.

Wasn't it *her* triumph, wasn't it? Wasn't he her triumph over Pittsburgh? Carrying her so far from her beginnings she couldn't possibly end up there. How could she possibly take him home to Pittsburgh? What could he possibly think of her, when he saw what Pittsburgh was?

Well, one thing Pittsburgh was, was a hell of a lot more fun than the Hearst castle. Why didn't it melt in the rain, why didn't it stop raining? Wasn't there a God? Hadn't He sent her this man?

"And this is the indoor pool," said Freedom.

A million miles long. A thousand miles wide. And Norman hated swimming. "Forgive me for doubting," she said, giving birth to her own square vaulted echo, from inside the grotto.

There was actually a grotto at the far inner side, where the water was shallower so they would have a foothold and there was only one statue in a little lesser grain than the Carrara which was everywhere else, and this one called "Abundancia." "Forgive me for doubting," the voice came back.

So she actually began to allow the castle, to every now and again find one little feature that didn't make her angry, that wasn't disruptive. It got consistently harder, as Freedom showed them the Graces by Boyer after Canova: three white neo-classical lesbians, they looked to Evelyn, and in spite of all that they still weren't interesting.

Now the pool, that was different. That cost a million dollars to build in 1933, according to Freedom. So it was right that it was totally outrageous, mosaic-ed up to its fig leaves. Had they had fig leaves on, the two statues on the far end? She couldn't wait to get back and take a better look. All for the sake of art.

"I have an idea," Evelyn said. "Freedom, why don't you take Norman around the rest of the place. Mr. Sterne and I, we'd like to go back to our room and nap."

"Yeah, I could use a little nap," Sonny said.

"I'm not tired," Norman said.

"Good," said Evelyn.

"You're going the wrong way," Sonny said. "I think our rooms are up that way."

"We're not going to our rooms, my darling. We're going swimming." She looked at him, smiling for the first time that day.

"Shouldn't we go back and get suits?"

"You're joking," said Evelyn. "After they went to the trouble of building us a grotto, for a million, in nineteen thirty-three? Oh wait. What about towels?"

"What about them?" Sonny said, grinning.

"Right. We'll ruin our clothes. Let Hearst's mother worry."

They ran past the unending greenery (no lawns), all of it flowers, along the balustraded staircases, holding on to railings, and each other. The flowers, like all of the art, came in too many varieties to consider seriously, but Hearst had been unable to get their colors to clash. Still, every few steps Evelyn could feel herself getting a headache from what was underneath her feet (now yellow and black diamonded and harlequined mosaic), or around her eyes. Where was the sky? Where was the million-dollar view? Obscured. Obscured, goddamit. Oh, excuse her for that. How could any woman need a view when she had Sonny? And Norman wasn't with them.

"I liked it best"—he was holding on to her elbow, pulling her tight in beside him as he raised the umbrellas above their heads—"when Freedom told us the facade of the Casa del Sol was all Mediterranean style. Moorish arches, Florentine wrought iron, a Roman sarcophagus."

"Well it is consistent," Evelyn said. "It's all the ugliest."

They ran into the poolhouse. And just as if worries were wishes, there were towels on the chair inside the door.

Evelyn opened her raincoat, letting it slide to the floor, as if clothes didn't matter. But she folded her slacks neatly, running her fingers along the press, because he was watching, and the whole thing was suddenly as exciting as if it hadn't been set against an unending mosaic.

"There are goldfishes in the bottom of the pool," she said. "Real goldfishes. Fishes made of gold."

"I got plenty to look at," Sonny said, arms folded.

She stood as tall as she could, remembering to hold her breasts as if they were something to be proud of. His eyes were as clear as the skies should have been, she could see for miles and miles in them, she could see their horizons together, limitless, shot through with sun.

"Aren't you coming in with me?"

"In a second. I want to watch you go in the water."

"I'm not a very good diver."

"I didn't marry an athlete."

That's right. He had married her. He had really married her. And had taken her to a castle. What matter that it was a castle—how could she put it delicately?—in less than exquisite taste, what matter that the earth had been raped, and they couldn't see the sky? What matter that the place seemed to be one continuous clutter of feather and flower and bird and mermaid and God and Madonna and Elephant?

She arced through the air, hit the water, tried for the bottom, reaching down for the fish that was made of gold. A million dollars, in 1933. What investments she could have made in 1933 with a million dollars.

She surfaced for air.

He was almost undressed, hurrying, seeming to pull himself out of his trousers, dancing backwards out of his socks. God, he was handsome, funny, strong, clever, when he wasn't being frightened of the road, when he was only being anxious to be with her. Funny. Handsome. Strong. Clever. No. Not clever, brilliant. Today the castle. Tomorrow the world.

She watched how the dull illuminations seemed to lighten his hair, streaking it silver, even the part that was palely yellow. She watched as he dove, neatly. The result of an older brother, Evelyn supposed, the East River. New York poverty had advantages over Pittsburgh poverty. He surfaced in front of her, kissing her breasts on the way up for air.

"Come with me to the grotto." She laughed, and kissed him.

She turned on her side and stroked past the little gold boys, blowing on little gold trumpets on little red sailfish in mosaic on the blue mosaic-ed walls and the yellow mosaic-ed walls, and the orange mosaic-ed walls, and the green mosaic-ed walls. "I'm closing my eyes," Evelyn said. "Tell me when we get to the grotto."

He touched her instead. She floated into his arms, letting his body pull hers toward him, velveted by the water. She put the whole of her being into his hands, her hips onto his fingers, his thighs, pressing herself against him, onto him, warmed by the pool and gentle insistence. Her eyes were closed. No pictures but those in her head, loving, spacious.

"Oh, my darling," he said.

She wanted to make it last, to stretch it out like the ray of sun to the one patch of honest scenery. But the tempo of the decor seemed to have affected both of them, and they were moving too fast, moving too fast, moving too fast.

"I'm sorry about that," Sonny said.

"Sorry about what?" asked Evelyn, her arms still around him, body floating away from him.

"I got a little excited."

"Well, that's what it's all about, isn't it?" She smiled.

"I mean it was over too quickly."

"Not for me," she lied. If it was good enough for him, it was good enough for her. It had to be. He'd satisfied her before. He could do it again. She didn't deserve to be satisfied all the time. That was pagan.

Still, it sent a little chill through her, missing that one. The one that was meant to be monumental, Roman, decadent.

"Are you sure?" he said.

"Couldn't you tell?"

"I was too busy being carried away."

"So was I." There was no point in hurting him. No point in opening up discussions. Certainly not that one. Men were so sensitive on that one. Even worse than women. Twice as worried, twice as silent on the subject.

Besides, sex wasn't everything: there was also money. She laughed aloud because she was such a good kidder, even of herself.

Mostly, she looked at Sonny during lunch, even though the vertical lines of that Gothic dining room were all to the purpose of driving your eyes upward. Evelyn had looked upward once, so mainly she looked at Sonny. Was there a ceiling that wasn't decorated? With decorations beside the decorations on the ceiling with decorations beside.

She had a terrible headache.

The flags of the Palio Della Contrata of Siena fluttered cluttered above them. "Each of them represents a different religious war," Charley Nestor offered, as the butler served a salmon mousse to each of them. The mousse was set inside individual silver fish molds, with one lapis lazuli eye staring at each of the guests, whose number now stretched to ten, none of them Winston Churchill or Errol Flynn, or even Arthur Lake.

"You want some ketchup?" Charley Nestor offered her a bottle of Heinz, along with history. "When the Chief was a kid and there was nothing up here but a hill, imagine, they used to come for family picnics, and bring ketchup in bottles, and mustard in jars, so he still leaves a bottle of ketchup and a jar of mustard on the table, no matter what's being served, to remind everybody of the simplicity of the old days. When there were picnics."

"How cute," said Evelyn. "With salmon mousse."

The length of the table was so great, so narrow-seeming to Evelyn, for all the churchly height of the walls ("An illusion," Charley Nestor guided, "an illusion because of the wooden vertical lines that the room's taller'n it's long, it isn't true, it's an illusion"), the room itself was so Gothic and spectral that missing weren't only Hearst and his Constant Companion, but also Bela Lugosi. Evelyn felt chilled. Actually chilled.

"Which one's the flag for men and women?" Sonny asked.

"You consider that a religious war?" asked the minister from Pasadena.

"You consider it anything else?" Sonny drank some wine. "Women in religion have been receptacle to or mother of greatness, never greatness itself. Forced to sit upstairs in *shul* . . ."

"You're a Jew?" asked the minister.

"Yes," said Sonny. "Are you a Gentile?"

The minister laughed. "Continue."

"But those who give us our religion, besides our teachers, are our mothers. Telling us to believe in something that doesn't believe in them, except as mothers of men and seductresses."

"Is there anything else?" asked Evelyn, and tinkled her own laughter into the tunnel that was a room.

"So there's got to be battle in them," Sonny said. "Having to tell us to believe, at the same time hoping we'll defy them. Mother-son. Grown man-grown woman. Of course it's a religious war, it's a test of faith."

"How come Mr. Hearst is so friendly with Arthur Lake?" Evelyn asked.

"Well you know," said Charley Nestor, "Bill started the comic strips."

"I didn't know that," Evelyn said. "I thought it was the Spanish-American War."

Silence.

"Oh I see," said Evelyn, after a moment. "The funnies. Blondie."

"Besides which, he's a regular guy. Arthur is. Not like some of these Hollywood phonies," said a Hollywood phony.

"You think that's an outrageous premise?" Sonny asked the minister. "That the battle between men and women is a religious war?"

"I don't think any premise is outrageous that gets you young people thinking about religion."

"Young people," Sonny said, laughing, and raised his glass in toast. "That's nice. Look who he's calling young people."

"Well, what do you think we are?" Evelyn darted.

"I don't know about you, but I'm entering middle age."

"That's right," she said coldly, and sat up straight, and turned the fish around so the eye faced someone else. "You don't know about me. You don't know about me at all. Not for a second do you know about me." She shoved her plate away, and the silver fish spun around. "Is there anything to eat besides Pink?"

One of the wives reached for a silver bell, in between Heinz's ketchup and Gulden's mustard.

"Forget it," Evelyn said, throwing her napkin on the table. "I'm not hungry." She got up and left.

Sonny covered his eyes, his hand an open shade over the glare of the error. He sat for a moment, his chin on his chest. He took a deep breath, and exhaled it audibly.

"I'm terribly sorry," he said, not looking at anyone. "Excuse me."

"I don't even know what I said," Sonny said, when he caught up with her in the room.

"I know that too. You don't even know." She was holding a gold-tipped cigarette from a box by the bed, lit it with a gold-tipped match. "You have no idea. The smartest man in the world, and you haven't the least idea."

"Tell me exactly what I said, and I'll apologize."

"I don't remember." She shook her head. "It's this place. Not being able to see outside. It must be beautiful out there. And we're shut in like prisoners with this . . . art." She hurled it like the expletive it should have been. And gave it the full fury it would have had if it also included Norman. "Why do we have to stay here? It's the dream of a lifetime, only it's a nightmare. Can't we say your mother died? He'll forgive you for that one, he's eighty-eight."

"I have to talk to him, I really want to meet him. I really need him."

"And what about me? Do you really need me?"

She was toying. She was playing. She was only kidding. Sort of.

"Is this a contest?" he asked angrily.

"That's right. Who do you love more, me or William Randolph Hearst?"

"Back off," Sonny said. "I don't play these kinds of games."

"Really?" she asked. "I think you're doing rather well."

"You're not going to make this a test of my love for you."

"That's right. I'm not. I don't have to. You already did."

"A lot depends on tonight," he said. "Like maybe your own financial future. I need this magazine to go. I need the money."

"Don't make me laugh." Evelyn lay back on the yellow spread, closed her eyes, and tried to visualize sky.

"I told you I was broke."

She opened one eye and saw his eyes were pleading, and he was serious. "What do you mean by broke?"

"What do *you* mean by broke?" Sonny said.

"Oh no," said Evelyn. "You couldn't be as broke as that."

"If the truth were only known," said Sonny. "If they ever called in all I owed on one particular day . . ." He saw the dismay on her face. "I'm going to make it all back, there's nothing to be afraid about."

"Afraid?" She covered her eyes. "Afraid?" She sat up, eyes still covered. "How much do you need?"

"Every penny I can get my hands on."

"I've got twenty-five thousand eight hundred dollars in safety deposit boxes. You can have it all." She lowered her hand. *"You son of a bitch! You son of a bitch! You son of a bitch!"*

"You married me for money?" Sonny said.

"Of course not. I love you. But why didn't you tell me you were broke?"

"I did."

"I didn't believe you," Evelyn said. "It's Arnold, isn't it? You gave him your money. Him and his whore!"

"Watch what you're saying."

"Your big seat of power. Your wonderful brother." She started rampaging around the room, a wind contained by other people's walls. "The Titan! The Zealot! Who disapproved of *me.* The Usurer! The Usurer!"

"I'm going out for a walk."

"Find a cliff!" Evelyn shouted.

He spent two hours in the library, almost peaceful with its books, studying ancient songs, ancient bindings, hoping for some kind of answer, some deep-seated wisdom that would keep him from the rashness of anger. Too much anticipation, all right, he could forgive her that: the castle was a sarcophagus for aging, wasted dreams. On a sunny day, perhaps, Clark Gable came splashing across the Neptune pool, but that was a long time ago. It was wrong to try and recapture the past, the past had value for history, not honeymoon.

And Norman. Oh yes. That had been a mistake, but what choice had he had? What choice? That was his son. That quiet, frightened, very brilliant boy. What chance did he have against her gusto, how could he prove it wasn't a competition, how could he prove that to Evelyn?

Why did he have to prove anything to Evelyn? Who the hell did she think she was? Who was she? A very beautiful woman who expected never to be disappointed. That wasn't what life was about.

She had offered him her money. He smiled to himself. The good specter of the castle. The invisible hostess had done as much for Hearst.

And had called him a son of a bitch in the very next breath. Arnold had been right about her. "The Titan. The Zealot." And she had been right about Arnold.

Arnold. Arnold would have laughed at the phony majesty of everything. Arnold would have played tennis in the rain, even though he didn't know how to play tennis. Arnold would have roared his way through the sepulchral weekend, making jokes, making friends, making love.

Not with a fucking lion jumping on the hood of the car. Not with a freak show of dimming lights, dimming memories, ugly design. Not closed in like they were with no view of the sun, no view of the sea, no hint of air. For the sake of the host, the castle was heated to over eighty degrees. Even Arnold might have grown angry and uncomfortable.

She had no right to call him a usurer.

Sonny breathed in very deeply, and chuckled. She didn't really mean it, she had just run out of invective.

He would go back to the room, and they could lock Norman in the children's tower for a little while. Sonny took two books Norman might enjoy reading at once, and actually laughed aloud. Two hours. Two books. How bad could the children's tower be? And he wouldn't actually lock him in it, he would just suggest it needed exploring, and give him the books, and leave Freedom outside.

And he would make the love to her that he'd saved since that train ride to Tennessee, his diva, slashing fire, hurling light.

Magnificent. Her fury was magnificent. A little too fast to flower, but that was probably explicable, accumulated. All those days on the train.

He went back to the room with flowers that he'd picked, and then planted in an urn, a little lighter clay, a little less ornate than the rest. He rang their bell, and shouted out loud that he was a messenger from Western Union, and what he was carrying was love.

"*Love,*" he started singing rather badly, holding the pot like it was a guitar, "*your magic spell is everywhere.*"

The door opened and he held out the urn, grinning. A chambermaid with fresh towels over her arm looked at him blankly. "*Busca la señora?*"

"I think so," said Sonny.

She yelled to someone inside. A younger girl, with a can of furniture wax in her hand, came out of the bedroom as Sonny walked in. She and the older woman exchanged some words in Spanish.

"You look for your wife?" the young girl asked. "She going."

"Going where?"

"She going to Mexico. She say tell you she always want to see Mexico, and since she be so close she going there to get a divorce."

He laughed. Then he went inside to fondle her, lie to her, tell her the truth, get her smiling again, start laughing together, because it was all going to be all right. They would have a wonderful life together, once the living of it started, once they'd left the unsealed tomb. There'd be no going to Mexico. The eleventh commandment: Thou shalt not go to Mexico.

She was gone.

He was frantic by the time he found Freedom. "About a half-hour ago, sir," Freedom said. "I let one of the other drivers take her, because I wasn't sure of your plans . . ."

"You know where she went?"

"To the airport, sir. In Bakersfield."

"Get the car. Find Norman."

He arranged for someone to bring the luggage, which the maids would pack, in another car. He left regrets and apologies for William Randolph Hearst, and left with his own regrets.

For a while she was frightened he might not come after all. It was an hour till the departure of the plane for Los Angeles, with connections to New York, but she was afraid she might have mixed him up, leaving that message with the maid. He'd know better than to believe she was going to Mexico, didn't he? Besides, she'd been careful to leave exact word with Freedom, giving him eighty-five cents to cover time and charges to *Bakersfield,* the *airport,* she had said, tipping him a quarter, so he'd be sure to remember.

What if Sonny didn't get there in time? What if he made Freedom drive forty-five miles an hour? No. There was no peril that could equal her leaving.

She would make him beg for a moment, but only a moment. She didn't want to degrade him. She simply needed to upgrade herself. To let him know she would stand for no nonsense. Unless he asked her nicely.

Just an instant. Then she'd kiss him. And he'd whisk her back to the castle. And they'd start all over again. And tie Norman to his bed. And she'd charm William Randolph Hearst, and enchant that dull company. And find one piece of furniture she could stand. And live happily ever after.

He was running across the small airport lobby. She'd never seen him run. His eyes were streaming, and his arms were open. She ran inside them, even though she didn't mean to.

"Don't you ever leave me again. Don't you ever leave me again." His arms were around her, and he was holding her hard. "Don't you ever leave me again."

"I didn't leave you this time. I couldn't have gone. I would've come back to the castle." She smiled up at him. She could make a grown man who was brilliant cry. There was nothing in the world she couldn't do. "Come, let's go back."

"We're not going back there. I'm going to take you to San Francisco. I'm going to give you a real honeymoon."

"But I want to go back to the castle."

"No you don't. You hate it."

"I love it, I swear. It just takes some getting used to."

"We're going to San Francisco, and that's that."

She was genuinely disappointed. But she couldn't tell that to him. That would have involved being honest, and how could you be honest with a man you could fool so completely? How could she fool him so completely? Maybe she was brighter than she thought.

"Let's go back to the castle."

"I couldn't do that to you."

"Do it! Do it!"

"You've been unselfish enough already. This is your honeymoon. Not a business trip."

And that was that.

So she never got over the feeling of the party missed, the moment vanished, the music undanced to. Damn him to hell. Oh, not Hearst. For Hearst she felt actual pity, especially when he died, very soon after. Getting old was bad enough. But having so much, even all of it wrong, and having to lose it. They were right about that, the playwrights. You couldn't take it with you.

Pity.

She really felt it for Hearst. When news of his death came, Evelyn went into semi-personal mourning, somewhere between the moment's stopping the presses of all his employees and real tears shed for a friend. She bought three maternity dresses in black, with becoming necklines, and mentioned his name in the *Kaddish* on Yom Kippur, because she had to do something. Sonny actually made them go to temple and stay through the whole service. So as long as she had to be there, and the dress was black, and the occasion arose, she stood when the rabbi asked mourners to stand. And she whispered Hearst's name under her breath, during the prayer for the dead.

She looked at Sonny, standing beside her, in the long well-dressed row, mourning the actually known. And she wondered for one fleeting instant if it was possible that one man was not the total solution.

Perish the thought.

SIX

THE PLACE ARNOLD CHOSE for the official launching of his senatorial campaign was Gallagher's on West Thirty-third Street. He had made it gently clear to Rosey di Bonaven that there was to be none of the smoke-filled room crap the public associated with politics, so Rosey had suggested the ballroom of the Waldorf-Astoria, where there was plenty of space, and air-conditioning to waft away the smell of cigars. But the Waldorf was right for celebration, when his victory became fact. In the meantime, Gallagher's had good steak for hungry supporters, a tight enough atmosphere so the machine people would feel comfortable, and ample room for Arnold to bounce around in a dignified way between press and soon-to-be-aides.

Flaming filets on swords flashed through the evening. Waiters in special jackets that Arnold had had designed—red and white

413

striped, "Sterne for Senator" spelled out in white stars on blue campaign badges the size of a grapefruit on their lapels—hustled crisp roast potatoes, French fried onion rings, hot garlic bread, and petit pois (Sonny's choice) from table to table. And in between the lushness of plenty to eat, and plenty to drink, various somewhat notables found plenty to say.

Daisy di Bonaven talked continuously through some informal speeches, it being one of the few evenings Rosey had agreed to let her come out. She told Evelyn a number of scandals that hadn't yet broken in the Administration, along with revived outrage at the Teapot Dome, as could be avowed to by her friend Roxy Stinson Brast, whom Rosey hadn't allowed her to invite for some reason. Evelyn smiled sweetly and nodded as if she were listening, all the time wondering why she hadn't been seated at Arnold's table.

She was a great deal prettier pregnant, she knew, than any of the women there undeformed, although she spent much of the evening telling the ladies how lovely they looked, especially Sarah Sterne, whose dowdiness was enshrined in brown chiffon. But her own chic little splendor was wasted at a table with the Di Bonavens, was needed by Arnold, as colorful as he was. A pretty woman was an asset to any campaign, she knew that, as little as she knew about campaigns. She had marked Eleanor Roosevelt, and Bess, and now Mamie, and thought the world had to be ready for a woman who knew how to dress, in between being good to orphans.

Still, she kept on smiling through the pre-keynote speeches, and Daisy's soft ramblings about the truth being known. She tried not to show her discomfort at being someplace other than the number-one table, where Sonny was, and most of the glory. She surrounded herself with her own bright radiance, remembering she was soon to be the Senator's sister-in-law. In law, that was something. Not the wife of a President, but she'd never met Stevenson, and thought he had very little chance, even though Mamie wore bangs. Besides she loved Sonny, she really did, she was glad she had married him. The Senator's sister-in-law. She raised herself up very straight, sat very tall, as she would at quiet dinner parties in Virginia and Georgetown, where the best of them lived, she knew that from the Washington *Post*, to which she was already subscribing, reading only the social and fashion pages; the news she left up to Sonny.

He was on his feet now, the Senator's brother, tinkling his glass with his fork, smiling and clinking the room into silence. "There's a lot of smart people here tonight," he said, when he had their attention. "I feel privileged to be among you. I feel more than privileged, I feel lucky." He grinned. "For a man from Wall Street, that's a very unusual feeling."

"If you had any idea about Rosey's people's tie-ins with the market and big business . . ." Daisy started to say. Evelyn touched her arm, warned her into silence, and indicated with her smiling proud eyes that she wanted to listen to Sonny's speech.

"But this isn't the stock market, this is a whole different horse race, and we're getting close to the starting gate. Everybody here knows something about that track, how slippery it can be. But fortunately we're backing an entry who for my money is a direct descendant of Man o' War."

There was applause from the press table, started by Joe McCreery, which spread through the rest of the room. Evelyn clapped politely, anxious to have interruptions, even favorable ones, gotten over with as quickly as possible, so she could hear the rest of the speech. Rosey di Bonaven apparently shared her enthusiasm for the coming words, as his hands were motionless at his sides.

"That's what this is going to be," Sonny said. "A soldier's campaign. My brother is a soldier; Arnold Sterne is a fighter. He fought his way up from the curse of poverty to the blessing of affluence this country affords. And when the safety and the very existence of this country were in peril, Arnold Sterne fought for this country. He is a soldier. He is a soldier who will settle for nothing short of victory. He will bring us that victory. We will help bring that victory to him. Ladies and gentlemen, members of the Party, members of the press, members of the family . . ." He grinned very wide and saluted Sarah and Ellis and Baby (who had flown in from California,) and Evelyn with a glass of champagne. "I am proud to drink a toast to the next Senator from New York."

"I'd like to join you in that one," Rosey di Bonaven said, springing to his feet. "I only regret that he couldn't be with us this evening."

A silence deeper than embarrassment, heavier than anger coated the room. Sonny tried to laugh. "This is no time for bad jokes, Rosey."

"I know that," Rosey said. "It's not even a time for good jokes. And that's what Arnold Sterne is, is a joke. Our Party will not endorse a joke. We have our man. And he sure as hell isn't Arnold Sterne."

A slow flush of fury ate its way up Arnold's face, stinging the roots of his white-yellow hair into red, dotting the top of his massive forehead like a scab. "Sit down, Rosey," he said almost quietly, but so everyone could hear.

"I finished my dinner," Rosey said, wiping his mouth with a napkin, throwing the napkin on his plate. "I got nothing to stay for. Come on, Daisy."

"But the dessert . . ."

"Come on, Daisy. Come on, all of you guys."

"Sit down," Arnold said, up on his feet now. "Sit down."

"And if I don't?" said Rosey. "What are you going to do, soldier? Fighter. Beat me up? Kill me? This ain't the back of a barroom. You can't kill me, Arnold Sterne. You're dead." He pulled Daisy's arm, which was still touching Evelyn's.

"Lunch tomorrow?" Daisy said very sociably to Evelyn. "I could try and get Roxy to join us . . ."

"Shut up," Rosey told her, and hustled her toward the door.

"You don't think it ends here!" Arnold shouted after him, blue veins in his forehead visibly pulsing, as Sonny held his shoulders. "You don't think it ends here!"

"It's ended," said Rosey. "It's over."

They spent most of the night in the living room of Sonny's apartment—Arnold, Joe McCreery, a few of the men who were not tied to Rosey, a very few men. Sarah had been taken home weeping by Ellis and Baby. Evelyn had brought back a Baked Alaska that hadn't been served, what with the turmoil and confusion. She served it with coffee in the foyer. Only no one seemed hungry. It was all very confusing to her. So she didn't try to understand any of it: Rosey's rancor, what had caused it, what would happen to Arnold now, why nobody ate such a beautiful dessert. She took the catalogue for the coming Saturday auction at Parke-Bernet into the bedroom for study, and told Sonny where she would be if he needed her.

"You could run independent," Joe McCreery said. "I would back you to the hilt, maybe even deeper with Rosey out of the picture."

"That's you," Arnold said. "You're an honest man. He's got the unions sewed up, he's got the big politicos sewed up, he's a fucking sewing machine. I couldn't get out of his way."

"Maybe that's what you have to do," said Sonny, at four o'clock in the morning when the champagne was wearing off, and the Scotch was wearing in. "Maybe that's just what you have to do, is get out of his way. Take a different path."

"Barefoot?" said Arnold. "Sawing logs? Carrying a crucifix?"

"Maybe something a little more Houdini than that," Sonny said, worrying his big jaw with his fingers. "You've always been a great escape artist, Arn. This isn't the moment to throw away the magic. Out of the clutches of other people, brother, that's where you need to be."

"And how do you suggest I do that, dreamer?"

"I gotta make some calls," Sonny said. "Excuse me." He got up from the wide blue silk wing chair and went into the den. He made his calls, apologizing for the hour, but they were all owed, or were owers, the men he startled from their sleep. Bankers who would know, who would know for sure, in aggregate opinion, how the vista looked a little to the south. He came back into the living room, grinning.

"We got any more champagne?" he said.

"Oh, cut the shit," Arnold said. "I'm tired. I'm whipped. I'm throwing in the towel."

"It's my house," said Sonny. "Evelyn keeps very good track of the linen. The laundry can't short her. There's no wasting, no losing, and no throwing in of towels."

"Just let him go on. Pay no attention to the persiflage of hope," Arnold said. "He could never shut up and go to sleep when the two of us were together. Thank you all for staying with me as long as you did."

"Stay a little longer," Sonny said, and winked, and went to get a bottle of champagne.

"Let me lie down," Arnold said, following him into the massive kitchen with its chopping blocks and two outsize re-frigerators. "Let me go home and go to sleep. You go to sleep. We both need to lie down."

"No we don't," Sonny said, finding the champagne behind the cheeses, where Evelyn hid it from the help. "The house in Metuchen. The one you let Jeanne and Roan Anderson live in, as part of your very generous wedding gift. Whose name is it in?"

"The company's."

"Your company's, right?"

"One of them."

"So the deed is in your name, basically, legally. They still in South America?"

"They better be."

"So no one's living in the house? Bring in some glasses," he said. "They're in the closet over the sinks."

"You're drunk."

"You're right," said Sonny. "Just get the glasses."

"Gentlemen," Sonny said, when they were back in the living room, bottle opened, glasses filled, in very tired hands. "I would like you to join me in a toast."

"Christ," said Joe McCreery. "I'm about toasted out. I think I'm going to puke."

"I don't think so," Sonny grinned. "Will you raise your glasses to the next Senator from New Jersey?"

There were screams of outrage in the Jersey newspapers, cries of "carpetbagger" accompanying the move, the announcement of candidacy, the promise of good intentions. "I am not native to this state," Arnold said at the first big rally. "But I am native to this country, and I live in this state, and I intend to do this state proud."

There were boos between the cheers, but Arnold kept right on smiling, right on talking through the garden club parties where he promised the ladies with big hats and tiny sandwiches there would be among the bills he intended to introduce a Federal Charter for the National Garden Club Organization. Right on promising the Negroes in a school auditorium in Newark that they would finally have a voice in government. Right on pledging to take care of the labor unions, so that some in his own party started calling him commie, which really made Arnold laugh. Just as the ladies made him laugh with how whole they gulped it up and how daintily they ate their sandwiches. But he took a certain sadistic pleasure in going up to Bernardsville and watching them swallow it, just as the Negroes swallowed it in Newark, thrilled to be even addressed, excited to be collected into an auditorium, supposing somebody cared.

It was to be five years before the first civil rights laws would be passed, longer till they began to be enforced, but Arnold couldn't guess at that, didn't even want to wager a guess that such laws would ever happen. He had taken his clue from Harry Truman, whom he had always regarded with something akin to respect as an avant-garde Boy Scout. If Truman's promise of civil rights had had echoes of greatness, it could thunder through New Jersey. Besides it was innovative, soothing to Arnold's own conscience, which appeared from time to time.

His campaign staff was headed up by Sonny, over Evelyn's strenuous objections. "Head Campaign Director," she said, in between shopping. "All that running to New Jersey. New Jersey, for God's sake. That's almost as bad as Pennsylvania."

"He'll be a Senator."

"And your own business will go straight down the drain. You're crying poverty and you're wasting your brain on thinking up things for Arnold."

"He'll be Senator."

"You'll go broke."

"As long as it doesn't keep you from shopping," Sonny said. It seemed to end the discussion.

For the chairman of finance, Arnold and Sonny had enlisted the aid of a Seth Arkens, a disillusioned member of the old New Jersey machine, who had lost the primary for Congress two years before and gone back into banking. There was actually little need for a chairman of finance, as Arnold didn't need anyone else's money, but Seth pointed out to him he had to look like he needed it if he wanted to win. So Seth spent a part of his day soliciting small contributions, and the time left over working with the chairman of special interests, which included minorities, labor, veterans, women, and miscellaneous factions. The chairman of cats and dogs they referred to him in private, Sonny and Arnold and Seth.

In his presence they called him Governor Manton, although that title had been invalidated many years before, and in the interim he had become a lush. Still there was something special about having an ex-Governor, so they kept him in a paneled office, in the center of the action when he was sober, up to his ears in Joe Pape's Finest when he was not.

Seth ran the intricacies of the campaign about which Sonny could not possibly be aware: keeping track of the man who handled the scheduling, the woman who handled the candidate's mail, the assistant campaign directors, three in all, for North, Central, and Southern New Jersey. He was clean and hard-working and honest, if honesty could be carried in the carrot they dangled in front of his nose: Administrative Assistant to Senator Arnold Sterne. The idea of going to Washington could not help but be exciting to a failed politician from New Jersey.

Sonny took care of the more oily things, plugging in to the

420

political machinery of the state. There was no way to get to the incumbent governor, whose own campaign would be a year after the senatorial race; nor would any of the declared or undeclared gubernatorial candidates pledge their support. They were all hanging back waiting to see what would happen . . . wondering what this phenomenon was—this upstart, this Arnold, this man who refused to be killed.

So Sonny studied Seth for style, and in between trying to make quiet deals smiled at the happy little volunteers, the offspring of socialites, who wanted to work in campaign headquarters because it was such a nifty thing to do. Working the precincts was something else; they were not very interested in that. So he and Seth marshaled county chairmen to organize the precinct level below them, and report their successes to the assistant campaign directors above them, who were mostly former state legislators who had lost.

"It's a loser's campaign," said Seth one night.

"It's a soldier's campaign," said Arnold.

"Tell that to MacArthur," said Sonny.

"Forget about MacArthur. We all will soon enough." Arnold sat back and looked at the fire burning hollow in the great iron fireplace in the Metuchen living room. "We are not concerned with the recently cashiered. We're concerned with the cashierers. How do we get them?"

"Stay with the big issues," Seth said. "Corruption in government in Washington. That's always a good one. And how about throwing in with Joe McCarthy?"

"I think he's dangerous. I'd rather stay away from any of that bullshit."

"Do you think it's bullshit?" Sonny said, smiling. "I thought you thought there were communists in the most unlikely places."

"Only Columbia Law School," said Arnold, making a thoughtful bridge over his nose with his fingers. "I want to steer clear of McCarthy."

Seth took a cigar from the humidor on the coffee table in front of him. He punctured one end with a metal nail file he carried in his pocket, lit a match, and carefully sucked in the flame. The action of inhaling made even deeper hollows in his very angular cheeks, leaning into the cigar a sadder round to his shoulders. The smoke drifting upwards gave a grayer appearance to the pallid color of his face. Only his hair, his thick chestnut hair, seemed to give him the stature for battle.

"The war's winding down," Seth said. "Eisenhower's said he will go to Korea. Can we use that?"

"Why not?" said Arnold. "I will go to Ceylon."

Sonny laughed. "I will go to Park Avenue, or Evelyn will hand my head to me." He reached for his hat.

"It's a very fine head," said Arnold. "Don't let anybody try to hand it to you. Especially a woman."

"We talk politics," Sonny said. "We talk money. When we're drunk we can speak of brotherly love. But we don't talk women— that's an old agreement. Agreed?"

Arnold nodded sadly. "Agreed."

"You will go to Ceylon," Sonny said, laughing, as he headed for the door. "You will go to Ceylon. You character. You nut."

"You potato!" shouted Arnold.

"I love you, too," Sonny said.

When he got home he was half-expecting her to be sitting on the antique opium bed she had gotten the week before at Midtown Galleries and placed directly against the wall underneath the Jackson Pollock. The Pollock had been turned on its side ("What difference does it make?" Evelyn had said) to accommodate the opium bed, strung with dark lacings of wood like an unyielding hammock. He expected her there, inhaling her own fury, at his lateness, at his concern for his brother, at his love for his son, at his life. When she wasn't there, angry, ferocious, he felt a swift pang of disappointment.

The rages had almost begun to amuse him; the skin, he adored. Nothing had ever felt quite that good to him, except for Catherine in the early days, before touching was out of the question because it might endanger her life. Nothing physical, nothing passionate, nothing smacking of living could ever hurt Evelyn. He loved her. He was smitten. The fact that she made scenes, the fact that she got angry, had become to him an affirmation of the blood that was coursing inside her—a little too heated, maybe, but better than cold.

"Evelyn?" he said into the darkness of the living room, the den, the guest rooms, the kitchen, turning on lights everywhere she was always so careful to turn them off. "Evelyn?" He turned on the light in their bedroom. Empty.

The bed had been turned down neatly by the servants (only two now, what did they need with four, when Heinz was a Nazi, and all Nazis had the efficiency of three, Evelyn maintained). He looked in her closets. Not empty, but it seemed to him there were some clothes missing. "Evelyn?" He ran into Norman's room. Not very likely, but maybe . . . maybe he had had a bad dream, and she found it in her heart to console him. Norman was sleeping. Alone.

The baby's room? He turned on the festival of lights, the network of nursery rhyme lamps, Jack and Jill, Old Mother Hubbard, waiting in crouched wooden positions underneath paper shades gaily painted for that soon-to-be arrival. All blue. The room was papered in blue, the crib dancing flowers of blue. ("I should do it yellow, that's neutral, in case it's a girl," Evelyn had said. "But I know it's a boy, I just know it, it's got to be a boy, so it will be. I know it, don't you think?")

It was like her to be angry, but not spiteful, never spiteful. Where could she have gone? What if she hadn't even come home? What if something had happened to her, because he hadn't called all day to find out how she was, if she was even safe and secure in her home, because he'd been too busy with Arnold. Arnold. You and your goddamned Arnold, she would have said, just after the mugging, the rape, the fall on her blossoming belly. What had happened? Where was she?

He started to sweat, and took some Alka-Seltzer from a shelf in the bathroom cabinet, and went to the kitchen for some ice water. There was a note, neatly typed, in the refrigerator, set into a cake.

My sometimes love,

I figured if you're so busy with your goddamned Arnold you don't really need me around. I am making a quick visit to my family, whom I also love, but do not devote my entire life to. I should return in time to have your heir in Doctor's Hospital, where I hope you can spend a few minutes.

I also hope you find this note before Norman, who will probably eat it.

Love,
Evelyn

Pappy did not believe in dreams, he believed in stories. Stories he loved. But one of the stories he hated with all his soul, so he put it out of his repertory, out of recollection. That was what frightened him most, that such a story could get stuck in his head and dance itself out while he was dreaming. He fought so hard to get it out of his eyes he woke himself.

He sat up in bed and listened to the industrial silence, faraway freight trains, a late passing automobile. Missing were the footsteps, but he knew they were coming. He went to the window and looked at the distant puffs of red from the steel mills, belching up to the sky. He narrowed his almost lashless eyes and searched for something beyond the smoke. He smiled at the sky, a questioning smile.

The pain in his chest could not be indigestion. Not the way Tillie cooked. He slipped into the trousers he kept on the chair, in the event of national emergency, and carried his shoes and socks with him into the living room. He pulled the cord on the old-fashioned lamp, with the Chinese floral vase for a base, and a beige silk fluted shade, still covered with cellophane from the original sale so it wouldn't get dusty. A yellow light moistened the room, blunting the edge of darkness. Slowly, he turned the big chair in front of the television so it faced the door. He sat down in it, eyes unblinking, not even looking as he put on his shoes, lacing them carefully as he stared down the door, dared it to open. Listening for footsteps, he tied his shoelaces. It couldn't get him with his shoes on.

"Uncle Jerry!" he whispered. "You're looking for the landlord! He lives upstairs. First apartment to the right."

The pain was worse. "Uncle Jerry!" he shouted. "You don't want me. You want Mishkin. A terrible person. He lives upstairs."

"Moisch," Grandma said from the bedroom, feeling his panic, hearing his fear through deafness. "Moisch, who are you talking to?"

"Eh, Tillie," he said. "Go back to sleep. It's between Uncle Jerry and me."

"Who?" She was at the doorway in her nightgown, barefoot, slipping her hearing aid into her ear. "Who are you talking to?"

"Nobody. Go back inside. You're barefoot. *Uncle Jerry!*" he told the door. "Upstairs. Mishkin. The stingy man. The one with no joy."

"Uncle Jerry?" Grandma peered down at him, her plump little bosom moving quickly in concern. "We have no Uncle Jerry."

"Everybody has an Uncle Jerry." Pappy laughed, holding his chest. "The last person you want to see."

Grandma ran to the telephone and called Sadie. "He's talking to somebody called Uncle Jerry. I think that's his name for the Messenger of Death. He's standing in the living room, yelling at Uncle Jerry, telling him to go after the landlord."

"He's had a heart attack," Dr. Solomon said to the family, assembled now, white-faced, in the waiting room, except for Evelyn, who was off in a phone booth with her bag of coins, calling up specialists, trying to get through receptionists, placing calls to the Mayo Clinic to try and get the name of the best man in Pittsburgh. She came back with the numbers of six different doctors, the best in their field, according to six different people.

"We'll want a consultation," Evelyn said.

"You can consult whoever you want to," said Dr. Solomon. "He had a mild coronary. Everything that needs to be done can be done by the staff here. But you can consult if you like."

"Will he be all right?" Evelyn asked.

"A very good chance. If he doesn't get too excited."

"Help! Murder! Police!" yelled Pappy, when he woke up from sedation in the oxygen tent and saw the man in the next bed, a network of needles joining him to life, food, breath. *"Nurse!"* he screamed, when she ran into the room. "What are you doing to that man? It isn't enough he's dying, you make him a pincushion?"

"Go to sleep," said the nurse.

"Where's my wife?"

"She's waiting outside. They're all waiting outside."

"Ask my wife to come in."

"No visitors."

"Ask my wife to come in."

The nurse ended up doing all that he said, including taking out the oxygen tent so he could have a cigarette. "This is against hospital regulations," she said, as she moved the oxygen outside.

"It's against my regulations to die so soon."

"You're not going to die. But you shouldn't be smoking."

"Almost dying makes me nervous. I need something to relax. What's with him?" Pappy indicated the bed next to his. "The pincushion."

"We're trying to save him."

"With torture," said Pappy. "Don't ever save me like that."

Grandma came into the room, crying, and stayed that way.

"I don't need this," he said to Sadie. "I don't need the *hilalyah* worrying at me. I'm not finished. Evelyn!" he shouted to his daughter, waiting on the bench outside the room, coin purse ready in her hands. "Take them away to Miami Beach, Florida, so I can get some rest."

"You'll be out of here in no time," Evelyn said, standing in the doorway, unable to move close to him, he looked so pitifully frail. "It's a warning. That's all. It's a warning."

"I don't need a warning," Pappy said. "I always knew it was dangerous, living."

"Mishkin is dead." Grandma wept softly. "In his sleep."

Pappy sat up, color returning to his cheeks, his bald dome glistening pink. "Mishkin? The landlord? The raiser of rent?"

Grandma nodded.

Pappy raised his eyes to the ceiling. "Who knew he'd be a listener? He needed somebody from the building. Get the *hilalyah* out of here, Sadie. I wish to speak to *mein* eldest daughter."

So there wasn't just sex and money; there was also life and death. Evelyn hadn't thought about that before. Fleetingly, perhaps, when her best friend died, as a kindness to her, in a way. But nobody had ever fallen out of Evelyn's life who was at the core of it, an essential part of the pattern, making it more real.

"What are you standing there?" said Pappy, and patted the bed beside him with blue-veined white hands. "Come here. Come here. I want to talk."

"It isn't good for you to talk too much."

"Come," he said. "Come sit beside me."

He reached for her hand, intravenous needle in his arm. She tried not to pull away.

"So look who's here. The Princess of Schventiensky, marrier of millionaires. How much will you pay them to save me? Retail?"

"Stop it. You're not going to die."

"We're all going to die. But I think this time I fixed it. Uncle Jerry took Mishkin." Pappy laughed. "Mishkin is shoveling coal."

"Behave yourself," Evelyn said briskly.

"Why? I'm alive. How much would you pay?"

"Anything." Evelyn's eyes filled with tears.

"You must really love me." Pappy patted her hand. "Either that or he's as rich as everybody says. Is he?"

"Of course." Evelyn looked away. "Of course."

"And you're happy with him? Tell me the truth. This is me, here, your father. On his deathbed, maybe."

"I love him very much. He isn't exactly what I thought. The answer to a maiden's prayer."

"You wasn't exactly a maiden." Pappy fixed her with a gray-eyed gaze. "What do you want from a man? Walter M. White, D.D.S., so he shelled Indian nuts. He made a neat little pile. He loved you. A very nice fellow. What was so wrong? He couldn't scale buildings in a single bound?"

"He bored me."

"Tish tish."

"He had no ambition."

"Really?" Pappy said. "The Lieutenant-Commander? Receiver of the Navy Cross?"

"That was an accident."

"Maybe so is life."

"Anyway, I don't want to talk about Walter."

"I hear he's doing very well. His sister Corinne told Grandma."

"I'm not interested," Evelyn said. "What is he doing now?"

"You're not interested," said Pappy. "Let's talk about Victim Number Two. Abraham Sterne, the Village Rich Man. What's the matter with him? He wants to move in with our family?"

"Why did he do that, why do you suppose Walter did that?"

"Maybe he liked to laugh. Maybe he liked your mother's cooking. Maybe he liked a place with love in it. They wasn't exactly the warmest, his people. So what's the matter with Sterne?"

Evelyn looked deep in her lap. "The first time I saw him, he was in a chauffeured limousine. I thought he was the most impressive man I ever met in my life. Little did I know he was afraid to drive."

"Tish tish. As bad as all that."

"And his son . . ."

"And your daughter? He's taking care of her?"

"Yes but . . ."

"Yes but," Pappy sighed. "Your whole life is going to be yes but. Did I ever tell you the story of my life?"

"Many times. Different facts."

"Here's the truth coming now. There is no Schventiensky. I'm sorry to rob you of your inheritance, Princess, but there's only life. That's the only present. God's a very generous person, but He's also an Indian giver. You got to use it, before it gets taken away." His pale eyes misted with tears.

"You're not going to die."

"Sure I am. That isn't the question. The question is, are you going to live?"

"He's going to be all right," she said to the family waiting outside. "He's still full of insults."

"Good for Pop," Murray said.

"What'd she say?" said Sammy.

"He's going to be all right."

Sammy started to cry, then so did everyone else in the family, except Evelyn, who went to the ladies' room, locked the door, and sat on the toilet and wept.

The man with the needles in him died the next afternoon, while Pappy was taking a nap. The bed was vacant for only twenty minutes. When Pappy woke up and saw the man in the bed next to his, with no terrible paraphernalia attached, he thought the hospital was indeed capable of wonders.

"Look, Tillie, how they fixed him. He looks so much better. Younger even."

"Eat something," Grandma said, spooning some chicken soup into his mouth.

"Go feed him. Do you know him? Did he talk yet? Will he live? I don't like being with diers."

"He's a math professor from Carnegie Tech," said Enid, who was there with her husband. "You want us to move you to a private room?"

"Your sister the traveler already offered. I like to have company if they're alive. Maybe he'll wake up. There's much to explain to a man who thinks numbers."

Grandma was there again at suppertime, trying to feed Pappy. "Feed him," Pappy said. "Help the Professor."

The Professor was lying in a semi-raised position, eyes open, lips set in a joyless smile. His dinner was on a tray in front of him, untouched.

"You want to eat something?" Grandma said.

The Professor nodded slightly.

"Where's your family?" said Grandma, all rounded and warm in a yellow dress with pink flowers, life colors, arguing with darkness.

"I have no family."

"I'll feed you. Let me help." Grandma drew up a chair next to his bed, and reached for the cup of chicken broth, moving it close to his lips, spooning it carefully into his mouth. He smiled at her and swallowed, and smiled and swallowed, and then he just gurgled and didn't swallow anymore. Grandma still sat there, spooning the liquid into his mouth. It ran from the corners.

"KEEP HER AWAY FROM ME!!!" Pappy yelled at the family later. "She killed a man."

"Stop it," laughed Evelyn.

When it was certain that he would be all right, that it was only a matter of rest and convalescence, when Pappy was already planning which friends he would have to go around and shake hands with to say hello, to show them he'd beaten Uncle Jerry, Evelyn went back to New York. She did not phone ahead to say she was coming, because she wanted Sonny as frightened as she was at not knowing for certain.

It was almost midnight when she got back to the apartment. Sonny was waiting in the living room.

"Why didn't you tell me your father had a heart attack?" he said, his shoulder moving.

"How did you know?"

"Your sister Enid had the courtesy to call. She thought I might be worried."

"She thinks your brother is going to be Senator," she said. "She's never been guilty of an unselfish act. Her husband wants to go into politics."

"Why didn't you tell me your father had a heart attack? Why didn't you tell me that's why you had to go?"

"It was only a man dying," Evelyn said. "I wouldn't want to do anything to disturb Arnold's campaign."

"Is he all right?"

"He's got a better chance than Arnold."

"I don't want to fight."

"Then excuse me. I'll sleep in the guest room."

"I'll sleep in the guest room," Sonny said.

"It's your house. Yours and Norman's. I'm just a guest."

She locked the door, hoping he would break it down. He didn't. She had beaten him again. Goddamit. Goddamit to hell.

The cocktail party was not exactly a cocktail party. There were no hors d'oeuvres and there were no women; the drinks were hardly cocktails. There was *grappa,* a white Italian brandy, passed from hand to hand in bottles, and of the six men who were in the small bed-sitting room, only Roan Anderson wore a suit. The rest were in work shirts and tight denim trousers; they were unshaven, they were drunk. Only Roan Anderson wasn't drinking. He was watching the other five. When they were drunk enough, but not too drunk, he said what he had to say.

There were some words in Spanish that he couldn't speak, like "insatiable." But he did manage "thirst for power," and "evil" and "death of freedom." Phrases like that soared in the Latin tongues, even from his mouth. Words like that could inflame, especially in Spanish, especially when men were drinking, and also wanted to live in America, the land of the free, the last free land there was. Free. That meant a country for the poor, where the poor could get rich and live free. Live any way they wanted to.

But not when a tyrant was going to change everything. Not when a man with a "thirst for power" would go to Washington, D.C., and use his "evil" influence to change the laws, so the doors would be closed, the dream would vanish, there would be a "death of freedom."

Did they understand? They understood, even through *grappa* haze. There was only one way to deal with a tyrant. Only one way to make a dream last. They were all willing to make the forceful sacrifice. No one had ever spoken to them as if they were men who could change things. Everyone volunteered.

Roan Anderson chose Felipe, the one with no wife, not even a wife he only pretended to love.

"Well, I'll tell you one thing," Seth Arkens said, at campaign headquarters. "It's going like a son of a bitch. There's no way to accurately predict these things, no matter what the pollsters say." The corner of his thin-lipped mouth moved downward in a wry smile. "The pollsters had me down for a shoe-in the day I lost. But I just have a feeling. With all the resistance, with all the haste, I think you have a fair chance, Arnold. I really do."

"I don't know that I want a *fair* chance," Arnold said. "I'd sure like to bottle it up."

"There's no way to do that," Seth said. "It's been uphill all the way, and the way hasn't been that long. I think it's amazing your chances are even as fair as they are."

"*Good* as they are," Arnold corrected. "You got my speech for tonight?"

"Sonny and the boys are just finishing it up."

"You think this suit looks too affluent?" He got up and moved to the round wall mirror, surrounded by white stars emblazoned on blue, underneath a poster that held a magnified view of his face, and looked at the real reflection. His dark blue suit was a little too shiny for his personal taste, but Seth had advised him that it would look better in the spotlight, from the platform, forcing the eyes of the audience up to the massive imposing features of his face, surrounding him with a subtle glow, just as the thick white yellow of his hair would cloak him with a fierce halo.

"The suit is right," Seth said. "And don't forget the Murine for your eyes. Your eyes have to shine like it's from inside, from passion. Sincere passion. Two drops in each eye, just before you get on the platform."

"Here's the speech," Sonny said, coming from the inside room.

Arnold scanned the pages quickly, took a pencil, and scratched out his opponent's name. Arnold had gone through his entire campaign never mentioning his opponent. He was particularly careful about that. It gave him great pleasure to consign someone else to oblivion, at least as far as his own sphere of influence was concerned.

"I like it. It's direct. It's honest. Politically honest, anyway." He gave a huge grin and hugged his brother. "Thoughts like those, Sonny, you could be in politics yourself."

"I never cared about politics."

"You cared about anything that cared about you back. Maybe when they start knowing what you are in Washington, you'll love Washington."

"I love law and religion and ingenuity."

"Well I guess that lets out politics." Arnold grinned. "Strikes me as a shame. How many people you figure will be there?"

"I been goosing the north, central, and southern chairmen," Governor Manton said. "And we got a lot of women, and the niggers—"

"Negroes," Arnold corrected.

"Start calling them 'Negroes,' they'll want to be called something else," Governor Manton said.

"Try to lay off the sauce until after the rally," Arnold said.

"What sauce?"

"What rally?" said Sonny.

"So how many people?"

"Between five and seven thousand."

"Is that good?" Arnold asked Seth.

"It's better than between three and five."

"And you really want me to wear this shitty suit?"

"Just make the speech," said Seth. "Make the speech, and try and sound like you mean it."

"I always mean everything Sonny says," said Arnold.

Arnold was halfway through the speech, thundering music over, Sarah and Ellis and his daughter Althea done up like daisies on wooden bridge chairs behind him, Sonny on the chair just to his right, beaming with the words, eyes shining with something more than Murine. There were two spotlights, one coming from the right rear of the hall, one coming from the left at the front of the platform, so Arnold was caught like a vision from near and from far. He was so busy hearing the echo of his own voice from all corners of the hall that when the shots rang out he almost didn't connect, it was just a part of the excitement.

But Sonny had written the speech, and checked the loudspeaker equipment, and nowhere in any of it was anything that could sound like that. He jumped and shoved Arnold backwards so the bullet aimed straight for his head grazed his temple. And the two of them were on the floor, and people were screaming, and Sarah was praying in shrieks.

"Turn up the lights!" Seth shouted to the engineer. The hall was flooded with brilliance. The police rushed up and down the aisles, finding the man, who was raging in Spanish, words like "tyrant," "dictator," that's what it turned out to be when people could remember the words, when it was over, when someone could translate, when people were calm enough to try and understand. But now the man stood waving his pistol like an angry fist at the skies, aimed it at the police who were coming toward him. "Freedom!" he screamed in English, before he was shot.

"Oh my God," Arnold whimpered. "Oh my God."

They were moving the wounded would-be assassin out of the aisles, out a side entrance. The hall was filled with screams, but Arnold was deaf to everything but the beating of his heart, which he could hear in his head. He reached up and touched his temple, where the bullet had ripped like a piece of flame. His hand was covered with blood, but his head was still on.

"You all right?" Sonny said.

"I'll kill him. I'll kill the bastard."

"I think he's been shot."

"The son of a bitch. Is he dead?"

"I don't know. The important thing is you're alive."

"My God," Arnold said. "He really wanted to kill me. Somebody wanted to kill me."

"Take it easy," said Sonny. He was down on his knees, covering Arnold, because his first instinct had always been to cover Arnold. He was down on his knees to cover Arnold, and also because he couldn't stand. His knees were shaking as if he were a frightened animal. His mouth was dry. An animal marshaling its adrenalin for running.

"Don't move," he said. "We can't run."

"Somebody tried to kill me."

"Is Arnold dead?" whispered Sarah, praying.

"He's all right." He turned to Arnold. "Are you all right?"

"Not a cough in a carload," Arnold said, smiling weakly.

"Then get up and talk to them. Get up and talk to them."

"Now? I can't find my mouth."

Sonny turned and surveyed the crowd, all on their feet now, some screaming, some running, some standing paralyzed, their eyes on the stage, their hands held over their mouths. "It's just below your nose," he said. "Close to your brain. And closer to Washington."

Arnold got to his feet unsteadily, and walked over to Sarah, kissed her, kissed his son, and his daughter. "He was crazy," he whispered to Sarah. "He had to be crazy. And I'm all right. You just sit there. Sit there and look like a Senator's wife."

"Okay." He managed the beginnings of a smile. He stepped to the microphone, the blood from his forehead dripping into his right eye. Making no attempt to stop the flow, he held up his hands for silence. Silence was what he got, in stunning waves.

"It's okay, it's okay," he said very softly. "Everybody's all right. Are you all all right out there?" He searched the lighted hall, shielding his eyes with his hands, squinting through light, squinting through blood. "Okay, let's settle down. Turn off the lights so I can talk to my friends."

"I don't think that's such a good idea," said Seth.

Arnold covered the microphone. "I've lived through my own shooting," he said. "Turn down the big lights and put the spotlights back on."

Seth had the engineer do what Arnold had ordered.

"Okay," Arnold said into the microphone, his voice still wavering. "I knew that some people didn't want me to run. But I'll make you one bet. *That guy wasn't from New Jersey!!*"

The audience erupted into one massive cheer.

"Well if that's what I get from you for being alive," Arnold canted, "you know how great it's going to be *living* here? Being able to *do* for you people? Because this is what I call a *new lease on life,* and I'm taking it out with YOU! You want to take it out with me? Because I am ready to FIGHT FOR YOU! Apparently," he managed a chuckle, "I was almost ready to die for you."

There were no cheers. But Arnold could feel it building.

"I *live* in New Jersey. *New Jersey* is where I *live!* Where my children *live*. Where my family *lives*. And I swear by Great God Almighty I'll do it proud. I'll do it proud! Thank you for coming, and if anybody else doesn't want me to run, I'd appreciate their letting me know in some other way."

Laughter. Nervous laughter, but laughter nonetheless.

"And for those of you who want me to run, who will vote for me to win, I will do everything I can for New Jersey. *New Jersey! The* state where a man gets a second chance!"

Screams. Cheers. For He's a Jolly Good Fellow. To the beat of a brass band.

"Jesus Christ," said Sonny, when they were getting down from the platform.

"I left him out," said Arnold. "But that's about all."

" 'Great God Almighty,' " Sonny quoted. "You never cease to amaze me. What happened to the man who believed in just Natural Order?"

"Tonight was not Natural Order," said Arnold. "I have to go someplace and lie down."

"Were you afraid?"

"I was scared shitless," said Arnold.

It was not exactly a landslide election. There were those who said Arnold Sterne won by a gunshot.

SEVEN

Spring, her senior year in high school, had been a season of choice for Chris. In New York her mother waited tight-lipped for the birth of the baby: on the phone Chris could hear the invitation to spend her vacation with the Sternes of Park Avenue, one of whom was wasting all his time on that goddamned Arnold's campaign in New Jersey, delivered through a mouth pulled almost lipless with despair, anxiety, anger: all the things Chris had at school when it wasn't even Easter, when the dogwoods held no promise of pink blossoms.

In Pittsburgh, where there was Grandpa, recuperating from his heart attack, they were clearing up the smoke, they were planning on leveling the slums downtown to make the city beautiful, a true Golden Triangle, where the Allegheny met the Monongahela and the Ohio. And Grandma would hug her and Murray would call her Baby Elephant, and she could play with Sadie's children, and the recent spawn of Sammy and Pegeen the *shicksa,* and maybe even make friends with Aunt Enid. She was called that now, little Enid, all grown up and beyond having to go into the closet with the telephone, so someone could tell her he loved her, and she could answer without the whole family listening, "I love you, too." Aunt Enid was married, and they were clearing up the smoke, and Pappy was alive and Grandma would hug her. All things were possible in Pittsburgh.

"I hope you don't mind," she practiced in her head in the cab moving up Park Avenue from Grand Central Station, with Lionel Lindenbaum dropping her off at the canopied entrance, not even asking her if she had plans for Saturday, or any plans at all. "I've decided to spend my vacation in Pittsburgh."

"Jesus Christ, are you fat," Evelyn said, when Chris came through the door.

Evelyn herself was strangely swollen, even for having a baby in her stomach. Her eyelids were heavy with more than the burden of carrying a child. She had been weeping, that much was obvious to Chris, but Chris didn't ask her why. There had to be joy in the birth of a baby, and Evelyn was joyless, fluttering, sorting her papers, doing her accounts on the floor of the living room where she could lay everything out and go over it, over and over again.

"I hope you don't mind," Chris said, putting her bag back outside the door. "I've decided to spend my vacation in Pittsburgh."

"That son of a bitch Pell's Delicatessen," Evelyn said. "I'm tired of their overcharging."

"How do you feel?" Chris said. When's the next plane.

"I feel like a cow." Evelyn got up clumsily from the floor. "But at least I have a reason."

"When is the baby due?"

"In about three weeks," Evelyn said. "But I may have a Caesarian."

"Is there anything wrong?"

439

"I don't think I can go through that again. My God. The agony. They say you forget the pain the minute you see the baby. I've never forgotten the pain. What you did to me."

"I'm sorry," said Chris. "When is there a plane to Pittsburgh?"

"Why do you want to go to Pittsburgh?"

"I want to see Grandpa. I want to see everybody. I want to see Pittsburgh. I really want to go home."

"But honey, you are home," Evelyn said, opening her arms. "Come, kiss your mummy."

On the train to Pittsburgh (it made more sense, Evelyn said, it was only eight hours and Sammy could meet Chris at the station, and she might find someone interesting on the trip who had a son who didn't mind fat girls), Chris wept over Lionel, and wrote in her journal, which she had promised Lionel she wouldn't keep anymore, but nobody kept their promises, she knew that much at fifteen. She thought about the baby that was due, wondered if it would mean sibling rivalry, since she understood about Sibling Rivalry, being a charter member of the Philosophy and Psychology Club at Coventry Hall. She loved the baby, she really did, she loved it unborn, she would love it to life. Babies were wonderful, babies were future, this baby would be a part of her, even though it would only be half. She had already made a joke about it, she had invited her class to a "coming-out party" when her mother had the baby, and Dr. Mann had considered that to be in very bad taste. She was only welcoming it with a joke, a joke was a happy thing. She tried to explain that to Dr. Mann, she was thrilled about the baby.

"It's in very bad taste," the principal had repeated.

What? To have a baby? To acknowledge birth as a glad celebration? Death was such a dark mystery; Pappy had almost died, there were very few jokes to be made about dark mysteries. Birth was a light mystery. A mystery of light.

Light. Morning in pale white radiance started to sparkle the metal rails outside the train window. Morning, making its way through the still smoky skies around Pittsburgh. Morning. A very good time. Especially when there was no one to share the night.

Sammy was waiting on the platform, waving to her, beaming a kind of Evelyn-smile, his face still open and young. Only the hearing aid, with the cord running down into his pocket where the controls were kept, testified to the passage of years, and certain mistakes. "Hey, you look fine," Sammy said.

"Thank you," said Chris, and hugged him. A hug with a prayer in it, that he wouldn't mention how fat she was. "How's Pegeen?"

"She's terrific. Pappy was wrong about all *shicksas* being run-arounds. She won't even run around with me."

"How's the baby?"

"He isn't a baby anymore. He's a little *goy*." Sammy laughed and carried her bag to the car. "All yellow and pink, a regular Gentile, except for his nose. Blue eyes, blond hair, and smack in the middle of his face, a map of Israel."

"Chauncey Mosk," Chris said, as she got into the front seat of the '46 coupe. "You do have a mean sense of humor."

"Why?" said Sammy. "A name like that, he'll have to have dignity." He chuckled about it, and everything else they could think of to exchange all the way to Grandma's apartment. The family were already calling it that, even though Pappy was still there.

Chris asked for no details of the sickness, it was enough, a heart attack, an attack on that wonderful old man's heart, that was detail enough. They talked only of his surviving, and Sammy laughed about Uncle Jerry and how he took Mishkin, and how in a couple of days Pappy was planning to go around and shake everybody's hand.

"You want to come with me, Christmas? Whatever your name is?" Pappy hugged her. "You want to come with me, say Hallo to the living?"

"I want to say hello to you," she said, feeling him so deeply, she was for a moment in time, miraculously, skin and bone. He was smaller—she couldn't believe how tiny and frail he felt in her arms.

"An ample bosom," Pappy said. "That feels good. I like an

ample bosom. I like the way it feels. I like the way it sounds. I read that in a magazine by the hospital."

"How are you feeling?"

"Alive."

"Come," Grandma said. "I made breakfast."

"I ate breakfast on the train."

"It isn't the same. Come. Eat. You'll feel better."

"She ate enough," Pappy said. "There was a fellow in the hospital, your grandmother fed him after he was dead."

"You can diet when you go back to the convent," Grandma said. "Come. I made waffles."

"How *do* you do?" Murray said, at lunchtime when he had an hour off, and rather than just eat at the drugstore, he could come say hello to Chris, and have a bowl of chicken soup that Grandma had made the night before, which he had eaten for dinner. "What's new, Baby Elephant?"

"She looks very pretty," Grandma said, ladling a matzoh ball into a bowl. "She's just pleasantly plump. She can diet when she gets back to the orphanage. Eat your lunch and get married and stop criticizing other people."

"I was only kidding," Murray said, cutting the matzoh ball into fine pieces with his spoon.

"I have a slow metabolism," said Chris.

"They can speed it up," said Murray.

"I'm on thyroid."

"You should eat less."

"You should get married," said Grandma to Murray. "Be quiet and eat."

They passed like a parade through the first day of her arrival, the members of the family, a few at a time. Blazing her back into origin, connection, the happiest time, even with one bathroom. Pegeen came in with Chauncey, a fat-legged less-than-a-cherub.

"Eh, Christian," Pappy hollered. "What do you think of the little *shagetz?* He has spirit, no? Even with that nose, he has spirit."

"My mother wants me to fix my nose," Chris said, wrestling with the baby.

"Let it stay as plain as the nose on your face," Pappy counseled, and took Pegeen's chin in his hand. "Look at this one. She could almost be a nice Jewish girl, as hard as she works, even with such a skinny nose. How's it going on the highway?"

"We're thinking of putting in custard."

"A *goyische kopf*," Pappy said. "A very pretty face. But a *goyische kopf*."

"Frozen custard," said Pegeen. "It's like ice cream."

"That wouldn't be so bad."

"How's your mother feeling?" Grandma said to Chris.

"Okay."

"Another baby," Grandma said. "I can't wait."

"The mother can," Pappy said.

"Don't speak bad about Evelyn," said Grandma, clearing off the table. "Her daughter is listening."

"Her father is talking," said Pappy. "Come over here, Chriscross, I want to tell you the story of my life."

Sadie came by with the twins, and her daughter, and Enid came over with her husband, who seemed very pleasant to Chris, especially after hearing about him from Evelyn. Hymie came over to pick up Sadie, and Enid and Harvey went home, and Murray arrived in time for dinner.

"I made stuffed cabbage, sweet and sour like you like it, Chris. Come. Eat. It isn't so fattening."

"She makes it with rice in the meat," Murray said. "Rice is carbohydrate. That's starch. Fat people have a hard time using up starch."

"How come such an expert isn't married?" Grandma said.

"After dinner," said Pappy, "I'll tell you the story of my life."

"Do you remember when you was a little girl, and I used to take you in my lap?"

"I remember," said Chris.

"I took you in my lap and I told you the story of my life. Do you remember that story? It comes in several sizes. Which one do you like the best, where I crossed the ice on one silver skate and a peg-

443

leg escaping the Russkies? Where I swam the Black Sea? Where I hid under the bridge while the Polish army ran over me on horseback?"

"Whichever one you like best."

"You want to sit in my lap?" He was grinning, teeth in, head shining pink in the glow from the lamp, the one with the cellophane still on the shade. He was seated in the big blue armchair from Evelyn's living room, the one it didn't pay to recover. And there was room on the chair for Chris.

"Now then," he said, a gentle hand around her shoulders. "Do you remember when you was little and I told you about the Big Bear that chased me? The bear that didn't like children, so I ate him?"

"I don't think I remember that one."

"Then that's the one I better tell you. It was a Litvak bear, but it came originally from Schventiensky."

"I like it already."

"You do?" said Pappy, and hugged her. "Then so will I like it. Listen. This happens to be a true story."

Sleeping on the sofa (they had offered her the convertible bed, the twin-size pull-out that came—miracle!—from the big square footstool courtesy of Mr. Castro, but she had chosen to bed down on the couch), Chris was suffused with Grandma smells. Just around the archway, as immaculate as that room was kept, the kitchen radiated cooking odors, nothing stale, nothing old or rank, just the warm suggestion of food, the presence of Grandma, preparing, mixing, like a Headless Horseman of Love, doomed or rather blessed to ride the earth in search of someone to feed, and well. Beneath the quilt there were corners of light perfume, sense-filled specters of Grandma's soapy clean skin, with touches of lilac: history through the nose.

It amazed Chris to find delight in something so simple, when love, true love as she knew it with Lionel and her mother and anybody else who might pay attention, was so complex and riddled with pain. She supposed her mother was right about her, she was not only fat, she was provincial. Loving Pittsburgh, with its funny architecture, with its curlicues and cornices on bank buildings, its semi-stately columns on libraries and official sites of commerce, the transported recollection of immigrants. Shady Avenue: the name alone gave promise of protection, even when there weren't many trees.

She had no right to seek grandeur in any form, no claim to the heaths of Thomas Hardy, no connection with the purple moors of the Brontës, no matter how much sorrow was in her heart. The smell of Grandma, the sight of uninspired two-family houses with only a shrub budding green along the sidewalk, the feel of a baby, the sound of hello sung warmly through cacophonous bleats of too many people talking all at once, the taste of stuffed cabbage was all she needed to make her feel alive and welcome, what right did she have to expect anything from life, no wonder Lionel didn't care about her. What difference did it make when she was under Grandma's quilt?

Hymie drove them up to the highway, Pappy in his long underwear with clean shirt and trousers, much too big on him now, for the occasion. Chris was in blue jeans and a flowered shirt Evelyn had bought her, a size too small.

"A fine day," Pappy noted. The sun worked its way through the early morning haze, summoning a different kind of red to the sky, from the glow that shone around steel mills at night. "A genuinely fine day," he said, beaming back at the sun, lowering his head like a gentle bull to butt back at the morning with his shiny pink dome.

"Shakne!" Pappy shouted, when the truck came to a halt at the top of Route 345. "Shakne!" he yelled as he got down from the cab, and went over to the big fruit stand with its prices posted on big cards: Lettuce 2 for 25/ Plums—Cheap/ Peaches first of the season. "Shakne, where are you, look, here I am, what do you know, still alive, I beat him!"

"Don't run!" Hymie cautioned.

"Shakne!" Pappy shouted, and laughed and ran to the stand.

445

The big sour man in the work shirt sorting the fruit, putting out the boxes of apples and pears and all kinds of vegetables, turned and smiled. "Moisch," he said, his smile gaping toothless in front, where the cigar was wedged. "Moisch," he said, "how are you?"

"Shake my hand," said Pappy. "Shake it hard. Look. I'm still here. How are you?"

They went down to Craig and Centre, to Pappy's old location, and Pappy shook hands with everybody at the stand, and told them about Uncle Jerry, and how they should maybe hose off the fruit to make it look better. "It doesn't take much water," he said. "It pays in the long run. Fruit should jump into your eyes."

"You sold me the stand," Willie said. "I run it my way."

"No battles," Pappy said. "Nobody's looking for a fight. I was only coming to shake hands. Have a cigar."

"I'm happy to shake hands with you, Moskowitz," Willie said, putting the cigar in the green cotton apron pocket.

"Harder," said Pappy, shaking hands and chortling. "Look how I'm still here." As he spoke his eyes moved around, checking the neighborhood. "This is a very good location, Craig and Centre. You can see the people coming from there, they can see you coming from here. Up and down the avenue. A very good location. If you don't want to hose it, polish it. The fruits should shine like jewels you can eat."

"Sandy," Willie called to his helper. "Come shake hands with Moskowitz. He used to own this stand."

"You got a helper? Let him polish."

"Hello, Mr. Moskowitz," Sandy said. "Nice to meet you."

"You got a good handshake. Let me tell you about how I fooled Uncle Jerry, and then I'll show you how with such a good handshake you can polish fruit."

They drove to the produce center, and he ran around to the men unloading trucks, opening crates of vegetables and fruit. "Shake hands!" he said. "I wanted to be sure and say goodbye. I

446

want to say Hallo. How are you? If I don't see you, have a good time."

There was one other place Pappy wanted to go, and he didn't want Chris to go with him. "Drive past Sammy and Pegeen's, by the highway," he instructed Hymie. "The first grandchild can play with the newest."

"I want to be with you," Chris said.

"We'll pick you up on the way back to Grandma's," Pappy said, and stared out the window, eating up the afternoon with his eyes. "You should see their stand, they did very good. Hot dogs and Coca-Cola and Frostee Freezees. Orange juice mixed with vanilla ice cream. To me it sounds disgusting but the travelers like it. You'll spend an hour with them, at the house. It's a two-minute walk to the stand. You can eat hot dogs."

"I want to be with you."

"I don't think so," Pappy said.

She squeezed herself almost into him, via his arm. "All right," Pappy said. "All right. She can come with us. But you'll stay in the truck."

"Where to, old man?" asked Hymie.

"You know the place. As long as we're driving around. Get it over with. I won't come again till I have to."

"For Christ's sake," Hymie murmured.

"A very nice fellow, Jesus." Pappy nodded his head. "A good magician. You shouldn't talk about him, swearing, even if he ended up Gentile."

"I wrote a paper on Catholicism for my thesis for the Philosophy and Psychology Club," Chris said.

"Those words are all English?" asked Pappy.

"It's really a wonderful religion," said Chris. "It's nice to have something that can give you all the answers."

"Nothing can give you all the answers," Pappy said. "Right, Hymie?"

"I ain't sure."

"Du hörst?" said Pappy. "And he's practically a professor."

"I met with Cardinal Dougherty in Philadelphia," Chris said.

"The baseball pitcher?"

"He's the Cardinal of Philadelphia. Cardinals are just below the Pope. A friend of mine from Coventry Hall arranged for me to meet him, for my paper on Catholicism. A Cardinal. In robes."

"Don't tell me," Pappy said.

"He's a wonderful man. He offered me his ring—held out his hand, and you're supposed to genuflect, that's kneel—and kiss his ring. But I just shook his hand. He looked surprised. He's a really nice man. Smiling and pink, like a very round version of you."

"Flattery wouldn't get you no place," Pappy said.

"He said he thought I was an Irish colleen."

"Well you ain't," Pappy said. He sat up a little straighter as the truck moved over the curve at the top of the hill, and they could see it stretching in front of them, an endless field of markers, tablets, crosses, and Jewish stars, stretched out row on row, neatly, exactly, like candles on an infinite grassy birthday cake. "The second gate," Pappy said.

"What are we doing here?"

"You wasn't invited. You came along. Don't be a critic."

"They called him in the hospital," Hymie said. "A person came with folders offering him a chance to pick out his spot."

"How morbid." Chris shuddered and looked down in her lap, hoping that what she didn't see would have less existence for her.

"What's morbid?" said Pappy. "What is that meaning, morbid?"

"An unhealthy preoccupation with things like death."

"No kidding," said Pappy. "An unhealthy preoccupation." He digested it for a moment, and then he smiled. "Well, it isn't exactly the healthiest thing in the world, dying."

"Let's go home."

"We're going home," Pappy said. "As soon as I pick out my location."

He wandered up and down some newly grassy knolls, walked on the paths that ran by the cluttered places, searched for the shade of a tree.

"This is a good location," Pappy said finally, smiling, satisfied. "When the sun is shining there'll be plenty of traffic. On a fine day I'll get to see everybody coming and going. They'll be coming from here," he pointed up the path. "They'll be going from there," he pointed the other way. "Maybe they'll stop to visit."

"Please don't talk like that," Chris said.

"Why, it isn't morbid. It's the truth." Pappy slapped a hand on her shoulder. "Everybody dies. How lucky can a man be, he can pick out his spot. *Hallo!*" he shouted to the graveyard. "How's everybody feeling?"

"Cut it out, Pop," Hymie said. "Nothin' can't hear you."

"How do you know? You ever been dead? You think they picked such a location for nobody to wonder how they was feeling?" He raised his head to the sky, took a cigar from his shirt pocket, and lifted it to a thick white cloud that hovered fatly over the neatness of day.

"Have a cigar!" he said. "You can keep it. I'm no Indian giver." He waited, and the cigar stayed motionless in his palm. "I hope You're taking care of these people," he said to the air. He shook his head from side to side, and looked at the ground. "What kind of a thing is that to try and make a man understand. Death. You didn't have a better problem to give us?"

"You shouldn't challenge God," Chris said.

"Why not?"

"It's like—" she lowered her head. "It's like making a joke. Making a joke about some things is in very bad taste."

"Sez who?" said Pappy. "Look at the joke He plays on me, on all of us. I forgive Him. He'll forgive me. He has a sense of humor. A sense of humor, you can forgive everything. Almost everything." He winked at the sky and put the cigar back in his pocket. "What kind of a thing is that to make a man understand?"

449

Walking back to the truck she asked Pappy if she could have the cigar to send to Cardinal Dougherty.

"I don't want no Pope praying for me."

"He's a very nice man. I'd like to send him the cigar. It's just a way of thanking him for letting me have the interview."

"You wouldn't ask him to pray for me?"

"Not if you don't want me to."

"Send him the cigar," Pappy said. "You like him so much, send him the cigar. But tell him no prayers. And tell him you're sorry, you're not becoming a Catholic."

She looked at him, surprised, because she had no idea how obvious she was. She thought he could read her mind, maybe even her soul.

"The mother wanted Errol Flynn. The daughter wants a movie star from the church. You think Jesus Christ in person could make you understand?"

"What?"

"Why we die."

"I want to understand why we live."

"That's a very big order," said Pappy. "That's two truckloads and a half."

"It's her mother's fault for putting her with the nuns." Grandma started weeping.

"I haven't done it yet. I've only been considering it," Chris said.

"She's sending my cigar to the Vatican," Pappy chortled.

"I'll get the pot roast." Grandma blew her nose.

"Did you make it with carrots and potatoes?" Murray said.

"Is the Pope Jewish?" said Pappy.

"Don't eat the potatoes," Murray said to Chris. "Starch is the hardest to use up."

"A Catholic," wept Grandma, spooning some braised celery from the roast, heavy with beef gravy, onto Chris' plate.

"She wants to become a saint," said Sadie.

Sammy looked over at Chris. "You can ride through France on a circumcised horse."

Everybody laughed except Grandma, who didn't hear any of it, she had turned down her hearing aid to be in closer touch with her grief, unimpeded by sound. She was crying very openly, which was something she seldom did. Making sure everybody had plenty on their plates, which was something she did always. Then she went into the kitchen to sit down on the hard wooden chair and cry into her Kleenex, which Murray had brought from the drugstore.

"Why'd you upset her like that?" Chris said to Pappy. "What'd you have to say anything for?"

"What did you have to meet with the Prince of Philadelphia? Anyway she likes to cry, your Grandma. Go. Tell her to come in and eat. She'll feel better."

"I'm not hungry," Grandma said, turning up her hearing aid. "Go. Eat. Become a Catholic."

"I'm not going to," said Chrissie. "I was only thinking about it. Please come in and have dinner. The pot roast is wonderful."

Grandma looked up. "Even without paprika?"

"Even without paprika."

"I worried about that," said Grandma. "The doctor said cut out spices. For Grandpa's heart. I was worried about salt, but salt you can put on at the table. Mainly I was worried it wouldn't be good without paprika."

The obstetrician's room was filled with a definitely better class of people than she had ever awaited birth with, Evelyn noted. They were mostly young, or at least younger in actual years than she was herself, although she looked much better than any of them, even very pregnant. There was one woman dressed in a sari, very elegant, very wan. She flew in to see the doctor from Bombay, every few months, to try and become fertile; Evelyn knew that from the receptionist. She looked very rich, all spun up in gold threads between the strands of beige silk, and she had a diamond in her right nostril, and her eyes were cloaked lightly with tears. Evelyn couldn't imagine anyone wanting a baby that badly, unless of course the kingdom was at stake.

"Are you a Maharani?" Evelyn smiled, coddled in innocent admiration. "You look so regal and beautiful, I thought you must be a Maharani."

"No. I am Cella Talbot."

"Evelyn Sterne." She shook the light brown small-boned hand, trying to return the touch with the gentleness she thought had to make for manners in India.

"You're not the wife of a Maharajah?"

"My husband is English. With the diplomatic service."

"That must be thrilling," Evelyn said.

"It is an existence." Cella looked away. "Without a child there can be no life."

"Imagine," said Evelyn, who couldn't.

"You can get dressed now, Mrs. Sterne." The doctor removed his rubber glove.

"And it's really a hairline incision?"

"That's all that it is," the doctor said. "I can definitely promise you a very small scar. Very small. But it would be a scar."

"That's better than having my vagina stretched all out of shape." Evelyn had been reading articles constantly, since the women's magazines, the tonier ones, were starting to allow for "labia," and words like "orgasm," and even "menopause," which naturally didn't concern her—those she clipped out and mailed to Grandma. But she knew for an almost fact that the birth of the baby, that terrible tearing, would stretch her vagina out of shape. "Isn't it?"

"I don't think so," the doctor said. "You're the one who's asking for a Caesarian."

"I don't see you putting up such a terrible battle not to make fifteen hundred dollars."

"I've told you the risks, which are minimal. I've also told you it isn't really necessary, but if you prefer it, at your age—"

"My age," she flared. "What do you mean my age?"

"If you prefer a Caesarian, if it will ease the psychological pressure on you—"

"There is no psychological pressure on me." Evelyn held her stomach. "Let's make the date for the day after tomorrow, maybe my husband can even come in from New Jersey for such a blessed event." She smiled, softening at the thought of Sonny, back at her bedside. Holding their son. Their son who would be all perfect, even more perfect without having to pass through that unyielding tunnel, the operation was a break for him as well as herself. Caesarian babies were pretty, she knew that for a fact. A very pretty boy. A brilliant boy with a massive expanse of forehead like his father had, a brain that would twinkle with Sonny's mind and hers, a fine combination. Light-eyed, light-eyed, a light-eyed boy who could leap society in a single bound. Who could make it all right for her at last.

Oh yes, she'd been angry from time to time, she didn't quite understand why. She had thought Sonny would fill her like a raging tide, not a tide of rage. But she still felt empty, she still could feel the beating impatience, unfillment, even with the next Emperor of the United States kicking inside her belly.

"And what kind of scar will it be again? What kind of incision?"

"I'm doing a low elliptical. Very common. Not dangerous. Hair-line scar. But I do prefer not to do surgery if it isn't—"

"My vagina would be all out of shape."

"There is a slight relaxation of the vaginal walls."

"I don't need a slight relaxation," she said. "Let's do it the day after tomorrow."

On the way into anesthesia she cried a little, because there was always that terrible possibility. They could make a mistake, people died all the time, from inappropriate anesthesia. A woman had died the day before from a miracle drug. Some

4 5 3

miracle. Sonny was holding her hand as they wheeled her down the corridor, her hair a mass of dark tangles, her lower part prepped. His face was a shade lighter than his hair, blanched, lacking color. Fear was in his eyes. Sweat was in his palm.

"There's nothing to be afraid of," she said, smiling her radiant smile. "It's a very ordinary operation. I'll be back in a jiffy with your son." She waited until she was in the operating room itself to let the full extent of her own fright flood through the room.

"I've changed my mind," she said to the doctor. "Let me up. Let me up. Let me out."

"Relax," he said.

"Count backwards from one hundred," said the anesthesiologist.

When she woke there was nothing but white, and she thought she had died. The ceiling was white but it seemed too hazy, too frosted to be a ceiling. And the lights were all in prisms, and she was dead.

"Am I dead?" she asked the nurse.

"Very much alive." The nurse smiled down on her. "And so is your little girl."

"I had the most terrible dream," she said to Sonny when the room came back again, another room this time, with Sonny standing there smiling, not looking at the intravenous feeding that was going into her hand. Her tongue was very thick, and she could hardly get the words together, but she could get the thoughts together in her head, and they were black, black terrible thoughts, the kind you could only get in a very bad dream. She had failed in the dream, she had failed herself completely. She had failed Sonny and life and purpose; she was being dragged down into her own dark empty insides.

"How is our son?" she managed.

"Our son is a beautiful daughter."

"Oh God." Evelyn started to cry. "Oh God. It wasn't a dream."

"She's absolutely perfect," Sonny said, stroking her hair, the heat on her cheeks. "She has ten fingers and ten tiny little toes. and her mother's figure, and they say they can't be sure for six months, but I think her eyes are going to stay blue. She's absolutely perfect."

Evelyn turned her head away. "She's a girl."

EIGHT

IT WAS A CLUB. The most exclusive club in the whole country, maybe even the world, and they couldn't keep Arnold out. They couldn't call him Jew behind his back and turn down his application, goddamit. God Bless America.

Arnold, like all semi-good men who had achieved an impossibility, had begun to believe the things he had promised in his campaign. He would do something for New Jersey. He would do something for his country. He would do something for the world. Why not? He was actually going to be sworn in as Senator, in Washington, D.C.

Also in the chambers with him, among the older faces, was thick-browed, intense Stuart Symington of Missouri (known to his friends as, but not called aloud, "Sanctimonious Stu"), the former Secretary of the Air Force. Arnold had never met him when they had the air in common. Now they had the earth in common, the country that spawned them, the clay their feet might be made of. Which was better than manure, which some wags contended was still on the boots of that lean, retiring Westerner with direct but courtly manner, Mike Mansfield (of Montana). A swearing-in ceremony. Jesus Christ. All things were within the realm of imagination, and doing.

Even as he stood being whipped into fervor and patriotism by the thought of oratory and innocence by association, Arnold considered the wisdom of hiring a topnotch P.R. man to start a campaign, to make the 83rd Congress of the United States the Do-Something Congress, a fiery contradiction to the Do-Nothing 80th Congress, as Truman had called it. Do-Something Congress. Not bad. Why not Do-Everything Congress? Why not, indeed?

He began to see why not, within a few minutes of the opening day when they convened at twelve noon. The Chaplain Reverend Frederick Brown Harris delivered the invocation. Before the swearing-in ceremony could begin, the action of the Senate started.

Brian MacMahon, Senator from Connecticut, had died after his election. William A. Purtell was announced as his replacement. Thomas Kuchel was appointed to take the place of Richard M. Nixon, who had resigned from the Senate on becoming Vice-President.

The administration of oaths was delayed by bickering over the seating of two Senators, Chavez of New Mexico and Langer of North Dakota. There was a debate as to whether they were allowed to take oaths without prejudice to the resolution of the challenge. And another between Senators Robert A. Taft and Lyndon B. Johnson as to whether or not the effect of an oath without prejudice was without prejudice.

Arnold was starting to wonder the same thing and a number of others. The greatest day of his life, and it was cluttered with lobbyists, arguments without meaning.

Once the Senate adjourned at 1:09 (they were finally sworn in) Arnold gave himself over to some practical considerations. His office was too far down the hall. He would lose an important four minutes a day. He had tried getting the incumbent to resign before the new administration began, so he could pick up the rest of his term, which would have given him seniority (a nicer office). But there were still some things he couldn't do.

He was only a freshman Senator, six years away from his next election, running down the hall so he'd be only half an hour late, starting his day with a waiting room full of people he couldn't possibly see, but he had to, so he did; trying on the floor of the Senate to get the attention of Styles Bridges, President Pro Tem, who looked through Arnold as Arnold couldn't yet look through other people, he was only a freshman Senator, with an assassination attempt behind him, which seemed to impress Styles Bridges (Republican, New Hampshire) not at all. There were too many people returned from the dead in that election.

The home Arnold lived in, at least, satisfied him: a rambling farmhouse in McLean, Virginia. Farmhouse. What cool minimizing these people dealt in. In Arnold's terms it was an estate, a mansion set back among trees, swallowing acres of fields with gardens, a tennis court, glassed-in poolhouse, with a roof that could be rolled open in summer. But the realtor called it a farmhouse, so a farmhouse it was.

Evelyn had found it for him. Evelyn had offered her assistance (anything to escape the wail of the child, the dark of the city, the glow that had seemed to desert Sonny in Evelyn's eyes when Arnold was actually elected). Sarah was proud and happy and totally out of her depth in the height, and with real estate people, so Arnold accepted Evelyn's offer to house-hunt for him. She was an excellent shopper.

Poor Sonny. At least turn it to the good, Arnold thought. So he let her run loose in his chauffeured limousine, meeting eight realtors daily, examining properties, deciding what to do with Arnold's money. Arnold's money.

She suspected it was mostly Sonny's, but said nothing, not for a while. She just decided to spend it in the wisest way for her. "A guest house is of paramount importance," she said to the real estate people, already adopting a little of the rhetoric she heard in the gallery in the few minutes she could sit still to observe procedure. "A guest house, or at least a wing where guests can stay." And meet Presidents.

All the time Evelyn was on her house-hunting crusade, Sonny was in New York, trying to breathe life and income back into his faltering investment business. It was a time of cool prosperity in the field of banking, but Sonny had taken too many time-outs from the game. And brother who was Senator, or no brother who was Senator, banks were still wary of him: investors wanted him to tell all over again why they should throw in with Sterne and Sterne when the better part of the company of Sterne was going to Washington. The greatest battle of his whole career had been won for Arnold, and still Sonny had to go through the drill as if he were in boot camp.

A soldier's campaign. Fine for Eisenhower. Fine for Arnold. Not so fine for Sonny, who had been kept out of war and was filling in the latrines of Arnold's past, potential Arnold scandals. And holding off the railroad. And trying to embrace the banks. And have lunch with Clifton Sanger.

"The brother of the Senator," he said through very tight teeth to Sanger's secretary on the phone. "He knows who I am, I think. His wife sent flowers to mine, some years ago; I'm sure he'll remember."

"I'm sorry, Mr. Sterne, but Mr. Sanger and his family are in Curaçao for the winter."

How long did winter last, how long would Sanger freeze him out, how soon did they forgive you for having some smarts? "When will he be back?"

"Perhaps the end of February," the secretary said.

"I have some very important matters to discuss with Mr. Sanger."

"I'm sure."

"Is there someplace I could write him? The address in Curaçao?"

"He needs a complete rest. I'm instructed to forward no business mail. I'm sorry. When Mr. Sanger takes a rest, it must be a complete rest."

Of course. How exhausting it had to be to have five generations of banking behind one. One really needed a complete rest. One's heart bled for Clifton Sanger.

"You'll call me when he gets back?"

"Of course. I have all your messages."

The 83rd Congress convened on January 3rd, 1953. By that time Evelyn had the other Sternes nicely ensconced in their farmhouse. She had selected some of the furniture at auction, the rest she had had trucked in from the Big House in Tarrytown, arranging to have the property sold by a broker from Mamaroneck, one from Rye, one from Stamford, Connecticut, and one from New York City. She assumed they would never be at a cocktail party together.

But meantime, how gay, how exciting was Washington, where she stayed in the guest wing all by herself, and wondered if it should be redone in flowered wallpaper like the Blair House, where she had actually been to a reception. Where Dolley Madison gave her teas. And Dolley Madison's cousin designed the wallpaper. A little too flowery for Evelyn, a few too many birds caught in flight on the walls, but not wrong for Washington. So perhaps, just perhaps, she could revise her opinion about the best walls being plain, and painted in white, or neutral colors. It was Washington, after all. No place to be neutral.

There were parties nearly every night, embassy receptions, informal, stilted little get-togethers thrown together by hostesses at the last minute (a month in advance). Arnold was too tired to go to most of them, so Evelyn did the decent thing and accompanied Sarah, who was so excited by it all and didn't have a thing to wear. Evelyn took her shopping. And dressed her well for a plain dowdy woman. And bought a few things for herself, simple and usually solid colors, so she wouldn't disappear in the wallpaper. Wouldn't look printed, and drab. As if she could.

She met diplomats from Africa, where she didn't particularly want to go, so she simply smiled while they canted at her, lightly sang-song their stories. She made no attempt to remember their names, or try to keep them from all looking alike. European

460

officials, however, became a part of her notebook (Mark Cross, black leather, very smart, compact, it could fit into the daintiest of evening bags, along with its tiny gold pen, and its tiny white pages—plenty of room for names and addresses—she wrote very small and used shorthand—and telephone numbers, ETOile 4692, that was her particular favorite, ETOile). She was especially kind to the wives of Pashas, or whatever they were, those who were allowed harems, their poor wives. But she wasn't exactly cool to the Pashas themselves.

Sarah actually seemed to bloom from all the excitement, if one could find a bloom on a faded rose that had never been more than a dandelion, and Evelyn—well, Evelyn actually shone. She kept her jewels to a minimum, and never was beaded or sequined, as she knew now that the glimmering part of her was her smile, accompanied by her eyes. She used both to the maximum, casting her teeth like pearls before connections, and kept the diamonds that Sonny had given her in a wall-safe at Arnold's. The jewels that she actually sported on crisp black silk were antique, distinguished, black pearls, cabochon emeralds, small necklaces twirled out of tiny rubies cut to look like beads. Understatement. The key to Washington. She knew that at once, even without meaning to listen.

In her political views, she was totally liberal or totally conservative, depending on who was talking to her about what. Most opinions could be fielded with an understanding nod, while her eyes moved around the room to see who else was there. Most passes could be grounded with a compliment ("How lovely your wife looks this evening, what a lucky woman she is to have a man of your stature in love with her"). She agreed to no assignations, disagreed with no strong arguments, because she understood the purpose of practically every party was for people to lobby for something or other in the hall.

She did agree to have lunch with some of the wives who seemed right in the center of things, hoping they would carry her along to the parties where even Arnold wasn't invited. She never took Sarah with her to luncheons: big parties were one thing, but luncheons—Sarah never knew what to say. And Evelyn did,

Evelyn almost always did. When she didn't, she would change the subject to clothes. With those, nearly every wife in Washington needed help and understanding, which Evelyn could get for them wholesale, with her old and ever-improving connections.

"Power!" bleated the columnist over lunch. ("Be careful of her," Arnold had warned over breakfast. "She's a dangerous woman. She'll stop at nothing to get ahead." "Look who's talking," Evelyn didn't answer.) "That's what this city is about, is power. The center of the world is here."

"I love your gloves," said Evelyn. "Italian?"

"What does he really want, your brother-in-law?" Charlotte, the columnist, said.

Evelyn wasn't sure if the lunch would be reported in the newspaper in the society section. Still she was picking up the bill, and ordering a third martini "straight up" for Charlotte, who had a hangover from the night before. Evelyn played with her celery, stringing it out, so Charlotte would forget her question.

"What does he really want, Arnold Sterne?" Charlotte said in the midst of her third frosted drink. "You can tell me, honey, I'm not working. I'm here with you as a friend."

Damn. It wouldn't be in the column, three martinis or no.

"Arnold's just what he seems to be." Evelyn bit a carrot stick. No point in the patience required by celery. No point in the truth, even shaded. "A very sincere man."

"Ha ha ha," said Charlotte. "The noblest Roman of them all."

"I didn't say that. He's from New Jersey."

"Yeah, I heard," Charlotte said. "Has he got a mistress?"

"Not that I know of." Where was she now, that madwoman? Faded. Her skin getting withered in South American sun. Over. Finished. So much for blondes.

"Are you sleeping with him?"

"I'm married to his brother."

"Well hell, honey, this is America. You can tell me."

"My husband is a fantastic man. Brilliant. Inspired. The inspiration behind Arnold. But you won't print that."

"Of course not," said Charlotte. "The steak bits here are good. You want some steak bits?"

"Fine," said Evelyn. "Two steak bits," she instructed the waiter. "I'd like mine medium-rare. How would you like yours, Charlotte?"

"For dinner," said Charlotte. "I never eat lunch. So many parties. So many dinners. I don't know why I stay in this place." She smiled. "Power." She swallowed it with some gin. "It's invigorating."

"My husband is a true idealist," Evelyn said.

"I'll bet. Just like Arnold Sterne."

"Well not exactly."

"What's Arnold really want?"

"Sonny, that's my husband, he's in finance. Or he's back in finance again now that Arnold's elected. He's a fabulous man."

"Yeah, you told me. How come if he's so terrific he isn't in politics?"

"Politics is Arnold's field. My husband's in investment banking."

"You said that. If he's so terrific, how come he's in New York and you're in Washington?"

"Arnold always comes first. With Sonny. And so, with me. I like to do whatever I can to make him happy. And there are some things I can do that Sarah—Mrs. Sterne—is just a little shy about doing."

"Like sleeping with Arnold?"

"Cut it out, Charlotte."

"Just asking. I have no intention to print."

"I'm organizing his household for him."

"The farmhouse in McLean. I hear he spent three hundred fifty thousand dollars. Just between us."

"I have no idea what it cost," said Evelyn. Two hundred and eighty-five thousand, with her handling it. "I'm only here to help."

"Isn't he lucky."

Well, no. The dream of a lifetime was lightly dusted with dross, incredibly dreary detail. Arnold would awaken at seven-fifteen, already exhausted at the thought of the calls he hadn't returned the night before. Already anticipating the race down the corridor (four minutes added, of waste). He was worn out from a speech he had usually made someplace in New Jersey, from the plane trip, from the breakfast he would have to attend, sponsored by utility executives, or executives from something important to New Jersey. They were conventioneers in masks of public servants, costumes of labor unioneers, guys coming in to Washington to have a good time. But they had to make it look official, so they would drag Arnold Sterne, whose ass was already dragging from the night before, to a breakfast meeting so their visit would look official. Breakfast was the time they could usually pin him, like a butterfly on toast, because there could be not too many claims for conflicting engagements at breakfast. Poached eggs. Poached eyes. Looking at him with runny whites.

In the back of his car, in the dim light of Washington morning on the way to his office, he would try and pick up as much as he could from the New York *Times* in eight minutes, from the Washington *Post* in seven, counting on Seth to have read them carefully, to have circled what was really important. As if Arnold would have a chance to do anything about it.

Running down the hall (in his next term he'd have a better office) checking his watch (it was already 9:27, twenty-seven minutes late), he'd hope against fact that his waiting room would be empty. There was a committee meeting at ten, and he had promised Seth and his legislative assistant he'd give them a half hour to brief him on everything under consideration by the committee. This committee. That committee. What committee was it today? What was today? Committees were to develop information and shape legislation. But when did the Senate get the chance to legislate?

He entered his office by the private door (Oh yes, the main door did have his name on it, Mr. Sterne, New Jersey, Welcome, with the seal of the state beneath, flashing a little liberty and prosperity). He opened the door to peer at the waiting room where, if there were miracles, no visitors would be.

Crowded. Jammed. People there was no way to ignore. Governor Manton, that old rummy (old bourbon, now, Arnold guessed they could call him, the conversion to Joe Pape's being permanent), waiting on the couch with his wife. Election favors. The Chairman of Cats and Dogs, there with his wife, who looked to be a little of both, anxious to see if indeed her husband had entree to a Senator's office.

A delegation of union people, the ones who made gestures of contributing funds to a campaign that hadn't really needed any, votes to a campaign that did.

". . . anxious to know what you're going to do on the arbitration bill . . ."

"I'm kind of anxious myself," Arnold said.

"Well we're watching."

"Rest assured," Arnold said, and wished he could do the same.

"I'm sorry, Seth," he told his administrative assistant, who had circled all important news in red but didn't have time now to explain clearly what was under consideration by the committee.

Arnold looked at his watch. He was already late for the committee hearing. But there were twelve more constituents waiting outside, and two self-appointed representatives of constituents, and constituents were important. Everything was important. Important and meaningless.

"How are you?" he said to as many as he could, and tried to seem like he cared. The ones that would vote for him again, regardless, he very sincerely hoped, he turned over to his aides, to his staff, to anyone he could. He moved through his day, listening to demands against the public interest, assuming he got to the newspapers and the issues and could ever determine what the public interest was.

He already had some small suspicion what it wasn't. Joe McCarthy was way up the hall, but Arnold could smell him. Lethal gas. A sour breeze. Ferreting out "flies in the ointment," as McCarthy sometimes called the commies who were everywhere. Flies in the ointment.

Well, the frost was off Whittaker Chambers' pumpkin, so any new old phrase would do. Hiss was in jail, and Vice-President

Richard Nixon was no longer a member of the United States Senate, where Arnold hoped to get in time for the vote, on whatever the issue was. He hoped Seth could tell him, before the roll call.

He would inevitably be at least an hour late to the committee hearing (there was a veteran with a disability file that had to be attended to at once, at once, the head of the New Jersey Veteran's Administration would say, watching Arnold to make sure the file was pulled *at once,* "Remember the Maine. Remember the next election"). On the way to the hearing, Seth would brief Arnold, both of them running, one talking, the other listening, Arnold absorbing only enough to enter the hearing room confused.

He was too smart to ask the wrong questions, which most of the other Senators would be doing, having had exactly the kind of harassing morning Arnold had had. Once in a while someone said something that got to the core of the issue, but by his second month in office, Arnold considered those questions accidents. As soon as the answers were starting to make sense it was time to leave the committee to get to the Senate floor to read press releases his head speechwriter gave him into the Congressional Record.

In time for lunch. "You can't skip this one," Sonny told him from New York. "He's a very good man and he's willing to act as the chairman for the finance committee for your reelection. I just won't be able to handle it. I'm over my head. I'm drowning."

"Don't drown, little brother. If it's really that bad, I'll throw you a rope."

"Don't worry about saving me. Save the country."

"But if it's a question of dollars . . ."

"I don't need your dollars. I'll do okay. If I can keep off the railroad, and the banks . . ."

At such moments Arnold would be tempted to tell Sonny that most of the dollars were actually his. But he didn't trust Evelyn. He didn't trust her at all. House. Furniture. Dresses. Christ, she was worse than Defense spending. As grateful as he was for her help, he saw her tight-fisted extravagance, doubted her love for

Sonny. If he waited it out, maybe they'd divorce, maybe she'd find some Mideastern potentate with enough oil to grease her for good.

In the meantime he had had a very long talk with his son Ellis, who was graduated from law school at Harvard (America!). He explained to him about the income from Joe Pape's Finest. That it really belonged to Sonny; Arnold was merely protecting him.

"I'm afraid he'll blow it," he told Ellis. "Or she'll blow it. He doesn't even know he still has it. But if anything ever happens to me . . ."

"Don't worry, Dad," Ellis said.

"He gets it all."

"Don't worry, Dad."

Don't worry, Dad. To the Senate Dining Room for lunch he couldn't eat, because he was so busy introducing the chairman of finance for his reelection to all the Senators in the room.

Don't worry, Dad. It was after two o'clock, and the afternoon's schedule was worse than the morning's. Helped by his staff when they weren't in his way, he managed to get through it—the week's accumulated letters—the tiny percentage of mail that had to be signed personally, too monumental to trust to his signature machine. HAVE NEVER RECEIVED YOUR REPLY TO MY PERSONAL LETTER came fifty to a hundred wires a week, in changing language, the message always the same.

"Send out a personal apology," Arnold said. "Seth, try and get a signature that comes off blue, so when they wet it with their fingers it looks like I did it myself, in ink."

There were usually a minimum of three afternoon committee sessions on his schedule so he went to the one being televised. Television. The changing nature of government. People could see. Arnold figured it would be harder to fool them.

Usually he missed one vote out of four on the floor of the Senate. Sometimes he would arrive just in time for his name to be called from the roll, and answer, "Aye," unless he saw a particular distinguished colleague shake his head, when he changed his vote to "Nay."

What were they doing? Where was it going? When did the treadmill end, the business of politics finish, and government begin?

But there was no time to worry because he was late for a caucus, and there was paperwork in his office, and sixteen phone calls he had to return even though it was after six. He finished by seven if he was lucky, and there were still eight people who would be insulted the next morning. And Sarah who would be insulted at night.

"But I don't even see you," Sarah said on the phone. "And it's going to be such a lovely party. Evelyn talked to Charlotte, and Charlotte's covering the party. She says maybe the President will be there. Or at least Mamie. You've got to go."

"I'm too tired," said Arnold. "Go with Evelyn."

In a way, he supposed, Evelyn was a godsend, if you considered the social hand of God. And he was saving his brother from a fate worse than Jeanne. If Sonny's business was going so badly, all she could do was sap the little strength left (the great strength made little, but Sonny would restore, Arnold was sure, as long as Evelyn was out of his hair).

Arnold really didn't mind having her buzzing around the house in McLean, it was big enough. She did most of her buzzing in other people's homes, embassies, places of national significance. On those rare occasions when there was not anyone else's place to visit, she would zip up to New York to slip Sonny a quick one, and a kiss to the baby, and a stern reprimand to the nurse not to neglect her, dear Angela, wasn't she pretty, her eyes had stayed blue after all. And to pick up some outfits from Traina Norell where she got absolute wholesale for the cute wives of those wonderful men in Washington, and some smart little numbers for herself at Loehmann's because things were going not too well for Sonny, that son of a bitch Arnold, it was all his fault, she was sure.

She didn't know how she could stand to stay in his house, she would think as she got into a cab to take her to the train back to Washington. Except that he wasn't totally thoughtless, being seldom home.

She went once to see him in action on the floor of the Senate, from the very special gallery reserved for the families and most important constituents of the Senators. She went once and stayed a full hour, trying to see the government in action, to figure out why only seven of the ninety-six desks were occupied. She listened to the debate droning on between two of the seven who were actually in attendance, and didn't understand the issue, doubted whether they did.

She looked for reassurance at the faces of the tourists who came in at fifteen-minute intervals to the visitors' galleries and listened, and looked as awed as she when they entered and confused as she did by the time they left. Some of them seemed not to be from Milwaukee. Still they appeared baffled at the silently ordered disorder below.

Whispers on the floor. The voting bell sounded. Senators scurried like self-trained Pavlovian dogs from all over the vast complex of buildings, in time to vote, however they did. On whatever the issue was. What matter to Evelyn? Or anyone else, for that matter.

So she'd seen Arnold vote (the wrong way, the first time). Big deal. Big man. Poor Sonny. She did love him so. She couldn't stand to see him suffer.

"Power!" said Charlotte at cocktails. "That's what this city represents."

"I can't wait for the cherry blossoms to come out in spring," said Evelyn. "My first husband, Lieutenant-Commander Walter White, received the Navy Cross here. From the Secretary of the Navy. He later committed suicide."

"Your husband?"

"Forrestal. But it wasn't spring when we were here. I so love Parisian architecture. So smart building this city all white on a model of Paris."

"You been to Paris?"

"I adore that pin. What is the stone?"

"Sapphire," said Charlotte.

"So deep. It almost looks black. Beautiful."

"I've never been to Paris," Charlotte said. "Why do I need to see Paris? I'm in *Wash*ington." She spread her arms on the syllables, like a song. Beige crepe flowed down her inner arms as she flung them as wide as the wings of a thought. She threw her head backwards, and the one loose blond lock that coiled deliberately from the tight bun of her hair touched the man behind her.

He was nobody. Evelyn was sure of that, the moment he turned around. Another tourist.

"Hi, you pretty ladies."

"We're waiting for someone," Evelyn said, and lowered her eyes.

"*Washington, Washington,*" sang Charlotte, and slid into a whisper. "When there's power, real power on the spot where you sit, you'd have to be a fool to go anyplace else."

"If you had power, you could go anywhere," Evelyn said without thinking.

"You know what power is? Real power, I mean?"

Evelyn thought for a moment, as it might make the column. "Courage," she said. "Confidence," she added, lacking enough of it. "Confidence is power. The courage to have confidence." She twirled the straw in her frozen daiquiri and tried to remember what she had said. Sometimes the thoughts that slipped over her tongue seemed curiously like Pappy's. Naturally she had difficulty understanding them. She licked the frozen lime and rum off the straw, and forgot the words.

Well, whatever she'd said, Charlotte certainly didn't agree with her.

"Bullshit!" cried Charlotte. "Power is the ability to make other people afraid. When they're afraid, people will do what you want them to."

"How can people do anything if they're afraid? Fear paralyzes people. Mentally. It makes them run, but the part of them that can move into real action is paralyzed." She'd read an article.

"Bullshit," said Charlotte. "Not if you have real power. That can really make them hustle. I've lived here all my life, you can bet I've seen some asses move."

"I'll bet," said Evelyn, spying a tall dark stranger (very distinguished, well dressed, moved like he could dance, oh hell, he was meeting that woman in the corner).

"Evelyn! Evelyn!" Daisy di Bonaven signaled from the door to the cocktail lounge. "Oh, I'm so glad I caught you." She stumbled across the room in too high heels, too loose dress, her hair only partially combed.

"I hope you don't mind," said Evelyn to Charlotte. "I asked a friend of mine to join us."

"She's a friend of yours?" Charlotte narrowed her eyes, and watched Daisy trip to rest.

"I was so frightened they wouldn't let me out of the hotel room," Daisy wheezed. "Rosey told me I didn't dare come, they're watching us every minute, and then one minute they weren't watching me so I hid in the linen closet, and I waited until there was no one in the hall."

"Daisy di Bonaven . . . Charlotte Dean."

"Yeah, I know," said Charlotte, and signaled for another drink.

"I tried to get Roxy Stinson Brast to join us," Daisy breathed. "But when I had her on the line, one of Rosey's helpers ripped the wires out of the wall."

"Do tell," said Charlotte, drinking tolerantly.

"You have no idea what's going on. I tell you, the whole thing's about to blow sky-high all over again."

"Sure," said Charlotte.

"How pretty you look," said Evelyn, hoping that Daisy would straighten her harlequin glasses, which were slightly askew, so you could see half of one of her eyes.

"It was hard fixing up in the linen closet," Daisy said apologetically. "But Roxy could confirm everything. Everything. Roxy Stinson Brast," she offered Charlotte. "She was right in the center of the Teapot Dome."

"That was before my time," said Charlotte.

"Well, it won't be, it's all going to happen again."

Evelyn saw the expression of bored disbelief on Charlotte's face. "We were discussing the architecture of Washington before you got here, Daisy, how it's all so pretty," Evelyn said. "Set out as it is to look like Paris."

"And right at the center," Daisy said, happily informed, "is the Capitol. It's all laid out to revolve around the Capitol, you know."

"Well don't tell them that at the Capitol," Charlotte said. "Or they might really do something in Congress. It isn't good for the country to think there's something as powerful as the President. The people don't want to know that a lot of people can run things. It's too hard to remember the names."

Evelyn thought about that, for a minute. Even in the midst of it all, knowing almost everybody, she couldn't remember too many Senators' names, and certainly few Congressmen, even her own. Yes, she thought, and ate some nuts. It was really easier just liking Ike. And the Vice-President, whatever his name was. Checkers. No. That wasn't it.

"Roxy could confirm it all," Daisy whispered. "Charlotte Dean. You're a reporter, aren't you? You'll believe me. You're a woman. You have to believe me."

"I'm a columnist," said Charlotte, eyeing, sipping.

"It's going to come out, all of it, and it's going to be even worse. My poor Rosey. They're going to point a finger at my poor Rosey."

"Your poor Rosey," said Charlotte, "has been the juice to one of the crookedest political machines in this country."

Daisy blushed. "No one's denying that. Rosey's a crook, but he isn't stupid. He'd have to be stupid to do anything to hurt this country. He knows he couldn't exist in any country but this, not as well. He may be a crook, but he's a good American."

She reached over and drank some of Evelyn's water. "I tell you, it's all going to hit the fan. Something's cooking that's going to shake this country to its foundations. Its *very foundations*."

"The Constitution," said Evelyn, pleased she knew what was in the country's foundation.

"And you know what's in the Constitution?" Daisy asked.

"No," said Evelyn.

"Well, you ought to read it sometime," said Daisy. "It's a very nice document once you can make your way through the words. I get a lot of time to read when they lock me up."

"Would you like a drink?" Evelyn said, feeling somewhat uncomfortable.

"I don't think I better mix it with the medication," Daisy said, leaning slightly. "They give me this medication to perk me up. You've got to believe me, Charlotte. Corruption. Political espionage. It's all going to come out."

"Sure," said Charlotte, drinking. "Sure, I believe you. But like the Taft man said, Ike's politics are unassailable," she quoted. "He's pretty much for home, mother, and heaven."

"No wonder she dresses like that," said Evelyn.

"I'm not talking about the President," said Daisy. "I'm talking about—" She paused, as two big men came into the bar, with Rosey di Bonaven between them.

"Hello, Rosey!" said Charlotte Dean. "Sit ye doon."

Rosey shook his head. "Come on, Daisy. How are you Evelyn, nice to see you."

He didn't look as if it were nice to see her. He looked very drawn, and his eyes were darting more than usual. From side to side, it seemed to Evelyn, as if from the man on his left to the man on his right.

"Just get up, Daisy," Rosey mumbled hoarsely. "Just get up, and come on."

"But I'm having a good time! I'm with friends."

He leaned over and whispered something in Daisy's ear. She went very pale. "But they can't do that, this is America!"

The two men moved in closer to Rosey. Daisy went paler, and got up. "I'm awfully sorry," she said to Evelyn.

"So am I," said Evelyn, not sorry at all. Obviously she was annoying Charlotte, and Rosey was of no further use to Evelyn now, she knew Senators.

"You'll call me?" said Daisy, as Rosey hustled her out. Accompanied by the two other, very imposing men, who were surrounding them.

"Of course I will," said Evelyn, not intending to. The woman really knew how to make a fool out of herself.

"Please," Daisy whimpered. "Don't forget to call. I've got something to tell you." Rosey moved her out of the bar.

"Poor Daisy," said Evelyn. "How he chases around."

"The woman's a fool," said Charlotte. "She's nuts. What do you even see her for?"

"She's harmless," Evelyn said. "And she's filled with the most exciting stories, if you can believe them. I'm surprised you didn't at least listen to her. I mean I don't listen, but then, I'm not a columnist."

"I only print scandal I can nearly prove," said Charlotte. "She's been in a mental hospital."

"She didn't commit herself," said Evelyn, with some small understanding.

"She's crazy," said Charlotte. "You can't believe a word she says."

"Really, I think she's sort of sweet. Like a demented Barbara Frietchie."

"Barbara Frietchie? She must have been before my time."

"The poem," Evelyn said, briefly recalling Walter's recitations. "You know, the woman in the Revolution who waved the flag at the British soldiers. 'Shoot if you must this old gray head, but spare this country's flag, she said.' Or something like that," said Evelyn.

"Well, we're about as far away from the American Revolution as we can get."

"Oh," said Evelyn. That being settled, she began to reexamine the room for men. "That fellow in the corner, the one with the redhead." Vermillion. White skin. She couldn't last. "Do you know who he is?"

"Sure," Charlotte turned. "Jeremy Dayton Adams, Democrat, Kentucky."

"Senator?"

"Congressman."

"Not as important."

"It's important to the Congress, but let's not tell them that either. Anyway, there's a hell of a lot of them. There's only ninety-six Senators, and you've got one," Charlotte said.

"What do you mean, I've got him?"

"Come on, quit kidding me," said Charlotte. "I'm wise about you and Arnold. I won't tell anyone. You can tell me."

"If there were any truth to it, Charlotte, you'd be the first I'd tell. I know what a good friend you are."

"You do?" Charlotte studied her for lies, couldn't find any. A columnist, not a journalist. "You have any idea what's going on in my life?" she said, and wept into her fourth martini. "You have any idea what's going on with that bastard I'm married to? That fourth-rate politician. That creep from Loosyana?" She gave it the pronunciation they used in New Orleans, where she had gone a few times in spite of its not being *Wash*ington. "That bull of the bayou. He's having an affair with his secretary."

"You poor thing." Evelyn patted the small crown of curls at half mast above the martini glass. "I know exactly what you're going through. My first husband did that all the time."

"My husband's secretary is a *man,*" Charlotte growled, and reached for a hanky in her purse. "I've threatened him with exposure in my column, I've threatened to name him, *name* him, not even using initials, and the bastard just laughed. He laughs at me. He says go ahead and do it, I'll come out the bigger fool."

"You poor thing," Evelyn said, and looked at Charlotte more carefully. Thin lips, hardly any lips at all, little breasts, slitty eyes, sagging thin inner arms, oh yes, she could see where a boy might be more appealing than that. "You poor thing," said Evelyn aloud, patting, patting.

"You tell that to anyone I'll kill you in this town. Remember. I have *power.*"

"You don't have to threaten me," said Evelyn. "I'm your friend."

"It's hard to tell in this town who your real friends are," Charlotte wiped her eyes, "except just after an election." She blew her nose. "Walter White. Walter White? The guy who went into highway construction out of Boston after he left the Red Cross?"

"You've heard of him?" Evelyn said, delighted, before she remembered they weren't married anymore.

"Hell, sure, I heard about him. The Governor of Tennessee was our house guest last week while my husband was in the office punking Lonny's ass. Anyway, he was our house guest, and we were talking about the politics of Tennessee. They're different from the North, you know. A little Western for a sort of Southern state. Homespun."

"I don't attempt to understand politics," Evelyn said, "regardless of direction."

"Well, it's a kind of strange state, Tennessee is, kind of old world and insular, but a little stylish. A little stylish. On the face of it they have nothing but bourbon and the TVA and banks and that Southern crap, but they're starting to build superhighways, they may get very big government contracts, because you know what may be in the ground in Tennessee?"

"Power?" asked Evelyn.

"Oil," said Charlotte. "That may be bigger than power."

"Oil?" said Evelyn, trying to visualize the terrain of Tennessee that the derricks would have to rip up, whether there were trees or flat fields or meadows or hills. What difference did it make if there was oil.

"Oil. So they brought this highway construction expert in from Boston. Walter White."

"Couldn't be the same one."

"The Governor was very high on Walter White, very high indeed. Said the man came right in there and threw his shoulder to it like a native. Love of state, love of land, all that crap. Wouldn't be at all surprised, he said, if Walter didn't start getting into politics now that he's settled there. Said he wouldn't be surprised if Walter White rose very high, very high indeed."

"It couldn't be the same one," said Evelyn. "My husband's a dentist from Pittsburgh. My ex-husband," she added. "My present husband is in finance. Investment banking. He's in New York."

"So why are you here? Is he punking his secretary?"

"No, of course not."

But it started occurring to Evelyn that he might, so she moved back to New York, sending notes, flowers, little gifts bought wholesale at the PX to which she still had a card (turning yellow, but what did the guard care when she smiled) to all her new and wonderful friends in Washington. Telling them how much she loved meeting them, how much she would miss them, how much she looked forward to seeing them again. And soon. Love (and kisses to the women).

> Let us develop the resources of our land,
> call forth its powers, build up its institutions,
> promote all its great interests and see whether
> we also in our day and generation may not perform
> something worthy to be remembered

it said on the wall. Chris had been in Washington only once before (twice before really, there was the layover on the way to Florida, but she didn't consider that really seeing Washington) when her father had received the Navy Cross. At that time she had been to the Washington Monument, all the way to the top, made her way round the colossal statue of Abraham Lincoln, realized she could no longer remember the Gettysburg Address.

Never before, however, had she been inside the Senate, the House of Representatives, the places where the glory came into actual being, where mottoes of purpose and courage were inscribed along the walls and ceilings, where plaques of white marble commemorated the actual heads of Jefferson, Napoleon, Suleiman, Maimonides. She drank it all in like a tonic for her brain, letting love of country invade her even though she couldn't understand why Napoleon was up there, or Joseph McCarthy was in office.

The last was one of the few opinions she shared with Arnold. The whole Sonny Sterne entourage, Norman, baby Angela, the nurse, drum-majoretted by Evelyn, had arrived to spend Easter week with the Arnold Sternes of McLean, Virginia. Sonny said he couldn't spare the time; Evelyn said there was nothing to lose except money, and a week to clear his brain might be just what the SEC ordered.

Chris was in her freshman year in college, and had already run away twice, to sing her songs to publishers who told her that talent alone was not enough. ("You could write the score to *Oklahoma,*" Evelyn had advised her, "and nobody would listen because you're fat. Why don't you have your nose fixed, that will change everything.") She had made an appointment with Dr. Aufricht whose office was only a block away from the Park Avenue apartment of the Sternes. Dr. Aufricht took pictures of her stretched-out face from every possible angle, and reluctantly agreed to do the operation. "A sculptor should see what the statue really looks like before he finishes the features," he said. "Why don't you wait?"

So she read Tennyson and Coleridge and fell into deep spells of romantic longing, and went to the office of the president of the college and told her Bryn Mawr had nothing to offer her, she needed to be in New York to help the theater. This she knew for a fact from some friends she had made at the Actor's Studio, when they were trying out a Tennessee Williams play in Philadelphia, and she went backstage and introduced herself and started singing her songs.

"We need you in New York. At the Studio!" the actor who played the streetcleaner said. Although he didn't have blue eyes, it was an invitation. The Actor's Studio had spawned Marlon Brando with whom, like most other girls in America, she was in love. Also everybody at the Studio was reportedly in analysis, so they had to be terribly interesting and open. Lionel Lindenbaum was at Haverford, just twenty minutes away from Bryn Mawr, and he hadn't even asked her to a prom. "I have a project for the Studio," the actor said. "You could write the music."

"What can I learn from Chaucer and Shakespeare?" she said to the president of the college, a very tall, very austere-looking woman who seldom smiled on campus, spoke with the marbled diction of the Main Line, and didn't even know Chris' name, Chris was sure. "Chaucer and Shakespeare are over: the theater is now. I must leave the past and move on to the future. So I'm going to New York to save the theater."

"Fine," said Miss McBride. "Try to be back for exams."

She was. She didn't mean to be, but she was, because the actor from the Studio wasn't sincere, and after she had written the entire score, he told her that her music wasn't French enough. And the publisher said talent alone was not enough. So she went to Sonny's apartment and hid in bed for two days, alternately weeping and reading Virginia Woolf, telling Evelyn she meant to quit college.

"Oh my God," wailed Evelyn. "They told me this would happen at the beauty parlor."

Sonny came in to her room in the midst of Chris' second day of mourning. He looked very tired, and very vulnerable, so Chris considered the possibility that he might be a human being even if he lived in the realms of coin.

"You don't have to say anything," Chris said. "The only reason I was going to quit college is that there wasn't any reason to stay. Now I have a reason to stay. You won't let me leave."

He smiled a very tired smile, but the little of energy in it crept into his eyes. "That isn't the reason," he said, and pointed to a portrait on the wall above her bed, that was maybe a Rembrandt (Evelyn wasn't sure, she hadn't had time to have it authenticated since the auction).

"There's your reason," he said very softly, indicating the warm brown and red tones of the painting. "All art will show itself in its time. Don't rush the calendar."

So she went back for exams, and continued writing songs and plays and a few secret poems she didn't tell Lionel about—as if he would ask her. When they saw each other by mistake, coincidence (she had planted herself in front of his dorm), the most he'd ask her for was a cup of coffee, and that proffered with a growl.

She gave an oral report on Freudian symbolism in the works of Virginia Woolf, particularly *Mrs. Dalloway,* in freshman composition class, in which she contended that Septimus Smith was a phallic symbol. "His knife represents a penis," she said, and three girls from Brearley grew very pale, and the teacher took her aside after class and asked her if she'd ever considered going to Bennington.

She had considered what she considered every possibility. None of them satisfied her, least of all being someplace she seemed to belong, like Bennington, where everyone was odd. All art would show itself in its time. What a very smart man Sonny was. A very kind man, she owed him the benefit of the hope.

And money for tuition and books and clothes. Her father had called her for the first time in several years, just when she was graduating from Coventry Hall.

"We've settled in Tennessee," he said. "It's a very fine place. Room to grow. Room to learn. Plenty of room for you."

"Thank you, Daddy," she told him.

"You can come and live with us and go to the University of Tennessee."

"I've been accepted at Bryn Mawr."

"The University of Tennessee is better."

"I don't think so," Chris said.

So they stopped speaking again.

And Sonny was paying for everything—her size twenty dresses, her new nose if she decided to get a new nose. Her books. Her Easter vacation in Washington, D.C., where it was written in very high chambers:

something worthy to be remembered

"I don't understand what Napoleon's doing on the wall in the House of Representatives," Chris said that night at dinner at Arnold's.

Arnold was determined to stay through the whole meal, in spite of the phone calls that kept coming in, announced as urgent. "Why shouldn't he be?"

"Jefferson's up there. He deserves only the best company."

"Napoleon was a great man."

"But he wasn't just," Chris said.

"Who says great leaders have to be just?"

"Don't you think it helps?"

"It doesn't help achieve greatness if you have to keep worrying about justice."

"You think Hitler was great?" asked Chris.

"No, I think he was foolish. He made a mistake."

"The idea of world conquest?"

"The Jews," said Arnold.

"You're kidding," said Chris, and tried not to eat her potatoes.

"Of course he's kidding," said Sonny. "He's always been a kidder. The thing that I look forward to in this country is seeing what happens with Presidents and war. It's always been that you could judge the importance of a war by whether or not it produced a President. Maybe the day will come when you can judge the importance of a President by whether or not he produces a war."

"Oh, stop beating around the bush with thinking and conversation," Evelyn said. "Why don't you ask him? Try to shore up your ever-failing finances. This is supposed to be a period of unprecedented prosperity. And you are on the unprecedented balls of your ass. Get some tips from Arnold on tunnels or something, Arnold could help you with that, couldn't you, Arnold?"

"No."

"You wouldn't be in Washington if it weren't for Sonny."

"The table is no place for arguments," Sonny said.

"Then why don't we adjourn to the bedroom and really get into it," Evelyn said.

"Why don't you drop dead," suggested Sonny.

"I was just thinking the same about you."

"Stop, stop," said Sarah.

"Big man, Arnold Sterne. Big man. Small enough to twist things before, but now that he's Senator, no undue influence. Christ. The whole country is based on exchanging favors. You really believe the promises you made? They were *Sonny's* promises. And now you won't lift a hand to help your brother."

"I happen to take my office seriously," said Arnold.

"Your office," Evelyn snorted. "I've seen your office. Some decorator."

"Leave the table," Arnold said coolly.

"Who do you think you're talking to," Evelyn flared. "I am not one of your loyal legion of followers. Get your hands out of the salad, Norman! I see what you've done to Sonny, Arnold. You've turned him into a blob. How do you think I feel when I have to drag him out of bed every morning to get him to go to the office, because he can't face it anymore. I don't know why he even bothers to get up."

"She tells me that every morning when she wakes me," Sonny said, and tried to smile.

"The only thing that sickens me more than getting him up in the morning is going to bed with him at night."

"Okay," Sonny said, and threw down his napkin. "That's it. Get out of here." He got up from his chair, his shoulder moving. "We'll continue the discussion upstairs."

"I haven't finished my dinner."

"Oh yes you have. Let's get out before I drag you out."

"I am not impressed with threats of physical violence."

"How about actual violence?" Sonny was breathing very heavily.

"Oh that I like," Evelyn said. "You still think you have it in you?"

He started moving around the long wooden table toward her. She ran from the room, Sonny chasing, trailing her screams of *son of a bitch, son of a bitch!*

Arnold lowered his head into upraised palms. "Potato," he said. "Potato."

"I agree with what you said about Hitler," Ellis offered his father.

He had come down from his law firm in New York, and made a pass at Chris, because he had no sense of discretion at all, Chris was sure. Or as her friends from the Actor's Studio put it about such men, they would screw a fire hydrant.

"It doesn't strike me as strange that you agree with such a dumb thing, Ellis," Chris said.

"Like mother, like daughter," Arnold said. "He really bought a package. *Schmuck*. Potato. Poor son of a bitch *schmuck*."

"Can I have some more bread?" Norman looked up from the book to the right of his plate.

"I don't think he's a *schmuck*," said Chris. "I think he may be the smartest man I know."

"I used to think that too," said Arnold. "Until he married your mother."

"Well, we all make little mistakes," Chris said. "Even Hitler made one little mistake."

Later that night when Chris and Sonny were the last two up, and/or speaking, Sonny was talking about the plans they were making for the astronauts to go to the moon. "Can you imagine? They're going to the moon one day. And they've got it planned down to the last detail, they even know how many cigarettes an astronaut will smoke on the way to the moon. How many cigarettes. Imagine." There was fire in his eyes, the first time in a long time she had seen enthusiasm sparking there.

"It occurs to me sometimes that had I taken a different path, I might have been a scientist," Sonny said.

"What made you go into banking?"

"Oh I don't know." He turned his head sideways so the light from the fire picked up the silver in his hair, "Greed. Wanting to eat. Arnold." He waved his hand. "One of those things."

"You would have made a fine politician," Chris said.

"Oh, I don't know . . ." He rubbed his eyes.

"You would have been a statesman!"

Sonny laughed. "You think so?"

"For sure. A great statesman."

"Then I wouldn't a gotten elected," Sonny said.

It was July 21, 1953, six months after Arnold had been sworn in in chambers, right up there, and in all that time, he had yet to speak on the Senate floor. He wanted the moment to be right, he wanted an issue to be introduced that meant something, he believed Sonny's promises, yes, Evelyn was right. So far he had limited himself to the Ayes and Nays, he refused to thrust himself out in the center of that arena until he had something that really was an issue, that would actually make a mark.

Besides, they hardly recognized him. The procedural rules were infinite. The chair recognizes the chair recognizes the chair. But he'd learned enough in almost seven months. He had traded a couple of favors, spoken to a few wives, promised a few votes. ("Give me a break introducing this bill, Charley, you got my pledge on the bridge authority. Let me get this one in, Ronny, I promise you your dam.")

". . . and let the peace that is God in His highest mercy continue to bless this land . . ." the clergyman for the morning invoked.

". . . the secret is uninvolvement," whispered a Senator on Arnold's right to the Senator three desks away.

"Let the love that is mankind's joy in its highest order pervade this country . . ."

"I go along with you, there, Al," the Senator whispered back.

"Let the meaning of brotherhood flow from these chambers, like a sea of grace, to all corners of this great nation . . ."

"Then I can count on your vote?"

"You got it."

". . . And from this great nation, to the rest of the world. Amen."

It was going to happen: he was finally getting on his feet. Arnold at last would be up there, recognized, by God, introducing his resolution. With people paying attention, as many as were present.

He had noted on the way in to the floor of the Senate, that on the Senate calendar it was the legislative day of July 6th, although the actual date was the 21st. The calendar roared on, but not the Senate. Fifteen days behind time itself.

That day Joseph McCarthy took the floor to defend Roy Cohn. Cohn had been mentioned in less than flattering terms by Senators Monroney of Oklahoma, and Lehman of New York. Senator McCarthy was taking the time to read aloud in the

Senate a letter that Lehman once wrote to Alger Hiss. "Lehman is no communist-fighter," Joe McCarthy said.

Later in the day, Lehman took the floor to defend himself, pointing out that the letter was written long before the mess with Klaus Fuchs and Hiss was even beginning, that since the letter was written the people of New York had returned him to office, to his Senate seat with an outstanding plurality. Joe McCarthy answered, "Did I correctly read the Senator's letter? I will read it again."

He read it again. Arnold was getting not only thrown but angry. It had been his intention to introduce only his resolution, to set aside the month of August as New Jersey Garden Club Month. By the Senate passing his resolution, they would be according proper recognition to the outstanding work done by these clubs, it said in Arnold's text. Please the folks back home, it said in his country boy heart. Also, there was going to be a National Garden Club convening in Washington shortly, and there could be national votes out there, if Arnold wanted to try for the Vice-Presidency in the near future, it said in his very smart head. Lock in the wives of the cronies, the big machine people, with roses outside their windows.

"Mr. President." Arnold addressed the chair. "Would the Senator from Indiana yield?"

Senator Capehart mumbled his assent, long enough for Arnold to introduce his resolution. "Mr. President, today I have submitted a Senate resolution." (He received a wink from Taft, the Majority leader, a gesture that summed up a relentless amount of finagling that had been done to pave the way for the resolution). "Mr. President, I submit the resolution and ask for its immediate consideration."

"The resolution will be stated," said the presiding officer.

At that point the legislative clerk then read the resolution (S. Res. 107). "Is there any objection to the immediate consideration of the resolution?" Taft said.

Arnold felt the anxious pause; Taft looked at the acting Minority leader. "The chair hears none, and it is so ordered."

Arnold could hear the premature echo of greatness. "Mr. President, I move the adoption of the resolution."

"This is on agreeing to the resolution. All in favor say Aye. (Ayes) Opposed: Nay. (Nays) The resolution is agreed to."

"Mr. President," said Arnold. How many were watching? More coming in. "I move to reconsider the vote by which the resolution was agreed to."

"I move to lay that motion on the table," Taft said. "All in favor: Aye. (Ayes) Nay? (Nays) the resolution is agreed to."

Then back to the chamber again came Joe McCarthy. "Mr. President, I ask unanimous consent that the vote by which Senate resolution 107 was agreed to be reconsidered."

At which point, "Mr. President, reserving the right to object," several Senators said. There was much confusion. "Mr. President, I object," said the Minority leader. He was objecting to the reconsideration.

There was gavel pounding. McCarthy trying to recapture the floor. People coming into the Senate.

"Mr. President," said Senator McCarthy. "I renew my request to ask unanimous consent."

At which point several Senators, entering the chamber, seeing it was McCarthy speaking, objected automatically. It ended with a quorum call.

He had slipped it by McCarthy. The resolution passed. Everybody was there to hear Lehman defend himself. They were all coming to hear. A garden club was not big enough.

"Mr. President," said Arnold. "Before I make my remarks, may I propound a parliamentary inquiry to the chair?"

"Will the gentleman yield?" said Joe McCarthy, after bigger game than gardens.

Arnold smiled and looked up. "I would yield to my distinguished colleague from Wisconsin . . ." Arnold paused, "if I could ascertain that he were my distinguished colleague."

Once, on the floor of the Senate, Senator Sumner had been beaten senseless by the nephew of Andrew Pickens Butler, whom he had verbally attacked. That was the only such violent incident in the history of the Senate.

"He can't do that!" Joe McCarthy shouted. "Senatorial immunity or no, he can't talk about me on the floor of the Senate. The rules protect me."

"This is a parliamentary inquiry," Arnold continued. "Mr. President, under the rules of the Senate, would it be in order to call the gentleman from Wisconsin either a fool or an idiot?"

There was no hesitation. "The chair rules that under Rule Nineteen, Paragraph Two, no Senator in debate shall directly or indirectly by any form of words impute to another Senator or to other Senators any conduct or motive unworthy of or unbecoming a Senator."

"This was not a debate, Mr. President, this was a parliamentary inquiry. Nonetheless, I shall not call him either a fool or an idiot. Nor will I speculate as to what I would have done, had the chair not so ruled, with the wise knowledge of the rules that befits a presiding officer of this, the world's greatest deliberative body. Had the chair not so ruled," Arnold scratched his chin, "I might have gone so far as to call him an enemy of the people, and that would have been inexcusable, what with the rules being as they are. Had the rules not been so, we could speak of a member of the government whose main interest is subversion of the laws when the business of government is to uphold those laws. But as the chair has ruled, I may not say these things, I shall not say these things. Still, I might have observed, as Churchill said, the truth is incontrovertible."

"I'll kill him. I'll give that son of a bitch a verbal caning, I'll drive him to the wall, I'll drive him out of the Senate!" Joe McCarthy said later.

"You mustn't get excited," said one of his aides. "You're into something bigger than being upset at a personal opinion."

"Expressed on the floor of the Senate? I should have struck him on the spot."

"Wise that you didn't, sir."

"Where the hell is that bastard?" McCarthy said in the Senate cloakroom.

487

"You looking for me, Senator?" Arnold said, smiling.

"Who the hell do you think you are? You know how much I could get in damages. You've slandered me. You've defamed. I don't know if there are any precedents in these cases . . ."

"I'll find out for you, sir," said a little dark-haired aide, and scurried to check the books.

"But I'll have your ass, Sterne, I'll have your ass torn to pieces and flung to the dogs . . ."

"For what?" said Arnold. "You'll have other chances to interrupt."

"You said I was not your distinguished colleague. You called me a fool and an idiot." The little eyes darted with rage. "You called me an enemy of the people."

"Oh no. I was tempted to call you those had the chair ruled otherwise. But you heard how the chair ruled. Otherwise."

McCarthy narrowed his eyes, a remarkable feat. "You're a commie!"

Arnold started to laugh.

"I'll find it out," said McCarthy. "I'll find it out. About you or someone in your family."

Arnold crossed his arms in front of his gray suit. "I'll find someone in your family who's *cra-zy.*" He sang the last two syllables.

"I'll have your ass," McCarthy said. "I'll ruin you."

"Oh you have no time for me. You've got much better people to ruin."

McCarthy stepped back and looked at Arnold appraisingly. "You know that's the first right thing you said. I don't have the time for you. You're a very lucky man."

He started to walk away, turned and looked back over his shoulder. "But I may make the time."

NINE

HAVING ESTABLISHED, except through facts, in a speech in
Wheeling, West Virginia, in early 1950, that there were 205
members of the Communist Party shaping the policy of the State
Department, having named Dean Acheson "The Red Dean," Far-
Eastern expert Owen Lattimore "the top Russian espionage
agent in the U.S.," having charged that U.N. Ambassador Philip
Jessup was "preaching the Communist Party line," having doc-
tored a photograph so that Senator Millard Tydings was purportedly talking with former U.S. Communist Chief Earl
Browder, so that Tydings (who had chaired the 1950 Senate
Subcommittee that branded McCarthy's Wheeling charges a
"hoax") lost the next election, having accused the Voice of
America of constructing radio transmitters where they would be
ineffective (which MIT and RCA experts later disproved, by
which time one of the engineers had committed suicide), having

done all that, but still wanting to show more of "Americanism with its sleeves rolled up," his own personal definition of McCarthyism, Joe McCarthy continued to stampede.

He had not been without supporters, besides the fear-ridden American public. "Traitors in the high councils in our own government," had said California Congressman Richard Nixon, "have made sure that the deck is stacked on the Soviet side." "McCarthy may have something," had offered Massachusetts Congressman John F. Kennedy. In 1952 Truman's Attorney General, J. Howard McGrath, had ordered six detention camps readied to accommodate alleged saboteurs and spies. Two of them might have been Truman and Acheson themselves, whom McCarthy had described as "The Pied Pipers of the Politburo," adding, with usual gentleness of tone, when speaking of the President, "the son of a bitch ought to be impeached."

Eisenhower himself had been deeply angered by McCarthy's pronunciamento that General George C. Marshall, Chief of the U.S. General Staff in World War II (later Secretary of State), was "a man steeped in falsehood . . . an instrument of the Soviet conspiracy." But the same Republican convention that nominated "Ike" (liking him) invited McCarthy to address the delegates, hailing the Senator as "Wisconsin's Fighting Marine," while the band played "The Halls of Montezuma" as McCarthy waved and smiled and beamed to the cheers that accompanied him to the stage of the Chicago International Amphitheater.

And the band played on.

Only a gentle fistful of Republicans had ever taken on Joe. Margaret Chase Smith had said, in 1950, that she did not want to see the Republican Party "ride to political victory on the Four Horsemen of Calumny—fear, ignorance, bigotry and smear." But she was only a woman, McCarthy didn't worry too much about those, because nobody listened to women, Senator or no. He could ruin her when he had more time, like he would one day ruin Arnold Sterne.

In 1953 he got busy overreaching, taking on the Grand Old Party itself, accusing the Administration of sending "perfumed notes" to those doing "blood trade" with Red China, believing himself to be, as the *Christian Science Monitor* said, the second most powerful man in the country. "The Senate," that newspaper said, "is afraid of him." So, apparently, was everybody else.

By the middle of 1953 diplomats were handed notes by State Department officials, suggesting they conduct their conversations elsewhere, the place they were sitting in was wired. Opinions that were nonconformist were being reported.

Even Eisenhower was reluctant to fight him. In private the President described McCarthy as "a lawless man," but declined to take him on publicly. "I refuse to get into the gutter with that guy," he said.

"It is not the less fortunate . . . who have been selling this country out," Joe McCarthy cried, "but rather those who have had all the benefits: the finest homes, the finest college educations. And the finest jobs in government. The bright young men who are born with silver spoons in their mouths are the worst." He had seized on something as old and new as America itself, a recurring theme in history, the little Match Girl, her face pressed against the cold window, dreaming of the warm turkey inside, the cakes, the salvation of privilege. The big city smart-alecks who had it all, versus the true blue rednecked American from the backwoods craning to seize the wonder, because it was their birthright, it said in the Constitution, to which Joe McCarthy paid little attention: it was only a document.

He rampaged onto the college campuses, where the blue-blooded silver-spooned bastards were, ferreting out communists in education. One of the places his committee headed for was Bryn Mawr College, where Owen Lattimore's brother Richard was teaching Classical Greek ("A coverup," said McCarthy. "He's his brother. He must be a commie").

"We want to question your faculty," said McCarthy's representative. "There is strong suspicion that the head of the Greek Department may have communist ties."

"What nonsense," said Miss McBride. "Do go away."

There was little that even the maddest of madmen could do in the face of quiet intelligence, even from a woman. So they left Bryn Mawr alone, and headed for bigger game. As did Chris.

In the summer of 1953, the new Humanism that Thomas Mann had predicted in 1943 (to appear very shortly, Mann had said), the wave of compassion, higher purpose, that would lift the country and the world into a period of transcendence had not yet begun to rear its lovely head. But Marlon Brando had.

Being recently turned sixteen, somewhat confused as to the meaning of higher purpose, knowing it wasn't in Joe McCarthy, suspecting it wasn't in Arnold Sterne either, Chris turned her eyes from the flag, and onto the movie screen. There was no doubt in her mind that Brando epitomized the higher purpose of sex, and even though she wasn't interested, Sonny had suggested that one day she might change her mind.

Summer seemed as good a time as any for changes, and one or two people she had met at the Actor's Studio seemed to be very sincere. Janice in particular was not only sincere, she was funny, and very friendly with Marlon. She had actually taken Chris to meet him, let Chris hear his voice bellowing her name down the hall, "Eh—Jaa-ni-ice," as beautifully animalistic as if she were "Stel-la." Janice had sung Marlon one of Chris' songs, while Marlon accompanied on drums, invisible drums, on a desk, on his knees, on Chris' chest. Smiling. What wisdom was in his eyes. What magic in his fingertips. What mystery in his smile.

"Nice, very nice," he murmured, eyes half-closed, grin Dionysian, so Chris wasn't sure if he meant her song or her chest. But it didn't matter. She was committed to him. For the rest of her life if necessary. For the summer, certainly. Lionel Lindenbaum had gone on vacation, and hadn't even told Chris where.

So she wangled an invitation to visit Janice at Falmouth, Massachusetts, where Marlon was summer-stocking his own production of *Arms and the Man*. Accompanied by a cast of his friends, and some hangers-on, of whom Chris was the newest, although she did not consider herself one. She considered herself only a lover of the arts, of which Brando was the finest hour, for the moment at least, spreading the glory of words and emotions through a slight veil of imperfect diction and hostility, which anyone with the least bit of perception could pierce. She was nothing if not perceptive. And sixty-five pounds overweight.

"Hey, hey," he muttered over blueberry breakfast, where ten of them sat in the outdoor niche of a cottage kitchen, eating at a wooden table, grownups at camp. "You don' wan' any cream on your blueberries?" Marlon Brando actually said to her.

"No thank you," said Chris, praying he could X-ray, along with his other great powers, to how pretty she might be underneath.

"You fin'lly on a diet?" Marlon said.

"Oh come on," said Maureen Stapleton, who was there appearing in *Three Men on a Horse* in the evenings while Brando rehearsed his production during the day. "Leave the kid alone."

"I was oney askin' if she wanned the cream."

"You're in no position to judge anything, Natural Beauty," Maureen said. "No one knows the meaning of true unhappiness unless they weighed a hundred and eighty-two pounds in high school."

At that moment Chris considered the possibility that Maureen Stapleton might be a greater artist than Brando. Without question she was the finest actress in the world, although Chris hadn't seen her in anything yet.

"Listen," said Marlon to Chris, "it's nothing to get embarrassed about. It's okay if you want to eat. I just happen to think most girls are prettier thin."

He said it perfectly. She wanted to die of shame.

"Skin-deep, Eighth Wonder," sang Maureen to Marlon, "try to remember that one."

He went into the theater to inspect the rehearsal set: the flats were all gray, the living room mournful and somber. "This is *Shaw,* not Gorki!" he yelled at the stage manager. "It looks like *The Lower Depths!*"

Intellect! (Heartbeat.) Chris could hardly believe it. She would write a song about him, a book about him, she would go to parties where he might be, become mute at parties where he was, befriend his cast-off women, she would know exactly what he wanted so when she finally became worthy of him . . . thin enough, pretty enough, good enough . . .

"Okay, chub." He indicated her. *"Company onstage!"* he shouted. "Phil, Marie, find Sam. You, outside." He nodded to Chris. "Closed rehearsal. You can see the Dress. Not before."

In the afternoons, she would go for walks with Wally Cox, who was there in *Three Men on a Horse.* The cheeriest mind she'd ever found in a seemingly mcek man's body. He knew every stratum of the terrain that welled up around them, what stone formed the hills that he climbed, was a secret explorer of uncharted ravines which he'd go through with friends twice as big, twice as daring. But somehow they always took the easiest path, his friends did. "Sometimes, ending in blind alleys," Wally lilted.

"I, on the other hand, oftentimes choose the more difficult path. Nature has ways of fooling us, you see, because she doesn't like to give herself away. More often than not, the most treacherous trail, if you handle it with appropriate caution, will get you home safely, a long time before the others.

"Only last week, Bobby and I went out climbing. He's very strong, you know, he thinks. I chose the top trail, and he thought that I was crazy. At one point he fell twenty feet and was struck unconscious. I, on the other hand, made my way safely through this very narrow-seeming wedge in the rock; true I bloodied my hands—I moved through balancing myself on two toes and four fingers—that's all there was room for in the rock, which was decomposing sandstone."

Geologic description along with adventure stories. What a remarkable man he was.

"The sadness is," Chris said, "nobody realizes that you're death-defying."

"Not the sadness." He grinned a silly-boy grin, eyes shining through his spectacles. "That's the wonder. The mystery. The happy part."

Sometimes, only rarely (one hour out of two) she would drift the conversation over to Marlon, with whom Wally had been friends since boyhood (the two of them actually referred to their "boyhood") in Libertyville, Illinois. "But why does he have a contempt for movies?" Chris said. "He's revolutionized a whole industry. Don't you see? They'll be finished with pretty boys now, it'll be nothing but actors, and interesting faces, and he'll be directly responsible for changing it, he's a great revolutionary force for acting, he's a dynamo, he's changed the whole face of an industry," she said, trying not to sound as if she were really excited about Marlon Brando. "He's the greatest thing in our lifetime to happen to the movies."

"Thank you, thank you, thank you," said Wally softly. "Thank you, thank you, thank you." He looked up and smiled at her. "I have to say that, because Marlon never will."

He kissed Chris goodbye on the cheek, the night he went away (knowing that her lips and her heart, like all the rest in Falmouth, belonged to another). "Adieu, Real Person!" said Wally.

"You think I'm a real person?" She still wasn't sure. She needed all the validation she could get.

"Well, look," he said and turned her around very gently, so she was facing the sea. And could see all the cottages that sloped down and up intervening hills, dotting the night with brightness. "Look at all those lights out there," he whispered. "Does any one of them represent you?"

"No."

"Then how can you ask such a question?"

Right. When there were so many more important questions to be asked: Would Shaw be pleased with the production? Would Sukie Howell and Paula Schwartz from Denbigh Hall really go to Washington this summer, tear off all their clothes in McCarthy's office, and yell "Rape"? Would it be more effective if some boys from Haverford did it? Had there been any truth at all to Bridey Murphy? Would the chlorophyll really be working if Marlon Brando ever spoke to her within breathing distance?

He played Sergius in *Arms and the Man*. He was terrible. She saw no reason to love him less, because he couldn't do comedy.

Joe McCarthy could. Joe McCarthy had done his act on some people in the theater who could never get work again until they were too old to play the parts they were born to play, and had to settle for character roles, when they were meant to be a STAR!!!! Joe McCarthy could really do comedy, and not just in the Senate. Joe McCarthy was a regular roadshow, traveling all over the country, using different names in different places—in different times, but always a star attraction, getting the Hollywood Ten and a number of very big talents who would never work again (ha ha), even the ones who weren't in jail would be punished (so there!). Joe McCarthy had really gotten his act together: all those different faces, all those different times, brought back together at last for the first time in person: McCARTHYISM! What a show!

So a lot of lights that might have lit up old Broadway went out before they had a chance to shine. Chris met a number of them that summer. Through the blacklisted actors she met, she met an unofficially blacklisted poet. Unofficially. That meant that the chances were good that he'd be skipped over for a number of prizes he deserved, and that those spoken of in loud whispers would be his house guests from time to time.

Limited income. It meant that, too. Fortunately, he didn't have to worry about money, as his wife was Clifton Sanger's younger sister. Their houses were adjacent in Marblehead, Massachusetts; Eloit Beniel and Clifton Sanger, the banker. Fortunate opposites.

Eloit Beniel was in his late fifties, his smile strung down sad at the edges, a poet's smile, a poet's laughter in the sorriest moment invading his eyes. His hair was already white, his shoulders slightly bent, as if from the weight of reminding people that words had some meaning. Even in the middle of madness. Even at the edge of a rope.

The one he held on to was not so frayed as those of his friends, who did not live on inherited income. He and Lahdee (Lahdee Da, her full nickname, known to intimates as "Lahdee") got by very nicely on forty to sixty thousand a year, depending on whether or not they were entertaining those who could no longer afford to entertain themselves, or had no wish to, having had opinion about themselves lowered in recent years. The rest of Lahdee's income from the Sanger estate, they gave to a number of causes, starting with friends, moving to friends they thought they might have made, had they the time. About three or four thousand came in yearly from his poetry, plus the fees he received from the colleges that would have him lecture, ever decreasing, what with the way things were going nowadays.

Still, he didn't mind, Eloit Beniel told Chris. He believed those who wanted to hear him would read his words, and those who didn't deserved to remain ignorant, "And confused," he added, "not having the clarity of my poems."

"But that's awful," she said. "You should speak. You're a wonderful talker." She herself had spent three hours listening to him, over coffee, even though Marlon Brando was performing in the barn. "You should have a guest lectureship somewhere, you should teach poetry at college."

"If I taught poetry," he said softly, "I might not be able to write it. Few are the men who can talk about words who can put them on paper. Fewer still are the men who can judge words, and write them."

"Would you read my poems sometime?" she asked him.

"Sure, I'll read your poems," said Eloit Beniel, leaning back into deeper shade of night, where the leaves of the trees touched the benches they sat on, warming wood against dew. "I'll bet you're a very good poet."

"A tyro," said Chris. "The man I love told me my poems were immature."

"How old are you?" Eloit sucked on his pipe.

"Sixteen."

He laughed.

"Well, that's me," Chris said. "Lionel's almost twenty."

Lahdee was as warm, as giving as Eloit was poetic and abstract. She fell frequently into hugging, of which Chris was often the recipient, telling Chris that when she was a girl, she, too, had had a weight problem, and there was nothing wrong that a little love couldn't make right. Chris was quick to realign herself with parental, poetic affection, as she couldn't see herself as camp follower, even summer camp follower when the order of the camp was theater, with a few games organized during the day by Mendy Wager. *Arms and the Man* was nearly concluded, summer meant nothing special at all to actors, there was no way she could tromp after them when they went their separate ways. There were too many women waiting in cars, and by their telephones, and on tropical islands and in India for Marlon Brando.

So when the Beniels said Chris would have to visit them in Marblehead sometime, she asked if the following week would be too soon. "Are you crazy?" asked Evelyn, when Chris returned to New York, to buy some bathing suits, which she had been too wise and modest to take to Falmouth. "You can't hang around with those people. Your uncle's a Senator. Joe McCarthy hates his guts."

"He's after Arnold," Chris said. "He isn't after me."

"He's after anybody he can get. Stay away from those people."

Parents? Love? The lure was irresistible.

As irresistible as friendship had been, Muggy, Bethie, Rooney Cortega, her third-best friend. Rooney, like Chris, came from a broken home, accompanied by fanfare. Rooney's father had been South American royalty, a famous composer, who ran off with the wife of his conductor, leaving the mother with three children, very small. Rooney's mother had remarried to a great deal of publicity, all of which Chris had been too young to read, Rooney too young to remember.

All Chris knew about Rooney was that she was sensitive, hurt, and much too tall, giving them the shared instant understanding of sisters. Rooney had come over for dinner the first week of

June, before summer (and Marlon Brando) really took hold. Rooney had run through the giant apartment of the Sternes like a very long bird, flapping free wings, finally barefoot.

"All of the people you could have connected with at Bryn Mawr," Evelyn said very quietly after Rooney went home. "And you had to pick up another freak. No shoes."

"Maybe she felt comfortable here."

"Really?" said Evelyn. "Where was she brought up, in a barn?"

Not exactly. The home Rooney lived in during the school year was a few blocks from the Mayor's mansion, an exquisite town house, very formal, on East End Avenue. Chris was invited for dinner there a few days after Rooney had flown through the Sterne apartment. The dinner was served by a butler and a maid (hamburgers on a silver tray), and Rooney's mother wore a diamond on her index finger. It flashed at Chris the whole time Rooney's mother served herself, with oversized sterling utensils.

"Her index finger?" said Evelyn contemptuously, insisting on a full report of the origin of the species that flew.

"It didn't seem strange on her hand," Chris said. "She has very graceful hands. It was the biggest diamond I ever saw. I guess you'd think it was vulgar."

"There are no such things as vulgar diamonds." Evelyn filed her nails. "There are only vulgar aquamarines."

"Anyway their house is beautiful. Rooney's stepfather is the chairman of the Knickerbocker Fine Arts Museum. I guess they lend him the paintings when they're not on display. The walls are covered with Renoir and Van Gogh and Pissarro . . ."

"The chairman of the Knick . . ." Evelyn swallowed, and tried to speak slowly. "Cortega," she said. "Rooney Cortega. Was her mother Elizabeth Cortega? The Countess?"

"I don't know," Chris said. "Rooney just called her 'Mother.' "

"And her stepfather?" Evelyn drank some water. "Isn't he Clifton Sanger?"

"Yes, do you know him? He's the chairman of the Knickerbocker Fine Arts Museum."

"And what about the *banks?*" Evelyn shrieked. "And what about the *stables?* And the *railroads?* What's the matter with you, don't you know *anything?*"

"I knew he was the chairman of the Knickerbocker Fine Arts Museum."

"You said that three times!" Evelyn lit a cigarette. "My God, the things that impress you. *Lend* him the paintings. You think they *lend* him the paintings. He *owns* the paintings, you silly child. When are you going to learn what's really important?"

"When are you going to learn what's really important?" she was shrieking again, now, as Chris was packing her suitcase to go up to Marblehead. "Visiting Communists, for Christ's sake, with McCarthy after your uncle, and your stepfather practically on the balls of his ass. Have you no sense of values at all?"

"They're very nice people. He's a brilliant poet. She's a wonderful woman. They may be the nicest people I've met in my life."

"Everybody's the nicest people you've met in your life. When are you going to start sifting? You certainly didn't inherit your judgment from me. I should have let you go with your father, where is he now, that son of a bitch, he still owes me child-support for you, from nineteen forty-one till this very day. Why don't you go back to him and let McCarthy start chasing his tail instead of Arnold's? That's all Sonny needs at this point in his life is a finger pointing Communist at his brother. Eloit Beniel. Of all the people in the world you have to visit. You're still under age. I think I'll forbid you to go. Unpack that bag."

Chris took a deep breath, to stop the pounding in her brain. "The Beniels live next door to Rooney in Marblehead."

Evelyn sat down. "You mean that sweet little thing from Bryn Mawr who's too tall? Your girlfriend who was so comfortable here in our home that she took off her shoes, and her mother married Clifton Sanger?"

"That's right."

"So if you went to stay with the Beniels, you could see your friend, Woomey." Evelyn stood.

"Rooney," said Chris, folding clothes.

"And become even closer friends than you are. And get even friendlier with her family." Evelyn grew taller with each sentence, as she swung herself out into her own clasped palms. "And maybe she'd invite you to stay another week. And we could come up and visit you, and stay at a hotel." She was almost singing; then she saw Chris' face and tried to talk calmly, with reason.

"And Sonny could meet Clifton Sanger. You know you really love Sonny, that's a good choice on your part. You know how important it would be for him to meet Clifton Sanger. How he's wanted to meet Clifton Sanger. Go ahead. Go. Stay with those nice communists."

"It was never established in a court of law that they were communists."

"Don't be silly, I've read his poems. He believes in sharing. But that's all right. Have a good time with them. And get friendly with the Sangers."

"Why, Mother," Chris said, smiling. "You're teaching me to infiltrate."

"It's a shame you're so fat. You are clever. And people seem to like you. They'd probably love you if you were thinner." Evelyn lit another cigarette. "Maybe we could have your nose fixed. No. I guess there isn't time."

Mornings they sailed. Lahdee was Captain, having been raised on what Eloit called "the Sport of Gentiles." Chris tried to pick up all the terms, and not get in anyone's way. Mainly she lay back in occasional sunlight and smiled as Eloit sang sailing songs, and helped his wife tack with the breeze.

Afternoons he read aloud from his poetry. And talked of philosophy. And politics. And their friend Alger Hiss, who had been convicted of perjury, perjury only, on the testimony of a nut, in Eloit's opinion. Time would vindicate Alger Hiss, Eloit was convinced of it. But time would not alter the public's opinion that Hiss had been found guilty of being a communist.

"Which is not the truth," said Lahdee.

"Truth has little to do with public opinion," said Eloit, and listened to some of Chris' poems.

Her fifth night there they were invited to dinner at the Sangers'. Chris watched the great Clifton Sanger himself ignoring his brother-in-law, lending the main part of his concentration to the paella Chris had prepared in the Beniel kitchen, for four hours, and brought over in a giant pot.

"Where did you learn to cook?" Sanger said.

"I taught myself," Chris said. "My grandma's a fabulous cook. My mother won't let me into the kitchen. She's afraid the help will quit if I get in their way. So I cook whenever I can, in other people's houses."

"I can't understand how I never married you," Clifton Sanger said.

Chris laughed too loud. "My mother said, 'I can always get another daughter, but I'm not sure I can find another maid.' "

"We who have been well brought up," said Elizabeth Cortega Sanger, "never discuss family at table."

Eloit Beniel belched. Rooney and Chris exchanged clumsy glances. Rooney's older brother held hands under the table with his house guest, a junior at Princeton. The younger brother was off in Newport, preparing for a regatta.

"When the Beniels have had enough of you, why don't you come stay with us?" Clifton Sanger said.

"We're expecting the Hertfords next week," Mrs. Sanger said.

"Fine," said Clifton Sanger. "Chris can do the cooking."

"Whoopee," said Rooney.

"I don't know what they teach you at Bryn Mawr," said Mrs. Sanger to Rooney. "It certainly can't be language."

"You really want to stay with those tight-asses?" Eloit Beniel said, when they were back in his house, and Chris was putting the rest of the paella away in a Pyrex dish.

"I like Mr. Sanger. He's a very nice man."

"It's men like Clifton Sanger who've put this country where it is today."

"You're talking about my brother," said Lahdee. "It isn't his fault he's rich."

"Exactly," said Eloit.

"He's been very good to Rooney," said Chris. "She's my third-best friend."

By the second day Chris was house-guesting with the Sangers, Rooney had been upgraded to her second-best friend, dreams and hopes having been exchanged on a roommate basis. Chris was in love with poetry and Marlon Brando, Rooney in love with music, which she couldn't tell her mother because of her father's being a composer who had deserted them. "But it gets in your blood," she said. "You understand that?"

"Of course," said Chris, remembering *Streetcar,* and the soft lilt of Eloit Beniel.

The Sternes flew up for the weekend, Evelyn ensconcing them, and baby Angela, and the nurse, in a hotel that wasn't restricted, Sanger having failed to get them into the better one that was. "I'd tell you to have them stay here . . ." said Clifton Sanger. "But we seem to be full up."

The Hertfords were there. And a playwright. And Rooney's younger brother, who was vaguely depressed and sunburned, having lost the regatta. And Rooney's older brother and his house guest, a senior from Harvard. And Clifton Sanger's son from a previous marriage, and his daughter and her fiancee, a banker from another dynasty.

"But they can certainly come for dinner on Saturday," Clifton Sanger said to Chris. "You can do the cooking."

"Saturday we have the O'Neills and the Bensons," said Mrs. Sanger. "Plus the family, and the Campignons, they're motoring in from the Vineyard. They're bringing lobsters. We can't have more than eighteen."

They ended up being invited for cocktails, Sonny and Evelyn Sterne, Sonny strangely subdued, Evelyn checking Elizabeth Sanger's tanned fingers for what was proper for summer jewelry. "We've never actually met," Sonny said, wearing a bright red jacket, and a striped tie that went with the thin white piping on his trousers. Sanger was still in his yachting outfit from the motorboat outing they'd had that afternoon, to which the Sternes had not been invited. ("We're full up, the rules of the waves," Elizabeth Sanger had said. "Besides they probably don't have rubber soles. They'll scuff up the deck, and you know how you are about your deck.")

So they ended up being invited for cocktails.

"We've spoken on the phone a number of times," said Sonny, wondering if he shouldn't have worn a turtleneck, as Clifton Sanger did. "Or at least I've spoken to your secretary," he said, taking a stuffed mushroom from the tray being passed on the veranda by one of the maids. "You sent my wife some flowers, when she was ill."

"I'm glad to see she's looking so fit," said Clifton Sanger, watching Evelyn with admiration. She was moving around the twilight, dressed in appropriate white slacks, a little blue blazer, a sailing cap on her dark red-black curls, as if she had been on the motorlaunch after all.

"I've been really anxious to meet you," Sonny said, honesty being the best policy when one didn't have time to beat around the bush. "There's a merger that's coming up, and I thought perhaps your bank might be interested. We're a little undercapitalized, but the risk is minimal, and the prospects . . ."

"You in finance?"

"Investment banking," said Sonny, trying to catch Sanger's wandering eye. "Sterne and Sterne."

"Arnold Sterne?"

"Arnold's my brother. I'm Abraham."

"Chris said your name was Sonny."

"It's a nickname," he said. "A very old nickname. From when I was young."

"Mine used to be Poopey," said Clifton Sanger. "I don't know where they come up with these things. My mother still calls me Poopey. There's no way to tell your mother to shut up. Haven't you found that to be true?"

"My mother is dead."

"I'm sorry," said Sanger. "Would you like another drink?" He moved his head slightly to the right, and a butler hurried over. "Gin and tonic," he said, putting his own glass on the tray. "With lime. Lightly pressed against the glass, Louis. Not squeezed. Sterne? What will you have?"

"Scotch and soda," said Sonny, putting his glass on the tray. "Anyway, this is really a pleasure for me. A very lucky coincidence, Chris and Rooney being so friendly."

"She's a nice girl, your daughter, it's a pleasure to have her with us. A hell of a cook."

"Thank you," said Sonny. "About the merger, it's really a very simple issue . . ."

"I never talk business on holiday," Clifton Sanger said. "Call me in the city. Excuse me. My other guests." He walked away.

"Why, sweetheart," said Evelyn, coming over to Sonny. "You look like your world just collapsed. Mustn't let it show on your face. Try to appear somewhat bored, like the really rich."

"Shut up," Sonny whispered.

"Why, honey, what happened, didn't he fall for your line? A rich smart man like Clifton Sanger?"

"Go charm the rest of the guests," said Sonny, "Leave me alone."

"Don't take it out on me," sang Evelyn. "After all, I bought it all, hook, line and sinker. And that's what it was."

"Go to hell," Sonny murmured.

"I prefer Marblehead," sang Evelyn, and wafted off into the evening breeze.

Chris went out to dinner with them, and the Beniels, who were expecting house guests. They left a note on the door, giving them directions to the restaurant.

"I don't care how much you think you owe this country," Eloit Beniel said to Sonny, waving the corkscrewed tail of a steamer clam. "You're a banker. It's okay for you. What about your daughter?"

"What about her?" said Evelyn.

"They call these piss clams," said Chris. "Even the Sangers call them that."

"Your daughter is a poet," said Eloit. "Poets should not have to struggle their way to impoverished recognition. If she were in Russia, they would dedicate trees to her."

"If," Sonny said, "she wrote about what they wanted her to write. Otherwise she'd be in very big trouble."

Eloit closed his eyes, and chewed for a moment. "You say there are tax advantages on municipal bonds?"

"Very big tax advantages," said Sonny. "In the main, they're tax free."

Eloit dipped a steamer into the broth. "You seem like a nice enough guy," he said. "Put all your money in public utilities."

"Eloit!" the man in his crumpled gray suit said from a few feet away. "What the hell kind of greeting is that, a note on the door."

"Milton!" Eloit got up from the table, and embraced his friend.

"Naomi!" said Lahdee, hugging the tired woman with him.

Sonny looked up. For the first time in a long time, Chris saw pure pleasure, unabashed joy and warmth invade his eyes. "Milton Radnitz," said Sonny, and started shaking his head, shaking Milton's hand till the tears came to both sets of eyes. "Milton, oh Milton, you son of a bitch." On his feet, hugging him. "Where have you been? Where have you been?"

"Abela, Abela!"

"You know each other?" said Eloit Beniel.

"Of course, of course, of course," Sonny said, hugging the very bent shoulders. "We went to law school together. He was my best friend. My best friend."

"Don't say it too loud," cautioned Evelyn. "Chris is staying with the Sangers.

"Where have you been?" said Sonny, pulling up chairs for the Radnitzes. Looking in the eyes that had been old at twenty-two. Empty now. "Where have you been?"

"In jail," said Milton Radnitz. "Where else?"

506

After she left the Sangers, Chris went to Elizabeth Arden's. "Two sons," said Evelyn. "Two sons! And Sanger likes you. You've got to be crazy not to get thin."

Chris decided to do it for Marlon Brando, even though she might not ever see him again, and Lionel Lindenbaum, whom she would see at school the end of September. They were not unlike, both being brooders, blue-eyed, and hardly aware of her. Yes, she would do it, she would starve herself, and appear like a beacon of love and light. She would never eat again, and find embraces.

She fasted her way through the rest of the summer, the tree-cloaked part of it at Maine Chance, Elizabeth Arden's little hideaway, which the girls (there for "Teenage Time," special cut-rate) renamed "Fat Chance," except for Chris, who considered it "Last." There was breakfast in bed (on a tray, half-grapefruit, black coffee) which Chris didn't eat, and lime-buttermilk sherbet and No-Cal, which she likewise skipped. Swiss Kriss, a herbal laxative, she indulged in at bedtime, so she had a constant case of the runs in between exercise classes, conducted on the dock by a woman who'd never been overweight in her life. How could any of them believe she understood problems, even as she instructed them to stretch?

She stayed at Arden's in Maine until it was closed, and spent the rest of the summer fasting in Evelyn's apartment, playing with the baby, and fainting occasionally. When Norman came home from camp, she took him to museums, and drank water while he lunched and teaed and dined. On Labor Day she went on the Sanger launch, which was in New York, anchored in the East River, and declined to have even an oyster. Clifton Sanger told her she really looked considerably better. By the third week in September, she was ready to weigh herself. She'd lost thirty-two pounds. Half a beginning. She let herself go shopping. Size sixteen. More than ideal, less than perfect, but a different size, at least. She bought a number of "flattering clothes," dark and "very slimming," the saleswoman said at Best and Co. She had her hair cut so it fell soft around her face, and hid a lot of the cheeks that were still there.

"Are you the new Chris White?" said a sophomore friend from Haverford, as she sat garbed in navy wool by the fireplace in Rockefeller Hall.

"We heard there was this new girl at Bryn Mawr," said Berkeley Harris, a very nice fellow, a little too clean-cut and blond for her, but a nice fellow nonetheless. "We wanted to see."

She let herself be indulged in glow for at least a minute and a half, trying to keep down the words struggling out of her throat. She managed to be silent for an extra thirty seconds, and tried to swallow the thought before it burst from her, very casually, by her own estimation, although it sounded more like an anxious scream. "Where's Lionel?"

"He's transferred to Columbia," said Berkeley.

She went upstairs and started eating. At the end of three weeks she'd gained back all the weight she'd lost in nine, plus another eight pounds. A hundred and ninety. She took the mirror off her wall and rededicated herself to art.

And a little learning, which was probably a dangerous thing, according to Joseph McCarthy, who managed to pull a great many students at Bryn Mawr away from their books that following spring. ("Watch the hearings," Evelyn said. "You can see G. David Schine, he's very handsome, his father owns hotels, maybe we can get to him through the Shumanns, I used to work for them, maybe we'll go to Boca Raton for Christmas, and we can get friendly with someone who knows the Schines, he'll be out of the Army by then, oh God, the possibilities are endless if you'll only stop eating.")

Chris had cheese and crackers in the television room at Goodhart, the only place on campus with a TV set. It was right down the hall from the Soda Fountain, where she could run and get sodas; the crackers were very dry.

Crackers in general stuck to the inside of her mouth. There had been some famous suicides among undergraduates at Bryn Mawr. One girl had hanged herself from the Gothic turret at the top of Rockefeller, but that wasn't as impressive as the story about the girl who spread rat poison on Hi Ho Crackers and ate them. Chris was not considering suicide, although she knew the only philosophic question, according to the existentialists, was suicide; and that Zeno, the founder of the Stoic Religion, had stubbed his toe at 98, broken it, and was so disgusted with himself he committed suicide. But philosophy was nothing that women were bright enough to concern themselves with, the professor of philosophy at Bryn Mawr told Chris. So suicide, along with philosophy, was not the center of her interest. Still, crackers stuck in her throat.

As did the words of Joseph McCarthy. She watched him wheedle his way through the early days of the Army-McCarthy hearings, watched him bulldoze the Secretary of the Army, Robert Stevens, throwing the meetings into incredible confusion with his constant cries of "Point of order," his not hidden accusations of communism in the ranks of the Army itself, flourishing at Fort Monmouth.

She searched the screen for someone she could recognize besides Roy Cohn and Bobby Kennedy, and Karl Mundt and Stuart Symington, whom she liked, but could not love. She hoped that Arnold would be there, baiting, even though she didn't trust him, and finally set her eyes on someone she could.

His name was Joseph Welch, he was the counsel for the Army. He seemed to Chris a guru among Brahmins, a reedy-voiced gentle-seeming Bostonian, with a rumpled coat and a big bow tie and a manner that suggested if he had a son, the son would not care what a girl looked like, that he might be concerned with what was really inside. Just as Welch himself was softly concerned with what was really bothering Roy Cohn, who seemed, for the first time to be floundering. He was asking Cohn why he had not indeed gone storming after the Army, proclaiming that Fort Monmouth was a breeding ground, a nest of communists.

Needling him, as McCarthy needled witnesses, only gently, very gently. Cohn was searching for words, claiming bad memory, as McCarthy's victims were usually forced to do.

McCarthy, who had said, "I am glad we are on television. I think the millions of people can see how low a man can sink. I repeat. I think they can see how low an alleged man can sink."

And now Roy Cohn sat squirming, as Welch continued his questioning. "When you find there are communists and possible spies in a place like Monmouth, you must be alarmed, aren't you? I don't want the sun to go down while they are still in there. Will you not, before the sun goes down, give those names to the F.B.I.?"

Roy Cohn shifted position. "Mr. John Edgar Hoover and his men know a lot better than I . . . I do not propose to tell the F.B.I. how to run its shop."

Welch smiled, as if he knew, along with the informed public, that at one point McCarthy had threatened to investigate the CIA. "All I am suggesting," said Welch, "is that we just nudge them a little."

"Surely we want them out as fast as possible, sir." Cohn was sweating.

"May I add my small voice, sir, and say whenever you know about a subversive or a communist or a spy, please hurry." He smiled.

Welch tenderly was cutting Cohn to pieces. McCarthy, verging on hysteria at seeing his ally taking the kind of punishment he so much enjoyed administering to his enemies, who were everywhere, sprang to his feet.

"I think we should tell Mr. Welch that he has in his law firm a young man named Fisher who has been for a number of years a member of an organization named as the legal bulwark of the communist party . . . Mr. Welch, I just felt that I had a duty to respond to your urgent request that before sundown, when we know of anyone serving the communist cause, we let the agency know . . . I have been rather bored with your phony requests to Mr. Cohn here that he personally get every communist out of government before sundown."

Joseph Welch raised a tired, lined hand to the left side of his face, seemed to be covering the brain beneath the thinning hair on his head from the onslaught. "Jesus Christ," said Alice, Chris' fourth-best friend, who hoped to go to law school at Yale. "What is the relevance? What is the relevance? Oh my God, that poor guy Fisher. Oh my God. Poor Joe Welch."

Joe Welch seemed to be able to hear Alice. He seemed to be able to hear everybody who had ever been disgusted with Joseph McCarthy. He turned to the Senator from Wisconsin, turned on him, the calm demeanor erased, emotional, honestly indignant. A sharp contrast to himself. An even sharper contrast to McCarthy.

"Until this moment, Senator," Joseph Welch said, "I think I never really gauged your cruelty or your recklessness. Fred Fisher is starting what looks to be a brilliant career with us. Little did I dream you could be so reckless and so cruel as to do injury to that lad. I fear he shall always bear a scar needlessly inflicted by you . . ."

"Amen," said Alice. "So he was once a member of the National Lawyers' Guild, for God's sake, I'd join something with that name."

Welch sat, hand outstretched in front of the microphone, as if in a plea, an angry plea. "Let us not assassinate this lad, further, Senator. You have done enough. Have you no sense of decency, sir, at long last? Have you left no sense of decency?"

He was finished speaking; he walked away into the corridor. He walked out of the hearing room as if it contained something vilely contagious, as if it held a plague a humane man, in spite of his humanity, could not afford to go near, if he wished to survive. If he wished the human race to survive.

"Poor Fred Fisher," said Alice. "He'll be ruined."

"Maybe not," said Chris, angry and excited and appalled. "Maybe he's shown him up for what he really is. Maybe McCarthy's shown himself up. Maybe it's over. Maybe there's hope for this country after all. Again. Finally."

"English major!" said Alice, who majored in political science and knew better.

TEN

THE CALL CAME in early fall of 1955.

"You shouldn't run up the stairs, Puffy," Chris said to the dormitory maid. "You're getting older."

"We're all getting older," Cream Puff said. "How often do you get a long distance call."

Who was it? Her father? Were they speaking again? Lionel Lindenbaum? Had he discovered the error of his ways at Columbia? The Editor of the Princeton *Tiger?* Were they going to let her submit something, after lengthy correspondence, even if she was at Bryn Mawr and a girl? Her mother? No. The rates hadn't changed.

"*Hallo!*" Pappy said. "It's me. In person. Long distance. How about that?"

"Are you all right?"

"I'm almost perfect. This is my first long distance call in my life. How about that? I thought it was time. How are you?"

"I'm fine. How's the family?"

"Together," he said. "I have something very important I need to tell you. That's why I called long distance. Are you ready?"

"I'm ready."

"Remember when I told you the story of my life?"

"I remember."

"You remember when I told you the story of the ferocious bear and how I bit him?"

"I remember."

"You remember the endings of those stories, when I said how everybody lived happily ever after?"

"I remember."

"I lied about that," Pappy said. "It couldn't always be happy, or it wouldn't be life. And it couldn't be ever after or it wouldn't be life. Everything else I told you is ninety-nine and forty-four one hundredths percent pure. I'm hanging up now. I love you. Have a good time."

"I'm in love, Dad," said Ellis.

"I'm happy for you," Arnold said into the phone.

"No, I mean it this time. She's wonderful. I'm deeply and permanently in love. If I have your approval, I intend to marry the girl."

"I can't give my approval till I know her. And something about her."

"That's why I'm calling. I'd like to bring her down to the farm this weekend."

There were some very big issues riding, some politicking that had to be done at parties, but what the hell, it was his son. "I'll tell your mother to make up the guest room."

"Three guest rooms," said Ellis. "I'm bringing her parents and her brother."

"And what about the rabbi," Arnold said. "Are you bringing him too?"

Ellis laughed. "I guess it does sound like we're closing in on you."

"Indeed it does," said Arnold. "But I can take it."

He couldn't really. He found her insipid, a typical spoiled New York princess with an excellent nose job and a pain in the ass for a father. But everybody had to live.

"We're thinking of spreading out from merely accounting," Sharon's father said at dinner, "We're thinking, my son Marc and I, of moving it from an accounting firm to something of greater consequence."

"Well if there are going to be consequences," said Arnold. "I think it's a good idea to make them greater."

Ellis didn't even smile. No sense of humor. His son was a bore. Pity. Well, he hoped they'd be happy together, boring each other. It was pointless to try and head Ellis in a different direction. Anybody smarter would probably see right through him, a dangerous thing in a marriage.

Arnold's daughter, Althea, was away at school, a bright young girl, maybe she'd shape up and capture a ring that was better than brass. And maybe Sonny would leave Evelyn one day soon, and be the man he had started out to be. And maybe Arnold would be Vice-President in '56; things were moving up, things were looking good, there was no point in interfering with natural order. He had no time for petty arguments like "She isn't good enough for you," when she was.

"We've been talking seriously of starting our own insurance company," said Mr. Rafiel, Sharon's father.

"As seriously as that?"

"American Frontier Casualty Company, we've drawn up the papers, how does that sound to you, Senator?"

"Very bold," Arnold said. "Very impressive."

"For a man your age, with your good medical history, we could offer you . . ." He took a notebook with charts out of his jacket pocket. ". . . Oh, a million-dollar policy at a fairly low premium."

"That low," said Arnold, trying to eat his dinner.

"If you paid, for example, the first premium payable trimonthly of, say, three hundred dollars before your fifty-second birthday, we could get you an excellent rate."

"You've made my day," said Arnold.

"So what do you think?" said Ellis, when they were alone in his father's study. "Isn't she beautiful? Isn't she wonderful?"

"So long as you've got your health," Arnold said.

"I don't understand."

"I was afraid of that." Arnold got up from the big wing chair, and stared into the fireplace. "Doesn't it strike you that her father's a little pushy?"

"Well, he's got a way to go if he's going to be in the same league with a Senator. You can't fault him for being ambitious."

"I guess not," said Arnold. "I guess not."

A few Senators and White House aides and Congressmen were kind enough to come to the wedding, which Arnold wanted kept small and in New York, but Harry Rafiel wanted big, and in Washington. "Don't worry, I'll pay for everything," he said.

"In that case," Arnold said, "I guess I'd better buy the policy."

The Senate censure of Joseph McCarthy had taken place on December 2nd of 1954. Since that time he had moved like a ghost through the corridors of the Senate, dropping into hearings, when he heard there were photographers present, asking a few questions, most of them incoherent. The photographers were not interested in pictures of Joe McCarthy. So he went home, bewildered, and drank, and talked endlessly of the past. And of Arnold Sterne, whom he was going to get one day, even though he'd given up on just about everything else, cast aside the advice of die-hards who wanted him to continue the battle. "Like shoveling garbage against the tide," the old leatherneck told them.

Arnold Sterne, however, was garbage into the tide: that was

one of the last clear convictions McCarthy had. Sterne was rising high, much too high for the good of the country, which McCarthy was still convinced he loved. "Check the records," he told one of the last of his loyal aides. "Get some financial stuff on him. He used to be in banking. There's got to be fraud somewhere. The man is a crook. See what you can dig up."

"How about communist affiliation?"

"If it comes up, sure, use it. But I'm afraid that may be over. Get something people today can chew on, like fraud. Fraud's always good."

"There's people checking around my records," Sonny said to Arnold on the phone. "Old files have been stolen, I don't know what the hell is going on."

"Deny everything," Arnold said.

"How can I deny when I haven't been accused? It's like I'm fighting something invisible."

"Nothing's invisible," said Arnold. "Nail the creeps."

"Again," Sarah said, watching Arnold pack the one clean shirt, the extra tie. "Again you're going someplace."

"It's only a speech, Sarah. Only a speech. The ladies of the New Jersey Garden Club. Very boring."

"Not as boring as I am," Sarah said. "Are they?"

"Sarah, it's politics. Those women started out as my biggest supporters. I can't ignore them now, just because issues have gotten greater, and the audiences more important. I can't forget the little ladies who gave me my start."

Sarah sat down on the bed, clung to the big wooden post at the foot of it; as if there were arms there that could give her comfort. "The little ladies. No. You can't forget the little ladies."

"Sarah, I'm going to be Vice-President. It's a different kind of romance, I swear it. I have no time for nonsense. Not anymore."

"How long has it been, Arnold? Twenty-nine. Almost thirty

years." She looked at him with suddenly lively eyes. "I know I never really excited you. I didn't even hope for that. It was enough that you wanted to marry me, that you wanted to be with me. That you wanted to have your children come from me."

"And after thirty years, you're going to start nagging."

"I don't mean to nag." She rested her head on the bedpost, so he couldn't see her face. "I just want to be with you sometimes. Sometimes." She started to cry. "You're my life, Arnold. I don't mind about the other things. I never even hated that woman. I tried to understand. I just want to be with you sometimes, you're my life."

He saw the small tired shoulders moving with silent sobbing. And something in him was very nearly touched.

"How'd you like to come to dinner with me, Sarah?"

"Tonight?" Her face looked almost pretty, streaming tears, streaming love for him. "But what about the ladies?"

"You'll sit on the dais with me. You can listen to my speech. You can have some chicken in cream sauce and overcooked peas. We'll hold hands under the table."

"You'll take me with you to New Jersey?"

"You're Mrs. Arnold Sterne. I'd be proud to take you anywhere."

The plane left out of National Airport. It was a two-propeller job, one that specialized in charter flights, most of them chartered to Arnold Sterne. He had considered buying his own plane, but he figured if they investigated the financial holdings of the candidates, the public might take that badly, Arnold's owning his own plane. He helped Sarah up the small rickety step landing, and into her seat. She was beaming. Actually beaming. The nation should be as easy to pin as Sarah.

"Okay, Joe," Arnold said to the pilot. "We can take off."

Sarah reached across the armrest and took his hand. "I love you, my husband," she said.

He smiled at her, so busy trying to examine the sheer simplicity of her statement, the pleasure in her eyes, that he wasn't even looking at his notes. "What a woman you are, Sarah. What a woman you really are."

"I wish . . ."

"Well, don't get shy with me now, Sarah. We're on a dinner date."

"I wish I could go on a trip with you. A real trip. Someplace special. Besides New Jersey I mean. We haven't ever really taken a vacation, Arnold. Not a long vacation. Do you think we could go someplace special. I mean, when you have time."

"I don't know when I'll get the time."

"But when you get it, can we go someplace special?"

"How about Ceylon?" Arnold said. "They have moonstones on the beaches of Ceylon, how'd you like to gather moonstones with me, Sarah?"

"Oh I'd love it, Arnold. Are there really moonstones?"

"Guaranteed," Arnold said. "Like pebbles on the sand. Moonstones on the beaches of Ceylon."

"I can wait for that." Sarah sat back in her seat. "I know how busy you are. I know how important you are, Arnold. You're the most important man in the country, practically. The most important man in the world, if you ask me."

"I should ask you more often," Arnold said, and smiled, and kissed her, actually kissed her on her small loving mouth.

He was one of those kids, you know, those smart-aleck kids that used to take their parents' car without permission. This evening, though, he took the keys to their plane.

Arnold was hugging Sarah, holding her gently against himself, and he saw the little yellow one-propeller plane spinning its silly circles, taking its dips, doing its loop de loops, like a little cardboard airplane from a cereal box, twirling its way through dusk. "Joe?" he said, almost quietly. "Joe . . . Joe . . . *Three o'clock, Joe! Three o'clock, Joe. He doesn't see us. He doesn't see us!!!*"

"Arnold!" Sarah screamed, as the yellow wing tore into the right propeller.

"Can you save it, Joe?"

"Try, sir." Fire. Spinning toward earth.

"Arnold!"

"You're with me," he said, in the two seconds that were left, holding her fiercely against the trembling. Two seconds that seemed a lifetime, being all there was that was left of a lifetime. "You're with me, Sarah. Hold on."

The path of the wreckage stretched for over a half mile. There were pieces of fuselage strung in the trees, burning wreckage cutting a path like a fire trail through the bushes. Parts scattered. Bodies burned beyond recognition. What they could find of the bodies. The parts that were buckled into the burned-out seats, the torso of a man, it looked like, and a hand, holding on to the hand of what must have been a woman.

There was a bulletin in the middle of "The George Gobel Show." Evelyn was very annoyed when the announcer said, "We interrupt this program to bring you the following bulletin." She loved George Gobel. Or at least she liked him a lot; it was easier watching him than listening to Sonny snoring, exhausted, the Blue List open across his face to shield his eyes from the light, from the facts, from the television.

"Two private planes collided tonight over National Airport in Washington, killing the pilots of both planes, and the passengers, Senator and Mrs. Arnold Sterne. Further details on the eleven o'clock news. We return you to your regular programming."

She sat for a moment, biting her nails, absolutely stricken. Maybe it was only her imagination. Arnold was a very smart man. Maybe he'd arranged a little something to bring him even further into national prominence. Maybe he'd only been hurt. Maybe he wasn't even on the plane at all. Sarah. He wouldn't

5 I 9

take Sarah with him unless he had to. Maybe it was just a curious mistake. There was nothing Arnold couldn't get out of, not like Sonny.

"Sonny?" she shook him. "Sonny."

"What is it?" He pulled the Blue List off his tired eyes. "You still sorry you bought the breakfront at Parke-Bernet?"

"The television. The television just said . . ."

She couldn't get the words out. She didn't have to. The telephone rang. It was Ellis.

"Yeah, Ellis," Sonny said, still lying on his back on the bed, rubbing his eyes. "What's up?"

Joe McCarthy turned off the television. He went to the bottle on the table beside his bed, and poured himself a drink. "Well, it's over," he said to no one, his last vigil cancelled. There was no one listening. "He has been struck down by a greater sword than mine."

The funeral was in Washington. Sonny had wanted it to be in New York because that's where Arnold really belonged. New Jersey thought it should be in New Jersey. But Ellis wanted it in Washington, that's where Arnold had found his greatest glory. Arlington National Cemetery, as befitted a Senator-Soldier. Ellis was thinking of going into politics himself.

"My poor father," Sharon cried. "He only just started the company, and he's ruined. He's ruined. He's going to have to give us a million dollars. Where is he going to get it?"

"Will you shut up and stop whining," Ellis said. "I have to make the arrangements."

They had collected the bodies, what was left of the bodies, and put them in closed coffins. ("Walnut," said Ellis. "Nothing but the best. I want this done with dignity.")

For two days Sonny had wept. She had listened to him weeping. Reached out occasionally to comfort him. "Oh, honey," she said. "I know. I know." She didn't know at all. She had no idea.

She couldn't begin to connect with his grief. She herself felt more anger than sorrow. Only Arnold could pay one premium of three hundred dollars on a million dollar policy and get in a plane crash.

Before the funeral, at the entrance to Memorial Chapel, North Post, Fort Myer, Evelyn paused. "A million dollars," she said to Sonny. "Dead, he's a bigger man than you are alive."

The torment that was raging in Sonny's soul was matched only by the torment raging in his offices. They were closing in on him, the screamers, the hysterics, the ones who believed that Arnold had been all of him that was good. Where were the missing files? "Leave me alone," he tried to tell his creditors. I'm not in business this week. I'm in mourning for my brother."

"So are we," said the manager of the Credit Bank of Long Island. "Our shareholders seem to feel that now that Arnold Sterne is no longer connected with your company . . ."

"He hasn't been connected with it for years," Sonny said.

"But the confidence in Sterne . . ."

"Will you leave me alone? Will you leave me alone?" He stopped taking calls so there was only Evelyn, telling him not to be depressed, why didn't he just declare bankruptcy and kill himself.

"You bitch," he shouted. "You'd like that, wouldn't you? You'd like me to just lie down and die."

"Not at all," said Evelyn. "I'd like you to live. I'd like you to stand on your own two feet, now that Arnold isn't here to carry you. Arnold believed in you, Sonny, he was a brilliant man, you must have something. Why don't you go into politics? Take his place. Of course . . . That's what you should do is take his place."

"I can't do that. It's too late for me to start into politics. I have no political ambition. I'm all I can be."

"No, you're not." She looked at the once powerful man lying prone on his bed, his face a bloated mask of sorrow. Sorrow at loss. Why not turn it to gladness at gain? She loved him, in her own way, she was only terribly disappointed. It hadn't been the way she thought it would be. Nothing was.

Maybe she could make him into something. She'd done it with Walter, gotten him the Navy Cross, quite without meaning to, of course. There was still time. She'd give Sonny courage. That was all he needed. That and a fortune.

"You're not all you can be." She moved to the bed, and sat on the edge, and touched his face. "You're more. You're so much more."

"Sometimes you can be so kind," he said. "I don't understand you."

"How could you?" said Evelyn. "I don't understand myself." She touched his lips, his very dry lips, swollen, and peeling from the salt of sadness. "But you can still be something. You're something already. You've just got to be the most you can be."

"I thought I was a failure." He almost smiled.

"That's how I feel sometimes about myself." Evelyn lit a cigarette. "I don't know why I'm so unhappy. I must be unhappy. Otherwise I don't know why I'm so angry." She blew out the match. "Maybe it's that goddamn Arnold again, getting a million like *that!*" She snapped her fingers.

Sonny sat up and slapped her.

"Why do you have to make everything into a fight?" She held up her hands, as Sonny got up, towering over her.

"My brother is dead! My brother is dead! Can you understand that?"

"I understand that his son has twenty-five million dollars of yours, and he's not giving it back."

"What are you talking about?" Sonny pulled back from the uplifted arms, trembling, and shoved his right hand against his trouser leg so it wouldn't shake.

"Your shares in Joe Pape's that you signed over to Arnold. They're worth twenty-five million."

"We sold them at ten, eleven, something like that."

"You gave them to Arnold, I knew it!" She looked at him triumphantly. "All during that business when Arnold was in trouble, when Catherine was dying." She had suspected it all along, she had stored it in her mind for the ripe time, overripe, when she could use it. "When you were so busy bragging, trying to win me with how brilliant you were, telling me about the trial, and how if you'd taken a different path, you might have been a great lawyer, all that different path bullshit you're always shoveling out, and the reward of Joe Pape's Finest. And never mentioning it again, not after Arnold had all the trouble, Arnold needed bailing out. Never mentioning it again, the glory of Joe Pape's, the income of Joe Pape's." All the time the money was starting to get tight again at the banks, where was the gentle leverage of bourbon shares? He'd given it to Arnold. She'd known it all along.

But she still wasn't sure. "We have the same masseuse, Sharon Sterne and I, Arnold's accomplished daughter-in-law, that dummy. She told the masseuse that her husband would inherit a third of the biggest distillery in the South."

"You're lying."

"No, I'm not." Only a little. Sharon had told the masseuse they would have a massive inheritance from something mysterious. Evelyn cut through the mystery. She could speculate as well as Sonny, that was for sure.

"Why don't you call Ellis and very subtly ask him what he's doing with his share of Joe Pape's?"

Sonny sat down on the chair by the window. "My God, they're in mourning. How can I talk to them about money?"

"How can you talk to them about anything else? They're horrible people. What do you have in common now that Arnold's gone?"

"I'm sorry to disturb you at a time like this," Sonny said. Oh Christ, his hat was actually in his hand. He put it down on the table in Ellis' living room.

In the dining room, closed off and shrouded, the *minyan* sat *shiva,* on hard wooden chairs that Sharon had rented from an agency that specialized in picnic equipment. Among the ten men that made up the *minyan* sat Sharon's father, glazed, and her brother, recently and unexpectedly out of business. The rest were mostly Ellis' friends from Harvard, and the law firm.

"I wouldn't disturb you for anything in the world." He started to cry. "Oh, Ellis." He covered his eyes. "I know how hard it is to lose a father. A mother. But he was my brother, Ellis, I'm a part of this too."

"I know that, Uncle Sonny," Ellis said coldly. "What did you want to talk to me about that we couldn't discuss over the phone?"

Sonny blew his nose, and wiped his eyes. "We took care of each other, Ellis, we always took care of each other. Mostly it seemed like he took care of me, but I promise you, I also took care of him. They're closing in on me, Ellis. The banks. The railroads . . ."

"Are you coming here for a loan?"

"No. I would if we loved each other, Ellis, but I don't have any illusions about that. I called Joe Pape. He told me the shares were never sold. That the shares still belong to me."

"They belonged to my father. You signed them over to my father."

"But he was desperate, Ellis. I signed over my life to your father. Because he loved me. Because I loved him. I signed them over to save him. If he didn't have to sell them . . ."

"Then they still belonged to him. So now they belong to me."

"And he never said anything? He never told you they belonged to me?"

"He never mentioned anything at all," Ellis said. "If you'll excuse me—"

Sonny turned toward the wall, put his face against the plaster and paint and started to shriek, a terrible animal wail.

"For God's sake, Uncle Sonny. There are people sitting *shiva*. They can hear you. Sharon's lying down, she's very edgy, she's pregnant. And this whole thing's been very hard on us, you're not the only one."

And still Sonny kept up his awful, wounded bleating.

"It's only money," Ellis said. "Try to control yourself. It's only money."

"No it isn't," Sonny sobbed. "No it isn't only money, Ellis. My brother is dead. My brother is dead. And you're what he's left us."

In November there was a play due at the Studio and three songs for Janice's act, and Chris thought as long as she was in New York, she might as well give Lionel Lindenbaum's family a ring. They'd moved. Their number was disconnected.

"Oh my God!" Evelyn shrieked from the bedroom. "Oh my God! Oh my God! Oh my *God!*"

Chris went to the doorway of the bedroom, assuming Sonny was finally killing her. Norman sat in the living room, playing chess with himself, changing seats with each move, changing brilliant imaginations.

Evelyn was huddled on the bed, in a long green satin robe. Sonny sat in the wing chair to the left of the television set, laughing, laughing, laughing.

"What happened?" Chris asked. "I thought you were killing each other."

"That comes later," Evelyn said. "First I have to kill myself. Your father's just been elected Governor of Tennessee."

Sonny grinned. "It was on the news."

"Now I know where to send the summons, that son of a bitch. He still owes me child-support from the time you were four. How could this happen? How could he be Governor of Tennessee? What the hell's in Tennessee?"

"The Reelings live in Tennessee. So does Joe Pape," Sonny said, in a somewhat quieter voice.

"The first Republican Governor of Tennessee. Can you imagine?" Evelyn chewed on her handkerchief. "The first Republican Governor. I didn't even know he'd become a Republican."

"You should have stayed with him," Sonny chuckled. "He would have been President."

"You're right," said Evelyn. "Oh for God's sake."

"I think you should try and get him back," said Sonny. "Send him a wire of congratulations."

"With a summons in it," Evelyn said. "What a good idea. You really think I could get him back?"

"I think you should try," Sonny said.

In early December, Pappy died.

What was in the coffin in Pittsburgh wasn't Pappy, Evelyn ranted. That wasn't her father, why did they have so much makeup on him, what was the yarmulke doing there, for God's sake, she wanted to see his head, his wonderful shiny head, the man in the coffin was dressed up so stiff and neat, that couldn't be Pappy, Pappy was a bald-headed man in long underwear leaning over the radio to hear it better, and laugh. And laugh.

"I told them we should have closed the coffin," Murray said.

Grandma sat in the corner, weeping quietly. Friends consoled her. Friends tried to console her.

"I lost my best friend," Grandma said. "I lost my best friend."

They came from the produce companies, they came from the highway, they came from downtown from places Evelyn couldn't even remember. And they remembered Pappy. Evelyn couldn't get over it.

"I can't get over how many friends he had," she kept on saying. "Who are all these people?" she whispered to Enid. "Are any of them anybody?"

"We should close the coffin now," Murray said.

"Not yet. Not yet," said Grandma. "I want to kiss him goodbye."

After the service, the cortege of cars, most of them rented, made its way through the icy rain to the cemetery. Halfway up the small hill was a good location. (He could see people coming from here, going from there.) The gravesite was barely twenty feet above the place where the car was parked, but so shrouded in fog it was hard for Chris to see the people already standing around it. It was as if a veil of ice had been suspended over that portion of the graveyard, obliterating the reality of it, sending the open grave into spectral shadow: as though death were the true illusion.

And the coffin was almost in permanent terrible place. There was sleeting, bone-chilling cold. The coffin suspended over the gape in the earth, balanced on three mechanical bars, placing Pappy over his own private piece of land.

Murray had passed around umbrellas, but there was no way to have enough protection from the bitter wet of that day. The rabbi droned on. Grandma wept. Everyone wept.

It all seemed so final, that closed box, the rabbi reading the last unhelpful prayer, against a sky so gray, a chilling wind so heavy with sleet it tore at their cheeks, iced off the temporal warmth of tears. No green trees broke the barren line of hills. Skeletal black and gray wood branches arched bleakly up to an even bleaker sky.

In between the narrow cement pathways for the living were thousands of stone markers, gray-white, hung with frozen rain. Sammy and Murray each had a hand holding Grandma's elbow, each angled his umbrella to cover her. Chris signaled Pegeen that there was room for her under her umbrella, but Pegeen shook her head, and stood there, crying straight into the wind, mascara running down her pale pink cheeks, penciled-on dark black eyebrows disappearing in the rain.

Grandma was very much shorter than anyone else standing around the grave, looking even smaller in Evelyn's old mink, turned to an orangey russet, the only bright color in the day. She was crying into her hands, while Sammy and Murray held her by the elbows, and tried to be reserved, like men who knew about life. They failed. They started to cry, and held each other's umbrellas while each of them reached for handkerchiefs. Enid was weeping quietly, leaning on her husband's arm. Sadie was crying loudly, hanging on to Hymie, who was crying into a hand-kerchief of Sonny's, which Evelyn had brought for each of the men.

But loudest of all cried Evelyn, wailed Evelyn, screamed like the banshee Pappy told her she better not grow up to be, Evelyn. She stood all alone at the far side of the grave, howling with such ferocity and pain it sounded like laughter.

Sonny was sitting in the darkened bedroom when Evelyn got home. "I'm sorry about your father," he said. "I'm sorry I couldn't come to the funeral."

"That's all right," said Evelyn. "There were plenty of people there. I don't know how he knew so many people. And they all bothered to come. Imagine that. They bothered to come."

"And I didn't," said Sonny. "Is that what you're saying?"

"It didn't matter. I know you have trouble. Pappy would have understood. That was something he understood very well. Trouble." She looked at him carefully. "How does it look?"

"Colder than the grave."

"Nothing's colder than that."

"I am. They won't carry me anymore. I'm signing an admission of no intent to pay. That way at least they won't prosecute. They'll just close me up."

"Really close you?"

"I'm afraid so," Sonny said. "I'm sorry about your father. I'm sorry about me. I should have done better for you."

"How much do you need?"

"Oh, I don't know. Ten, twelve million." He looked up and tried to smile. "Your father leave it to you?"

"How much do you really need?"

"If I could get my hands on a couple of hundred thousand, I could maybe get above the waves. Maybe get the railroad to back off for a while. Maybe. Maybe they'd let me stay afloat to try and save a little of what they'd be losing. But I haven't a cent. I haven't a chance of raising a goddamn penny. Nobody trusts me. It's like the good chance went out, when Arnold did."

"I'm tired of hearing about Arnold." Evelyn wiped her eyes. "I have four hundred thousand dollars. You can have it all."

"You have what?" Sonny switched on the lamp by his chair, and looked at her, very carefully.

"Four hundred thirty-six thousand," said Evelyn. "You can have it all."

"Where did you get it?"

"I saved it from the household accounts, and made some investments."

"You saved it from the household accounts?" He was on his feet.

"Well, you know how you love being overcharged. So I didn't let the stores do it. I did it."

"You're wonderful!" he ran to her, and lifted her into the air, hugging her, laughing, and laughing. "You're absolutely wonderful. What an embezzler you would have made!"

"You're right," said Evelyn, "and I had to marry you. You son of a bitch."

ELEVEN

Several times, during her undergraduate life, besides the moments Chris ran away from Bryn Mawr to give herself to the theater and art, she had run back to give art and the theater to Bryn Mawr. She had organized pageants on May Day, which they celebrated traditionally with a Hymn to the Sun at sunrise sung from the turret of Rockefeller, strawberries at breakfast, hoop-rolling down the hill that stretched between two vast parallel lines of giant oak trees, populated with curious squirrels, hiding from all the hullaballoo of blooming young girls beating their hoops with a stick. (The first one to reach the bottom would be the first married, said the superstition, explaining the fervor with which the race was run.) Then they would twist gay streamers in varying colors of spring around the Maypole, weaving in and out, the girls with the streamers in their hands. And as things grew more open with passing years, the boys from Haverford would come over and steal some panties from the dorms. And Chris would sit in the window of Pem East conducting an Elizabethan pageant, a colloquy of words and bodkins and Punch and Judy and very gay madness, in the style of those who felt a part of the Renaissance, having studied Shakespeare very closely, and life hardly at all.

Even the loyalist of undergraduates accepted that Bryn Mawr was an Ivory Tower, heavily studded with Gothic design. The Cloisters was the perfect name for that portion of garden and trees and silence in the center of the library, with a pool in the middle (very small, but still a pool) where tradition demanded the senior girls swim three times around the night before their final comprehensive exams and where (rumor had it) Katharine Hepburn had swum nude (as did everyone who made the three time round). The Cloisters was also the setting for Lantern Night, when sophomore girls in cap and gown sang a little more gaily in Greek (*Pallas Athena Thea*) than the somber Greek song sung by the freshmen, in cap and gown, waiting to receive their lanterns from the sophomores who would make them their lantern girl. All of it very warming, strange, none of it practical and modern. Except for the realization that life went on outside those walls.

Determined to bring some reality in to speckle the fine light and dark traditions, Chris had organized an original musical late in her sophomore year, with sketch contributions from Haverford, Swarthmore, and Bryn Mawr, and a cast from all three colleges. And a public performance (DEBUT! at last!) in the Radnor High School Auditorium. Admission: $1.25.

"I'm afraid not," Miss McBride had said to her. "No student from Bryn Mawr can be a part of a commercial theatrical enterprise using the name of the college."

"Are you forbidding me to do it?"

"Not at all," said Miss McBride. "I wish you nothing but luck and success with your show. Either that, or I hope to see you continue at Bryn Mawr."

So that had been that.

But Junior Show at Bryn Mawr, that was not a commercial

enterprise. That was a college show, a part of tradition, *Charge the Ivory Tower!* Chris wrote the music and lyrics and most of the libretto, and played the comedy lead. And it was very good for a college show, except that Lionel Lindenbaum hadn't been there to tell her she was wonderful, and that Evelyn felt Chris would have been better in the ingenue lead, if she had only been as thin and pretty as Muggy, and had her nose fixed.

"Mrs. Sterne!" Miss McBride had hailed Chris' mother, after the show as Chris walked back to Rockefeller to take off her makeup and try to come down from the exhilaration in her bones, which were tingling, she could feel them even through the barrier of too much flesh. She could feel her spirit soaring. Soared. High over gray turrets. Warming cold walls. Racing to cover ancient stone with ivy. Life. Art. Victory. Junior Show.

"Mrs. Sterne!" Miss McBride called again. Remarkable woman. She even knew Evelyn's name, when Chris had been sure she hadn't even known Chris's.

"I just want to congratulate you." Miss McBride held out her hand, and shook Evelyn's with a grip that made Evelyn stare. "Tonight was the most exciting theatrical event at Bryn Mawr since Kate Hepburn was an undergraduate."

"Thank you," said Evelyn, a little glazed, looking at her hand.

"Mr. Sterne?" Miss McBride shook Sonny's hand. "You must be very proud." She smiled at Chris. "So should you be."

"Who was that?" Evelyn said, when the woman had moved off into the night.

"The president of the college," Chris said.

"I thought she was the cleaning woman," said Evelyn.

"She has a strong handshake," Sonny said. "She seems to be a fine woman."

"As good as they come," Chris said. "A tribute to mind."

"Someone should help her with her clothes," said Evelyn. "Kate Hepburn. Imagine. A college president who's a name-dropper."

"She was her lantern girl," Chris said. "Miss McBride was a sophomore when Katharine Hepburn was a freshman. She gave her her lantern."

"A thrill a minute," said Evelyn. "Why didn't you go to a co-ed school? You might have met someone."

"I've met a lot of people," said Chris.

"Women," said Evelyn.

And now Chris was graduating. They stood on the grass outside Rockefeller in casual ranks, waiting to line up for the Processional to Goodhart. "Is this going to be in Greek?" asked Evelyn. "Or can we hope for something we can understand."

"We can always hope for that," said Chris.

She had gone in to see Miss McBride, early that morning, to say goodbye, and thank her, and apologize. "I'm sorry I didn't get as much out of college as I might have. I wasn't ready. I was too young, I guess. Also, I was crazy."

"Well, you weren't as crazy as you thought you were," Miss McBride smiled. "You are graduating. Congratulations."

She held out her hand. The best grip Chris had ever felt in her life. She returned it for the first time with equal strength, and no embarrassment.

"Have a fine life," said Miss McBride.

"I'll try to."

"I suspect that you will."

They were starting to move into lines now, in the rich fine green of a June morning. Ordered, tassels in place on the caps on their heads, ready to be switched to the other side of the cap, when the ceremony was over. Square-headed scholars, wearing the dark black chorus gowns of every other campus in the country, eager to have it over, to have it begin.

Evelyn stood, dressed neatly in a chic black suit, searching the crowds for Sonny, for Mrs. Clifton Sanger. Or anyone else of some import.

There was a man getting out of a cab on the corner, where the street ended and the green of the campus began. A very handsome man he looked to be to Evelyn, who observed him from the back, which in his case was broad, well-tailored, with fine shoulders. Yes. And he stood up quite tall once he was on the lawn, and his hair glinted finely silver. The woman he helped from the cab was quite pretty in an unspectacular way, small, well-dressed if you didn't subscribe to *Harper's Bazaar*. But they had a certain happy assurance about them. The woman actually leaned on his arm. Evelyn felt something akin to envy. Imagine being able to find a tall well-dressed man you could lean on.

He turned around, and for a moment, Evelyn was sure she was confused. Not possible. But even as Evelyn dismissed the reality, Chris was running across the lawn, shouting, for all the world as if she were still a little girl.

"Daddy! Daddy! Daddy!"

And that's who it was. "Oh shit," said Evelyn, "and me without a subpoena."

She watched them embracing for a moment. So there he was, the Governor of Tennessee. "So you're the Governor of Tennessee," Evelyn said as she made her way toward him. "I've heard so much about you."

"Hello, Evelyn," Walter said.

He was actually holding out his hand; Evelyn shook it. "Congratulations on everything."

"This is my little girl's day for congratulations," said Walter, hugging Chris.

"So self-effacing," said Evelyn. "So upright. So staunch. So ready to show up when the bills are no longer due."

"Mama, please!"

"I told you never to call me that. Why didn't you let me know he was coming?"

"I didn't know," said Chris. "Isn't it wonderful?"

"Wonderful," Evelyn said coldly. "Just wonderful. How are you, Dolores?"

"Very well, thank you, Evelyn."

"You're looking very well." Dolores was. Evelyn couldn't understand it. She searched the blue eyes for the terrible pain that had to come from living with Walter, even if he was Governor. None. The woman looked actually content.

"You haven't put on any weight, Dolores," Evelyn said.

"Neither have you," said Dolores. "You're looking younger than ever."

"Well, that's what I am, is younger than ever. I mean it's hard to believe from looking at me that I'm a woman who's owed fifteen years of child-support."

"Not today," said Walter.

"You're right, not today," Evelyn murmured. "But only because your daughter the traitor didn't let me know you were coming or I would have had a brass band to welcome you, Governor, with a process server in the drum."

"Excuse me!" Chris said to Evelyn, as she took her father's hand and started to lead him toward the hall.

"I will not excuse you. Don't you dare go with him. Don't start getting sentimental because he comes to a graduation. Anyone can show up for a graduation, even if it is in Greek."

"Evelyn, please, I beg you." Walter looked at her very kindly. "Give us a moment together. Let's not quarrel. Let's treat each other with the respect due fellow human beings. This is a day for beginnings."

"You want to take me out?" Evelyn smiled, her cutest smile. "I heard you were one of the richest men in Tennessee. Is it true?"

"As Teddy Roosevelt said, 'I am only an average man, but I work harder at it than the average man.' "

"I think I believe you," said Evelyn. "Poor Dolores. You've stood up very well."

Sonny was in the bathroom, the one off the lobby in Rockefeller Hall, which had been temporarily converted into a men's room (BOYS, said the sign. FATHERS ALSO WELCOME). Sonny was smiling at that, the whole time he was peeing. That's what he was now, he was a father, and that was about all. The boy was over. The man? Well, the man should be at the top of the heap, and Sonny wasn't in the gutter, he'd made his way back pretty nicely with that great crazy lady's four hundred thousand, but he wasn't exactly at the top of the heap.

He washed his hands, and dried them with a paper towel, watching his face in the mirror. Older. Sure, a lot older. But wiser maybe, like they said. A professor. He might have made a fine professor. Had he taken a different path . . .

There was an impatient knock at the door. "What the hell are you doing in there, growing daisies?"

Sonny threw down the towel, and opened the door. "I'm sorry," he started to say. Standing in front of him was Clifton Sanger.

"Sterne!" Sanger said, and held out his hand, held out his smile in actual greeting. "How the hell have you been? I didn't know you had a kidney condition!"

"You gave it to me when I met you in Marblehead," Sonny ventured, smiling.

Clifton Sanger laughed. "Wait just a second, will you, I got to take a leak."

"That's how I felt in Marblehead. Only I was afraid to say. That's what gave me my kidney condition."

Sanger was laughing. Sonny waited outside.

"So how the hell are you, Sterne? Come on, let's sit down by these steps here. We've got some time. How the hell are you?"

"How the hell did you even remember my name?"

"I followed your career for years before I even got to meet you. Very bold. Very daring. Very shaky. But balls, man, you've got balls, I've got to say that for you."

Sonny looked at the gray-haired even-featured man beside him. He tried to see inside his eyes to find out what kind of joke was going on. Sanger didn't seem to be joking. He could laugh, but he didn't seem to be joking.

"How come you didn't tell me that in Marblehead?"

"I get crazy on vacations," Sanger said. "I'm consigned to all these vacations, and it makes you crazy when you really enjoy working to take so goddamned many vacations."

"Nobody's forcing you."

"I don't even like that goddamn house in Marblehead. I just bought it for the kids, and my wife, they need places like that, but when I get up there I go crazy. I'm sorry I brushed you that time, but I hate to see somebody pressing. You don't need to press. You're a very smart man. I've watched your career for years."

"You've watched my career," Sonny said, very softly, looking into his palms, amazed.

"Wish to hell I could have had a career like that. Fighting my way up, taking on the whole goddamn establishment, stopping at nothing." Clifton Sanger thrust a fist in the air. Then he lowered his hand. "But I was the whole goddamn establishment, so I stopped at everything."

"I wish I could cry my heart out for you," Sonny said laughing.

"So do I," Sanger said, slapping him on the shoulders. "So do I. Let's do it!"

"Let's do what?"

"Let's cry our hearts out for each other. Let's get in some trouble together!" Sanger got to his feet, brushed off some stone dust. "I'm so tired of taking these goddamn vacations. And they won't let me have any real fun at my place. The goddamn banks that I own own me. *No* speculation. No wild hunches. No more than minimal risks. Hell, the office could run without me, I can't stand being in an office that's being run by something that owns me that I own. That's why I take so many goddamn vacations. How's your daughter? Nice girl, graduating today?"

"Yes," said Sonny, getting to his feet. "Yours?"

"Yes. Stepdaughter really, but I love her like my own."

"Mine, too," said Sonny.

"But then, you should have seen my own children," Sanger laughed. So did Sonny. "So what do you say?" said Clifton Sanger as he put his hand on Sonny's shoulders and they marched toward the gathering girls.

"What do I say about what?"

"Doing some business together."

"I thought your company wouldn't do business with me."

"Well, that's my company. That isn't me." He turned and looked at Sonny. Looked at him very hard. "Yes, I do. I trust you. I can *afford* to trust you. How about five million?"

"Five million what?"

"Five million dollars. I can get my hands on five that the bank can't dole out to me. We have unwritten rules, you know, we legion of bankers, never toy with capital, only income from capital. I'd like to break an unwritten rule. My stepdaughter's graduating today. But my life isn't over. I can get five million loose. You want to play with it?"

"You bet your ass."

"One condition," Sanger said. "You'll have to let me come in pretty often and play with you."

"It'll be my greatest pleasure," said Sonny, beaming.

"Good luck!" Miss McBride strode by Chris, smiling, signaling a hand to her.

"Who's that?" Evelyn said. "The president-washerwoman?"

"The finest woman in the world, besides Grandma."

"You're going to have to learn to evaluate," Evelyn said. "The finest woman in the world. That woman. Grandma. Honest to God. Besides, what's so good about that? The most it is is a woman. You must learn not to have such an overblown opinion of women. Women are nothing. Look. I'm young. I'm beautiful. What's so great about me?"

"A lot of things."

"Really? You really don't hate me and resent me just because I'm younger and prettier than you?"

"Not for that," said Chris.

"But you do hate me."

Evelyn was ready, her eyes narrowing, waiting to spring. "For what? Speak it out. No. Be like your stepbrother, the potential lunatic. Keep it all inside."

"I love you. But I hate you for calling me fat."

"It's the truth," Evelyn said. "I only say it for your own good. You're the fattest girl in the graduating class. That's what matters to me. I don't say that to hurt you. Talent is more than skin-deep, and in your case it has a lot to pass through. I say it for your own good. Mummy loves you."

Chris turned away.

"But it's nice that the president thinks you've got talent, even if she dresses like that. The finest woman in the world. You're just going to have to start developing some sense of values, Chris."

"You're right about that."

"Maybe Sonny can send you to live in Europe, now that his finances are on the mend."

"My father's invited me to come live with him in Tennessee."

"Isn't he generous," said Evelyn. "Is that your graduation present?"

"He says that Nashville is the Athens of the South."

"You haven't seen the Athens of Athens yet. Go to Europe. Maybe you can capture a count or a prince or go to Queen Elizabeth's reducing specialist. Maybe you can sail the seven seas and find adventure, and try to lose weight."

"I'll go anywhere you say," she said. "But I have a feeling I'll end up here. I think I really love this country."

"Oh my God, an overweight patriot. Just what the doctor ordered. What's so great about this country? Any country that could elect your father Governor . . ."

"That wasn't the country. That was a state. He isn't President."

"Well, he may be," Evelyn said. "He would have been if I stayed with him. Even Sonny said so." She smiled with something like pride. "If he gets elected, I'll know exactly where to send the summons. Boy, I'd like to be a fly on the wall for that subpoena."

Chris laughed.

"Well, it isn't impossible for him to be President. 'My wife has a fine Republican cloth coat.' I can just hear your father saying that. At least if it were cut with a little style. Poor Dolores. She

539

probably doesn't even have a mink. This country. Why don't you sing 'God Bless America'? You could, you know. You look like Kate Smith."

Chris started to cry.

"Now don't get upset. I say it for your own good. If you lost weight and went to Aufricht, you could get anybody. Aly Khan's got a son. Very handsome. You'd be a Begum or something. Stevenson's boy Borden, if he gets elected, although Sonny says he doesn't have a chance, he's a statesman. But there's always Javits. He's got a son. Or a nephew. Everybody important has a son or a nephew."

"How about a daughter?"

"What about a daughter? Anyone can have a girl. Use your life. Youth is beauty. Fat is old. I want you to be everything you can be. Get thin and marry well."

"And that's it?"

"You don't think that's enough?"

"Was it enough for you?"

"Of course not," said Evelyn. "But I made mistakes. I picked the wrong men. At least I think I did. Grandma and that woman. Well, your values will change as soon as you get thin and see Aufricht. I just want you to have the best."

"Thank you," Chris said. The music for the Processional began, and Chris stepped exactly in line, wiping the corners of her eyes with the tassel on her cap. She raised her cap high on her head, as she started to move to the music.

One day perhaps, she might emerge, with some understanding of love and truth and God, and where Lionel Lindenbaum moved to; one day she might shed the skin she was in and emerge. In the meantime, it was nice to be graduating.